Tackling Tanner

Cliff J. Cavender

Cavender Books

Contents

Dedication   1

Content Warning   2

Prologue   3

Chapter 1   5

Chapter 2   14

Chapter 3   20

Chapter 4   25

Chapter 5   29

Chapter 6   37

Chapter 7   41

Chapter 8   51

Chapter 9   63

Chapter 10   73

Chapter 11   83

Chapter 12   95

Chapter 13   105

Chapter 14   112

Chapter 15   119

Chapter 16   125

Chapter 17 135

Chapter 18 142

Chapter 19 149

Chapter 20 164

Chapter 21 174

Chapter 22 190

Chapter 23 195

Chapter 24 201

Chapter 25 212

Chapter 26 224

Chapter 27 234

Chapter 28 239

Chapter 29 247

Chapter 30 256

Chapter 31 267

Chapter 32 273

Chapter 33 279

Chapter 34 282

Chapter 35 286

Chapter 36 288

Chapter 37 293

Chapter 38 300

Epilogue One—Nine Months Later 306

Epilogue Two 313

What's Next? 317

Dedication

To those who have ever felt shame for the damage inflicted upon them—you are
lovely, and you are loved

Content Warning

This book contains sexual assault and heavy drug use on the page. After much outlining, consideration, and writing, I have chosen to make these topics integral to the plot of *Tackling Tanner* for three reasons. First, given who Jimmy and Tanner are, it makes the most sense for them to run into these problems. Second, a significant number of men in the LGBTQ+ community deal with sexual assault and addiction. I wrote this story, in part, to shine light on how much more common these problems are than we think. Third, and most importantly, I wanted to show how self-love, romantic love, and platonic love can help heal the wounds that sexual assault and addiction leave on our bodies, minds, and communities. As always, read at your own caution, but I really hope you enjoy Jimmy and Tanner's story. It ends very happily, and it shows just how possible it is to thrive regardless of what damage has been done to us.

Prologue

Tanner Bash

I KNOW I SHOULD have eaten breakfast this morning. Because the banana and granola bar I stuffed down during half-time to compensate are threatening to make their reappearance.

I get in place along with my offensive line on a hot August day in San Diego. I grab hold of the ball and get ready to snap it to the Seals quarterback. The linebacker for the Portland Tigers towers above me, and I have to take deep breaths to still my nausea. Thank God star linebacker Kyle Weaver retired. 'Cause if this was him, I'd be done for.

I chuck the ball back to our quarterback, and then immediately get in position, my hands out and ready to block. The linebacker barrels into me, and my arms buck under his force. I press harder, digging my cleats into the turf.

But then the worst happens.

Panic, resulting from me not being strong enough, floods my body. Because slowly, but surely, the linebacker is dragging me through the turf. No matter how hard I dig in or push, he's still moving me. He's stronger than me. Fiercer.

More of a man than I'll ever be.

Suddenly, I recall a memory of me attending Church with my gramps. There, I learned that if I obeyed the Lord's commandments, I would be blessed. One of those commandments was that, as a man, I was to marry a woman and raise a family.

But I'm not attracted to women.

My arms weaken, and the linebacker manages to push me off my feet, and I fall to the ground. I feel banana come up my throat, and it takes all my strength to swallow it back down. But by the time I do, nothing matters. The linebacker tackles our running back just as he's gotten hold of the ball. That's our last down, so now we're forced to hand over the ball to the Championship Game two-time winners. And I slam my fist into the turf.

After we lose, I drag myself into the locker room. My teammates are passing around Gatorade and protein bars, but the last thing I want to do is eat right now.

My fellow lineman, Carter, puts his hand on my shoulder. "Come on, man, you gotta eat," he says, thrusting a cookies and crème protein bar in my hand.

"Fine," I say. Carter and I have been playing for the Seals for years, and he's been like a brother to me. I've learned to always take his advice, even when it's last thing I want to do.

As I chew on the bar that tastes like cardboard, looking away from my teammates as they undress—because, well, I don't like where my mind goes when I watch them strip—I get that weird fluttering feeling in my stomach. And it's not just 'cause I'm hungry. But because I'm pained. I'm retiring at the end of this season, which means I'll finally have time to date.

And how the hell am I going to obey God's commandment to raise a family if I get even get it up for a woman?

Chapter 1

Jimmy Dillon

MAN, IF I KEEP looking at my phone, I'm never going to get finish cooking this new recipe. Blinking my tired eyes, I set my phone face down at the far edge of the counter in my diner kitchen and walk back to the large pot of bubbling stew. My mind already beginning to race from having nothing to distract me, I glance over at my printout instructions, hoping that that'll keep my thoughts at bay. But it doesn't do much. This is why I never cook soups or stews. Too much sitting around and letting my brain stew itself. I'd much rather pick up my phone, get on the apps, and find some hot guy to fuck like I always do.

I hear the kitchen doors flap open. The light, yet confident footsteps tell me it's Lilah, one of my managers.

"How's it going, girl?" I call out.

She gasps and turns on the kitchen light. "Sweet Jesus, you scared me," she says, adjusting her glasses.

"Sorry," I say, setting my ladle down. I point to the window, the sun just barely shining through. "I like to cook with natural light."

She takes off her messenger bag, sets it on a hook, and grabs her apron. It's got this little drawing of the pink ball Kirby wearing a chef's outfit and holding a skillet. Cute as hell.

Lilah's as sweet as a peach. She's a short pale woman with pink-dyed hair, but she makes it look somehow natural. She and her wife Marissa became managers at my diner a couple years back when they moved to Glamour Springs, and they've done nothing but ease my load and make the diner more profitable. Lilah's always been the one to respect our employees and make our customers feel at home. And she always knows what to say to me, even when I don't want to hear it.

"What are you doing here so early?" She smells the air, then walks over to me. "And look at you cooking up a storm."

"I'm trying out this new stew," I say. "It's got local game."

She sticks her head over the pot and takes a big whiff. "Smells good. But you're seriously trying out another new recipe? Marissa and I already told you."

I hunch my shoulders a little and feel the heat of shame light up my face. "What? I can't use my own kitchen to experiment every now and then?"

She sighs and pushes herself up on the counter. We always tell our staff to keep their asses off of kitchen equipment, but when it's just me and Lilah, we do whatever we want. She's like the sister I never had. And God, I wish she was. Woulda made growing up with my overbearing mother a whole lot easier.

"I've told you," she says. "Our menu is fine. People love it. Your diner is the most popular eatery in Glamour Springs. Sure, we could add a few new things that people might like, but it's not worth getting up before sunrise to do. You got a life to live, Jimmy."

I let out a sharp exhale through my nose. Besides cooking, working out, and hooking up, there's not much I like to do. Well, there's baking. There are even some leftover cookies in the fridge I made the other day for one of our servers' birthdays. But God knows I don't like baking. Just like cooking the stew, baking takes a long time, which gives my brain the chance to conjure up dark thoughts in the voice of my mother. Best not to give it that chance.

"But Glamour Springs is getting bigger," I say, trying to think of some excuse. "Pretty soon, they'll bring in the big chains. How will we compete with those?"

The kitchen doors slam open, which means that Marissa, Lilah's wife, is here.

"Jimmy," she says, her voice low and forceful. She's carrying a heavy bag, showing just how toned her tattooed arms are. She's black with a huge afro and a nose ring bigger than Texas. In other words, the exact opposite of Lilah. And yet I've never met a more perfect couple. Maybe besides my friends Kyle and Michael.

"People like diners," she continues, setting down her bag with a thump. "They want a homecooked meal. Not some microwaved shit from a drive-thru. You're delusional. Our diner is fine."

Lilah walks over to plant a kiss on her wife's cheek. Her words used to hurt me, but now I know that she's a tough love kinda girl. And seeing how protective she is of dear Lilah, I know that woman's got a lot of love in her. I turn around to greet her, and that's when I realize how tired I am. And of course, while they're both looking right at me, I let out the biggest yawn.

"Are you sure you can handle a whole shift?" Lilah says. "Seems like you've been up for a while."

"Yeah, don't want you falling asleep at your desk again," Marissa says.

My face goes red from embarrassment. Having one of my new hostesses find me face down on my desk was not one of my finer moments.

"I'll be fine," I say. "Got some energy drinks in the fridge. I should be good to go."

They glance at each other, then back at me.

"You worry me," Marissa says, walking over to my stove. "This one of your new recipes?"

"It's stew with local game," Lilah says.

Before I can stop her, Marissa grabs the ladle and ours some of my stew into a plastic cup. She takes a sip, tilts her head back and forth, then frowns. And my stomach sinks.

She pats my shoulder as she throws the cup in the trash. "We're definitely not adding that to the menu."

Before Marissa leaves to take down the chairs in the dining area, she opens the fridge and takes one of my cookies out of the container. She takes a bite and audibly moans. "Now this," she says. "This is your masterpiece. Consider adding more baked goods to the menu. I know they'd be a hit."

And then she leaves, and I slump against the stove. I turn off the burner. No need to continue cooking that.

Lilah comes over and takes a place right next to me. "I'm sorry," she says. "You know how Ris can be."

I sigh, folding my arms above my belly. "Just kicking myself that it isn't good."

"Why is this so important to you anyway?"

I shift my feet, feeling the stickiness of the kitchen floor on my boots. And for the first time today, true exhaustion sweeps over me. There's only so long I can go on five hours of sleep a night.

"I'm just—" I exhale through my nose. "Just trying to stay busy, that's all."

"Jimmy," she says. "Did your mom try and reach out to you again?"

I let out a sharp laugh as I turn to the stove. I frown at the brown stew. This will be a bitch to throw out.

"Not since I went no-contact with her a year ago," I say. "But it's like her voice is always in my head."

"Saying what?"

I trill my lips. "The usual," I say. "That I'm fat, ugly. Unimportant."

She scoffs. "Okay, sure, you're not exactly skinny, but you're not unhealthy either," she says. "You work out like crazy, and people say you're like the handsomest guy in town."

I blush and smile at her. "They really do, huh?"

She whacks my arm. "You know that," she says, laughing. "Quit fishing for compliments. But what I'm saying is true. Your mama's just a curmudgeon. Get her out of your head."

I let out the biggest sigh I have today. I know Lilah's right. I know my mom just has it in her head that bullying me makes the world better—saying that if I was skinnier or had a college degree that I would be farther along in life or my ex, Joe, wouldn't have cheated on me.

I grab a dish towel and fling it over my shoulder. I don't want to think about my mom anymore. "Thanks, Lils," I say, patting her on the shoulder.

"Anytime."

"Now enough pity for me," I say. "Let's get to work."

She gets started with our food prep just as our cooks arrive. I make my way to my office, rubbing my sleepy eyes, ready to down some Red Bull to get through the day. But when I open my fridge, I want to sink into the floor.

It's empty.

"Marissa," I call out. "Did you finish off the last of my drink?"

"No," she yells back from the dining area. "That's all on you, honey."

I stomp my feet and stare into the empty fridge. Guess I'm white-knuckling it today. My AA sponsor says to be careful when it comes to sleepiness, but one day with an energy drink can't hurt. I know I should be sleeping more, but I just can't stay asleep for long. Once I'm awake, I'm awake, and my thoughts break into a sprint like horses in the Kentucky Derby. I either gotta experiment with new recipes, work out, or find some guy to sleep with. The fact that Glamour Springs is growing so quickly and becoming an LGBTQ+ safe haven is nice in some ways. There are a lot more options.

When we open up the diner, our regulars flood the place. I do my normal rounds, greeting people as they dig into our eggs and our famous pancakes. When I see Linda Higgins, Kyle's mama, she stands up to greet me.

"Is everything still on for catering the book event?" she asks, sitting down.

I prop my foot up on the step of the booth and rest my arms on the table. "All set," I say. "I'm excited to see Michael and Kyle again."

"Me too," she says. "And I'm so happy for my Michael. This is his second book tour."

Michael Cunningham, the pornstar turned romance author, ended up marrying my buddy Kyle, Linda's son. Just before he retired, Kyle was voted as the Sexiest Man Alive. The dude's like a brother to me, but I can't disagree with the public—he's a sexy guy. And it's pretty hot of Kyle to have landed a pornstar.

"It's impressive," I say, yawning. I feel sleepiness overtake me. "You take it easy, ya hear?"

"I will," she says, putting her reading glasses on her forehead as she looks down at her pancakes.

It's only been an hour, but I need to sit down and take a breather. I don't know which is worse: the pain in the backs of my eyes or this sleep deprivation headache. I skedaddle to the back of the restaurant, using the last of my energy to greet the new customers walking in. Then, once I reach my office, I shut the door and slump down in my chair. I rest my head on my desk and close my eyes. Just five minutes here is fine.

But then a loud noise startles me awake. I shoot my head up and look around, my chin wet with drool, and there's a sharp pain in my neck.

Marissa is standing over a large stack of papers at the edge of the desk, a stack I assume she dropped to wake me up, and she looks pissed. But Lilah is standing just behind her, concern all over her face.

"You did it again," Marissa says. "Falling asleep on the job. What has gotten into you? It's been two hours."

I drop my jaw. No wonder my neck hurts. I've spent hours laying in a horrible position.

"Jimmy, you gotta take care of yourself," Lilah says, sitting down in a chair next to the desk. "I'm worried you're gonna be too tired one day and fall in the kitchen and get hurt."

"And you're a liability," Marissa says, leaning on the stack. "What if you fuck up an order? Or set the diner on fire when you're here early experimenting with one of your 'recipes'?"

Lilah shakes her head. "You need to take a sabbatical."

I recoil, which lights up the kink in my neck. I grimace as I try to massage it, but I only make it hurt more.

"A sabbatical?" I ask. "You mean like a break?"

"Yeah," Marissa says. "Lilah and I have been preparing for this. Take a break and let us take over while you're gone."

I look between the both of them like they're crazy, feeling betrayed. "You planned this behind my back?"

They both nod.

"Jimmy, this has become a real problem," Lilah says.

I shake my head. "But I can't take a break. This diner is my life. I started it all by myself. I can't just abandon it."

"And you'll destroy it all by yourself if you keep showing up exhausted to work," Marissa says. "You need to take it easy."

"And we'll keep the diner going while you're gone," Lilah says. "You won't have to worry about anything." She approaches the desk and puts a hand on my shoulder. "Experiment with recipes. Rest. Do whatever you need to do."

"And we won't let you back until you're well rested," Marissa says. She gestures at me flippantly. "No more of this."

Lilah steps away, and I slump back in the chair, slightly more rested, but feeling the heat of anxiety grow in my chest.

A sabbatical? That's insane. What would I do instead of work? This is what I've been doing for years, and it got me through my breakup with Joe. And what the hell will distract me from my racing thoughts?

"But—"

"No buts," Lilah says, and both Marissa and I turn to her, surprised by her firmness.

"Jimmy, for yourself, just take the rest," she says.

I clench my fists under the table, then release them. I rub my aching head and sigh. There's no use fighting this. I'll get some sleep over the next couple days, then I'll come back. It'll be easy. I don't know how I'm gonna go the next couple days without working, but it'll be temporary. I'll be back here in no time.

"Fine," I say, standing up. "But I get to help cater Michael's book event this weekend. Then I'll take the week off like y'all are asking."

Marissa scoffs and folds her arms. "A week off? That's funny, babe."

I scowl. "What do you mean 'that's funny'?"

Lilah winces as if she forgot to add something. "We aren't just talking about a weeklong break."

Dread pools in my chest. "How long?"

"Multiple months," Marissa says. "At the very least."

My stomach sours like I've been punched in the belly. "You can't be serious."

"As a heart attack," Marissa says.

I stare at my messy desk, my chest tightening ever so painfully. *Months?* How the hell am I supposed to stay busy for months? To keep my mind occupied?

"At least three or so," Lilah says. "Jimmy, you've been working your ass off since you opened the diner ten years ago, and you've never vacationed at all. You need a break."

I fold my hairy arms and huff air out of my nose.

It feels like my world is crumbling before me. I don't know how the hell I'm supposed to go multiple months without my diner. Like Lilah's said, I've been working since it opened without a break. Hell, I can't even remember the last time I took a long break in all my thirty-eight years. And there's reason for that. I don't like my mind to be idle. Mom's harsh voice gets too loud.

But I can't argue with my girls. They're right. I'm becoming a liability to the restaurant.

"Fine," I say, rubbing my eyes. "Just let me help cater Michael's book event this weekend and then I'll take this goddamned sabbatical."

"Deal," Marissa says.

I look between both of them, hoping that one of them will start laughing and say this is all one big joke. But when they just stare at me expectantly, I know I'm not being pranked. This is the real deal.

"Well I guess this forced break starts now," I say, standing up.

"We'll be in communication about anything big," Lilah says.

"Sure, sure," I say, collecting my things. "I trust you."

As I make my way out of the office, I feel a tingle of emotion in my chest. These girls only did this because they care about me. And it was real brave of them to say something.

I pause at the door. "Thank you, girls. Kind of you to look out for me like that."

Marissa nods, and Lilah rubs my arm.

"We care about you," Lilah sees. "Rest up while you're gone."

Marissa pats me on the back. "Take it easy, J. You work hard, so you deserve a break."

I nod, feeling heat behind my eyes. I make my way out of the restaurant, chewing on Marissa's words. I get in my car, ready to go home and take this goddamned sabbatical. But all I can think about is the last thing Marissa said. I know, theoretically, I deserve a break.

But the echoes of my mom's words tell me that, in reality, I deserve no such good thing.

Chapter 2

Tanner Bash

WHEN THE FINAL PRACTICE whistle blows, my shoulders sag in relief. I jog with my fellow players on a perfect San Diego day to our locker rooms. I've been playing football for the majority of my thirty years, don't get me wrong. I love it like crazy. But today, I'm beyond exhausted.

As we undress, I feel warm, like the sun is still shining on me. I take my helmet and shoulder pads off, and suddenly my vision goes blurry, and I'm afraid I'll pass out.

Carter catches my arm when I nearly lose my balance, keeping me upright. "You good there, buddy?" he asks, letting go.

I wipe my eyes and wait for my eyes to refocus. "Alright, man. Thanks."

"You sure?" he asks, propping his leg up on the bench. Carter is about my same height, a little chunkier. But he's got such an earnest, kind demeanor, and he's a proven ladies' man. Yet he's settled, and he couldn't be happier. Wish I could say the same for myself.

I plop down on the bench, happy to finally get some rest. Carter's been my best friend in football for a while. Maybe it wouldn't hurt to be honest.

"I don't know, man. I—"

"Tanner Bash!" Coach Larson, our head coach, yells from his office.

"Yes sir?" I call out.

"Come here," he says tersely.

I stand up, and Carter pats me on the butt.

"Good to see you," he says.

"You too."

Once I'm in clothes that are somewhat presentable, I make my way to coach's office and shut the door.

"Sit down," he says, his hands steepled in front of him. He's in his forties, having retired from a New England team about a decade ago. And somehow, he's still got a pristine body.

"I'm gonna cut to the chase," he says. "What the hell's going on?"

I slump in my chair as his little office fan turns toward me, slightly drying off the sweat I'm dripping from practice. But I'm still hot as hell.

"What do you mean, coach? I'm working hard."

"No amount of work can make up for the weight you've been losing," he says. "305 to 280 since last season. That's a lot. And it's affecting your gameplay."

I shift in my seat. I'm not a small guy—6'4". I got huge arms, one of which has a tattoo of three hearts on it, and my torso is a perfect mixture of fat and muscle. But keeping up with a weight required of an offensive lineman is tough. And eating has been a chore more than ever lately.

"Sorry, coach," I say. "Been dealing with some issues."

"Issues?" he asks, almost scoffing. "What? You need a therapist or something?"

"I tried that a while back," I admit. "Didn't work."

He sighs and rubs his forehead. "Okay. Well, are you eating enough?"

I play with the callouses on my palms. Earlier this summer, I finally gathered the courage to talk to Kyle Weaver, the famous linebacker who came out at the Championship Game half-time show and an old friend of mine. And I confessed to him and his boyfriend Michael—well, fiancé now—that I'm gay. I thought that that confession would cure the sadness that keeps pulling me down. But it hasn't. I feel more depressed than ever. Kyle suggested therapy. I tried it, but it didn't go anywhere. And for the life of me, nothing tastes good. It's like in the past year God took away my taste buds or something. As a punishment possibly? I don't know. But it's been hell to say the least.

"I don't know," I say. "I'm trying. But eating's been tough."

"Do you have a chef?" he asks.

For the first time during this conversation, I look up at him, trying to hold back my scowl. "I don't need a chef," I say. "I can provide for myself." If I learned one thing growing up in a chaotic home with drug addict brothers and neurotic parents, it's that I can fend for myself.

He gawks at me. "You're saying that you can manage feeding yourself 7,000 calories a day?"

"I can," I say.

"But the scale says you're clearly not," he says, leaning forward. "And that's a huge problem."

I shut my mouth. He's right.

"You need to find a chef, and you need to get your calorie count up. Your performance in the opening game was god-awful. It was against the champions, so I'm not surprised we lost, but we coulda done better if you had your shit together."

Shame lights up my face. Which makes me angry. "So I gotta find a servant to cook for me? Got it."

Coach slams the desk and stands up. "This isn't a fucking joke, Bash. We have a real shot at making it to the playoffs this year, and I'm not gonna let your piss-for-an-excuse eating habits stop us from getting there. Either you find a chef and up your calorie count, or I bench you for the rest of the season."

Anxiety squeezes my chest. I remember when I spoke with Michael and Kyle, that's what they said this painful chest feeling was.

I can't sit out the rest of the season. This is my last one. As a kid, it was church, football, and video games that kept me above my crazy home life. But today, video games don't have the same effect, and I haven't been able to find a congregation like the one I used to attend with my grandpa. So football's the only thing I got to keep me sane. I'll do anything to keep it.

"Fine," I say.

Coach plops down in his seat, and for a second I think about how arousing that was: getting yelled at by a daddy.

No. I can't think this way.

Sure, I admitted I was gay to my buddy Kyle and his fiancé, and the NFO is more open toward gay people now that he has come out. But I want to be a family man—one that obeys the commandments of God. I can't do that if I'm entertaining thoughts of gay sex.

"I'll contact your agent," he says. "He'll help you find someone."

"Wait," I say. "Will you let me find one?"

He glares up at me. "Is this something you'll actually do?"

I nod. If I'm gonna be stripped of my dignity to make my own food, I might as well be able to choose who it is. Plus, chefs often live in with their players, especially in San Diego. If I'm forced to have a roommate, I at least want to pick them out.

He tenses his jaw, then he relaxes. "Fine. But we'll be weighing you at every practice. And I better see progress by next time."

I nod, relieved that I at least have some control here. "Thank you, coach."

"Now get," he says, looking down at some papers. "Gotta strategize for next game."

And I get out of there before anything else can go wrong.

As I walk back to my locker, I feel conflicted and stressed. Not only do I have to find a personal chef, but I also gotta deal with this gay shit. Kyle said he feels happy being true to himself, but I doubt I'd be happy being openly gay. True happiness comes from following God's commandments. But maybe there's something I'm not getting here. I have few days off before my next practice. Maybe I can go visit Kyle in Glamour Springs and get some advice on what to do.

By the time I make it back to the lockers, all the other guys are gone. Except for one. Fucking hell. The man I least want to see right now approaches and sits down on the bench next to me.

"What do you want, Whitacre?" I say under my breath. I don't even want to take off my clothes next to this guy, but I need to get out of here, so I bite the bullet. His eyes stay glued to my pelvis as I remove my underwear.

"How've you been?" he asks in a smooth voice. "It's been a minute since we've had some fun."

I groan to myself. Chris Whitacre is a closeted player and wide receiver for the San Diego Seals. When I got signed onto the team, I thought I was fortunate to have found another gay player. After practice, we would sometimes suck each other off. But then things started to get weird. He wanted commitment, which I rejected considering the state of gay NFO players at the time. And that's when he got creepy. He would ask for more and more sex, afterwards talking about our marriage and the kids we were going to adopt together. Fed up with him, I called everything off a year ago, and gradually, he just stopped bothering me.

But I guess he wants me again.

"What do you want?" I ask, not even looking at him.

"You already know," he says. He pulls open his gym shorts to reveal his massive dick.

My heart starts to race.

I'm still pissed after that conversation with coach, and I get hornier when I'm hungry. Like desperately so. I may want to be a family man, but that doesn't mean I can't fool around just one more time. It's not like I'm hurting anyone.

"Follow me," I say, low. He stands up, and I lead us into the shower area. I pick the farthest one back, the one that no one uses and is too isolated for sound to carry far. We both slip inside, and I shut the curtain.

"Can I film this?"

I give him the most disgusted look. "Absolutely not."

He shrugs and lowers himself. He takes his jacket off and sets it down carefully.

"Open your mouth," I command. We've done this so much that it's all I have to say.

He obeys, and his eagerness makes my breath quicken. I pull down my pants to reveal my already hardening cock. He looks up at me, asking for permission. And that's when I shove my dick into his mouth.

He gags once, then he composes himself. Good. If I'm getting off with a man once, I'd rather it be easy.

I push him back into the tile wall, and then I thrust my dick into him. He moans quietly as slobber drips out of his mouth. I may not love this, but it's hot to see how much Chris likes it.

Chris moans as he cums into his shorts, and hearing him so pleased with my body sends me over the edge. White hot pleasure strikes through me as I shoot into Chris's mouth. But when I'm done, I don't really feel relieved. I feel gross. Used, almost, even though *I'm* the one who fucked his mouth.

He wipes spit and cum from his lips and kisses my softening dick. "Let's do that again," he says. He grabs his things, stands up, and exits the shower, leaving me here like nothing happened.

I lean back against the tile and sigh. "Fuck," I whisper.

Guilt, shame, confusion, and anger flow through my body. I think I will take my time off and go visit Kyle in Glamour Springs. If there's anyone who can shed light on how I'm feeling, it's one of the biggest gay football players of the century.

Chapter 3

Jimmy Dillon

"Alright, Jimmy," Marissa says. "That's enough."

In the café at The Book Corner, we stand next to a large table covered in all kinds of sandwiches and salads, and at the very end sits a giant plate of my homemade cookies that I somehow gathered the patience to make. I've been fiddling with the presentation for the last twenty minutes.

"I know, I know," I say, finally but reluctantly stepping back. I was excited to have something to do, but I'm bummed that it's already over. After this, it's back to my months long 'vacation'.

"It's looks great," Lilah says. We watch as patrons peruse the bookstore.

"Thanks," I say. "Apparently, it's gonna be packed tonight."

"Michael's a big deal, huh?" she asks.

"He is." I'm proud of the guy. I remember calling him when he and Kyle had broken up, telling him what I had learned from dealing with something similar. He's since become a close friend. I'm glad he and my good buddy Kyle have worked out.

One of the plates looks off center, so I reach out to fix it.

"Ahh!" Marissa says, coming out of nowhere to swat my hand. "You did your job. Now go back to your sabbatical!"

I groan like a petulant child. "Y'all, I'm so bored. You gotta let me do something."

"Not our problem," Marissa says, setting down some plates and silverware.

Marissa and Lilah get caught up in providing water for the guests, and suddenly I feel lonely. I leave the table before I'm tempted to help again and get scolded.

I search the bookstore for anything to read. I've listened to Michael's stuff on audio, and I've loved it, but I'm otherwise not a huge reader. I would say I'm into TV, but I'm not really into that either. I like to be on the move, doing something, keeping busy. Which is why these past few days have been hell. I managed to find a hookup, but it just feels weird and kinda desperate to fill *all* my time up with random sex. I've gone to some AA meetings as well, but I can only go to so many before I get a little stir-crazy. I gotta find something to keep me occupied, or I'm gonna explode.

I make my way outside, and it's a bright day in Glamour Springs, Mississippi. It's Labor Day weekend, and tourists walk up and down the streets. I'm tempted to pull out the hookup apps again because I'm seeing a lot of gay men, but I resist the urge. For now.

When I discovered that Joe cheated on me—with a man he went on to date openly—something cracked inside me, and I lost all confidence. How could he—the man who broke my heart because he was too scared to be gay—go on and find another man to be with when he was too afraid to be open with me? Was I just not good enough?

Having sex with random men helped for a while. Until it became a habit. Now, I love the validation I get from watching a man cum under my control. Makes me feel hot, powerful, needed. But most of all, it keeps the negative thoughts at bay.

I'll admit, though, it's not totally fulfilling. It's always lonely to connect with someone and then watch them disappear, usually never to be seen again, only to let my thoughts pick up speed again until I'm able find someone else to get under me. But I don't know what I'd do instead. So, I just keep having guys over, hoping that this next guy will be the one to quiet my thoughts for good. Christ, sometimes I feel like I'm one of those cats that sits by its automatic feeder, batting it with their paw until they get what they want, convinced in their delusion that they make the feeder work. They say in AA that insanity is doing the same thing over and over again, expecting a different result. I don't drink anymore, but I'd very well say that my sexual behavior is insane. Per that definition at least.

As I watch a group of gay tourists make their way into a nearby pub—one of the more divey pubs of Glamour Springs that attracts the queers—I decide that that's my next destination as well. I could probably get one of them to sleep with me.

When I get inside, I get a better look at the guys, and it turns out I'm not really into any of them. I like beefier, bulkier types. Even bigger than Kyle Weaver. Beefy guys who could crush me. Think your stereotypical high school football bully but aged ten to fifteen years older. These guys are handsome, don't get me wrong, but they don't fit that criteria.

Hungry, I decide I might as well sit down and eat. Not like there's anything pressing back home. My good friend Rhonda takes my order, and as I'm waiting for my Dr. Pepper, I see a man that takes my breath away.

I swear it's like one of those slow-mo things in the movies. He walks in, uses his thick hand to push back his short but shaggy blonde hair, his sunglasses hanging effortless off the collar of his shirt. He's wearing a silver watch and a thin gray tee with loose-fitting shorts where, if they were a little tighter, would show what he's packing. And he's got the perfect amount of blonde stubble that makes his face gleam in the light. When he sits down at the bar, I'm at the perfect angle to see just how thick his back and chest are. The dude looks like he could bench press me if he wanted. And I'd let him do that and a lot more.

But he looks familiar. I can't tell from where, so I decide to take my chances and get a better look.

I swagger up to the bar a couple chairs away and order a non-alcoholic beer. Sober for over six years, I usually don't approach the bar like this. But it's not so much a temptation for me anymore. The only temptation is the blonde hottie sitting a few chairs down.

I don't recognize him from around here, so I suspect he doesn't know that this bar is where the queers usually hangout. Or maybe he does and that's exactly why he's here. Oh, my excitement swells in my chest at the thought. He is exactly my type.

Looking at his phone, he lifts his arm up, revealing a series of hearts tattooed along his forearm, and that's when I recognize him immediately.

That's Tanner Bash.

He plays center for the San Diego Seals. I know this because I keep up with my football, but I didn't recognize him immediately because he looks so casual here and so... hot. I don't know how I didn't see how beautiful he was before. But I have no clue why he's here. Maybe to see Michael and Kyle—that's the only thing that would make sense. I nearly gasp at the thought. If that's true, maybe he could set me up with this hunk. If he's gay, of course.

I get my non-alcoholic beer and thank the bartender, and that's when he looks up at me with those blue eyes, and I swear my heart stops. His gaze lingers on me for a little longer than would be normal for a stranger. Then, he looks me down, then up, taking in my full body. When his eyes meet mine again, they shoot back to his phone, and I swear I see a little blush on those thick pale cheeks.

Now, I may not be the sharpest guy around, but I know how to flirt. And what Tanner Bash just did was check my full body out.

Oh, he's into me.

Now I really gotta shoot my shot.

But then I look around. A man as hot and high up in the NFO as this should be swarmed. Hell, when Kyle Weaver comes into town now, it feels like the whole place shuts down. But the man is sitting there scrolling on his phone completely unbothered. Not even the other gays here are paying him any mind.

This is definitely my chance.

I stroll over to him nonchalantly, then sit one seat away. Not too close where it's creepy, but close enough so we can chat just the two of us. He doesn't look up from his phone, but that's fine. I'll get his attention soon enough. I clear my throat, ready to break the ice. I'll start with something small, not with the fact that's he's a professional football player. I want to make him feel human, normal.

"So you from around here?" I ask.

But the man doesn't even so much as look up from his phone. In fact, I don't even think he breathes. He could be a fucking statue for all I know.

My forehead breaks into a sweat, and I take a sip of my drink.

Chill, Jimmy. He could have just not heard you. Maybe say something a little louder this time. Plus, he's a visitor. It's not like he'll remember you if this goes south.

Alright, I'll try this again.

"You should try the burgers here," I say, louder this time. "Some of the best in town." Besides mine of course.

But then I swear my face goes red when he still doesn't react. He scratches his blonde stubble, and it's like he's one of those iPad kids. He can't look up from his damn phone. And that's when I get pissed. Here in Glamour Springs, we don't give each other the cold shoulder. And we sure as hell don't lead somebody on.

"Hey, man. I'm talking to you. I didn't know professional football players were such assholes."

And that's when Tanner Bash looks up at me and flashes me with the most disgusted scowl I've ever seen.

Chapter 4

Tanner Bash

AFTER CATCHING UP WITH Michael and Kyle at their cabin, I drive to downtown Glamour Springs to try and get a bite to eat—if I even can—before Michael's book event. I didn't know this was happening, but it felt like all the more reason to come.

I'm so conflicted inside, and it's only gotten worse in the last year. Before, I knew I was gay, but it was easy to stuff it down. There had never been prominent players in the NFO who were gay, and I sure as hell wasn't going to be the first one. After I retired, I was going to find a wife and get married. I was going to be the obedient Christian boy I learned would earn me God's favor.

But when Kyle came out, the American public became more tolerant toward gay players. Hell, a couple of college players came out, and the NFO even drafted one of them. And all this turned my attitude toward my sexuality on its head. Because suddenly, I could be gay. I wouldn't lose everything if I was. But then if I accepted this part of myself, how could I be a man of God and raise a God-fearing family?

I park in the lot of the first pub that I see. There's a rainbow flag next to the sign, but I don't care. It seems this whole town is pretty queer. Which is good for them, I guess. But I could never live in a place like this. The state of California is already too much. At least the weather's good, though. I can't stand the humidity and heat here. It's already making me cranky.

As I make my way inside, I mull over what my good friend Kyle said: 'integrity is the most important thing we have. When we deny what's in ourselves, we can never be truly happy'. But if the seed of male divinity is inside me like I learned in church growing up, then doesn't accepting my gayness go against this divinity? This divine integrity?

When I open the doors to the pub, I rub my tired eyes. I can't figure this all out now. At the very least, I'm hungry. So I'll eat and maybe get some shut-eye before Michael's book event. But when I lower my hands from my eyes, I see the most gorgeous man I've ever laid eyes on.

Everything about him is thick. His arms, his legs, his chest, his back, his belly. He has a thick, black beard that goes all the way to his chest, and it's perfectly groomed. He looks like a guy I could stick my dick into and practically cum from his looks alone. God, and that black hair—it's like he was dipped in ink. I wonder if he's just as fury under all those clothes—and just as thick. But when he looks at me, I look away so fast I nearly kink my neck. Speaking of kink...

No, I can't be doing this to myself.

I got all my gay desire out of my system when Chris Whitacre sucked me off. *But then why is it so hard to keep my eyes off this man?*

I order some food, and then he approaches the bar. I feel my underarms begin to sweat, so I pull out my phone and just start playing with the calculator. But not before I take in his full figure. Damn, this man looks like my dream guy. I look away before it looks like I'm checking him out, but when I feel the heat of his gaze on me, I know I held onto him with my eyes for a little too long. I'd better keep my eyes on my phone, or else I'm a goner.

I'm not a huge social media guy, and I don't have any texts, so this is the best I can do. 8 times 8 is 64. Who knew? Let's see. 10 times 10. That's one hundred. I knew that one. 11 x 11? 121. Cool, wasn't expecting that. 12 x 12 is 144. Huh, big number. 13 x 13—169. And that's when I picture him on top of me, his bearded face in my ass and my lips around his—

"So you from around here?" he asks me.

Oh, fuck. He's sitting right here.

I'll just pretend I didn't hear him. I'll keep putting in numbers. He won't know a thing.

And then he asks me something else.

Goddamnit. I swear if I let myself talk to this man, I'll be taking him back to my motel. This is the last thing I need to be doing right now. I'm supposed to be on the way to being a family man, not getting off with some random hottie from small town Mississippi. Isn't this the south? There shouldn't be gay men confidently coming up to me like this. Sheesh.

You know what? If he keeps trying to talk to me, I'll be an asshole. That'll be easy with how crabby this heat is making me. They're all about Southern hospitality down here? Then I'll be frigid and mean. That'll keep him away from me.

And that's when he shows how pissed he is, so I put on the meanest face I can.

"What the fuck's your problem, man?" I ask. "I'm not gay, okay? So stop fucking talking to me."

He recoils almost as if I punched him in the face, and he looks so hurt. I'm tempted to abort my mission to be mean and apologize instead, but then that would mean really talking to this guy. And I can't have that.

"Sorry, I just thought—"

"Thought what, exactly?" I say, channeling my inner douche. "That I was gay? 'Cause you're dead wrong."

By now, the bartender's watching us, and a table of gay looking guys have gone silent, listening in on us.

"I—I'm sorry," he says, getting up from the stool. "I'll be going."

"Good," I say. "Sheesh."

But as he sulks out of the restaurant, guilt burns my entire torso. By the time my food arrives, I'm not even hungry anymore. Usually, I can't determine why I'm not hungry. The best I can do is say it's the result of some vague sadness or whatever. But this loss of appetite can be directly traced. I should not have been so mean to that man. On the off chance that I do have one or two more gay sexual experiences, I doubt he'd ever reconsider doing anything with me. But more importantly, I did learn kindness in church growing up. And even though shooing this man away was to protect my own divine integrity, couldn't I have done it a little kinder?

No longer hungry, I push my food away and leave plenty of cash on the bar to pay for it. I wanna get a sizable nap in before the book event tonight. If I see this dark-haired hunk later, I'll consider apologizing. As long as his looks don't tempt me any further.

Chapter 5

Jimmy Dillon

As I sit there in the Book Corner watching my good friend talk about the release of his new book, I know I should be over the moon for him.

But I couldn't be angrier.

Who does Tanner Bash think he is?

Fucking telling me off in front of the whole restaurant? I'm no creep, but my chats were not uninvited. The man checked me out. The least he could say is that he wasn't interested, not embarrass me in front of everyone. Goddamn. I had to go to an AA meeting right after just to calm my nerves. Jesus, you'd think a whole lotta money and prestige would make people less stressed and more kind. But Tanner Bash is exhibit A as to why that's the biggest falsehood on the planet.

After the Q&A, there's a mix and mingle afterwards, catering provided by yours truly. Michael, the author, sits at a table, while Martha and Llewlleyn, the bookstore owners, help facilitate the signings. The people who aren't eating right away get in line for their book to be signed.

I hover over by the table, watching as those not in line take their firsts, then their seconds, and some even their thirds. I may wish that I knew how to cook more, but I'm damn proud of what I can manage to whip up. I love watching people enjoy my food. It makes me feel like I'm the glue holding the social event together.

Silas, a cowboy buddy of mine from Alabama, comes to my side. "Your food's a success as usual," he says, taking a bite of a deviled egg. "Mmm. I don't even like hard-boiled eggs, but you made these delicious."

"Thanks," I chuckle. Being around Silas always lifts my mood, at least a little. A few years back, he ran away from his abusive family in Alabama, wanting to find a safe place in the south to be gay. He found Glamour Springs, the queer safe haven of Mississippi and, well, the whole South. Martha and Llewellyn, the owners of this bookstore, took him in as one of their own. Now, he helps manage the place, but he's also been studying to be a physical therapist. Right now, he's even wearing his scrubs. But he's also got his cowboy hat on. He wouldn't be Silas without it.

He finishes off one of my mini burgers, which are a classic. "How'd you manage to get all this done?"

I shrug. "No sleep. And Lilah and Marissa helped out a bunch, especially with the salads. But I don't know if you heard about my little 'sabbatical'." I say with air quotes.

He laughs. "I did. My poor guy's on probation."

I grunt. "I just don't get it. I work hard. I just want to expand our menu."

"But sleep is important, man," he says. "And your menu's fine as it is. Maybe Lilah and Marissa are right. Maybe it's time to rest and explore other hobbies."

Other hobbies. Psh. Only things I care about are keeping my business afloat and getting laid to keep my mind preoccupied.

On the topic of getting laid, I'm still angry at that asshole Tanner Bash. Not just 'cause he rejected me. My ego isn't that soft. But I am angry that he was such an asshole about it.

And speak of the fucking devil.

As I watch Kyle greet Lilah and Marissa, the douchebag himself joins the conversation, carrying a plate of *my* food no less. Wish I poisoned it now. Kyle introduces him, and my girls shake his fucking hand.

"You alright there, boss? You look pissed." Silas says. He looks where I'm looking. "Ain't that Tanner Bash? Plays for the Seals, right?"

I blow air out of my nose, annoyed that Silas recognized him faster than I did. "Yeah, and it turns out he's a Grade A tool."

"No way. Why?"

I'm about to recount the story, but then I realize how embarrassing it is. And how I don't look too good in it either.

"Just shot me down," I say. "Was rude about it."

Silas frowns. "Is he gay?"

Curiosity replaces the anger in my body for just a minute. "I don't know," I say. But then I harden as I remember the whole incident. "But he checked me out. Real obviously too. And then I felt confident asking him out, which only led to him cursing me out in front of the whole restaurant."

Silas grimaces. "Sheesh. Yeah, sounds like an asshole. Possibly gay too."

"And here he comes," I say, my stomach twisting. Kyle's walking over with the devil spawn himself. Before, Tanner's plate was nearly full, but now it's almost empty, and he's digging into his last mini burger.

"Kyle Weaver," Silas says as they clasp hands. Meanwhile, I just glare at Tanner *Bitch*. He looks at me with complete surprise, as if I'm the last person he'd want to run into. Ditto, asshole.

"Good to see you, Jimmy," he says as he wraps his arms around me my shoulder. I hug the big guy back, grateful to no longer be looking at the douchey, yet somehow-more-handsome-than-before Tanner. I hate to admit that I wanna know how that blonde stubble feels against my skin.

"You, too," I say as we pull away from each other. "How many more stops you got?"

"Well," Kyle says. "We're going to Texas after this, and then we're done. Which is good. Because Michael wants to get back to writing his next book." Nearby, Kyle's fiancé Michael is signing hardcover copies of his book for a young gay couple.

"That man just doesn't stop, does he?" Silas asks.

Kyle smiles mischievously. "No, he does not."

"Hey, Tanner here," he says, inserting himself into the conversation. As he holds his plate up, I can see just how thick his bicep is. I'm tempted to just lean down and lick it and have him squeeze me so hard I—

"Good to meet you, Tanner," Silas says.

I just nod at him.

"Good buddy of mine from the NFO," Kyle says, putting his hand on Tanner's shoulder. "He plays for the Seals. We went to Miss U together."

I perk up at that. At Miss U, Kyle was part of the underground club of gay football players who all fucked each other. If Tanner went to the same school, and he and Kyle are friends, then that could mean...

"It's a pleasure," he says. He picks up one of the last of my homemade fries on his plate. "I gotta ask, who's cooking is this? It's fucking phenomenal."

Silas and Kyle shift to look at me, and I just fold my arms contentedly as it dawns on the asshole that I'm the one feeding his huge ass.

With food, that is. I'm not thinking about stuffing his actual ass with any-thing.

"That would be me," I say, nonchalantly raising my hand.

He drops the fry, and I swear his face has gone one shade lighter. I can't resist smirking at him. Didn't realize it was me he was complimenting. Hah. Fucking prick.

Kyle looks down at Tanner's plate, then up at his friend with wide eyes. "You're eating."

Tanner nods, then goes rigid. "I guess I am."

"You said food's been giving you trouble. Sorry," he says to us, then Tanner. "I know that's private. But this is a big deal. You've said it's been hard for you to stomach really anything as of late."

"No, you're right," Tanner says. "This is a big deal." He looks up at me. "Thank you for making such good food."

I want to reply with something snarky, but his praise is so genuine that it leaves me speechless. Out of anything that could happen today, I was not expecting to be rudely rejected by an NFO player only to have him genuinely praise my food hours later.

Lilah and Marissa come to join us, and I'm just praying they don't say anything embarrassing about me. I'm not trying to keep up my reputation with the mean hottie Tanner at all, it's just that—ah, fuck it. That's exactly what I'm worried about.

"You two mentioned you work at the diner nearby," Tanner says, making conversation.

"We do," Lilah says. "Jimmy here's our manager."

When Tanner locks on me with those blue eyes again, it's like I'm frozen in place. I need to go back to hating him or else I'll try to ask him out and embarrass myself again.

Kyle furrows his brow at my managers. "Didn't you two say that Jimmy's not working right now?"

"Yeah," I say, scoffing. "They put me on sabbatical against my will."

Marissa rolls her eyes. "It's because he's working too hard for no reason. It's not healthy."

"And you know what else isn't healthy?" I retort. "Sitting in my house and doing nothing all day."

"Not my problem you don't have hobbies!" she says.

My face goes red, embarrassed, especially with Tanner listening. I love Marissa, but sometimes she just makes me wanna—

"Wait," Kyle says, folding his big arms. "This is perfect."

We all look at him, curious.

"Tanner," he says. "You need a personal chef right now."

He nods.

"And Jimmy," he says, looking at me. "You're not working right now, but you're bored out of your mind."

"Clearly," I say, but then when I think about what Tanner might think about me being bored all the time, I decide to amend my answer. "Sometimes." I don't want him thinking I'm a loser or something.

"And Tanner, Jimmy's food is the only thing you've been able to stomach as of late. I know this sounds far-fetched, but what if Jimmy became Tanner's personal chef for the football season? I know you got an extra room on your property. Seems like fate to me."

Tanner and I balk, but the rest of the group just nods. "Live in San Diego?" Silas asks. "Sounds like paradise."

"That would be good for him," Lilah says. "A change of scenery sounds healthy."

"And it'll get him out of our hair," Marissa says.

I scoff. "Y'all, I'm right here."

And Tanner's just shaking his head, his face pale, as if we're discussing his funeral. Jeez. Didn't realize that living with me for a few months could be that bad.

"What do you think, Tanner?" Kyle asks.

"I mean," he says, scratching his stubble. He looks conflicted but also resigned as if this is bound to happen. "His food is good. He'd be paid of course. And I need a chef ASAP."

Everyone looks at me.

"What say you, Jimmy?" Kyle asks.

I cross my arms and purse my lips, thinking. Living in San Diego does sound really nice. I grew up here in Mississippi, only a few hours away. But the farthest I've traveled is Texas, and that wasn't a whole lot different than here. But living in San Diego? I can't imagine how handsome the men are—and how many more there may be. I love Glamour Springs, but the tourist turnover is only so high. And the beaches—golly. It's not like I'd be doing much here anyways. Lilah and Marissa don't want me working for the next few months, and I'd be cooking for Tanner, which would keep me busy. Oh, and fucking. I'll definitely be fucking many, many men. Fuck. In San Diego, I'd be sitting pretty.

"How long?" I ask.

"I would need a chef until we finish the season," Tanner says. "And that depends on the playoffs. This is my last year, so I'm hoping we make it. So at least through December."

"Fine with us," Marissa says. "That'll keep him away from the restaurant for that long."

I glare at her, then sigh through my nose. No point in fighting her now, especially with this opportunity. Tanner Bash may be an asshole—a hot asshole, but still—yet I'd be living in California for Christ's sake. Maybe it's time get out and explore. I think I'd be a fool not to take this opportunity.

"I'll do it," I say. But then I amend it so I don't sound so desperate to be around Tanner. "That'll keep me from going stir-crazy."

Tanner looks up at me, almost angry—maybe worried?—but I glare at him right back. He looks away before too long, and I get a sense of satisfaction. At the very least, I've established with my glare that I'm not gonna take any more shit from him.

"Well it looks like you got yourself a chef, Tanner," Kyle says, patting him on the shoulder.

Tanner blushes and puts on a boyish smile, and now I have to be the one to look away because it looks too damn handsome on him.

"Thanks," he says. And then he turns to me, but I keep my gaze focused elsewhere.

"And thanks for agreeing to help me out. Let me get your contact info, and I can give you payment details."

I cross my arms, ready to give him attitude. But the man is paying me after all. And, I hate to say it, but it looks like there's an important reason why he needs a personal chef—something personal. Even though he was a dick to me, I'll be the bigger man and make this just a little bit easier for him.

"Sure," I say, pulling out my business card. "Here's how you can contact me with the information. I'm assuming I'd need to move to San Diego as soon as possible?"

He shrugs. "Yeah, as soon as you can."

I sigh, not really bothered. It's an adventure, after all. Something to keep me busy. And now that I don't have the restaurant to keep me tied down, I don't see a reason to dilly dally here longer.

"I'll pay for your travel," he says. "Since you're already doing me a huge favor."

"Well alright," I say. "Getting the royal treatment."

With how rude he was at the restaurant, I expect him to roll his eyes. But I see him laugh a little. Oh Christ. Did I just flirt with this asshole? Marissa pats me on the back. "I'll miss ya," she says. "But I'll be happy you're gone."

I pull her in for a hug, then eye Lilah. "You two don't burn down the restaurant while I'm gone, alright?"

Lilah laughs and shakes her head. "That's why you're on a sabbatical—so the place doesn't burn down."

"Alright," I say, embarrassed. "I get it. Don't' worry, I'll be getting out of your hair soon enough."

And as we wrap up our group conversation, I can't help but sneak glances at my new employer, Tanner Bash. And, if I'm not mistaken, I catch him sneaking glances at me. My chest tingles as it dawns on me that it might not be random Californian men I'm sleeping with, but Tanner.

So long as I don't misinterpret his signals again.

Chapter 6

Tanner Bash

GOING TO VISIT MY buddy Kyle was supposed to give me more clarity about this whole sexuality thing. But it didn't, and now I couldn't be more on edge. Because, for the next four to six months, I'll be living with one of the sexiest men I've ever seen. And, Lord help me, I already know he's into me. If I wanted, I could flagrantly disobey God and pursue my homosexual feelings for this man as soon as he arrives.

But under no circumstances will I let this happen.

As I'm cleaning up my guest house, I get an uneasy feeling in my stomach. Sure, he'll be my chef, which I was in desperate need of, but I'm also in desperate need of finding a woman and starting a family. How am I supposed to do that now with a hairy hunk cooking for me all day? This is like my gay fantasy. And I'm not supposed to be living my gay fantasies.

Exhausted, I take a break from cleaning and stand up to assess my progress.

Jimmy Dillon, my new personal chef, will be staying in this small guest house next to the pool after he arrives tomorrow morning. It's got one small bedroom, an open kitchen, and bathroom. It sits on a small hill that leads down to the beach. Not much, but it'll be a nice place for a single man. Besides, he'll be over in my house most of the day cooking for me.

Oh man. He's going to be in my house most of the day.

I know it's crazy that I hired one of the hottest men I've ever seen to cook for me, but it's not like I had a choice. I needed to find a personal chef, and his food was the only thing I've been able to stomach in what feels like ages. It only made sense to hire him. Now, I just have to somehow keep my thoughts pure and eyes off of him whenever he's around. I can do that.

I hope.

Feeling uneasy about the whole thing, I decide to step outside, clearing my head of the scent of bleach and lemon. The sun is setting over the beach, and I find myself walking to my fence to watch it. No matter what mood I'm in, watching the sunset always makes me feel better.

I feel like I have one of the best NFO deals out of anyone. I get to play as a center for the San Diego seals. I'm paid handsomely, allowing me to afford this beachside property. It's smaller than most houses on the street, but I don't need much as a single man. When I marry and start a family, I'll have to relocate, but I can enjoy it while I'm here.

In church growing up, I learned that hard work earns us blessings, and this whole property feels like confirmation of it. I've come a long way from Georgia to be here, and I'm not gonna let some bearded, thick, handsome, gruff man from Mississippi get in the way of that. Speaking of which, that accent, man. Sheesh. He's got the swagger of a demigod, I swear, and that voice just puts me right at ease. It's even sexier than Kyle Weaver's accent.

What the hell am I saying? I should not be talking about a man this way.

I shake my head, then walk over to the edge of the pool. I sit down and stick my legs in the water and try to sigh out all my impure thoughts. My whole life, I've done well by always doing the right thing. Growing up, that meant doing good in school and football while my brothers were out getting drunk and knocking up girls. It meant going to church and listening to the word of God with Gramps when home got too rowdy. And now, since this is my last season, it means finding a woman to start a family with once I'm retired.

A tan man pokes his head above the hedges that divide our yards. He stands in the backyard of a huge, modern three-story house, and his backyard has a volleyball court.

"Tanner Bash!" he yells. "Football player extraordinaire."

I sigh. I'd rather be alone, but Yousef's a nice guy. I don't want to come off as rude, and I don't really have that many friends in the city besides Carter. So I try to be agreeable.

"What's up, Yousef?" I ask.

He walks around the side of the hedge wearing a blue tank top, white shorts, and bare feet, which is generally more clothing than I usually see him in. He's a gay, middle-aged Persian man who's been living in the home next to me for decades now. He's in what I've heard him describe as a... polygon? No, that's not right. Poly... something. Fuck it, I don't know, but he's got more than one partner, and there's always other guys coming in and out of their house. Personally, I think that's a little weird. Seeing men and women hold hands with each other on the beach is already pretty jarring. But having more than one partner of the same sex? That's pushing it.

"Mind if I join you?" he asks, slipping off his flip-flops.

I gesture to the pool, wanting to be friendly. "Have at it."

He walks over and sits on my side, far enough away to be respectful but not close enough to be personal.

"How's the start of the football season?" he asks.

"We lost the first game," I say. *And it's my fault because I can't keep my damn calorie intake high enough,* I want to say. But that feels too private.

He winces. "Bummer."

We both sit there in silence, and I'm starting to wonder why he came over here in the first place. This silence is making me uncomfortable.

"You mentioned the other day you were looking for a personal chef," he says. "Did you find one?" Even though he's lived in the U.S. for almost as long as I've been alive, I can still hear the Middle Eastern lilt in his voice, especially when he says any word with a 't' or 'd'.

"I actually did," I say, kicking my feet just a little bit, while Yousef's moving his feet steadily back and forth.

He smiles wide. "Congrats. When does he arrive?"

"Tomorrow," I say. "He's staying in this little house from here." I point to my small yellow guest house. "He's from Mississippi."

"Oo, a southern gentleman like you," he says. "Is he attractive?"

It feels like someone grabs hold of my heart and squeezes it.

"Oh, sorry, you are not gay."

I breathe a sigh of relief that it's not obvious. Because how am I supposed to build a nuclear family if people can guess I'm gay?

"Ha, no, I'm not," I say.

"A shame," he says. He stands up and kicks the water off his feet. "Well I'll have to come by and introduce myself once he's here. And, as always, the invitation is open for you, and this new chef if he'd like, to join us for our meditation sessions or weekly potluck."

I nod, looking at the bottom of the pool. Yousef and his polycule—there, that's the word—like to have a little get together every Sunday before the week starts. And it's not just the polycule—it's a collection of his friends. I've heard them get loud and boisterous, and it seems like they have a really good time. But it doesn't really feel like my scene. I'm not really a people's person—never really have been. Too much drama, no matter their race or gender or whatever. They also have a meditation session down on the beach every few days. I've thought about taking him up on the invitation, but it happens at sunrise, and that's way too early for me. Early morning practices are already enough.

"Thanks, Yousef," I say. "I'll let you know."

"Enjoy the sunset, and have a goodnight," he says, making his way back over to his house.

And I can't help but feel a pang of sorrow. Though a part of me wanted to be alone, another part of me really wanted him to stay here talking to me. But this first part of me—the stronger part—kept me quiet. I'll probably just play on my Nintendo Switch for the rest of the night.

I sigh, then stand up as well, kicking off the excess water back into the pool. At the very least, with Jimmy working as my personal chef, I won't be so alone. I'll just need to keep him distant, that's all.

Chapter 7

Jimmy Dillon

After I cum inside some beefy twenty-something, I get him off by sitting on his face, and then I gotta ask him to leave. I got an early flight to San Diego tomorrow.

"Um, I was wondering..." he says, fumbling to put his sweatpants on.

I hoist my jeans up and buckle them together, making my hairy belly jiggle. Then I grab my shirt. "What's up?"

"I'm here for a couple days," he says. "Maybe we can meet up again. This was fun."

As I slip on my shirt, I spot a shine in his eye, showing me just how earnest his request is. Which makes me feel bad. Normally, with these younger guys who don't have a lot of experience, I like to go a little bit slower with them, getting them off more than once and making them feel at home. That's what I wanted, at least, when I was in my twenties, so I try to pay it forward. I also like how they look at me like some sort of savior when I do.

Whenever a gay man comes out these days, their first stop is the app. For me, it was the bars, but result is always the same: sex. So, especially with the younger ones, I try to be kind. Thoughtful. Tender. Because, chances are, it's exactly what they need. I've had it more times than once where after I get a man to cum, he comes out to me. Other times, a man—usually a younger one—is going through a rough patch. He just wants to feel accepted. So, regardless of the reason for their distress, I just hold them and make them feel loved. That's all we need sometimes, really. Someone to hold and love us. And I'm glad I get to do it when I can.

But not tonight.

"I'm sorry, guy," I say. "But I got a flight at the ass crack of dawn. On any other day, I would."

He frowns and slips on his pants. "Alright," he says, picking up his shirt. But I can hear in his voice just how disappointed he is.

"Come here," I say. I pull him into my arms and kiss him on the forehead, and he hugs me tightly, nuzzling his furry face into my chest.

He doesn't cry, but I can tell just from how tightly he's holding me that I helped him more than just getting him off tonight. Once he's fully dressed, I take him to the door.

"Great having you over," I say. I open the door, but he doesn't budge.

"I know I'm not from here," he says. "But can I get your number?"

I close the door slightly, then rub the bridge of my nose. "I'm not sure if I'm the relationship type you're looking for," I say honestly. After the debacle with Joe, my ex, I began to prefer casual sex. And that hasn't changed.

"I get it," he says, stepping out the door. "Forget I asked."

He walks toward his car, and I'm about to close it. But then I look around my house.

It's perfectly clean. I did a deep clean today so I wouldn't be coming home to a dirty house, and I triple-checked every little spot to make sure I was thorough.

And I'm not tired.

Which means that I'll just lay in bed with my thoughts until I'm lucky enough to fall asleep—hearing my mom tell me I'm not good enough, that I should have sex with men more my age. And that's the last thing I want.

I pull open the door and step out onto the porch. "Hey, John!" I call out.

He's just about to get in his car when he stops. "Yeah?"

"Why don't you come in and spend the night?" I ask.

The guy pauses, then shuts his door. And then he comes walking right back to me.

Bingo.

I won't have a lonely night after all.

When he reaches the porch, our lips meet without a word. I drag him inside and slam the door. I break from the kiss to drag him upstairs.

Once we're in my room, the horny man practically tears off my clothes and gets to sucking me. When I feel that righteous sensation, my eyes roll to the back of my head. I lay back on my bed, and I have the feeling that once I get the both of us off, I'll be tired enough to sleep.

He sucks me greedily, almost getting me off that way, but then I put him on his side and stick it in him with a little bit of lube. He moans like the little slut he his, further turning me on. And then I get to pounding him.

I wrap my arms around his torso and dig my teeth into his neck.

He gasps. "Yes, Daddy," he says. "I need you inside me. I need you, Daddy."

And that gets me to climax. With one final thrust, I push myself inside him as hard as I can and squeeze his muscular pecs, groaning away the pleasure. He grabs my hands and kisses them over and over again, like I've just granted him a new life.

My dick still inside him, he gets off. As we're drifting, I remind him that I have to leave early.

"All good," he says, nuzzling his back into me. "Just wake me up when it's time."

"I will," I say, relieved I'm not sleeping alone.

My eyes falling shut, I feel contented knowing that, at least for just one night, I'm important. Desired. Needed. And, to be honest, that's the feeling I chase more than anything else.

* * *

After I convince this hot young man to let me go at four in the morning, my buddy Silas drives me to the airport in Memphis. We arrive at the drop off just as the sun is rising, and the air is surprisingly crisp.

"If you bring home a California boyfriend," he says, helping me get my luggage out. "Bring one of his friends for me too."

I laugh. "Come here," I say, giving him a big ole hug. "If I find any California man, he can be yours, so long as you let me fuck him first."

Silas chuckles as he pulls away. "Come on, man. You gotta settle down some time."

Just the thought gives me chills. I grab my backpack and sling it over my shoulders. "I'm still sowing my wild oats," I say. "Living my life after Joe took it away."

He shrugs, yawning. "Fine. More for me. Text me when you land?"

I grab my luggage and turn toward the exit. "Will do. Thanks for taking care of the house. Try not to burn it down! And no orgies without me!"

He laughs. "Take it easy, Jimmy!"

To my relief, I get through security and find my gate with relative ease. And once I sit down, I freeze to process what I've just done, like a printer finally catching up with its queue. Not only am I stepping into my third state ever, but I'm also flying for the first time. I guess I didn't give myself the time to process this last night—you know, with all the sex and cuddles and all. And I was too distracted talking to Silas' about his PT program on the way here to let it sink in. But now that I'm sitting here with absolutely nothing to do, I guess my mind finally processed it.

With my plane boarding in forty minutes, I decide to go to a nearby Dunkin' and grab some breakfast. Not super hungry, but that gives me something to do. And that does the trick. Because by the time it's time for me to board the plane, I've just gotten my food, and I'm chowing it down as I step in line. Apparently, Tanner Bash got me Business Select seats, whatever that means. All I know is that it means we're boarding first, which is great. Less sitting around.

And then, finally, I sit in my seat.

And I have nothing to do.

Quickly, the thoughts catch up to me.

I should have checked in with Marissa and Lilah before I left. They're completely taking over my restaurant, after all—the staple of Glamour Springs that I built with my blood, sweat, and tears. Well, did I really build it all by myself? Because I know that Martha and Llewellyn at The Book Corner helped me out with my loan, and I did get a little bit of ease from the bank because they were wanting to build more small businesses in Mississippi. And should I really be proud of it? Because the food there is really unhealthy, and I know how many people are going vegetarian or vegan these days. See, this is why I was exploring new recipes. We have to get with the times. Mom would say—

I sigh and close my eyes, rubbing the bridge of my nose as I feel a headache come on, from lack of sleep or self-hatred I don't know, but one thing is clear: in California, I gotta keep busy so I can keep these thoughts at bay. Or I'm gonna fucking lose my mind.

And, under no circumstances, am I going back to alcohol. Luckily, there are AA meetings everywhere. As long as I stay busy, I'll be fine. Which I should be. Tanner Bash is fucking ginormous. He'll probably need to eat a shit ton of food, which means more work for me. It's all good. I'll be fine.

So, as the flight's getting ready to take off, and my thoughts get more rowdy than ever, I decide to take one of those night-time antihistamines that's supposed to help you sleep. And I hope to conk out. So, when we take off into the sky, I don't really pay attention to the cool sensations of taking off the ground, and I don't bother to look over the shoulder of my neighbor to gaze out the window at the rising sun. Because Lord knows I'm not the one sensitive enough to understand and enjoy such simple things. After all, that's what Mom—sometimes literally—tried to beat into my head as a kid. And I've found it's best not to try and go against this message. Because any time I do, that makes the thoughts so, so much worse.

I manage to get some shut eye before our layover in Vegas, and I manage to carry over my sleepiness to the next connecting flight. So, by the time I land in San Deigo, I've managed to sleep almost the entire trip.

When I'm on the way to the luggage pickup, I get a text from Tanner saying that he's ordered an Uber to pick me up, and then the even bigger realization dawns on me.

I'm going to be Tanner Bash's private chef for the rest of the football season, the center for the second best NFO team in the country. The same jackass who so rudely rejected me when I came onto him. He may be hot, but he made it very clear to me that he was not into men. Guess he wasn't part of that underground Miss U football sex cult after all.

After I text Silas I've landed, I grab my luggage and head to the spot where he says they'll pick me up. Even though Tanner Bash may be an asshole, I've had worse bosses. And the pay will be phenomenal. Plus, I'm living in San Diego for fuck's sakes. If anyone else were in my shoes, they'd be piss-happy. My sponsor tries to hammer gratitude into me. Maybe this is one of those times where I should be grateful.

I step outside, and I'm immediately hit by salty, warm air. Not hot, humid air like back in Mississippi. But ocean air. The kind that clears your nostrils, your pores, and your soul. I've only felt this when I went down to the Mississippi coast with some buddies in High School. But that pales in comparison to this.

There are palm trees everywhere, and it feels like everyone's smiling, even when they're clearly not—and even then it feels like their souls are smiling. The sun shines brightly, and I'm even hearing people speak other languages—Spanish, I think? And an Asian language I can't recognize. Wow. I'm far away from Glamour Springs.

My Uber arrives, and he quickly hops out of the car to load my luggage into the back. He's a young Indian man with a bright smile. I try to return it, but I'm still a bit groggy from the antihistamine. Maybe living in California will give me a permanent facelift like all these folks.

In the car, Girish, my driver, talks my ear off, and his enthusiasm is so electric that he nearly zaps the antihistamine from my system. And, even though the GPS says the drive is forty minutes, it feels like five, and we're soon in one of the ritziest neighborhoods I've ever seen.

"So you'll be cooking for the football player Tanner Bash," he says, carefully looking over the steering wheel as we slowly drive down the street lined with huge beach houses. I can't see beyond them, but I'm pretty sure behind the row of houses to my left is the beach. The Pacific Ocean.

"I will," I say, noticing just how strong my accent is compared to his. Great. Nothing will out me as a Mississippian faster than my voice.

"So cool," he says. "I'm not his personal driver or anything, but he always reaches out to me when he needs a favor. And he tips well. He's a great guy."

"Huh," I say, hanging on to the handle above the window. "Didn't know Tanner was such a nice guy." *Because the dude yelled at me in front of an entire fucking restaurant.*

"He's quiet, but very kind. Especially for a celebrity."

Right. A hot celebrity. One who may be nice but is meaner to me than a cat dipped in water. Best I just do my job and steer clear of him lest I wanna get yelled at again.

We pull up to a smaller looking house painted a light pink. It's modest compared to the houses around it, but it's still sizable, and the lawn's well kept. We park in the driveway, and when I step out of the car, the sound of the waves fills my ears. And suddenly, everything else goes quiet. I can hear the sound of Girish taking out my luggage, and there's sound coming from where I think the beach is. But the sound of the water drowns them all out, and it calms me. My thoughts, too, which is saying something. I think I may like it here.

"Come on," Girish says. He hands me my backpack, and I try to grab my luggage, but he just shakes me off and grabs them himself.

"Go on back," he says. "I'll follow. You'll be staying in the guest house."

"Guest house," I say, trying to tone down my accent. Unsuccessfully. "Fancy."

"Oh, you'll really enjoy living here Mr. Dillon," he says as we walk up the driveway to the back gate. "I've been living in the city for five years now, and I don't think I'll ever leave."

Hearing the sound of the waves, the salt of the ocean clearing my sinuses, I don't think I can blame him. And oh, I can't wait to see just how handsome the men are. Maybe I'll find a California boyfriend after all.

And that's when I see him. Not my California boyfriend, no. But Tanner Bash.

In the tightest swim trunks I've ever seen.

He's floating in the pool, his entire body just resting on the surface of the water. How the hell is he doing that? His huge, muscular, bearish body just floats along effortlessly, and I have a perfect view of just how beefy he is without a shirt, his lightly hairy, semi-freckled body the picture of perfection. I like body hair, but a blonde guy with little body hair makes me weak in the knees. Like he's so hot he doesn't need hair to make him look better. And those sunglasses with his blonde stubble make him look just like the lifeguards I jerked off to in my head as a kid. Except, this time, it's a full-grown man with biceps strong enough to crack my head open. God, I wish he would. That'd fulfill my school bully fantasy.

And those trunks.

Jesus almighty.

Even from here, I can see the outline of his manhood. And God bless us all, he does not look small.

"Mr. Bash!" Girish says as we walk up to the pool.

Tanner immediately submerges under water and folds his arms over his body, and I immediately picture that one photo of Marilyn Monroe trying to cover herself while standing over a vent. But it's like Tanner's more embarrassed than coy. Which makes no sense to me. He's got nothing to hide and everything to show.

"Girish!" he yells. "And Jimmy," he says less enthusiastically, wading to the side of the pool where we stand. He rests his arms on the rim, and goddamn I have to look away because his arms have more bulges than the fucking Himalayas themselves. And the three hearts on his forearm only make him look better. Only a god's arms could look that nice, so I guess NFO lineman are the closest things we got to divinity on earth.

"Howdy howdy," I say.

He pushes himself out of the pool and walks over to a towel on a chair nearby, dripping carelessly everywhere. And boy does he look better out of the water than in. Seeing how embarrassed he was when we saw him, I'm worried he'll wrap the towel around his torso. But, to my relief, he wraps it around his trunks after he dries the top of his body off, giving me a full view of the America's hottest dad bod. Step aside, Kyle Weaver. Tanner Bash is your new Sexiest Man Alive.

What the fuck am I saying? I'm not crushing on my new boss, especially after I discovered what an asshole this man is.

"Should I take his luggage inside the guest house?" Girish asks.

"I'll take it from here," Tanner says, grabbing hold of one of my suitcases. "You go on ahead and go about your day. Thanks so much."

Girish nods and turns to me. "Nice to meet you," he says. "Enjoy California!"

I wish him goodbye, and as I grab hold of my other suitcase, watching Tanner's huge, muscular back as he walks to the guest house on the other side of the pool. As he walks, his ass cheeks swish, and each one is as round as the moon—just as big, too. I think I will enjoy California. Even if it means I can only look at the man in front of me.

He opens the door to reveal the cozy interior of the guest house: a small kitchen, a bedroom with a queen bed, a small living room with a couch that looks a little too big for it, and a TV.

"Attached to the bedroom is your bathroom," Tanner says, setting my bag next to the couch. He turns around and snaps his hands together near his waist, showing just how toned his arms and chest really are. I look away and set my bags down, and it hits me just how tired I am. I mean, I'm always tired these days, but I'm especially tired now.

"I'll let you get some shut eye," Tanner says, walking to the door. "You must be tired after your flight." The man's talking like a damn robot. Sheesh. The only thing warm about this welcome is how hot he is. At least he's not yelling at me.

"Sounds good to me," I say, rubbing my eyes.

"You wouldn't mind if I ask you to start working tonight?" he asks. "I hate to admit it, but I'm craving your burgers. I bought some of the ingredients already, and they're in my kitchen."

Christ, I'll be cooking in this man's kitchen, doting on his every nutritional request. Might as well strap an apron on me that says *Tanner's Little Bitch*. And imagine if he made me wear it naked.

Not happening, Tanner.

The man's straight. Even I know better than to go after a straight man.

"Sure," I say. "Should I just..."

"Come over after your nap," he says. "You get some rest."

"Roger that," I say. Then I plop myself down on the couch.

"See you later," he says. And he shuts the door.

Now, if I didn't have trouble sleeping, I'm sure I'd conk out right here. But laying on my dick this way, paired with all the mental snapshots I took of Tanner Bash's shirtless torso and ass, has me hard already, despite how much sex I had last night.

I turn over and take my dick out of my pants, opening my eyes just a bit to make sure that Tanner isn't there. I mean, I don't imagine that could be too bad, but I don't want to give him a reason to call me a pervert.

So I'll just be a pervert in my head.

But with all the things I'm imagining doing to him, I think that's the only suitable thing to call me.

Chapter 8

Tanner Bash

I SPEND THE REST of the afternoon doing God knows what. I dick around in the kitchen, making sure everything's clean. I shower to get the pool off me. Even though it's a saltwater pool, I still feel cleaner after a shower. I play on my little Nintendo for a bit. But none of this gets the thought of Jimmy Dillon out of my head.

I should *not* have agreed to this. Having my ideal male type living just across the pool? Cooking for me every day, getting all sweaty in the kitchen? Christ, when I walked past him, I caught a whiff of his natural odor, and I almost fainted. Because it was intoxicatingly sexy. I need to keep this man farther away from me than I thought. Maybe I can set a little rule for myself: I can't be in the room with him unless absolutely necessary. Yeah, that will work.

While I find myself dozing off on the couch, I hear a knock on my back door. And then it opens.

"Tanner?" he calls out. Oh man. That *accent.* God, why did you have to bring me a country boy? Do you even want me to get married to a woman? He shuts the door, and that's when I jump to my feet. I know I'll do my best to avoid him, but I can't really do that when I need to show him around the kitchen. So, just like the at the bar, I'll build a wall between us. Along with a mote and some barbed wire for good measure.

"That was a long nap you took," I say, walking into the kitchen. "Almost slept past dinner."

I don't look at him, but I can hear him scoff.

"Well, I did have a long flight."

"That I paid for," I say. I glance at him. "You're welcome, by the way." Okay, that was a little much, I'll admit. I don't need to be this mean.

"Uh, thank you?" he says, not thankfully at all.

I don't respond. Maybe I'll tone it down. I don't want to antagonize the guy, really. He's making my food after all.

He checks his phone. "It's only five. Didn't know Californians ate dinner so early."

"Sometimes we do," I say, shrugging. And when I feel a pain in my stomach, I'm reminded that I haven't really eaten at all today. As coach said, I need to be heavier by next practice. Which is tomorrow.

"I'm just hungry," I say.

I prop myself against the fridge and face him fully, getting in a good look of him. And man, how is this guy so effortlessly beautiful? His beard is full and rich, and his bushy eyebrows accentuate his masculine face. He's got a belly, and it's tasteful. Like the kind a hardworking man develops eating a little too much after a hard day's work. Like the deserved indulgence of a working-class man. And oh man, the hair. I can see it poke out of his T-shirt, and I get the sudden desire out of nowhere to have his toned, hairy forearm flexing as he squeezes my—

"You said you bought the stuff for hamburgers?" he says impatiently.

I shake my head and look away. "Yeah." I open the fridge and pull out a large board that holds the ground beef, lettuce, cheese, and tomato. I set it on the counter.

"Spices?" he says.

"I'm sorry?"

"You have spices?" he asks. "Like seasoning?"

Why did I think he said 'spicy' like he's from a goddamn romance book that I hear all these women are reading these days?

"Oh, uh, here."

I walk over to my cabinet where I know I have some seasonings. I pull out some pepper and salt. And cumin I think? But the labels are faded. I set them down in front of him.

He wipes his face, almost like he's embarrassed for me.

"I'll go to the store tomorrow," he says, putting his hands on his hips. Oh my, he is such a specimen. Like he's made of pure beef. I feel like the media really pushes men that are skinny with washboard abs, which is maybe why I didn't realize I liked men until later in life. Because once I saw men with a little more meat on them, ones that were husky and sweat easily, I was weak in the knees. To me, these were real men. If the media had shown me men like Jimmy Dillon as a kid, I'd have known about my sexuality a lot sooner.

But that doesn't matter anymore. Because he and all other men are off limits.

He rubs his hands together. "Well I better get started. If you'll let me run through your kitchen supplies, I think I can scrounge something together. You got buns?"

I swear my face goes red, and I tense my shoulders. "Buns?"

He deadpans. "Like hamburger buns? Or are NFO players so pampered they don't know what that is?"

I relax my shoulders. So he can be an asshole too. Got it. At least he wasn't talking about the buns attached to me.

"Sorry," I say, looking for an excuse. "You just have a strong accent."

"Aren't you from the South, too?" he asks. "Kyle said you're from..."

"Georgia," I say quickly.

He huffs. "Georgia, huh?"

"Yeah," I say, trying to cover up the bun incident. "My accent faded by the time I was in college. It's cool that you still have yours, though. I know the ladies must like it." *Fuck.* Did I really just say that? I'm just digging my grave deeper.

He smirks. "Men like it, too."

My stomach sinks to the floor. "Oh, right. Forgot you're, uh... let me grab the buns for you." Before I can embarrass myself any further, I grab the puns from the pantry. I toss them to him, and he catches them with more skill than I would expect.

"Alright," he says, clicking the stove on and reaching into one of the cupboards underneath to pull out a pan. "Dinner will be ready soon."

I nod, and I'm about to leave, but something stops me. I feel magnetically drawn to the kitchen. And it's not just because a hot man is—oh God, he found my old apron, and he's putting it on.

Okay, but I'm definitely not drawn to the kitchen because there's a hot man, now wearing an apron emblazoned with the words 'Kiss the Hot Chef' surrounded by flames I won at a Seals Secret Santa party a few years back, cooking for me inside. Really, it's because I can't remember when there was someone else besides myself inside this house. And it feels nice.

"So," I say, sitting down at my kitchen table. "How'd you get into cooking?"

Somehow, he found quality olive oil in my pantry to pour into the pan, and he's just set down a seasoned burger topped with cheese onto it. It lets out a satisfying sizzle.

"Had to," he says shortly.

"Had to?" I ask.

He glares up at me, then looks down at the pan, his face softer now. "I kinda had to raise myself," he says, moving the burger around on the pan with a spatula. "Dad wasn't around. Mom left me to fend for myself."

I suck air through my teeth. "That's rough, man." I hold back what I'm about to say next, thinking it's too nice, but I can't just be rude to this guy now. Not after him saying something like that. So I decide to say it.

"I'm sorry to hear that," I continue. "Musta been hard."

He chuckles, but there's no mirth there. "Tell me about it."

It's silent for a little bit, but it doesn't feel as tense as it once did. That's how I'd like it to be with us: distant but not tense. Professional. He is my employee, after all. Part of me wants to tell him that I had similar struggles with my family, but that feels too personal.

"So, is 7,000 calories a day manageable for you?" I ask. "To cook for me, that is." We talked and agreed about this before I secured his flights, but it's something to talk about. And I want to talk.

He nods. "Oh, yeah. No problem. I'll have to get a little creative, but I like cooking. I'm thinking three big meals a day. And I'll get high protein snacks for you for practices and games and stuff."

The way he's reciting all this as he's cooking feels... comforting. He's so sure of himself, like he possesses some self-knowledge that I haven't been able to find myself for some reason. Almost like the parent or older brother I never really had. Well, I did have parents and brothers, but they weren't self-aware like Jimmy seems to be. Once I was in middle school, I was on my own while my frazzled parents tried to keep the house afloat by managing the chaotic lives of my addict brothers. They tried to be there for me sometimes, but they were often too tired or busy or angry to take the time to talk to me. And when they did, they were distant, mean, or absent altogether. Like Jimmy, I had to support myself. But I don't near have the surety in myself like he does. And having him exude this confidence while he's here cooking for me in my kitchen, knowing that he's gonna be here at least for the next four months makes me feel—I don't know, safe? Something like that. Regardless, I like it.

And it's not because I think he's hot.

He asks me about how I think the Seals will do this season, which is easy enough to talk about. Football's been the one consistent thing for my entire adult life, after all. And I'm surprised to see that Jimmy's interested in what I'm saying. As he cooks, he focuses on me when he's not flipping a burger, and I can't remember the last time anyone looked at me with such purpose—like I'm the only thing that matters. Maybe when I was a team captain back in high school, or sometimes when I lead the other lineman. Definitely not growing up in my household. But he's looking at me like he sees and understands me, which I think I like. In a friendly way, of course. By the time I'm finished explaining our odds at getting to the playoffs, he places the last burger on a plate with the other s.

"Finished," he says. While we've been talking, he's cooked about six burgers. And they're sizable. He plops three on buns he was able to toast in the same pan and hands them to me, tomatoes and lettuce to the side.

"Thanks," I say. "This looks wonderful."

"Oh," he says, clapping, showing how thick his arms are. Seriously, how? I have to work hard to make my arms thick. And what does he do? Flip burgers? Not like that's a bad thing, but sheesh.

"Do you have condiments?"

I freeze, hearing the word 'condom' come out of his mouth, but I manage to pull myself together without him noticing.

"Oh yeah," I say. "In the fridge."

He nods and pulls out some mustard and ketchup I had on the side. "Hope you're okay with this," he says, setting the bottles down on the table. "I'll get some more things tomorrow."

"This honestly looks like the best dinner I've ever had in a while," I say, genuinely. "I've been craving your food ever since I tasted it back in Glamour Springs. It's been difficult for me to eat lately, but your food makes it easier. So, thank you."

He smiles without teeth, crinkling his eyes and making my stomach bunch up. Christ, he's handsome.

I look away, and he looks down.

"Hey, look," he says.

I turn to him, and he pulls out the part of his apron that says 'Kiss the Hot Chef', then looks up at me with a wider smile, giddier now.

"This is cute as hell," he says, laughing. "Why didn't you tell me this was what I was wearing?"

I laugh, then I realize what I'm doing and stop myself, blushing. Oh no. This is exactly why I came up with my rule earlier. If I say in a room with him, conversations like this might happen—conversations where we both laugh and smile at each other. Next thing you know, my nose is in his pubes with his cock in my mouth. And I stopped doing this kind of stuff after my last time with Chris.

I stand up with my plate. "I'm, uh, gonna go into the living room to watch TV while I eat," I say.

He shrugs. "Alright."

I walk into the living room, sad that the conversation is over, but happy that I won't be tempted any further. I sit, set down Jimmy's delicious looking burgers, and turn on the TV. I turn to the latest NFO game—Billings vs. Salt Lake City. I pick up my burger, take a bite, and oh my God—

"Who's playing?" Jimmy asks, walking into the room.

I look up at him, surprised, still chewing on his meat. And oh my God does it taste good.

Fuck, no, that's not what I meant. His burgers taste good. His cooking. *Not his meat.*

He plops down next to me, a little too close for my comfort. Naturally, I sit farther away, and he just gives me a dirty side eye. *It's not personal*, I want to say. *You're just too hot for me to resist.* I thought that telling him I was coming in here was enough to say I wanted to eat alone. But I guess he didn't get the message.

"Salt Lake vs. Billings," I say, swallowing. "And you really outdid yourself with these." I hold the burger up. "I don't know how you did it with just my ingredients." I look down at the plate. "And made so many."

He takes a bite of his and chews. "You said you needed calories," he says. "And I provided."

Lord he did. We sit together, watching the game for a bit. And now I'm not so sad he walked in here with me. It feels nice having a warm body nearby.

"Oh my God," he says.

I glare at him, not liking being startled. "What?" I ask. Surprises like this remind me too much of the house I grew up in.

He points to the entertainment center just below my TV. "Is that a Super Nintendo?" A boyish smile is spreading across his face, and it's contagious.

"Yeah," trying to keep my lip from curling up. "I got all the Nintendo's actually. Even the Switch 2."

He sets his plate down and walks over to the entertainment center. He sits down cross-legged and looks back at me. "Can I look through?"

"Be my guest," I say, trying not to smile at his genuine enthusiasm, but it's been forever since I've had someone so interested in something of mine.

"Oh my," he says. "You have—no way!" It's like he's a six-year-old opening up his gifts on Christmas morning. I want to be annoyed with him, to call him immature, but he honestly feels just so refreshing.

He holds up a cartridge to me, and I squint to see it. It's Super Mario Kart.

"Can we play it?" he asks.

I set down my plate and finish what I'm chewing. I haven't played on my Super Nintendo with another living soul in what feels like years, let alone Super Mario Kart. I think the last time I touched the game was back in college. There were a couple football buddies of mine back at Miss U who revived my love for the old console, but we've since fallen out of touch. I did grow up playing it, though, so that would be fun to play again. Especially with one so enthusiastic about it. I know I *should* say no—I need to stay distant from Jimmy Dillon. But passing up a social interaction to do something I'd really like to do with someone who's expressing genuine interest in me feels insane.

"Fine," I say. "But I gotta warn you. It's been a long time."

He gives me that handsome smile again, but I don't look away this time.

"I'll go easy on you," he says.

"Whatever," I say, trying to sound disinterested even though my heart has started to race. Which I don't understand. It's just a video game that I'm playing with my cook who I have a strictly professional relationship with.

He pulls out the console and sets it on the wood floor. He pulls out some controllers and plugs them into the console, but when he stretches out their cords, he frowns.

"Pretty short," he says. "Looks like you'll have to sit down here."

"That's okay," I say, finishing off the last of my second burger. Goddamn, Jimmy's cooking is good. It may be complicated trying to stay away from him, but I'm glad I hired him. I'll be up to my calorie count in no time.

I bring over my plate with my last burger and sit down next to him. I help him get it all set up, and pretty soon, the Super Mario Kart title screen is blaring on my TV. The theme song brings me back to my childhood, and I don't think that's a very good thing. Because my heart starts to beat faster, and my breath gets all quick.

"Oh man, this is awesome," he says. "Brings me back to hanging out with my neighbors as a kid."

I try to respond, but I just remain frozen. Like someone has taken my voice and my will to move.

"What do you wanna play?" he asks as selects on the two-player game mode.

"Uhh," I croak.

The little green one-up icon hovers between Grand Prix, Match, or Battle. My blood goes cold imagining doing the first two, and I'm too frozen to understand why. But Battle mode is what I did with my buddies in college.

"Battle," I somehow get out.

"Sounds good," he says. "But I do want to get some races in."

We select our characters, and I slowly let myself relax. Maybe I'm just uneasy playing with Jimmy. He's still pretty much a stranger at this point, a stranger I'm keeping at arm's lengths for obvious reasons. That's probably why.

But when we get to battling, the music of the battle stage brings me back to college when I remember having a group of friends I regularly did things with. The unknown unease I had earlier drifts away, and I melt into the game.

"Oh man," Jimmy says. "These controls are harder than I remember."

I focus on the screen, my tongue slightly out. "Not so much for me," I say. "This is muscle memory."

In a clean sweep, I manage to pop all his ballons while he he's having trouble moving away from the wall.

"Okay, that was a warmup," he says as my victory music mocks him. "Let's try again."

And we do. This time, he manages to drive around the course, but I still KO him without taking a hit. He glares at me while Yoshi, the character I selected, gloats. And I can't help but smirk.

That's when he smiles at me, and I can't help but smile back.

"I see you're enjoying yourself," he says. "Takes a lot to put a smile on your face, huh?"

I blush and look down at my controller.

"Guess I should let myself lose more often," he says. "A smile looks good on you."

"Play again?" I say, wanting to change the subject. "This time, for real. Best two out of three."

He picks up his controller. "You're on."

And to my surprise, he's actually more of a challenge. In the first game, he gets two hits on me. In the second, he manages to win.

"Alright," I say, genuinely enjoying myself. "Winning game."

"Psh," Jimmy says. "It's mine. And when I win, we get to do a race."

"Fine," I say as we start the game.

And this is the closest one yet. We both get each other down to our last balloon, and that's when Jimmy goes on the offensive. Just as he throws a red shell, I turn a corner, and it crashes against the wall. Then, using my lone red shell, I turn around quickly and snipe him with it. And the game is over.

"Oh man," Jimmy says, pushing me lightly. "You really got me."

I put my arm up to where he touched me and rub it. Not because I didn't like it, but because his touch sent a ripple of warmth though out my body.

"Good game," I say.

"Good game," he says in agreement.

"I'll be a good sport and let us race," I say, wanting to keep this moment going. "If you still want."

"Hell yeah," he says, his effervescent enthusiasm returning as if he never lost.

We quit the battle and go to the Grand Prix mode, but that sluggish dread returns, and I feel my heart speed up. Yet I don't pay it any mind. I'm having a good time with Jimmy, and it's so nice to have company with someone so kind. We select the mushroom cup. But the second the music starts, I immediately know where all of this dread is coming from.

Suddenly, I'm back in my nine-year-old body. I'm playing Mario Kart with my second oldest brother. He was fourteen at the time. We're playing this very racetrack, having fun.

And then I hear footsteps stomping down the stairs.

"Richard Bash," she says, her voice sharp and strong. "Tell me why I found your father's liquor underneath your bed."

"That was Matthew," he says, blaming our older brother.

And then the shouting match begins. My mom's yelling at my brother, him yelling back. Soon, my dad comes down and joins the fray. Ricky gets physical, and my dad tries to restrain him. He hits my dad and runs away, and both my parents chase him, all while this very same music I'm hearing now blares on the T V.

Crying, I try to finish the race for both of us, but the sound of stomping and yelling upstairs makes me realize how alone I am. How much I want to get out. But how I have nowhere to go.

"Tanner," Jimmy says.

"Tanner," he says again, putting his thick, hairy hand on my shoulder.

I startle to the present. "What's up?" My gaze meets his, and there's concern there. Genuine concern. For me.

"You just froze," he says. "Are you alright? Was it something in the burger?"

I look down at my third burger, suddenly not hungry anymore. "No, no," I say, trying to brush his hand off my shoulder. But I'm too weak to move it. So I put my hand on his instead.

And he doesn't move his.

Our eyes meet again, and suddenly the distance between us simultaneously feels minuscule and expansive at the same time. I want to close the distance, kiss him, make myself feel good after all the emotions I just relived. But that doesn't feel like a good idea for so many reasons. He's my chef, and I'm trying to be a man of God. This will not happen.

Using all the strength I have, I move his hand off of me and stand up. He clears his throat and wipes his nose, trying to act nonchalant as if we didn't just gaze longingly into each other's eyes. Good. Hopefully he still keeps it professional after this.

"Sorry, uh," I say. "I shouldn't have played that. It's just—video games aren't for me."

He looks up at me like I've said something silly. I don't think this is something a man with all the Nintendo consoles would say, but it's all I could muster up. "I got practice early in the morning," I say, scratching the back of my head. I start making my way to my bedroom. "I'll leave some cash for you to go grocery shopping and get whatever you need to cook for me this week. Yourself included."

"Alright," he says, and it sounds like there's hurt in my voice. Right. Because I've rejected him twice now.

I sigh to myself, lingering at my living room entrance. Better to distance myself than get close to this man. I have divine rules to follow, and pursuing Jimmy would break all of them at once.

"Thanks for dinner," I say. "See you later." But I hope I don't have to see him again for a long time. I scurry off to my bedroom, leaving Jimmy alone, pushing down the lingering emotions from my flashback.

I don't know what just happened, so I'll pretend it never did. That's all I know how to do, anyways. It will have to do.

Chapter 9

Jimmy Dillon

It was my mistake to try and be kind to Tanner Bash. I should have it in my head by now that he's a cold asshole who just wants me to cook for him. That's all.

After using Tanner's second car that he's letting me borrow to go grocery shopping, I walk into his kitchen with the last of the bags, and I put them in the last little square of free space the counters have. The rest is filled up with all the other groceries I bought both for me and him. And sheesh, California's expensive. But I can't complain. I didn't pay for any of it. Tanner's the one who left three grand on the counter for me. Said it was for all food related items this week. This is something I could spend on food on any given week *for my diner,* but I'm just cooking for me and Tanner. These next four months, I'm gonna eat like a king.

The house is quiet without him in it, which I don't like too much, but it's better this way. I prefer him gone. I'd rather not have him here, asking me all sorts of questions and smiling with that cute face of his, then running off after something random. We were just playing Mario Kart. He was all tensed up, and I asked what was wrong. And that's when he just pushes me away. Fine by me. I can see people say Tanner's a nice person, but what people say about him being quiet fits a lot more with how I'm getting to know him. Even though I was caught up in the way he talked about football. When the man does get talking, he lights up like the sun.

But no matter. I'll just ignore Tanner. I'll find a group of guys to fool around with here, and then I'll never even notice Tanner Bash around. Regardless of how hot he is.

By the time I've put all the necessary groceries away, set out what I'm cooking, and get some of Tanner's very nice coffee brewing, the house feels too quiet and my thoughts too loud, so I go and turn on the TV for some company. I tune into the ESB network and listen to commentary and thoughts about how this football season will turn out. That helps drown out the noise in my head.

And I get to cooking. Tanner said he got some protein bars to eat before practice, but he'd like to eat something substantial when he gets home as well as have a big lunch and dinner prepared. Easy. So I make some breakfast casserole, stuffed with plenty of protein, and once that's in the oven, I get lunch prepared. After that, I can set aside the food for dinner, but I'll also have some down time. That's when I plan on getting myself set up at a local gym, and if that doesn't take enough time, I've brought some of my AA books on the kitchen table so I can get some studying in. That kinda fills me with dread though. I'm already liking how this cooking keeps my mind occupied, and spiritual studying doesn't preoccupy me the same way. I'm not ready to be susceptible to racing my thoughts here in San Diego.

But I can worry about that later. I'll make some pesto chicken sliders for lunch.

Just as I'm beginning to brown the chicken, a tall, wiry man with tan skin comes to the back door. He's wearing shorts and a tank top, holding shrub shears, and he would startle me if he didn't look so friendly with that smile on his face.

He peers through the window at me, widens his eyes, then dashes. Okay, what the hell is going on? Is this the California version of a house burglar?

I sneak into the living room to turn off the TV and wait by the back door while the chicken's cooking. I want to make sure this weird man isn't trying to break in.

When he returns, instead of holding shears, he has a plate of what looks like a cake of rice with fruit on top. He knocks on the door, and I open it, more curious to see what he's holding than anything else.

"Can I help you?" I ask.

"Wow," he says. "You're more burly and handsome than I expected."

I blush and wipe sweat from my forehead. But then I squint at him. He's got an accent I don't recognize. Is he from the Middle East?

"Sorry, my manners." He extends his hand. "I'm Yousef, your neighbor. Well, Tanner's neighbor."

I shake his hand. "Beyond the hedge?" I ask. "In the giant three-story mansion?"

"That's our place," he says. "Live there with my boyfriends."

"Cool," I say, happy to remember that California is kind to queers like us. No wonder so many live here.

"I wanted to come by and bring some Tahchin and introduce myself," he says.

"I'm sorry. Tah-what?"

He laughs. "May I come in?"

Without a word, I gesture for him to enter. He knows Tanner, so I think it's fine. He saunters in, and he's got the pep of a man in his twenties, but he has to be at least fifty years old.

"Smells good," he says, looking at the chicken on the stove. "So exciting to meet another cook." He sets the rice dish on the table. "This is Tahchin, a dish from my country. Think of it like a cake of rice with chicken in the middle." He picks up a Styrofoam container on the plate. "And then you pour this gravy on your piece when you're ready to eat."

I lean down to smell it, and it's somehow floral and earthy, and I get a strong scent of turmeric. My chicken starts to sizzle, and I know it's time to take it off the burner.

"Thanks so much for the food," I say. "It was nice to meet you, but I have to get cooking."

"You are from Mississippi, no?" he asks, not having heard me over the sizzling chicken. He sits down at the kitchen table.

I move the chicken to the plate and start lathering on some pesto to some mini-rolls I bought at the store. I wasn't anticipating having anyone else here, but the man seems nice, and more company means less time with myself.

"I am," I say. "Definitely far from home."

He smiles, holding his knee in a cross-legged position. "I hope you are enjoying the beach," he says. "That is one of my favorite things about living here. Best place I've ever lived."

I glance out the kitchen window, and that's when I notice that I can see the beach from here. Tanner's house is on a hill, so I can see down onto the shore. There are a few people walking around, and I'm briefly mesmerized by the waves crashing into the sand. I don't know how I didn't pay attention to this before. I must have been rushing so much to preoccupy myself that I didn't stop to notice.

"Oh man," I say, still staring at the water. "It is gorgeous." I turn back to him, intrigued by Yousef's charm. "Did you say you were from here?"

He shakes his head and uncrosses his legs. "No, I am from a city called Tehran, which is in Iran. I grew up and went to university there, but I was fortunate enough to get a Ph.D. here in the states. I began working in a tech company up in the bay area, and then I moved down here to retire."

"Retire?" I ask. "Already?"

He laughs. "Oh, you flatter me. I am older than I look—sixty-three."

"Wow," I say.

He blushes. "I was also fortunate to make a good amount of money that allowed me to retire and live down here in beautiful San Diego."

"I have to ask," I say. "What did you do that allowed you to retire in such a gorgeous house?"

He smiles. "Well..."

As I finish preparing the sliders, I listen to this man explain his cybersecurity expertise, fascinated. Back in Glamour Springs, it's mostly just black and white. I can only count on one hand the amount of times I've had a meaningful conversation with someone outside the country. And truthfully, I wish this number was higher. Because just by the way Yousef is holding himself I want to keep talking to him. He's confident and happy, and I get the feeling he has some experience and wisdom that I might find interesting.

He widens his eyes mid-explanation about how many millions his cybersecurity breakthrough made him when he spots one of my books on the table. "Is this yours or Tanner's?" he asks, pulling it to him. "I didn't know Tanner was in AA." It's a copy of AA's big book, sorta like the main manual.

"It's mine," I say, scratching the back of my neck, feeling embarrassed for some reason.

"I am also in recovery," he says. "Been for fifteen years."

A smile creeps on my face. "No way. I've been for about six years. Really changed me."

"Oh," he says, clutching the book to his chest. "The Twelve Steps are the best thing America has to offer."

I chuckle. "You think so?" I ask, finishing the preparation of the sliders. By now, the breakfast casserole is done, too, and I take it out of the oven.

He takes a whiff of it. "Wow, you are talented. I'd ask for some, but I know that Tanner needs to be a big strong boy. He needs all the food he can get."

I laugh, partly because I'm trying to imagine this gregarious man and the quiet, hulking Tanner having a conversation. I can't even picture it.

"And yes," he says, standing up. "I know so. And it's helped me in more ways than one. CMA is where I found the twelve steps, and I'd be dead if I hadn't."

"CMA?"

"Crystal Meth Anonymous," he says.

My stomach gets uneasy. I've heard that on many of the apps that I use, it's just as easy to find drugs as it is sex, if you know what you're looking for. And whenever I think about how many gay men I know drink or do hard drugs, my blood boils. It's one thing that gay men and queers alike have had to really struggle to feel at home with themselves. But to peddle substances to vulnerable people like these because they know that many of us are hurting? It's diabolical.

"I'm glad you found recovery," I say.

He lets out a heavy sigh, one where I can feel there's a lot behind it. "Me too."

There's a moment of silence between us, and I feel bad, like I should give him some food or say something more heartfelt, especially since he brought something that looks so good. But I'm at a loss for words. Maybe I can give him just one of the sliders.

"Here," I say, handing him one of the pesto chicken sandwiches. "Because you went to all the trouble of coming over."

He takes it in his hand and smiles. "Oh, thank you. You know I'm next door, and I manage the hedge that Tanner and I share, so don't be a stranger. I will leave you to your cooking, but don't hesitate to reach out if you need anything."

"Thank you," I say. "Hey, I do need a buddy to go to AA meetings with me."

He puts his hand on his chest. "I'd love to take you to the ones I go to," he says.

"Perfect."

He walks to the door, and there's a pang of sadness in my chest. I don't really want him to leave. Not yet. He's good company, and I want to talk with him more.

"Oh," he says just as he's about to walk out the door. "Some of my recovery friends and I do a little meditation session down on the beach every morning. Not an official meeting—some of us go to other meetings after. But it's nice and peaceful, and we're always looking for new faces."

"Meditation, huh?" Just the thought of that makes me queasy. Sitting alone with my thoughts and doing nothing? Absolutely not.

"I'm good," I say, shaking my head as I clean up the stove. "Meetings are good enough for me."

"Of course," he says. "Me and my polycule also do a weekly potluck on Sunday. If you'd like to join."

"Sounds awesome," I say. "I think I'll take you up on that." Wow. A gay, poly, Iranian man who's a millionaire global expert in cybersecurity. I am far away from the South. And I love it. Glamour Springs is a queer safe haven, but there's nobody like Yousef there.

He pulls out his wallet from his pocket, takes out a card, and sets it on the counter. "Old business card, but my number's here. Reach out so we can coordinate a meeting."

I take it and shove it in my back pocket. "Will do, Yousef. It was a pleasure chatting."

"It was all mine," he says, smiling. "Happy cooking!" And he's off, and I'm alone. Again. I know I said I was going to wait to cook dinner, but I figure I'd do that now. Something to do. Then I can deal with my boredom afterwards.

I decide to prepare some steakburgers and fries that I can just throw on the stove when Tanner's ready for dinner. Meanwhile, I try some of Yousef's Tahchin, and it's to fucking die for. I've never had anything like this. I should get the recipe from him.

Unfortunately, I finish cooking the burgers sooner than I would like. Now that I've prepared Tanner's meals for the day, I'm all out of shit to do, and Tanner isn't even home from practice yet. So I decide to do what I always do when I've got nothing else going on.

I get on the apps.

When I arrived in San Diego, I quickly hopped on the apps to finally check out the California men and to let the algorithm know where I was. In other words, so people would see and message me. And boy was I smart to do that. Because I've gotten nearly a dozen pushes and a handful of messages just from having my profile on display.

I scroll through who's shown their interest, and I'm pleasantly surprised to see so many men I'd like to fuck. When I made it to San Diego and saw so many conventionally attractive, smiling people, I got worried that these would be the type of men on the apps. But a lot of the men I'm seeing have something to hold on to. Just the way I like.

I hop into a conversation with a bearish man, and we cut right to the chase. He wants to get fucked, and he's wondering if I can host. Ah, the golden question. There's a saying around the community that a gay man can never have all three: the ability to top, host, or drive. I think it's bullshit, but when you're trying to hookup with a man, it's actually pretty rare for them to have all three.

Back in Glamour Springs, I did. And here, I always top, so we're good there, and I have Tanner's car to use freely. But I'm not sure if I can host. I better ask my confusing boss.

"Hey," I send to him.

He replies almost immediately. "What's up?"

I remember that those were the exact words when I caught him in his weird stupor last night. If I remember correctly, he almost looked pained. Like he was reliving some bad memory. I try to shake the thought from my head. Now's not the time to be thinking of ice-cold Tanner. But the image of his scared face lingers in my mind.

"You good if I have someone over to my little bungalow?" I ask. I don't specify who or why. He doesn't need to know. And why should he care? He's straight. He told me so when he rudely rejected me back in Glamour Springs.

"It's your place for the next few months," I say. "So yeah, you can obviously have friends over."

Jesus. Even in his messages, he manages to come off an asshole.

I just thumbs-up his message and get back on the app. I give the guy the info, and then I walk over to my little house to wait for him. But before I do, something on the beach catches my eye. I walk over to the part of the gate where I can see it clearly and try to get a better look.

There's Yousef. He's with a black man who looks about his age, and there's a third tan guy with him. Those are his boyfriends. They walk together closely, and Yousef is walking with that happy jaunt he has.

I've been in recovery for a while, but I don't think I'm at the level of recovery that he is. He feels like a sage. Like happiness radiates off him. I mostly go to AA so I don't drink. When I did drink, I did things I regretted, and it wasn't pretty. I'm lucky to have stayed sober all these years. But that's where my spirituality ends.

My phone buzzes, and I look down to see that my hookup is about five minutes away. That was fast. And while I've been on the app, I've received a dozen or so messages and pushes. I could get used to this. Glamour Springs was nice because it had a lot of turnover, but even then the options were limited.

The anticipation of which tourists would be there that weekend was what kept me going. But here, I have like ten times the options. And the validation. This is fantastic.

As I gaze into the ocean, I feel a disturbance in my chest, something that makes me uneasy. My sponsor's talked about moving from the bottle to the penis. That is, replacing my addiction for alcohol with my addiction for sex. But I don't think that's what I have. Sure, that could be denial speaking. But giving up sex? It's more than just getting off. It's getting to know other men in an intimate way. It's helping other men out when they're having a hard time, just like I did with that young man just before I left Glamour Springs. Besides, I love the way it boosts my confidence. I love looking into a man's eyes when I'm thrusting inside him, watching his face contort in pleasure as he's about to cum. Because I did that. I gave the man that pleasure. My mom drilled into my head, time and time again, that I was worth nothing, that I would never do good in the world. But is a man who brings this much sexual pleasure to another someone so worthless?

The man says he's parked out front, and I walk up to the gate to let him in. "Nice place you got," he says as I walk him back to my bungalow.

"Thanks," I say. "But it's not mine."

"Oh," he says, intrigued.

I look back at him as I open my front door. "Hm?"

"When your profile said you were from the South, I didn't think like South-south. That accent's hot, man."

For some reason, I think of what Tanner said about my accent. He didn't say it was hot, but he said it was cool how I don't try and tone it down, how that's something he felt tempted to do as soon as he got to Miss U. And for some reason, that feels more like a compliment than this.

"Thanks," I say anyway. I take him inside and lead him to the bed that I've only slept in once. Without pause, we immediately start to undress each other.

"I have a request," he says.

"Lay it on me," I say, unbuttoning his shirt.

"I'm way into dirty talk, but like not your typical kind of dirty talk."

"Alright," I say, opening his shirt. He's got a belly covered in fur, and I run my hands through it like it's freshly cut grass on a summer's day.

"I want you to talk to me—like, tell me what you're doing to me. But do it like nicely. Like you're praising me."

"So like a praise kink."

"That's the word," he says with a small smile. He looks handsome that way. But not as handsome as Tanner when he smiles, as rare as it is.

What the fuck did I just say? Yeah, no. I'm not going to think about how handsome Tanner is.

"I can do that," I say. I pull him onto the bed, and we get right to it. And I love it. I love watching his face twist in pleasure each time I shove it in him, the little moans he makes every time I pull out, like he's thirsty for more. And when I tell him what a good boy he is, how well he's taking my cock, he practically melts into my calloused palms. I get him to cum on his back in the first fifteen minutes. Afterwards, I lay next to him, honestly ready for him to go.

He rubs my belly, and I almost jump at the touch.

"You wanna get off?" he asks.

I look at him, then shake my head. "Honestly," I say, thinking of the joy that was plastered across his face and how I was the one to bring it. "I got exactly what I needed."

Chapter 10

Tanner Bash

AFTER I SNAP THE ball, I rush toward the linebacker and shoot my hands out to block him. My hands hit him like thunder, and I dig my heels into the ground, using all my strength to resist his and push him forward. We enter into a stalemate, neither of us moving the other. And when coach blows the whistle, I let go of him with a contemptuous sigh.

The linebacker puts his hand on my shoulder pads. "That was good, Bash," he says. "Held your ground."

"But I didn't move you," I say as players gather around our coach. We slowly join them.

"Hey," he says, hands raised in defense. "Just pointing out where you're working. Better than the first game of the season."

I take off my helmet and spit out my mouth guard into my hands, not even caring that my face is turning red from embarrassment. Everyone else's face is red from the hot, long practice that coach just put us through.

"I've seeing some improvement on the field," Coach Larson, our head coach, says once we're all gathered around him. "But if we're going to stand a chance against the Tigers, I'm gonna need you all to step up your game. Now most of you know how you need to improve." Coach's glare hangs on me for a minute, and I shoot my gaze down to the turf. "So I shouldn't need to remind any of you. Is that understood?"

"Yes, Coach!" We all shout in unison.

"Now break," he says, tucking his clipboard under his arm. "And get plenty of rest for our game against the Leopards this weekend."

We break formation, and then all of us start to jog to the locker rooms.

"Bash, stay here for a minute," Coach says. I groan to myself, but I turn around and jog over to him, completely soaked in sweat from today's practice.

Once I reach him, he looks around to make sure we're alone, then folds his arms and looks at me plainly.

"You weighed in at the same 280 this morning," he says. "What's going on, man?"

"I got a personal chef," I say, kicking my cleat into the turf.

"And is he even cooking for you?" he asks. "It's been over a week, and we've seen no progress. I had hoped you would have a few more pounds by now. How am I supposed to expect you perform well this next game?"

I clench my fists, then release it. "I've only had him for a couple days. I promise you'll see a difference by the next time I weigh in."

"You better weigh more by this next game," he says. "Or else I'm benching you like I said. And this time I'm serious. We can't have a repeat of last time."

Sweat drips down my forehead, and I wipe it away. That can't happen. Football's the only thing I'm really enjoying these days. Well, I did enjoy playing video games with Jimmy. Until I had that flashback.

"I'll do it," I say. Jimmy's food is good, anyways. I can force myself to eat more of it.

"You better," he says. "You're free to go."

I jog back to the locker rooms, and by now, most people are either showering or filtering out. Carter catches me just before I leave.

"You get that personal chef like coach asked?"

I think about handsome Jimmy cooking dinner for me. Man, those burgers were good.

"Yeah," I say. "But I'm hovering around the same weight."

He folds his arms and gives me a serious look.

"What?" I ask, taking off my shoulder pads.

He looks around, then leans in and talks quietly. "I'm worried about you, man. Usually, people have a hard time losing weight. You know, 'cause food is good. But you're not eating, and I just don't get it. It's not like you've been like this for a long time, either. I feel like this is only in the last year that you've been like this."

I stay quiet, not even knowing where to begin.

"I'm sorry, it's just—" he looks around again to make sure no one's around. "I was gonna ask you when we hung out, but you never got back to me."

"No, man, don't apologize," I say, wiping my sweaty face. "I've been the flaky one."

He gestures for me to sit on the bench next to him, and Carter's so nice that I can't say no. "What's going on, dude?"

I suck on my lip and let out a heavy sigh through my nose.

Carter's been a lineman in the NFO only a little longer than me, but by sheer coincidence I've followed him everywhere. He started out in Ohio, then I got drafted to the same team. Then New York for a bit. And now San Diego. We sorta saw it as a divine message that we were meant to be friends. He did, at least, and I was so flattered that someone cared about me that much to even consider me being part of their life divine at all. We've been friends all this time, so I know I should trust him. But even if I could be fully honest about what's going on with me, I'd have to know what's going on with me.

I wipe my eyes, feeling them stinging. "I don't know, it's just that—you know how I've always been a rule follower?"

He laughs and nods. "Oh yeah."

I can't help but let out a small laugh with him. When I was a young player, I took in every suggestion that my personal trainers, coaches, and senior players gave me, so much so that I didn't even know how to improve. Carter was the one who could see me struggling and decided to help me sift through it all.

"I can't describe exactly what's going on," I say. "But that—this rule follow-ing tendency feels like where this is coming from. My whole life, especially in football, there's been something to do. Some way to be right."

Carter scrunches his brow. "Like...?"

"Like in high school, it was get good grades and play well to get a good scholarship. At Miss U, it was to focus on my grades and do well in football. But now..."

"Hmm," he says, picking up on what I'm saying. "You're retiring at the end of this year, and there won't be any more rules to follow after. You must be nervous."

Suddenly, my throat gets tight. I think there is one more rule, actually—the one that I learned at church. I gotta build a family. But he is right—I am nervous. I just don't know why.

"I mean, I was taught to build a family, and once I'm done with the NFO, I can focus on that."

"But is that a rule, though?" Carter asks. "I mean, sure, I got a fiancé, but there's no rule of life out there that says you have to get married. You could be single the rest of your thirties."

His words make my heart race. Whenever things at home got too chaotic, it was Gramps' house I went to. And when I went with him to Church, that was the first place I felt peace. Because, all the sudden, there was a divine order to things. An explanation. Meaning. No longer was I subject to the chaos that defined my childhood home—the lies, the backstabbing, the sudden change of rules, the outbursts. I had scripture, the teachings of God's servants, telling me how to navigate hardship. I was around other disciples who also wanted the peace that came with obeying these teachings. It was like a divine compass was miraculously put in my hand, and so long as I obeyed God's laws, this compass would point me to the promised land of peace and happiness.

So that meant I needed to obey these divine rules. And one of the most important rules I was given in life was to build and lead a family. This was, and still is, my divine duty as a man. And if I'm wanting this compass to work, to continue to give me divine peace and guidance, I have to do what God tells me.

And that means I gotta be married to a woman.

Carter shrugs. "Hell, look at Kyle Weaver. Sure, the NFO isn't totally accepting of queer men, you could come out and find a man just as easily. If that was your thing."

Suddenly, I picture Jimmy—the way he put his big hand on my shoulder and tried to comfort me after I was sucked back into memories of my upbringing. His care for me felt so tender, so warm. More than anything, I wished I could have just fallen into his big, burly arms.

If what Carter's saying is true, I could open myself up to Jimmy. He did hit on me first, after all. So I know he's into me. I could see where it goes. Because, at church, I didn't just learn that it was a man's divine duty to lead his family. I also learned that a husband and wife were supposed to comfort each other, to support each other—that a wife would support her weary husband when he got home from work, and a husband would hold his weeping wife in his arms and kiss her tenderly until she felt better. And when Jimmy put his hand on my shoulder, I saw it, clear as day: Jimmy, my loving husband, and me, the weeping wi fe.

Carter waves in my field of vision. "Tanner, you good?"

I blink rapidly, suddenly feeling lightheaded. And starving. I told Jimmy I had protein bars to hold me over for practice, but I only ate a third of one before getting out on the field.

"Yeah," I say, wiping my face. "What were we talking about?"

"About how you feel you need to get married and how this might have to do with your lack of appetite."

"Right," I say, recalling the conversation. But then it all makes sense. Back at home, I never really felt like I could eat until I felt relatively safe. That was often why I would stuff my face when I got to Gramp's house. There was something about being in a stressful environment that made my stomach clench up and made even the best foods look unappetizing. And, assuming I still behave this way, I'm not eating now for the same reason. Because I feel unsafe. And only two things have changed in the past couple years for me. First, the end of my NFO career means it's time to start a family. And two, it is now possible to be an openly gay man as an NFO player.

And these are at complete odds.

"Well shit," I say.

"What'd you realize?" Carter says, shifting to face me.

I open my mouth to speak, but then I stop myself. Carter's one of my best friends, and I do want to tell him what I've realized, but I don't want to tell him that I'm gay. Sure, I told Kyle Weaver, the first man in the NFO to come out, as well as his boyfriend, but Kyle was already retired then. And he's gay. Carter still actively plays, and he's definitely not gay. And if I do tell him, that's like accepting that I really am a gay man and don't need to marry a woman. But if I can't marry a woman and start a family, how will I have the divine compass that is my relationship with God?

"Still working through it," I say, finally kicking off my cleats. My feet feel relieved, but that's about the only part of me that does. "Thanks for talking through all of this with me."

"No problem," he says. "I'm around if you need to talk."

"I know," I say, patting him on the shoulder. "Thanks, man."

Just as he's leaving, my phone buzzes in my bag. I pull it out to see a text from Jimmy, and my heart skips. No, I can't pursue him. I need to preserve my relationship with God. I need guidance in my life, and I can't have that with Jimmy. I just can't.

I open the text, and it's nothing special. He's just asking if he can have someone over. I say something cold so I can preserve that distance between us, but I let him. It's his place, after all. I'm surprised he's finding friends so quick after he moved here. I guess it's that charismatic personality he has.

Now alone in the locker rooms, I hear a door creak open and some footsteps. Just as I'm putting some fresh clothes on—I'll shower at home—the man I least wanted to see appears in the entry way.

I shake my head. "No, Chris," I say, not even trying to be subtle. "I'm not interested."

"Sheesh," he says, sitting down on the bench even though I basically told him to get lost. "You were talking to Carter for so long I thought it was him sucking your dick."

I scowl at him. "What the fuck's your problem?"

He scowls back. "My problem? You're the one who's always so flighty about sex."

"Dude, I don't owe you a fucking thing," I say. "Leave me the fuck alone."

He pulls down the waist of his pants, showing off his dick. Months ago, I'd be aroused. But now I'm just disgusted and annoyed.

I slip my tennis shoes on quickly and stand up. "I said 'no', dude. Fuck off."

"Come on," he says, the band of his shorts snapping back in place. "You're really gonna say no to head?"

I grind my teeth. After that realization with Carter, I'm still sure of myself. I'm sticking to my divine mandate. And besides, I told myself that Chris was the last time I'd do anything gay. And I'm a man of my word.

I pick up my bag. "You're a despicable man," I say. And then I walk out of the locker room without looking back.

On my way home, my mind churns. I keep saying I need to start dating after the season's over. But maybe I should start now. Carter mentioned a while back that he's got a single cousin he could hook me up with. I could do dating apps, too, if that fails. I've got options.

When I get home, there's a stranger's car in the driveway. Oh, right. He's got that friend over.

I park in the garage and carry my stuff inside. On the counter, Jimmy's got what looks like a breakfast casserole hot and ready and some chicken sliders in a plastic container. On the table, I spot one of those rice dishes that Yousef loves to make. And it looks like Jimmy's already had a slice. I wonder how they got along. Probably great seeing how kind Jimmy is. I hate that I have to be a dick to him, but it's the only way I can keep myself on the straight and narrow.

Starving from practice, I don't even bother getting a plate, I start eating the breakfast casserole straight out of the dish. And oh my God. How does he do this? This tastes better than what my favorite Miss U diner had, the one me and the guys would go to after a night of partying. And that's saying something. I hungrily shove spoonfuls into my mouth, not even caring that I'm getting it all over the counter. I need as many calories as I can get.

And that's when I spot him.

Well, them.

Jimmy walks out of the guest house first, followed by some bald bearded man. He's handsome, but not more than Jimmy. Or me, I'd like say. Jimmy puts his hand on the man's back and walks them to the gate. Through the kitchen window, I watch them, my stomach gradually twisting over itself, my appetite disappearing. When they reach the gate, the bald man leans in to kiss Jimmy, and Jimmy gives the man a small peck on the lips.

And suddenly, I'm white hot mad. Uncontrollably so.

I wait until the man's gone and Jimmy's back in his guest house. Meanwhile, I'm clutching the counter so hard my knuckles turn white. Then I stomp over to my guest house and bang on the door.

Jimmy opens it. "What are you banging for?" he asks, his face contorted in confusion, which somehow makes him more handsome. "Your food's all prepared as you requested."

"Who was that?" I ask, my chest on fire. But I don't even know where this anger is coming from. I just know that I have to get it out.

"Who was who?" he asks. Then his face relaxes in recognition. "That was just, uhh. A friend. You said I could have people over."

I fold my arms. "Your boyfriend?"

He scoffs. "I don't have a boyfriend."

"What?" I demand. "So this is some friend that you happen to kiss? Looks like a lot more than that."

Jimmy folds his thick arms and takes one step closer to me. His furry brows form a deep V, and his brown eyes threaten to swallow me whole. And all this, paired with smelling his sweet, earthy natural odor again, I'm tempted to step back. But I can't back down now.

"What the fuck is it to you?" he asks.

I stare into his eyes. How the fuck are they so brown? Like the rich, coffee brown, the same as the expensive coffee I like to buy and sift through my fingers before I make it?

"I don't want you having guys over," I say.

He huffs air out of his nose like a hairy bull. "And why's that?"

Because I can't stand to see you living the life I want to live, I want to say.

"I don't want strangers knowing where I live. I'm famous, after all."

"You're a center," he says, almost laughing. "I couldn't even recognize you when I saw you."

Incensed, I grab hold of his collar and pull him close, all my stresses of the day—coach, my realization, Chris—pooling into this moment and shattering any shame I might have about my behavior. I stare deeply into his eyes, my entire body on fire.

I'm 6'4". And even though I'm not the weight I should be at, I'm still huge. So Jimmy should be scared of me, him being a good few inches shorter. But he's wearing the most neutral expression I've seen on him, which I think would make me angrier. Yet it just pieces my shame back together, like I'm a puzzle that Jimmy can easily solve. In my household, I was never the angry one. I could never hold it together for very long.

I let go of his shirt, and I step back, nauseated by what I just did.

Jimmy straightens his shirt and folds his arms again. "You done?"

Feeling no more mature than a five-year-old, I nod my head like one. "I'm sorry, I don't know what got into me. If you need to quit or something, I understand."

Jimmy runs his hand through his beard, and just the sight of his handsome face alone makes me have to look away. And that's when I realize that I wasn't angry at him for having another man over. I was angry at him because I was jealous.

And not just jealous because I can't kiss a man while he can.

But because I wish I was the man he was kissing.

He folds his arms again, ready to speak. And I hope he'll forgive me.

"I'm not going to quit," he says. "It's not like my life will be any better back home right now."

I relax slightly, hoping what comes next is my forgiveness.

But then he steps forward, his face deadly stoic, and his face is only inches from mine. He sticks his hairy finger into my sternum. "It's clear to me that you got some issues," he says, pressing into me so hard I'm afraid I'll bruise. "But I won't be treated this way. From the moment we've met, you've been warm one minute, cold the next. I'm fucking tired of it. And you're never going to lay hands on me like you just did again, alright? Or else I'll be walking out faster than you can blink. You understand me?"

I take a breath, intoxicated by his smell, and nod. "I understand. I'm sorry."

He steps back and puts a hand on the door handle. "Good," he says, pulling the door open. "I'll be in later to start dinner. Enjoy the casserole."

And then he slams the door shut, and I feel like I've just lost a tough game after playing in the snowy mud: cold, tired, and disgusted with myself.

From now on, I'm keeping my walls up between Jimmy and me. And now it's not just for my sake. It's for his, too. Because Lord knows my feelings are too strong for the man for anything else to work.

Chapter 11

Jimmy Dillon

Right now, I'm sitting in the San Diego stadium watching the Seals, Tanner Bash's team, play against the Arizona Sparrows. It's been a month since Tanner blew up on me, and back then I'd have sworn I'd never be at one of his games. But after inviting me so many times to his games as a means of apology, the man wore me down.

Since the moment I thought Tanner would beat the tar out of me, we've developed a system. When I'm in the kitchen, he knows not to enter. And when I'm not cooking, I'm in my bungalow. Tanner's tried to make conversation beyond meal logistics a couple times, either through text or before I manage to slip out of the kitchen, but I shut him down. I know he probably thinks I'm mad at him or that I'm just trying to keep it professional. But it's honestly none of those things.

He scares the living shit out of me.

And no, it's not because he's a few inches taller than me or has been growing in muscle from eating all my high protein meals. I'm a big guy, too, and Tanner has the demeanor of a teddy bear. Now I know he couldn't land a blow if his life depended on it. It's because, that moment he grabbed my shirt, I didn't see the center for the San Diego Seals yelling at me.

I saw my mom.

That's what she always did, especially when I was a kid. Act all nice, then startle me with some physical reprimand over a new rule I didn't know existed.

And then she would put me down, in any way she could, using what mattered most to me. If I was doing good in a subject in school, she dwarfed my achievements by comparing me to what older students could do in the same subject. If there was a hobby that interested me, she would list all the ways how I wasn't cut out to do it. And all these words played on repeat from the moment she spoke them to me. My mom made it important for me to meet her standards by holding back her love until I did what she wanted. But even when I gained her love, it was always fleeting. No matter how much I fooled myself into believing that this time, finally this time, I had won her love, I was wrong. Because there was some other way I was deficient.

And truth is, no matter how handsome Tanner Bash may be, I don't know the guy. After playing Mario Kart, I picked up that he may have some emotional issues from his past like I do. But I don't know if that's just made him insecure or an all-out monster like my mom. And I don't want to find out. So, I don't have anyone over anymore, and I make sure Tanner's meals are perfectly prepared. I stay in my own quarters when I can and keep my lips zipped any time I don't need to be talking to him. I will do nothing to earn the man's ire or contempt. Plus, Tanner's straight. It's not like I'm missing out on any sort of good sex with the man, even though him getting mad that I was having someone over did feel strange. Like he was maybe jealous. And, even when he grabbed my shirt, there was a brief moment—very brief—where I was aroused. I mean, how could I not be with the bully fetish I have?

But I gotta admit that this self-imposed isolation has been hella boring. I don't know much about San Diego, and Tanner's my only point of contact. I mean, I've been going with Yousef to his AA meetings, but outside that he's busy with his polycule. There's all the men I've been traveling to fuck, but I don't know—none of them really interest me like Tanner does. He may be broody, easily angered, and quiet, but I like the way the man talks. The way he thinks. He's got this thoughtful outlook that's more interesting than half the people I know. Like, when he was explaining all about football, I loved watching him ease into himself. And he spoke so goddamn earnestly. Plus, when we played Mario

Kart, and I watched his walls gradually go down, I got the sense that Tanner was actually a very sweet and cool guy.

So that's why I finally gave in to Tanner's invitation to come to a Seal's game. I decided that I can experiment letting my guard down with Tanner, just a little bit, to keep myself entertained while I'm here. And, the second I catch a whiff of my mom in his behavior, I'll put that wall right back up.

Tanner snaps the ball, and the play begins. The quarterback dashes back, and Tanner manages to keep their huge linebacker at bay. The quarterback throws the ball out to the wide receiver, and he catches it with grace. Then he runs. And run. And runs.

Folks around me stand up, and I join them. I watch with rapt attention until, finally, the wide receiver crosses the touchdown line. The stadium bursts into applause, and I cheer as well, unable to help but feel a little bit proud of myself. Tanner has asked that I up the protein in my meals so that he can gain more weight. And so far, we have both been successful in that regard. So if Tanner hadn't been as strong today, could he have prevented that linebacker from tackling the quarterback? Maybe not. Even though there are a lot of reasons why a team wins, this is a little story I'm gonna keep telling myself. Makes me feel go od.

It's 21-14 with the Seals in the lead, and the clock runs out before any team can adjust their score. So they win, further solidifying their odds to make it back to the playoffs this year, which is impressive. The Arizona Sparrows have been nothing to laugh at this year, but the Seals still took home the win today. It's kinda cool being this close to a rising team. Maybe they'll end the streak of the two-time Championship Game winners, the Tigers.

As folks prepare to leave, I stand up and rush to the exit. I want to beat the parking lot crowd, but I also want to get home and finish preparing my post-game meal for Tanner. I know how much he likes to pig out after a game, especially one that he won. Plus, I wanna finish all this and retreat to my quarters so we don't have to talk. I've never had to prepare his meals for gameday while also being at the game myself, so I gotta be quick. I'm glad I got my workout in this morning. Trying to fit it in now would be a nightmare. And after all this, I can take my pick of the very hot San Diego men that hit up my DM's daily. If I rush, it'll be a good day.

When I get home, I take the chicken salad out of the fridge and start splitting the croissants I bought in half. It's the beginning of October, but it's still hot here in San Diego, so I figured he'd want something cool after playing in the heat. While I'm scooping the chicken onto the bread, I scan through my messages to see who I'm fucking today.

I get another message from this guy who won't leave me alone. He keeps inviting me to a parTy, which, after double-checking with Yousef, means he wants to do group sex with crystal meth. Yeah, no thanks. I've already had my toxic substance experience with alcohol. I'm not doing that again.

The door to the garage slams, nearly giving me a heart attack.

I immediately shove my phone in my pocket. Tanner isn't really a homophobic guy—he's good friends with Kyle Weaver, after all. But I don't want him knowing what I get up to sexually. Especially after he blew up on me. What is he doing here? It usually takes him at least another hour to get home after a game, talking to coaches and reporters and what not, whatever players do after games. How is he home so early? I schedule my time in the kitchen for a reason: to avoid him.

"Congrats on the win," I try to say flatly. But it's a little more enthusiastic than I intend.

"Thanks, man," he says, taking off his bag and setting it on a kitchen chair. He's wearing a sleeveless undershirt, and he's still carrying all the sweat from his game. Goddamn, his arms have gotten thick, even in the past month.

He eyes the food. "Looks amazing."

"Thanks," I say, focusing on preparing the last of the sandwiches. "You're home early."

"Just wanted to beat the rush," he says. "Besides, coach has been happy with my improvement, so he didn't have a whole lot to say to me after the game. Your food's helped me get back some of the muscle I've lost in the last year. So thanks for that."

I give him a lukewarm smile. "That's great. You're welcome."

Both of us sit there in silence for a minute, and I start to sweat. It's been forever since I've been alone with Tanner for this long. And I don't know if I like it. Which irritates me. Because I *shouldn't* like it. Tanner could be like my mom, after all. I gotta keep myself safe from a potentially toxic person.

"Whatcha got going on for the rest of the day?" he asks. "I feel like I don't know what you do in your free time."

I look up at him skeptically.

"Not that I need to, of course. That's your business. But I'm just curious seeing as you're new to the city."

The hookup app still open, my phone vibrates in my pocket, which is likely from another message from this annoying crystal meth guy. I may like to stay busy, but I don't need drugs to do that. I'm a recovery man.

"I, uh—probably just hangout in my bungalow. No plans."

He laughs. "I like how you call it a bungalow."

I laugh with him.

Fuck. I know I'm blushing now. He's usually quiet, but when he actually says something, it's so earnest.

"That's what it is, isn't it?" I ask.

"Yeah," he says, shrugging. We sit in silence, again, and it feels like I'm the one who just played a football game with how much I'm sweating.

I finish off the last sandwich and set it on the plate. "There," I say, walking around the counter. "Now I got a couple things—"

"Can you hang on a second?" he asks.

I stop myself just before I reach the door. "What's up?"

He waits until I've turned around to face him. He's sitting with his legs spread, and the sun shines in his blue eyes, making them brighter than the ocean I see every morning. Goddamnit. I shouldn't be thinking about this man this way.

"I know you've been trying to avoid me," he says.

My chest tightens. "I mean, no. What makes you say that?"

"I don't blame you," he says. He gets up and grabs two plates from the cupboard. He serves himself a sandwich, and then he puts another on the second plate.

"I was a real dick to you, and I still feel really bad," he says. "This past year or so's been tough for me, for reasons. And I think I took that out on you." He hands me the plate then sits down. But I'm still standing.

"Truthfully, I've tried to put distance the two of us," he says. "I want to keep things professional, but in the process I made things hostile. And I feel like a fool. I'm glad you came to the game today, and I'm hoping that things between us can be more... congenial."

I shift my weight from one foot to the other. He's being so kind now. Is this a trick or something?

"You're gonna be living in my house for remainder of the season—so long as you keep working—so I want us both to be comfortable. Does that make sense?"

I nod. "It does."

"Would you like to eat lunch with me?" he asks. "It looks fantastic."

I look between him and the table. Right now, I could either hightail it out of here and go find someone to fuck, then slink back to my bungalow and be bored out of my mind. Or I could have some stimulating—mentally stimulating—company with a man who's currently being nice to me. I don't see any big issue with that.

"I can do that," I say, sitting down at the table.

"Awesome," Tanner says picking up his sandwich. Then pauses. "I just realized—we could also pick up where we left off." He's pointing to his living room.

"What's—" And then I remember. A few weeks ago, we were playing Mario Kart, having a good time. And then he shut down. "You really wanna play video games again? You said yourself they weren't really your thing."

He shrugs, chewing. "I've got other games. And, wow, this tastes good."

I smile, holding back my blush. "Thanks."

"So you wanna?"

I think back on that night, how bright I saw Tanner's face and how enthusiastic he was. If that's the real Tanner—not the one who got angry and blew up on me—then I could stand to play a little bit.

"What the hell," I say, setting down my sandwich and standing up. "Let's do it."

"Hell yeah," he says.

We go to the living room and get everything set up. This time, we decide on Super Smash Bros. for the Switch, which I've played a few times with Silas. I remember it being fun, but when I start playing it with Tanner, I didn't realize what a fun game this could be.

"See, the cool thing about this game," Tanner says after our first round. "Is that they've done a much better job at making all the characters equal. The bummer about previous games is you could only really stand a chance as a select number of characters playing competitively. But here, that roster is much wider. And I think that makes the game open to more people."

I stare at him, my brows furrowed. "I think that's longest I've ever heard you speak," I say. "Maybe besides you explaining the Seals stats." *And I fucking loved listening to you*, I wish I could say. But that's too far for what we are.

He blushes this time, and that smile looks so good on him.

"How do you know all this?" I ask.

"I like to follow the competitive scene," he says. "E-sports is my weakness."

"Tanner Bash," I say. "I didn't take you for a nerd."

"What?" he asks, looking at me, almost defensive. "I can't have hobbies outside football?"

I laugh. "Joking. Let's keep playing."

We do round after round, and I think it will get boring, but Tanner's little point about there being so many viable characters proves to be true. Each time one of us switches up a character, it's like a whole new game, and Tanner's little points about each of the character's particular strengths makes me want to turn off the console and just stare at him while he speaks.

I know Tanner's kinda been hot and cold with me, and I know some of his behavior even resembles the way my mother used to treat me. But I like the

Tanner I'm hanging out with right now. He's so goddamn earnest, so different from so many of the guys I hookup with. With them, it's about getting off, and anything you say after that couldn't mean less. But with Tanner, it's like everything that comes out of his mouth has a purpose, and it's not just to sleep with me. He's just being himself. And I like who he is.

After one game where I manage to beat him, I feel like I'm on cloud nine. "You gotta keep your pointers to yourself," I say, slapping Tanner on the shoulder. "Or else I'll keep winning."

"Hope you're having fun," he says. "It's been so long since I've really played with someone like this. I have a buddy on the team I do stuff with, but it's been so long."

A buddy to do stuff with. Flashes of what I imagine Kyle Weaver's little sex cult was like back at Miss U, and now I can't help but picture Tanner as a part of it. But he's straight, right? He said so himself when he so rudely rejected me that day I met him. Yeah, he has to be.

He pulls out a little container filled with cartridges and cases of random games. "You wanna play something else? You could take a look to see what I have."

I set down my controller and peruse the container. And that's when I see best game ever made.

"You have Zelda: Majora's Mask?" I ask, pulling it out.

He smiles. "That's one of my favorite retro games. Such a classic."

I look at him imploringly.

"You wanna play?" he asks with a smile.

"Hell yeah, I do," I say.

I hand him the cartridge, and our fingers brush for just a moment, sending a jolt of electricity down my spine.

"Sorry," both of us end up saying unison.

I blush and look away, while Tanner just lingers there.

Put the cartridge in the damn console, I beg him in my mind. *Forget this ever happened.*

And then, to my relief, he does move on as if nothing happened. Which is good. Makes our relationship a lot less complicated. I may be a horny guy, but I'm not one to fall in love with a straight man. I have standards.

"So you've played this before?" he asks as the game's booting up. Outside, the sun is setting, and then Tanner's lights dim with it, like they're set on a timer. And suddenly the mood feels a lot more romantic.

"I have," I say. "Played this a lot in middle and high school."

"I forget you're older than me," he says.

"I'm only thirty-eight," I say defensively. "And what are you? Thirty-two?"

"Thirty," he says, smirking.

"Just a little boy," I say.

The title screen to the game blares, distracting both of us. I select a save file, and we get started. We open to nostalgic music and a macabre prologue scene.

"What about you?" I ask. "You grow up playing it?"

His mood, light before, turns heavy, similar to how he was when we started racing in Mario Kart.

"Yeah," he says. "But this game—this was actually something I played to distract myself, to keep myself busy from all that was going on in my house."

Keep himself busy, huh? Sounds pretty similar to me. And now I'm wondering what went on in his house. But he continues, and I listen.

"A lot of video games, especially for kids, tended to be lighter. But this one—with its dark themes and eerie atmosphere. I don't know. It made me feel right at home. Like it never sugar-coated things. It gave it to me straight. Like it respected me. And I guess that made me feel safe. If I could handle what was going on in this game, I figured I could handle life."

"Wow," I say, once I finally have control of the character. "I never thought of it that way."

He shakes his head. "Yeah, I know it probably sounds—"

"No," I say, stopping him. "It makes total sense."

Both of us sit in companionable silence as I get through the first little chapter of the story. When I'm hurt in the game and my health goes down, I take notice of the hearts in the top left and feel like they're familiar. That's when I glance down at Tanner's arm and notice that the three hearts look identical.

I point to the TV, then his arm. "Is your tattoo...?"

He looks at his arm, then blushes. "Oh, yeah. I got it a while back. I kinda like the idea of health in video games. Like, sure, you can get hurt, but you can also heal, too. From anything, really. And I like that idea. So I got it tattooed on my forearm."

I pause, my brow furrowed. This Tanner Bash is more thoughtful than I realized. And he's so genuine about it, too. So many guys I've slept with put on some sort of façade. But not Tanner. He just is who he is, which is cool.

When I finally get to the main hub of the story—Clock Town—Tanner perks up.

"What bit of lore do you have to share with me this time?" I ask, genuinely curious.

"Sorry," he says. "I know me sharing my trivial knowledge can be irritating."

"Tanner," I say, putting my hand on his knee. He looks at it, almost horrified, but he doesn't move to stop me. So I keep it there.

"I don't know why you put yourself down like that," I say. "I like hearing you talk. You're interesting."

He chews on his lips, his face going red. "Really?"

"Yeah," I say, leaning in closer to him.

We both linger there for a beat, then I gain my senses and pull back. I have more self-respect than to come on to a straight man.

"But it sounded like you did have something to share about the game," I say, resuming the quest I'm on. "What is it?"

He leans forward, looking closer at the screen. "It's less trivia and more something personal."

"Then I definitely want to hear it," I say, briefly looking at him. I can see a small smile on his lips, which makes me happy.

"I love the music of this game, but especially this hub. I said earlier how this game is really dark. But that makes the light moments so much more... powerful. And the fact that the hub of this game just feels so positive and upbeat—I don't know—sorta helps me see that no matter what's going on, even if the moon is crashing down, everything will still be okay."

I stop playing and just look at him.

He looks at me and almost giggles. "What?"

"How is it that some lineman who happened to curse me out in front of a whole restaurant manages to say something so thoughtful and profound?"

"You think I'm—"

"Yes, Tanner. I do think you're thoughtful and profound."

He fiddles with the stubble growing along his neck, and I just want to lean over and kiss him—his neck, jaw line, chin, lips—

"Jimmy—" Tanner reaches out and grabs my controller just as I'm being attacked by a monster. I manage to kill it just before I die, making little Deku Link finally safe. But I'm not. Because Tanner's hand is now holding mine.

I look up at him. "Tanner—"

"Please tell me I'm not the only one who feels something," he says, rushed. "Because if so then—"

"You're not the only one," I say emphatically.

He looks at me, then my lips, as if asking for permission. And I nod in response.

He closes the distance between us, and I wrap my hand around his neck and pull him against me. Our lips meet, sending fireworks throughout my body. He kisses me hungrily, desperately, as if this is the only chance he'll ever get. And I hold myself strong against him, giving him everything I have, trying to reassure him with my tongue that I'm an endless fountain and I'm not going—

He pulls away from me and looks down at the carpet.

I lean back, my arms propping me up, my dick almost fully hard.

"Tanner, I'm sorry—"

"No, I'm sorry," he says. He stands and brushes himself off like I got him dirty.

I get on my knees. "I didn't mean to—"

He cuts me off with the gesture of his hands. "This is my fault," he says. "I shouldn't have—God, I'm such a fuck up." He wipes his face. "This shouldn't have happened."

I look up at him, hurt and confused.

"I'm sorry," he says again. And then he scurries out of the room and down the hall into his bedroom. He gently shuts his bedroom door, leaving me, yet again, alone in his living room.

Chapter 12

Jimmy Dillon

FIRST, I WAS AVOIDING Tanner. But now he's the one avoiding me like the plague.

It's been two weeks since we kissed—since I tasted his delicious tongue. And holy fuck. That was so much better than 95% of the sex I've had. *The sex*, I'm talking about. Not comparing kiss to kiss, but his kiss to all the times I've had sex. Which is a lot.

And it isn't just that Tanner's hot. I feel fucking connected to the man. He just opens up to me, like he trusts me or something. And that sort of connection you can't just find with an electronic message or quick fuck. That's special.

At least *I* think it's special. But clearly Tanner doesn't think so. He won't return my texts, even when it's related to his meals. He just leaves a note on the kitchen counter with the answer to whatever question I've asked him. Which drives me fucking insane. Because this is like my mom all over again.

Whenever my mom was remotely vulnerable with me—the few times that she was—she would rubber band the complete other direction as soon as I thought that her vulnerability was genuine. She would cry about a bad day, and I would try to comfort her. Then as soon as I showed her my sympathy, she would lash out and insult me.

And how the fuck is Tanner Bash any different?

I avoid him, which makes him feel bad. So he comes and asks if we can be closer. I let him in. And what happens? I get burned. We fucking kiss, and he pushes me away.

You know, I should know better at this point. This is my fucking fault that I keep trusting Tanner even when he's shown me time and time again that he's not trustworthy. My sponsor said on a recent phone call about not going to the hardware store for bread, talking about another situation, but it fucking applies perfectly here. I can't go to Tanner expecting to get warm social interaction. All I'm going to get is ice.

I collapse onto the couch in my bungalow, exhausted. I just got back from the gym, and I've already finished preparing Tanner's meals for his upcoming game. But it's only 5PM, and it's a Friday. I still have the rest of the night ahead of me. I texted Yousef to see if he wanted to go to a meeting. He's become one of my good friends here, and he always down to chat about men or go to an AA meeting with me. But he said he had something with his boyfriends. And that's when I realized how fucking lame I am. Is my life really just work, fuck, and AA? Am I anything fucking more than that?

Bored, and hating myself, I get on my hookup app to boost my mood. Getting messages from horny guys saying I'm hot always helps my self-esteem.

But when I hop on, I have nothing. *Nothing.* I refresh just to make sure it's not a technical error, and when it's clear to me that no one has reached out—that not even one of my messages to men I think are hot have been responded to—I hear my mother's voice as loud as a siren.

Does anyone even like you? she would say. *Because if they did, you'd have more friends than Tanner and Yousef right now. You'd be out doing things. Men would be interested in you. But clearly they're not. And Yousef doesn't like you—he'd rather be with his partners. You aren't even good enough to be one of them. And don't get me started on Tanner. You're just too—*

I bang my fist against the couch and pull a pillow over my head to drown out her voice. But it's just constantly there, nagging me, pulling me down.

She's right, though, isn't she? I would be out doing things if more people liked me. Maybe if I was more handsome or less hairy or had less of a belly.

Or maybe even changing those things wouldn't be good enough. Maybe I'm doomed. God, fuck me. I fucking hate my mind. I wish I could just take a pill and fall asleep and not wake up. Because death is preferable than suffering these thoughts.

I pull out my phone again, hoping that by showing myself online, I can put myself on the algorithm and be visible to other profiles. And, thank fucking God, it works. I get one message.

But it's the last person I want to see.

The crystal meth man.

"Free tonight?" reads his message. Scanning our chat history, it's just a one-sided series of him reaching out and me never responding.

But this time I decide to take the bait. Because, at the very least, I'll be doing something to keep me occupied.

"What's going on?" I ask.

Bubbles appear in the chat immediately, and then he responds. "ParTy, if you're interested. Shown you to some of my friends. They want you to come too."

A burst of excitement rushes through my body, temporarily numbing the distress I've been feeling all day. This is the attention I've craving—men being into me. I need more of this.

"Where at?" I ask.

He sends an address, and then my heart starts to race.

This isn't just some normal party. From what Yousef has told me about his party days, a lot more than sex will happen here. There will be alcohol, cocaine, and worst of all, meth. I don't have any interest in doing drugs, but I do need something to do, something to keep these thoughts at bay. And this is my only option. It will have to do.

"Be there soon," I say. To which he replies with a thumbs up.

I slip on a nice shirt, jeans, and flip-flops, then head out the door. When I step outside, a cool breeze, scented by the salty ocean, makes me briefly pause. I stand by the gate overlooking the ocean and take in the sight. In my nearly two months of living here, I've only gone down to the beach once, and I didn't even stay for long. It was pretty, but I was bored, so I scheduled a hookup with some random guy and left as quickly as I came.

But part of me wishes I had the patience and mental fortitude to just sit on the sand and watch the water. I know Yousef does. He and his friends have that meditation group after all. But it's just not for me. I need to stay moving.

On my way to my car, I pass by Tanner's house, and I curse at him under my breath. If he just wasn't such an asshole, maybe I wouldn't be doing this. But it's too late now. I get in the car, punch in the address to the party, and get on my way. On my drive there, I try to quiet my mind by reminding myself that, at the very least, the guys will be hot there. And I flatter myself with the reminder that they wanted me, some bear from Mississippi, to join them. These guys, though wild partiers, are hot as hell, at least the ones I've seen. So their interest in me is way flattering.

After a thirty-minute ride, I arrive at some house bigger than Yousef's, which is impressive for San Diego. I'm not close to the beach, but I can still smell it, which comforts me. And I need the comfort because my heart is racing like crazy. I can't believe I'm meeting the crystal meth man. I have to remind myself, over and over again, that I'm just here for sex.

I step out of the car and make my way to the door. The entire house is white, and there are two palm trees in the front lawn. Sometimes, I still can't believe I made it all the way here to the California coast. It's unbelievable.

When no one answers, I take a step back toward my car. I could leave now. I could stop myself from going into a place where I know there's only trouble. But if I left, the thoughts would return, and I'd hear my mother's voice louder than ever: how I'm a coward for leaving, that these hot guys were never interested me to begin with. That I'm a worthless fuck.

I step back up to the door, but I don't knock this time. Instead, I just decide to let myself in, knowing that's how some guys are about their hookups anyways. They just want you to walk in and fuck them.

Standing in the foyer, I hear some muffled sounds coming from another room. I walk behind the stairwell into what looks like the living room.

And what I see blows me away.

There are at least ten guys, half of them naked and the other half with at least one article of clothing missing. Most are white, but I can see one or two Hispanic men. And it looks like a full-blown orgy.

A couple guys are kneeling on the ground, getting their faces fucked. Others are bent completely over, their holes getting pounded. This is the exact scene my homophobic parents would have warned me about as a kid, that this is all gay people do. I thought they were just exaggerating, but apparently there are some gays that do this. And I'm looking right at them.

Yet this doesn't really appeal to me. I like fucking, don't get me wrong, but I like it definitely more on the intimate side. This? This is purely mechanical, using other bodies purely for the sake of getting off. But even when I try to step back toward the front door, I can't. Because I'm afraid that if I leave, I won't get what I came here to get: praise and preoccupation.

One man finally turns and notices me, and to my relief, it's the man who messaged me. He comes over, shorter than I thought he'd be, but possessing a muscular, toned body with some dark body hair. He hugs me, and I awkwardly return it, confused by such an intimate gesture in what feels like a very non-intimate place.

"Glad you came," he says, his voice sounding completely different than what I imagined. With how much he was messaging me, I imagined his voice as something nasally and annoying. But it's deep and sexy.

"Yeah," I say, my voice scratchy. I stop myself and clear my throat. "Uh huh."

He rubs my arm and checks me out, his eyes lingering on my belly. And that's when I realize that every single man here has defined abs. Suddenly, I feel self-conscious, which is unlike me. Usually I'm confident about my body. Guys like a dad bod. But right now, I just feel like an ugly duckling, and I'm afraid the others will think the same.

"Let's get these off you," he says. Somehow, he manages to slip my shirt off with ease and finesse. He runs his hand through my hairy chest down to my belly. That's when two other guys notice and come over. The three of them get to fondling my body.

The guy who messaged me puts his lips against mine, and his kisses are slow and deliberate, more intentional than I thought they'd be. Slowly, I'm dragged over to the couch. The three guys plop me down. While I'm being kissed, one of the other guys starts undoing my belt, rubbing my hardening cock under my jeans.

This isn't so bad. This is exactly what I wanted: attention and action. And I haven't seen any drugs. For all I know, this could just be an orgy. I've been to a few of those, and while not my preference, I'll admit they're fun. So this is gonna be okay. I got nothing to worry about.

My guy kisses me, and another one is now sucking my dick with a finesse I didn't think possible. The third is lapping up my nipple with his tongue, sometimes finding his way into my armpit. It's rare that I'm worshipped by three subs, but when I am, I relish it and relax. This is the life.

My guy pulls away and looks me in the eyes. "Want some T?" he asks.

I furrow my brow, distracted by what these other men are doing to my body. "T?" I ask. And then it feels like all my muscles coil up inside my body. I know exactly what he's talking about.

The other guys stop what they're doing and look down at the coffee table as crystal meth man gestures to it. The step out of the way as my guy leans down to show me what I didn't see before. There's a white powder on the table—what I assume to be cocaine—but there are slightly larger white flakes mixed in with it.

"And cocaine," he says. "You want some? It's for everyone."

I look around. The other guys are getting it on like no one else exists. And, looking closer at them, they're sweating up a storm, which communicates to me that they've been at this far longer than I would think. I've heard of these sorts of parties going on for days—no rest, no food. Just sex and drugs. And just the thought of doing that makes my stomach curl in on itself.

"I think I'm good," I say. "If that's okay."

"Not a problem," he says, running his hands through my belly hair. "But I'm gonna have some more."

He and the two other guys worshipping me sit down in front of the table and lower their heads. They each arrange themselves a small line using some nearby business cards. And then they snort it all up. They each sigh and rub their now red noses in contentment after. One of them leans onto the other, laughing, while the other has a smile so wide I can even see it with his head only slightly turned. Then, the three of them turn around get back to pleasing me. The one sucking my nipple takes his spot in between my legs, while the other sits where his friend was. My guy returns to my side and kisses my lips.

"You are fucking hot," he says, pulling on my chest hair. "Not often we get a bear around here. You're just what we wanted."

I'm about to say something, but the man sucking dick sends a jolt of pleasure up my spine, taking away my ability to speak entirely. Crystal meth man gets to sucking on my other nipple, and now my entire body is lit up in pleasure. I like my nipples tended to as much as the next guy, but this is next level. In fact, I don't know if I've ever had my body worshipped to such a degree.

The guy's tongue massages my dick extra tenderly, and my body bucks involuntarily. The guy sucking my dick laughs, and he does the only thing that could bring me more pleasure. He lifts my thick legs and sticks his tongue directly into my asshole. Without missing a beat, crystal meth man releases his glorious hold on my nipple and moves to my dick. Now, all three of my greatest pleasure points are getting attention. I don't think this could get any better.

In heaven, I open my eyes to watch them. And I'm overwhelmed by what I see.

Before they took a hit, they were into it, enthusiastic. But after that bump, there's an enhanced energy to what they're doing, an almost manic one. As crystal meth man goes up and down my dick, his head moves back and forth, and I swear there's a smile on his face. The guy eating my ass is sticking his tongue so deep and pressing it into just the right places that it feels like I'm being fucked by Poseidon himself. And don't get me started on the guy worshipping my pec. He's lapping it up like a dog, sending warm chills all the way up my neck. And he uses just the right amount of teeth to hold it right where he wants it.

All three of these guys worship me with their backs arched and their fine asses in the air. They moan and worship me like I'm the last thing they'll taste, not even bothering to stop for air or energy. And that's when I know I'm a goner.

"Fuck," I grunt.

Somehow, they pick up their enthusiasm, and I practically cum a bucket into crystal meth man's mouth. The other two stop what they're doing to pay attention to my dick. Then, taking turns, they suck my dick, relishing the last of my cum and kissing each other to share it.

"Fuck," I say again, this time to myself.

But then, slowly but steadily, dread seeps into my chest, and my hateful thoughts toward myself that I had earlier in my house return. Yet these guys, even after my orgasm, are as energetic as ever, sucking me so good that I can't even get soft.

"Hope you got more than that," my guys says. And that's when my eyes immediately go to the table where all the drugs are. The drugs that turned these guys into sexual and confident godlings.

He looks at the table, then at me. "You want some? It'll keep you going longer," he says. He grabs a card and starts making a line. "Makes everything feel better too."

Christ. With how good that orgasm felt, the thought of anything better makes my head spin. And if I did take a hit, I'd be just like these guys, carefree and in the moment, just focusing on pleasure without a thought in my head. Isn't that what I've wanted all this time?

"Here," he says, getting out of the way. A line just for me sits on the table, and the other two slide out of the way to give me room.

Without a second thought, I slide off the couch and sit right in front of it. I look down at the powder, my thoughts racing faster than they ever have before. And if I take this, my thoughts will probably relax. I mean, look at all these men around me. They've been going for hours, if not all day. They haven't stopped because they were tired or sad. They've just continued to make themselves and each other feel good.

Crystal meth man leans down to kiss my shoulder, then trails his kisses up my neck. And suddenly my mind goes to Tanner.

The sex here was good—some of the best I've had. But it still pales in comparison to the kiss I had with him. Sure, the man's an asshole and probably no different than my mom. But I know that the man's not on drugs. He's in the NFO for Christ's sake. And our kiss transcended all that's happened here. That shows I don't need drugs to have that good feeling. In fact, even though everything around me suggests the opposite, my gut tells me that drugs could get in the way of this feeling happening again.

Riding on this thought alone, I stand up and pull up my jeans. I rush to grab my shirt before I can get a second thought.

"Where are you going?" my guys asks, standing up with me. I glance down at the other two, expecting their objections, but they've since left and joined some other group.

"Thanks for the invite," I say. "But I gotta go."

"Fine," he says with a shrug. "Hit me up if you wanna do this again. That was hot."

I nod, but I immediately make my way out of the living room. I'm not listening to anything else he might say. Because I'm afraid it'll keep me here.

At the front door, I slip on my flip-flops and step outside. As I breathe in the salty air, I feel my head clear, and I jog to my car. Once I'm back on the road, I want to blare music to keep myself distracted from what just happened. But the music is too abrasive against my sensitive soul right now.

What scares me most about what just happened wasn't that it was scary or bad or intimidating. No. In fact, it was the opposite.

What scared me most was that I wanted to be there. I wanted to feel like those other guys, to take a hit and keep the pleasure going. To finally take something to keep the thoughts at bay. But remembering Tanner's kiss—that's what stopped me. A stupid kiss with a stupid man. It wasn't my will or my desire to not get addicted to something else. It was a stupid fucking fleeting kiss.

At a stoplight, I pull out my phone and prepare a text for Yousef. The fact that I was so ready to just risk my life by putting my addictive personality over the open flame of meth, all for some temporary relief from my thoughts, just shows how fucked up I am. I can't keep going on as I have been. I need help. And I need to do something I've never done before. I don't think an AA meeting alone will fix this.

"I think I'm ready to take up your offer," I send to Yousef. I roll down my windows and take a deep breath, relishing the salty air coating my nostrils. The tension that's been in my shoulders all day finally gives just a little.

"I'll give this meditation thing a try," I send in a second text. And when the light turns green, I feel a little relief. At first, I think it's because I no longer have to wait at a long stoplight. I like to say moving, after all. But my gut tells me that it's something else—that maybe, just maybe, meditation might be the salve to my dark thoughts, the cure that I've been chasing all this time.

I sigh as a drive, still uneasy despite my relief. I fucking hope it can do something to stop the thoughts. Or else I'm fucked.

Chapter 13

Tanner Bash

WE'RE IN THE LAST thirty seconds of our game with the Vegas Marauders. It's 24-21 with us in the lead, and we have possession of the ball. As long as we don't turnover the ball, this game is ours.

The offensive line gets into position, my good friend Carter by my side.

He taps the back of his hand against my thigh. I look at him, and we both nod. We got this. Just a little longer. I place the football on the ground, and I wait until our quarterback gives the signal.

When he does, I snap the ball, then barrel into their linebacker. He's a good couple inches taller than me, but that doesn't faze me. Just as coach has asked, I've been gaining weight. I'm a good 295 pounds now—not ideal, but in the area of where I need to be. And I hate to say it, but I wouldn't be here now if it wasn't for Jimmy and his cooking.

Digging hard into the turf, I manage to stay in place, then drive him backward, giving our quarterback enough time to throw the ball out to the tight end. He's tackled quickly, but we shaved nearly ten seconds off the clock with that play.

I see their defensive line getting into a slightly different formation, and I communicate with Carter and the others to mirror them. We are not going to let anyone through. When it's time, I snap the ball, and then I rush out to block their linebacker before he can reach our running back.

But there's a problem. One of their huge defensive ends breaks past Carter's hold and darts straight for our much smaller running back. If he tackles him now, we'll be out of downs, forced to turn over the ball to them. And with how close we are to our own endzone, they could very well score take the win. So, I break my hold of the linebacker and sprint with all my strength to reach our running back before the defensive end does.

Just as the defensive end is about to reach out and tackle him, I throw myself in between them and manage to push him off just in time. Our running back rushes out from behind us, and I do my best to catch up. But I realize I no longer need to. He's rushing down the field, and by the time he gets tackled, there's too little time for the Marauders to both gain possession and score. The Vegas crowd isn't too happy about the outcome, but I couldn't be happier. We won.

After the game, I'm questioned in the locker rooms about my last save, and I just tell them that a team looks out for each other. If anyone just happens to drop the ball, I help out where I can. And they do the same with me. That's why we've been successful so far this season. We even get some questions about our thoughts on our progress so far this season, if we'll make it to the playoffs. We just say that's what we're aiming for.

"Hey man," Carter says, sitting down next to me after a lot of the questions have died down. "Haven't gotten a chance to say thank you. And I'm sorry."

I pat him on the shoulder. "There's no need to apologize, man. I meant what I said to the cameras."

"But I shoulda been more with it," he says. "I know it sounds crazy, but I just didn't get a lot of sleep last night. I feel like that fucked me up."

"I told you," I say. "You're good, man. We're a team. I'm on your side."

"Thanks, Tanner," he says, brightening a little. "I'm glad you were able to cover for me. Your playing has really been fire lately. I'm impressed."

I chuckle. He's right. The past few games, I've held nothing back. And thanks to Jimmy's cooking, it's not only my weight that I have back, but also my energy. If I hadn't been eating my share of calories this week, I know for a fact I wouldn't have been able to make that sprint to stop the defensive end.

But this also makes me feel guilty. Because, despite what Jimmy's doing for me, I've been nothing but confusing with him, and now I'm avoiding him altogether.

Fuck, man. Now I feel like shit. Even after winning a game, I can figure out a way to feel bad about myself.

"Thanks," I say, trying to be present in the conversation, but I'm angry at myself.

"And you're packing more," he says, patting my belly. "Looks like this new cook is working out."

I resist a grumble. He doesn't know the half of it.

"Yeah, I'm grateful I'm gaining weight," I say. Now that I really know why it's been hard to eat—feeling unsure regarding what to do with my sexuality—it's been easier to force myself to eat. But I'm not completely at ease. Because the only person I have any interest in lives in my guest house, and there's no way in hell I should have any interest in him. I need my divine compass. And the only way to get that is by marrying a woman.

"I'm grateful too," Carter says. "Or else we could have lost today."

I pat him on the back. "But we didn't," I say. "And that's what matters."

After we both shower, we put on some fresh clothes and make our way to the bus. We ride our bus to the airport, and then we all get off to wait in line to board our plane. It's crazy how fast we travel in the NFO. After all these years, it still impresses me. Standing in the back of the line, I relax, knowing it'll be a minute before I'm on board.

Someone taps me on the shoulder from behind, nearly startling me. I turn around and don't even bother hiding my scowl. It's Chris, our dickhead wide receiver, the same one who can't take no for an answer. The line moves up as more people get into the plane, but I don't budge.

"Hey handsome," he says, quiet enough for only me to hear. "Wanna have some mile-high fun?"

I somehow deepen my scowl. "How many times do I have to tell you?" I ask. "Are you dumb in the head?"

He chuckles. "Come on. It's been a while."

And that's to my relief. He hasn't asked me since that last time I turned him down, and I've cherished the silence. But he's asking again, so I gotta reject him.

"Even if I wanted," I say. "This would be the stupidest place to do it. We'd get caught so easily."

"Not if we sat in the very back," he says. "The flight attendants hangout in the front. We'd just have to be quiet."

I turn around to walk up to the end of the line. He rushes up behind me.

"Not happening," I say.

He chuckles. "I thought you might say that."

Unnerved by the confidence, I turn around again to see what he's about, and that's when my stomach sinks to the concrete ground. He's holding up his phone to me, and on it I see the huge ass of someone familiar—familiar because it's my own. In the video, I thrust into the face of somebody kneeling just in front of me, clearly a man but obscured enough by my thick thighs to not see who. And suddenly, my blood turns to ice, and there's a cold sweat forming on my forehead.

"What is this?" I ask. I think I know, but I don't want it to be true.

"You know," he says, a sadistic smile forming on his face. "This is the last time you agreed to have some fun."

My knees go weak, and I prop myself up on one of those portable metal gates next to me. "You sick fuck," I hiss. "You asked if you could film. I said no."

"And I guess my finger slipped," he says with a shrug. "And my phone just started filming."

The video starts over again, forcing me to watch myself reluctantly face-fuck the most disgusting man on the planet.

"Why?" I ask, almost crying.

He sighs, still holding up the video. I look around to make sure that nobody can see it, but everyone else is distracted getting on the plane.

"I've told you I like having fun with you," he says. "This is me making sure it can still happen."

"So you're blackmailing me?" I hiss. I look around again to make sure no one hears.

"I mean, I wouldn't put it that harshly. But if that'll get you to agree to more fun, then sure."

I run my hands through my still wet hair. I stare at the video, praying with all my heart to have it just disappear. But God won't do that. I've clearly disobeyed him by kissing Jimmy and enjoying it, and this is him punishing me. I haven't just lost the compass to peace. God's taken it away and watching me suffer. Because I deserve it.

But, watching the video again, I get hope. "You can't do that," I say. "The video—you can't tell it's me. You can't see my face."

Without missing a beat, he moves to a point in the video where I lower my arm, clearly revealing the tattoo of three hearts. And that's when it all sinks in. Chris Jenkins is blackmailing me to be his fuckbuddy.

"I know how much you've said you want to be a family man," he says. "It'd be a shame if people saw this and learned what you really are."

I make the most disgusted face I can. "You eavesdropped on my conversation with Carter?"

He shrugs. "I belong in the locker rooms as much as you do. It's not my fault you talk too loud."

The guilt I felt about Jimmy earlier turns into white hot anger in my chest. I want nothing more than to tackle this man and beat him silly.

"So if you want to keep this image," he continues. "I suggest you do whatever you can to prevent this video from coming to light."

I clench my fists so tight they ache.

Yes, the NFO is more accepting toward gay and bisexual men now. But this acceptance is gravely limited. These men, if they want to have, at the very least, three years in the NFO, need to be masculine and family friendly. What do I mean by family friendly? That means monogamy with a loving partner. And *DEFINITELY* no sex scandals. Straight men? They can be sluts or abusers all they want. But queer men? They have to be perfect.

And if it came out that I'm actually the type of man to fuck the faces of unknown men in the San Diego Seals locker room, my image as a respectable man would be shattered in an instant. I'd be lucky to have any woman interested in me at that point, let alone one who would trust me enough to lead a God-fearing family. Chris may be disgusting, but if I don't want my reputation ruined, I have to do what he says.

"What do I need to do?" I ask, struggling to keep my voice steady.

He steps dangerously close, and I'm tempted to step back, but that means he'll have to talk louder. And I want no one to hear this.

"Let me have fun," he says. "Whenever I want." When he finishes, I have to blink twice.

"That's all?" I ask.

"All? You act like it's easy to give me whatever I want."

I grab hold of the collar of his shirt and pull him close. "Listen here, fucker. I swear to God I'll—"

"Guys," our manager calls out.

I let go of Chris and push him away with all my force. He struggles to stand upright.

"Come on," our manager says, standing on the top of the stairs that lead into the plane. "Let's get home."

I turn halfway toward the plane, and I keep my gaze on Chris. But he shoves his phone in his pocket and walks on in front of me like we never had this conversation. Like he isn't fucking blackmailing me.

I follow and ascend the stairs after him.

"I went ahead and saved the last two seats for you," the flight attendant says to Chris once we're inside the plane. "As you requested."

Chris glances back at me with amusement, and I stare back at the two empty seats in horror. He's right. As long as we're quiet, anything just short of full on penetration could happen back there.

We make our way to the back seats. Once we're settled, I try to relax, to pretend like Chris's threat isn't real and none of this is happening. But once we're in the air and the seatbelt signs are off, Chris's hand rubs my crotch.

I look at him, my jaw locked tight and my eyes on fire with fury. But then he pulls out his phone and shows me the video in his photo collection. So, I take a deep breath, and nod with a sigh.

Slowly and methodically, he fishes my dick out of my shorts and starts stroking it. Knowing I can't protest, I lean back and close my eyes, pretending I'm asleep, pretending that I'm not being sexualized against my will. I have a hard time staying hard, but I know I have to for this to be over sooner. So, I try to conjure up any image—some person who I think will get me off. And when *he* comes to mind, my stomach nearly sinks, but my cock gets rock hard, so he'll have to do.

Jimmy Dillon, my charismatic personal chef.

Imagining his lips against mine, it makes it easier to finally cum. And when Chris's lips are wrapped around my cock swallowing it all, I try to imagine them as Jimmy's. Because that's the only thing I can do to make this bearable.

Chapter 14

Jimmy Dillon

IF I HAD KNOWN that Yousef's group meditation sessions happened at the ass crack of dawn, I might have reconsidered asking to participate in one.

We have chairs set up on the beach just behind Tanner's house. I'm sitting next to Yousef, and his boyfriends, Chewy and Xavier, sit to his right. There are a handful of other people I've never met before: a Hispanic woman, a white couple, and a gay black couple. Yousef has a guitar, and the white couple brought some small instrument I don't recognize.

After I nearly let myself snort meth, I decided that the way I was approaching my life wasn't really working. For years, I've tried to stay busy with the hope that my thoughts wouldn't overwhelm me. At first, alcohol quieted the thoughts, but after I got sober, I had to find other means. That's usually been in the form of sex. But when I walked in on that orgy, I realized that sex is starting to lose its potency. I found myself ready to risk it all by taking a drug I know has caused lots of misery just to feel better. So I reached out to Yousef, knowing he's in Crystal Meth Anonymous, and asked if I could attend his meditation sessions, so here I am at 5:30AM sitting on the San Diego beach. If sleep wasn't so hard to come by, I might actually be dozing off right now.

"We have a new guest with us," Yousef says, holding the guitar in his lap.

"I'm Jimmy," I say with a wave of my hand.

The others greet me and introduce themselves, but all their names sail right over my head. Except for the Hispanic woman, Maria—she's got an interesting little instrument in her hand in the shape of a bowl.

"So how does this meditation thing work?" I ask.

"That's the fun thing about it," Yousef says. "There is no way meditation is supposed to work."

"Just let your mind wander," his boyfriend Xavier says. "And be aware of your thoughts."

"But not too aware," the white woman says. "Because then you'll distract yourself."

Maria chimes in. "I don't even let myself think of anything," she says. "I just pretend as if I'm asleep."

Chewy, Yousef's other boyfriend, leans forward. "But what if you fall asleep? You have to empty your mind—not pass out."

Pretty soon, everyone's arguing with each other, and I stare at them all wide-eyed. I didn't know what to expect with this meditation group, but it surely wasn't this.

Yousef, the only one not arguing, leans over to me. "Gotta love it," he says, laughing. "Since you're new to this, all I want you to do is listen to the music. Don't worry about anything else."

"Music?" I ask.

He lifts the neck of his guitar.

"Ah," I say, only slightly less confused. Honestly, this feels ridiculous. I should have just asked that Yousef take me to a CMA meeting or another AA meeting. This meditation shit is not going to help. The only thing stopping my thoughts from running rampant is how sleepy I am right now. I know that once the sun is fully risen, my thoughts will run around like unattended children.

"Alright, everyone," Yousef says, and his calm, yet strong voice seems to silence everyone. I'm impressed. "Shall we begin?"

Maria lifts up her instrument in one hand, what looks to be a small brass bowl, and in her other hand she holds a wooden mallet. "Our normal improvisation?"

Yousef nods. "Let's keep it simple for my friend Jimmy here," he says. "He's never really done this before."

I lower my head in embarrassment, but I don't feel the stinging gaze of anyone in the circle. When I look up, I'm surprised to see all but Yousef and Maria leaned back in their chairs, their eyes closed. Nearby the waves lap against the shore, and the sun is just barely peaking over the horizon. There's a slight breeze, but I have a hoody warming me. Physically, besides my fatigue, I feel pretty good.

Maria then closes her eyes and holds the bowl out in front of her. She then extends the mallet and taps the bowl, sending out a deep ring. Then, she presses the mallet to the side of the bowl and circles the rim with it. The ring amplifies and deepens, loud enough to rattle in my ears. But it's not distressing. It almost feels like it's the call of an angel from heaven: scary and otherworldly, but ultimately peaceful.

After Maria's had the bowl ringing for a minute, Yousef starts strumming his guitar. Now, I don't know a lot about music, but at first glance I would think that these two instruments would clash with each other. But Yousef is striking the same note as the bowl, and they sound as unified as ever. Then, he ascends the scale on his guitar and returns to the original note. He does this over and over again, creating in my mind the image of scaling a mountain and walking back down its slopes. Now with everyone's eyes closed, including Yousef and Maria, I think it's time that I follow suit. I lean my head back into the chair and close my eyes. And, just like Yousef instructed me, I listen to the music.

I picture a mountain—more specifically, me ascending a mountain, even though I've never really been to a mountain before. But that doesn't matter. What matters is that I'm listening to the music.

I ascend the mountain again, but this time when I return, my mom is at the bottom. My heart starts to race, and I shift in my chair, but I keep my eyes closed. My mom opens her mouth to speak—no, to yell at me. But I can't hear her. Her voice is drowned out by the bowl and the guitar. I leave her in the dust of the foothills, and I climb the mountain again. When I return, she's still there, but she looks sadder than before. And though I can't read her mind, what I imagine is her own words catching up to her. In other words, her being a victim of her own words rather than me or anyone else.

When I ascend the mountain and descend a third time, my mother is gone, but I don't feel bad or worried or scared. I'm not afraid she'll return, nor am I worried that she's gone off and done something reckless or insane. In my head, I just know that she's gone. That she's elsewhere and safe. And, most importantly, that she's not there with me.

I try to ascend the mountain again, but that's when everything goes dark. The last thing I remember is trotting the path upward again, the harmony of the guitar and bowl ringing in my ears.

I wake to a tap on my shoulder. My eyes shoot open, and I find myself still sitting on the beach. But the sun is now well above the horizon, and there are a good number of people on the beach around. Most folks in the meditation circle are standing up now, their fold-up chairs in their arms, chatting with one another. I catch Yousef in my periphery. His guitar is laying down in the sand, and he's one of the few people still sitting. I sit up, realizing he was the one who tapped my shoulder.

"Oh my God," I say, sitting up. "How long was I out?"

"Well," Yousef says. "We did the meditation for about thirty minutes, and then we chatted for another forty-five-ish after that."

My eyes widen. "Are you serious? I've been asleep for that long?"

He laughs softly. "It seems like you needed it."

I look around, embarrassed. But nobody is paying me any mind. They don't seem to care that I conked out for the entirety of their meditation session.

"Why didn't you wake me?" I ask. "I wanted to participate."

"You did participate."

I roll my eyes, digging my toes into the warm sand. "No, I slept through nearly the whole thing." I think about me almost snorting meth to calm my racing thoughts, and I shiver. "I need to learn how to meditate properly to quiet my thoughts."

He frowns, his brow furrowed. "You know, there is no way to meditate properly."

I grunt. "You keep saying that, but sleep to me really doesn't feel like meditation."

"Meditation is meant to relax you, no?" he asks. "And if you are in need of sleep, what harm is there in letting yourself doze off while meditating? You have mentioned to me before how hard it is to sleep."

I slump back in my seat and rub my eyes again. I do feel much better than I did before the meditation, probably because of the sleep. "I guess," I say. "But I wanna take this thing seriously. If meditation can really help me with my thoughts, I don't want to fall asleep while doing it. I want to make sure I'm doing everything right so it can help me."

He sighs and pats my knee. "Jimmy—you have said that you have had trouble sleeping for years. That your thoughts keep you up by running wild."

I shrug. "Yeah."

"Then, if meditation has helped you sleep, doesn't it stand to reason that meditation did exactly what it was supposed to do? Calm your racing mind so much that you fell asleep?"

His words prick something in my chest, though I'm not sure what.

"I guess," I say.

"Then it sounds like your first meditation session was a resounding success," he says.

I nod, relishing in how well-rested I feel. I can't remember the last time I got a full eight hours of sleep. And even though I definitely didn't get that with this nap, my head feels clearer, and I feel more at peace. I remember that little vision of me running into my mom at the base of the mountain. After she had disappeared, that was when I felt calm enough to rest. I don't exactly know what it means, but maybe Yousef is right. Maybe I meditated exactly how I was supposed to today. Maybe I did it right.

I reach out and pat Yousef on the shoulder. "Thank you," I say. "For helping me with my first session."

"It's my pleasure," he says, his Persian accent stronger when he's enthusiastic. He stands up and folds up his chair. I follow suit.

"So I'm welcome back again?" I ask. "Even though I fell asleep?"

"You'd be welcome back if you feel asleep every time," Yousef says with open arms. He turns his head to the group, still chatting away with one another. "Isn't that right?"

"Oh yeah," Maria says. And the rest of the group chimes in with their agreement.

The little sting of pain in my chest, after hearing how welcome I am, gradually turns to warmth. Turns out meditation isn't so bad after all. And I didn't fuck it up. I wonder what the next time will be like.

"You guys do this every week?" I ask as we make our way back up to Yousef's house.

"Multiple times if we can," Yousef says. "If you'd like, I can add you to our email list. We communicate there whenever we want to do a session."

Maria puts her hand on my shoulder. "So glad you came," she says, her black hair flowing in the sandy wind.

"I'm looking forward to coming back," I say.

She pats me on the arm. "That's the spirit!"

When we all reach Yousef's house, he invites me in for the potluck, but I decline. I gotta cook for Tanner and workout later. I wish everyone a goodbye and walk past the hedge to Tanner's house. Alone again, the unease I felt before the meditation returns, and I wish I could go back to the company of Yousef and the others. I guess I gotta get to cooking before the thoughts take over my head completely. But this thought depresses me. Because I just did the meditation this morning. Is peace only going to be a reality for me when I'm meditating? Will my thoughts otherwise race as they always have?

Opening the door into Tanner's kitchen, I try to ignore the growing worries in my head and instead focus on what I imagined during that meditation: ascending and descending the mountain. Maybe this visual will be enough to keep me preoccupied.

I get some coffee going and get Tanner's food for the day in order. Then, I start cooking, welcoming the distraction. But when Tanner trudges into the kitchen carrying his game day laundry, all the peace I felt this morning vanishes in an instant. I don't know how the hell I'm supposed to feel serene with this goddamn confusing as hell man in my life.

Chapter 15

Tanner Bash

FROM THE MOMENT GIRISH dropped me off from the airport after my trip to Vegas, I've barely even left my room. I can still remember Chris's face when he showed me that video he secretly took of me—that smug smile, like he won possession of me. Now, he's threatening me, saying that if I don't do what he wants, he'll leak the video to the whole world. Then my goal of finding a woman and raising a family will be a wash. No one would want to date such a disgrace.

I roll over in my bed and stare out the window. My bag that I brought to Vegas still has all my sweaty, dirty clothes, and it's stinking up the room. I know I need to do my laundry, but after what Chris did to me on the plane, I haven't so much as wanted to get out of my bed.

I was *violated* by the man. Sure, he was the one who sucked my dick, so I guess I shouldn't feel so dirty, but I do, man. I feel fucking disgusting. I doubt God will ever give me back my compass again. I'm fucking soiled.

And the worst part? I let myself enjoy it. I closed my eyes and imagined that it was Jimmy pleasing me. That was the only way I could get through the whole thing anyways. But what kind of man of God would let himself enjoy such a thing?

And what makes my blood curdle is that fact that this isn't over. At any time, Chris could reach out and request that he fuck me or I fuck him. And if I reject him, my reputation and chances at starting a family will be as good as gone.

I just don't fucking understand. My whole NFO career, I've done the right thing. Fuck it—my whole life. I obeyed my Gramps and my parents as much as I could. I did well in school. I've been nothing but a team player on whatever team I've played on. Hell, I've even gained all the weight back to satisfy Coach Larson. And I've obeyed God's commandments as much as I could. And this is the reward I get? Violation?

It has to be because I kissed Jimmy. It has to be. Sure, I've fornicated with Chris on and off over the years before this blackmail. But I've never really enjoyed it, so I never felt so bad about it. That kiss with Jimmy, though? Fucking hell. I enjoyed that so much I haven't been able to get him off my mind. So this has to be what God is punishing me for. Not only am I breaking his commandments—I'm *enjoying* breaking them.

Laying over the side of my bed, I take a deep breath, and that's when I catch a whiff of my nasty clothes. It's time I finally wash them. After taking some time, I finally roll out of bed and throw some shitty clothes on that aren't too dirty. Then I grab my bag of shit and finally make my way out of my bedroom.

And that's when I hear Jimmy cooking.

Fuck.

He's the last person I want to see right now. And it's not because I'm still trying to avoid him.

I had to picture Jimmy to get through Chris violating me. And since then, while laying in my bed the past couple days, I swear I've jerked off to him nearly a dozen times. Imagining his lips against mine, what his beefy body looks like naked, what his dick feels like inside me...

Which is insane. Because I've never, not once, let a man inside me. Back at Miss U, I was the resident top, if that's what they still call it. I was the one who stuck my dick in another's asshole, not the other way around. Imagining someone else inside me like that felt invasive and weird.

But not with Jimmy. I mean, yeah, I'd imagine it to be invasive. Yet if there's anyone I'd want to invade my body, it'd be Jimmy. The tender care that he's shown me in the few interactions that we've had? Goddamn. There's no one I'd trust more to put it between my cheeks.

Okay, I gotta stop. I can't walk into the kitchen with a boner and greet him. But I don't want to be super distant and cold with him as I have been. I know the past couple months of having him here I've confused him, letting him in then pushing him away. I justified this by saying that I couldn't let myself fall for him. God would abandon me, after all. But now that God's certainly abandoned me—evident in Chris's violation of me—what's the harm in being kind to him? And I doubt it'd go any further than that. I know Jimmy tried to ask me out when we first met, so there is interest there, but he lives in San Diego now. He has so many more options than just me.

Once my boner is completely gone, I take a deep breath and brace myself to see Jimmy. When I walk into the kitchen, hes looks up from the stove, and I can tell he's surprised to see me.

"You're back," he says flatly, looking back down at the stove. His side profile, for whatever reason, makes him look more like a man than when I face him from the front. I can see just how well-groomed his beard is, and there are small wrinkles just at the side of his eye.

"Yeah," I say, setting down my bag.

"Thought you were still gone," he says. "You haven't been eating much of what I've made for you."

A pit forms in my stomach. Right. Because after Chris violated me, my appetite has been shot.

"Just haven't been hungry," I say.

"Aren't you supposed to be gaining weight?" he asks, flipping over the chicken breast he's cooking.

"Yeah, it's just—" I try to think of some excuse, but my brain is so groggy from being locked up in my room all day.

"And have you been home this whole time? Just in your room?"

I feel my face reddening, and I look down at my dirty bag of clothes. "I've just been... going through it."

He squints at me, his face so handsome as he does. He opens his mouth, I presume to ask me something. And then he shuts it and gets back to cooking.

That's when guilt flares in my chest. Before, Jimmy has expressed concern for me: when we were playing Mario Kart together that one time, as well as the night we kissed. And just now, I could see that he wanted to talk about what I was feeling, to see what was wrong. But he stopped himself, likely because he knows better now than to trust someone flaky like me. And honestly, I don't blame him. I've been nothing but shit to him. It just makes me sad that he's given up on me, and it makes me wonder if this is what I'm doomed for: everyone just giving up on me. God's done it, now Jimmy. So what hope is there for a woman to not give up on me? Especially if that video of me is ever leaked.

I sigh.

"Welp, gotta do some laundry," I say, picking up my bag.

"I have some stuff in the washer," he says. "Could you just move it to the dryer? I'll do the rest of mine later."

"Sure," I say, walking past him, and I can tell that both of us are trying our hardest to not look at the other. But I feel so magnetically drawn to him that it takes all my strength to look away. He's wearing that 'Kiss the Hot Chef' apron, and I love how sweaty he gets when he cooks, how focused. The man's just so damn attractive, not only physically, but emotionally too. More than anything, I wish I could just open up to him. Tell him everything. I know he would listen. But I've already betrayed his good will enough. I'll give him the peace he deserves.

I carry my bag into laundry room, happy that nothing went wrong during the conversation with Jimmy. Over the last few days, that's one of the few things to not go wrong.

I transfer Jimmy's clothes from the washer to the dryer. When I furnished the guest house, there wasn't any way to get a washer and dryer in there without costing an arm and a leg. And with how rarely anyone comes over to my house, let alone my guest house, I didn't think it was necessary. It's not ideal that Jimmy has to do his laundry here, but it isn't the end of the world.

I manage to fit about half of my dirty clothes in the washer. Then, I put in some detergent and start it, which makes my dampened mind feel a little bit better. I've accomplished something today. They say that with depression, it's good to celebrate the small things. I don't know if that's what I have, but it feels good all the same to congratulate myself for doing my laundry.

I set down my bag, ready to isolate myself in my room again, but that's when something catches my eye. Just next to the washer, tucked behind some jackets of mine, is a hamper full of clothing. I glance toward the kitchen, but Jimmy's still hunched over the stove, and he couldn't even see me if he looked up. He'd have to take a few steps back.

I pull out the hamper to determine if it is what I really think it is—what I really hope it is. And when I recognize some of Jimmy's shirts, my chest nearly soars with excitement.

These are Jimmy's dirty clothes. He mentioned he still needed to do some of his own laundry, so this must be what's leftover.

I pause, my heart picking up speed, as I reflect on what I'm about to do.

Ever since Chris fucking used me, I've been horny as hell. Which doesn't make any fucking sense. I feel like I should be hiding under my covers and recoiling at anything sexual. But that isn't the case. I've already jerked off to the thought of Jimmy twice today, and I'm still raging hot for him. This thing with Chris—it shouldn't be affecting me this way. But it is, and I can't hold myself back from my urges. And with how much Jimmy's smell intoxicates me, doing what I'm about to do has been one of my greatest fantasies.

My heart racing, I reach my hand inside and pull out one of his dirty shirts. It's a shirt with the Portland Tiger's logo over the left breast, and I've seen him wear it a few times while he's cooked. I glance over at the kitchen to make sure he can't see me. And when the coast is clear, I lift the armpit of the shirt to my nose and take in a big whiff. It takes all my strength to hold back an audible moan.

I don't know what it is about Jimmy, but from the moment I met him, I wanted to smell him. I've heard a thing or two about pheromones, but I never really understood them until I smelled Jimmy as he walked by me for the first time. He didn't smell bad, but he smelled like him—sweet, musky, manly. It made me imagine him all sweaty, leaning over me as he thrusted himself inside me

I take another deep breath of his scent, and I feel my dick getting rock hard. Goddamn, I feel like such a pervert for doing this—for taking his clothes and smelling them. But I don't give a shit at this point. I'm being blackmailed and coerced for sex. God's abandoned me. How much lower can I truly go?

Once I get enough of his shirt, I put it back right where I found it, not wanting to risk Jimmy knowing that I've touched his clothes at all. But that's when I spot it—his underwear. My brow actually sweating, I tiptoe over and peer into the kitchen. Jimmy's just placed a raw chicken breast in the skillet, so he's going to be occupied for a while. I'm good.

I sneak back to the hamper and grab hold of the underwear. They're black briefs, and I don't even hesitate. I lift those bad boys to my nose and breathe him like I'm out of air. And holy shit am I glad I did this.

It smells like his shirt but ten times as good, all of his man smell concentrated into such a small piece of clothing: sharp, musky, manly. I imagine how he must smell after a long day. If his underwear smells this good, I can't even begin to imagine—

"What are you doing?"

As fast as lightning, I throw the underwear back into the hamper. But when I still feel the heat of his gaze on the back of my head, I turn around slowly, and entire body lights up with the heat of embarrassment.

Jimmy glares at me, still wearing his 'Kiss the Hot Chef' apron, and I want to sink into the floor and be buried alive.

"Were you just sniffing my fucking underwear?"

Chapter 16

Jimmy Dillon

I STAND IN THE laundry room, unable to fathom what I just saw.

"Were you just sniffing my fucking underwear?" I ask.

Tanner just stares at me with doe eyes like I'm a fucking supernatural being. And I'm sure I'm staring right back at him with just as much incredulity. Because if my eyes don't deceive me, I just saw that man huffing my dirty laundry.

The man's eyes dart toward the kitchen door, then back at me. Right. Because he's gonna run away just like he always does. But, to my absolute—horror? Surprise? I'm not sure. But Tanner then does what I would least expect him to do. He falls back against the washer, slides down to the floor, and bursts into tears.

His wails echo through the entire laundry room. "I'm sorry," he says. "I'm sorry. I'm sorry."

Not knowing what else to do, I kneel down next to him, my anger quickly turning to tenderness. I know how to console a man when he's crying. I know I should be angry or disgusted or uncomfortable—or turned on—but this man is clearly distressed. I just want to comfort him.

"Hey, buddy. It's okay," I say, rubbing his shoulder. "Cry it out. It's good for you."

He cries harder, and I keep rubbing him. He then wraps his arms around me and pulls me in, weeping even harder into my shoulder. I'd always assumed that

Tanner had issues, but I didn't know they were bad enough to make him this vulnerable during a crisis.

"I'm sorry for being such a dick to you," he says, pulling away.

I look at him with a tilted head. "Really?"

"You're such a good guy to me," he says, wiping his eyes. He's just this huge man leaning against the washing machine, his eyes red and swollen from crying. It's a strange sight to see. But it's a beautiful one, I have to admit. Such a handsome, manly man being so vulnerable is a rare occurrence.

"And I've been nothing but shit to you," he says, holding back a sob. "And now you're comforting me? Jimmy, I don't deserve this or you."

He starts crying again, and it takes everything in me not to wrap my arms around him again. To swaddle him in my affection. To make him feel okay.

But my gut tells me not to get too close. I've been here before. I don't want to open myself up again just to be hurt by him pushing me away again.

"Tanner," I say. "Can you tell me what's going on?"

He looks up at the ceiling, a tortured wince on his face.

Suddenly, I smell something burning, and I remember I left the chicken on the stove.

I rush into the kitchen, smoke already filling the air. I take the skillet off the stove and toss the burned chicken breast into the sink without thinking. I turn off the stove and immediately turn on the fan for the stove and the microwave. I open the kitchen window and back door and pick up a plate to fan the smoke outside. All the while, I'm thinking about how Tanner Bash, the NFO player who I would think is straight had we not kissed, was sniffing my underwear.

He was, right? I'm not crazy?

And then he burst into tears after I walked into the laundry room to grab a dish towel. What the hell is going on?Once most of the smoke is gone, I turn off the fans. Tanner's pristine kitchen appliances have powerful, and very loud, fans, and they're just too much on the ears. That's when I realize that in the midst of all the chaos, Tanner's probably retreated back to his room. I bet he's going to pretend like what just happened never happened—like he didn't just have his nose buried in my sweaty briefs, like he didn't just break down into tears right in front of me. And then things will go back to normal. Because that's just the kind of person he is.

But he plods into the kitchen, his eyes still red from crying. Then, he sits down by the kitchen table and slouches.

"Need any help with the smoke?" he asks.

"No," I say, looking at him warily. "I got it handled."

"Sorry for not coming in earlier," he says. "Had to regain my composure."

"All good," I say. Like I would want his help anyways. I clean up the rest of the counter, deciding to abandon dinner. If Tanner wants to eat, he can eat some of the leftovers that he's been ignoring.

Out of nowhere, Tanner breaks the silence. "You wanna go get ice cream?" he asks as I'm cleaning the burnt bits off the skillet into the trash.

I look at him with a furrowed brow as I set the skillet back down on the stove. "Ice cream?"

"Yeah," he says with a shrug. "It's nice out, and I haven't been outside in a while. Plus, I need the calories."

"You've mentioned to me before that eating's hard. You can eat ice cream?"

"It's actually one of the few things I can eat easily," he says. "I just don't a lot because it's not nutritious. But I can make an exception tonight. If you want."

I shake my head and press my hands into the counter. I thought Tanner would run away from me like he usually has, but now he wants to go get ice cream? After he was just all up in my laundry? I'm sorry, I still can't get over that.

"Just to make sure I'm hearing you correctly," I say. "You want to go get ice cream? With me?"

He nods like he's a little kid who's just scraped his knee and wants to go get something sweet to feel better.

"And, if you want," he says. "I can tell you some of the things going on. And I won't push you away this time."

I look at him—this handsome, confusing man—and I can't help but laugh. I don't have anything going on for the night, so I could use a distraction. Tanner looks like he needs it. And he supposedly won't pull away from me like he's always done. If he's self-aware enough to say something like that, maybe I can trust him this time.

I sigh. I can't believe I'm about to do this, but what the hell.

"Sure," I say, tossing a dirty towel into the sink. "Let's go get some fucking ice cream."

Tanner drives the both of us in a pickup to this little shack about fifteen minutes away from where he lives. It's on the lip of the beach where the concrete sidewalk meets the sand, and if I didn't see so many people crowded around it, I would think it's some abandoned bathroom. It has a sign up top, but it's too scuffed for me to read it.

"This is some of the best ice cream I've ever had," he says as we get out of the car.

"Alright," I say, following him up to the shack. I agreed to come out here because clearly this man is distressed and needs some company, but I'm starting to regret it. Based on my experience, he's all over the place emotionally. One second, he's nice—the next, he's an asshole. And now I've just practically isolated myself with him, making myself depend on him for a ride home.

We get in line behind this young couple trying to wrangle the six kids running around them. The dad's wearing a BYU shirt, and both parents are exceedingly patient even though their kids are causing a ruckus. I've met a few Mormons in my life, and they never cease to confuse me.

"All respect toward people who choose to have kids," I say. "But could you imagine handling all this?"

Tanner's jaw tightens so hard I'm afraid I've insulted him.

"Sorry, was that—"

"You're good," Tanner says, relaxing. "I just—why don't we wait until after ice cream?"

I shrug. "Fair enough."

After the Mormon family orders, Tanner steps up to the glass. Inside, there are several people of Asian descent scooping up various ice creams and mixing in toppings like they're a fucking Coldstone pop-up. Tanner orders for himself, then turns to me.

"Know what you want?" he asks.

"Oh, you don't need—"

"I've been an ass," he says. "Of course it's my treat."

Nearly blushing, I tell him I want the chocolate peanut butter surprise. We step off to the side, and already the Mormon family has all their ice cream.

"Sheesh," I say. "They got roadrunners back there?"

Tanner laughs a little, his eyes still puffy from crying, and now I'm full-on blushing. Damn, this man's face card. I'm surprised he wasn't up against Kyle for Sexiest Man Alive. Guess they don't like guys who are bear sized.

Soon enough, we get our ice cream, and Tanner leads me over to a table that looks directly into the ocean. There's a slight overcast above, obscuring the sun, which is honestly better than if the sun were out. It's bright enough to see clearly into the ocean, but not so bright it's blinding.

"So you're a chocolate-peanut butter guy," Tanner says. "You like Reese's then?"

I grimace, grabbing a spoonful of ice cream. "Ugh, that processed crap? Absolutely not."

"Forgive me," Tanner says in a haughty voice. "Forgot we have a professional cook here."

I let out a genuine laugh. "I feel like sweets are more a baker's thing than a cook's. And I'm not really a baker." I put the ice cream in my mouth, and then I stare down at my ice cup, incredulous. "Holy shit. This is amazing."

Tanner smiles at me again, his spoon in his mouth. "Told you."

"No, seriously," I say, putting another spoonful in my mouth. "This is—is this custard? It's too creamy to be ice cream."

"It's a family recipe," he says. "The Zhaos migrated here from China in the early two-thousands and set up an ice cream shop here. They've blown up since, but they've refused to scale up despite pleading from the public. It's not technically gelato, ice cream, or custard. They call it Zhao cream."

I look up at the sign above the shack. 'Zhao's Shack', it reads. 'Home of Zhao cream'. And now, the line is stretching all the way to the street. We got here just in time to avoid the rush.

I turn to Tanner. "Delicious homemade Chinese ice cream? California's fucking insane." I take another spoonful. "And I fucking love it."

Tanner laughs as we continue eating, and I might just go up and buy myself some more after I finish this. If the line isn't all the way to LA by then.

"So you say you're not a baker," he says.

I exhale a bit, my mood deflating along with it. "Yeah, never been my thing," I lie.

"Why's that? Aren't cooking and baking similar? Sorry, as you can probably tell, I know next to nothing. That's why I need a cook."

My face hardens, and I set down my ice cream.

I used to love baking—well, at least until my racing thoughts got worse a few years ago. My mom had been hospitalized due to high blood sugar, and after months of not seeing her, I decided to go visit her at my father's request. And she did what she always does: she was upset, so I got vulnerable with her, and then she punishes me for it. She asked what I was up to, and I told her how I was going to start adding some baked goods to the menu at my diner. And that's when she blew up on me, telling me how I'll get fatter than I already am and how she doesn't want diabetes to continue down the family line, as if it was my fault that she was hospitalized for her blood sugar. I tried baking after that, but every time I put something in the oven and had to wait for it to be done, her thoughts gained more and more volume in my mind. And once that became unbearable, I scrapped all my pastry ideas and just stuck to cooking.

"I'm impatient," I say, not necessarily lying. "With most things cooking, I put it on the stove and watch it. I'm in control. With baking, you have to wait forever—for yeast to rise, for things to bake. I like to have most of those processes within my control."

He raises his brow as he finishes off the last of his ice cream. "So you like to be in control?"

I look at him confused, almost like I'm short-circuiting.

"Sorry," he says, shaking his head. "Don't know where that came from."

But I'm still looking at him like he's crazy. Because, goddamnit, he fucking is. He blows up at me for trying to talk to him in public. Then he invites me to play video games. Then he almost beats me up? And then I find him sniffing my fucking laundry. This man is a walking nutcase, and he's no better than me my mom.

"What the fuck, dude?" I ask. "You push me away after we kiss. And now you're fucking flirting with me? What the hell?"

He looks around, embarrassed that we're being overheard. All of the tables around us are filled up now, and the line's as long as ever.

"Look," he says, setting down his empty container on the mesh table. "I told you I'll tell you what's going on. Explain myself a little. But could we go somewhere private?"

I take a deep breath, exhaling some of my anger with it. If this was any other man, I'd turn him down. But I love the way Tanner gets when he talks about or does something he enjoys, and he even shows this genuine interest in me that no guy I've ever really slept with has. Not even my ex, Joe. And I want more of that.

I tilt my head toward the beach, the one I've seen remarkably little of during my time in San Diego despite living right next to it. "Down by the water?"

He nods without missing a beat.

We make our way down to the sand, and I immediately regret my suggestion. Tanner's wearing shorts and flip-flops, which I hate to admit look very good on him. But I'm wearing jeans and tennis shoes, which aren't necessarily beach friendly.

He steps onto the sand, then turns to me and notices my hesitation. "Don't worry. Won't be too bad. You can wash yourself off before you get to the car."

"Alright," I say with a sigh. Then I step onto the sand and follow him down to the water. This close, I can hear the waves crashing against the sand, and watching the water undulate makes me a little dizzy. My first time really looking at the water back in September, I had to go ahead and crash early that day because of the nausea. But now it just mesmerizes me in a good way.

Tanner finds the driest part of the sand, and we both sit down. It was hotter than average today, so the salty breeze is definitely welcome. The waves flow just close enough for me to watch the foam bubbles individually pop, and I suddenly understand why California has so many residents. Absolutely nothing can beat this.

"So you're probably wondering why I've been so confusing with you," Tanner says. "Nice one minute, distant another." He's taken his flip-flops off, and he's digging his toes in the sand. I love how big and hairy his feet are, and he almost looks like a child doing what he's doing. I wish I could do the same, but I got socks on.

"Distant is one way to put it," I say. "I think asshole is more fitting."

He looks down at the water with a chuckle. "Yeah, that makes sense."

We both sit there in silence for a minute, one that feels so long I'm worried Tanner will just up and run and leave me here stranded. But when he sighs, I have a feeling I'm about to hear honest, genuine Tanner.

"I never would have thought I'd be admitting this, but there have been some interesting... developments in my life. Things that have made me reconsider my inhibitions."

I scrunch my brow at him. How on earth am I sitting on the beach with a lineman stud who is now sounding like a Natasha Beddingfield song?

"What are these inhibitions?" I ask. Without thinking, I dig my tennis shoes into the sand, which gets some inside my socks. "Fuck."

Tanner laughs. "Just take your shoes off," he says.

"Fine." I slip off my shoes, then pull off the socks I've been wearing all day. Then, when I stick my toes in the sound, I let out an involuntary groan.

"Holy shit," I say. "Now I know what it's like for a woman to take off their bra."

Tanner nearly cackles at that, and I can't help but be caught up in his contagious laughter.

"Never heard you laugh so hard," he says.

I wipe my eyes. "Same goes for you," I say. "I can't remember the last time I've laughed like that."

We both gaze out into the ocean in companionable silence, and I feel a warmth in my chest. This is the Tanner that I want to be around, the one I feel seen by—the one who's himself.

"Anyways," he says. "My inhibitions."

"Right. Go ahead."

He sighs. "My whole life, I thought that by obeying God's law, I would be blessed. But clearly that's not the case anymore."

"Anymore? What happened?" I ask, enjoying the way the sand sifts through my toes. There's sand on the beach around the lake in Glamour Springs, but it's rocky and dirty. Here, the sand is as smooth as powdered sugar, and I feel like I'm a little donut getting sugared in the stuff.

He thins his lips and chews on them, like he's wondering if he should tell me or not.

"Sorry, you don't have to say if it's too personal," I say. Tanner's like a goddamn cat who's finally approaching me slowly. I don't want to do or say anything that will make him clam up again, and I'm afraid I might have just done that.

He looks at me, and I swear I can see a sparkle in his eye. A familiar one.

"I can't say right now if that's okay," he says.

I nod. "Of course," I say. I'm reminded of all the time I've fucked guys younger than me, guys that were unsure of themselves or otherwise going through a hard time. I've loved the way they look at me when I bring them pleasure, how their bodies curl in delight when I stroke their prostate over and over again. I love the power they let me have, and I love using this power to bring them the safety and love they're so desperately craving. And how afterwards, they gaze into me like I'm an angel sent from above.

And now, Tanner's looking at me the same goddamn way.

He looks back at the water. "To obey God's law, I did a lot of things that people might think are crazy."

I tense my shoulders. What? Did Tanner belong to a cult?

"Such as...?"

He sucks on his lip. "After college, I've sorta kept to myself. I never partied like the other guys have. I try to go to church when I can, but I haven't found a congregation here that I like. And I'm not a Bible reader. So I mostly just try to pray."

I shrug, releasing some of the tension in my shoulders. "That's not that weird."

He lets out a sharp laugh. "Well, there is one big thing that you might consider crazy."

I squint at him. "Tanner Bash, are you telling me you murdered someone?" I fake gasp. "Let me guess—in the guest house?"

He looks at me, sadness in his eyes, but he smiles anyways. "No. I'm gay." He looks back at the ocean. "No point in holding it back now," he says under his breath. "I've been abandoned anyways."

"What?" I ask, leaning into him. "What did you just say?"

"I said I'm gay, Jimmy."

"No, I mean after—" then I stop myself. The man just came out to me. I have no right to demand more of him. "So you're gay," I say. "I mean, we did kiss, and I did catch you sniffing my laundry. So it's a bit obvious at this point."

He blushes. "Yeah..."

I sigh. "Then why—" I stop and shake my head.

This time he looks at me with a furrowed brow. "What?" he asks, almost laughing.

I shake my head one final time. "No, it's stupid."

"Now I want to hear it even more," he says.

"Fine," I say with a sigh. "If you're gay, why did you so rudely reject me back in Glamour Springs? You told me 'I'm not gay'."

Some seagulls fly by, and Tanner wipes his face until his face turns red.

"Right," he says, blowing a raspberry. "That."

Chapter 17

Tanner Bash

"Yeah, what the hell was that about?" Jimmy asks me. "You had the whole restaurant staring at me. That was embarrassing as hell."

I readjust myself and dig one of my hands in the sand, wishing I could bury my whole body instead.

Now that Chris is blackmailing *and* violating me, I figured I've been abandoned by God, so it longer matters that Jimmy knows I'm gay. It's not like I would be having sex with him. That would be too far, even now. It's not like I can't be a man of God again. I don't think I'm *that* far gone.

But now that Jimmy knows I'm gay, it makes sense for him to wonder why I rejected him. Not unless I was really into him and had to push him away, which is the truth. I think the only way I'm getting out of this is by pushing him away now.

I make my way to my feet, brushing sand off my lap. "I say we head back."

"You're really doing this again, dude?" he asks.

"I'm sorry," I say, not knowing what else to say. "I'm bad news, Jimmy." Which is honest. Why else would God allow Chris to do what he's doing to me? I'm doing Jimmy a favor. "I shouldn't have told you anything."

"Come on, man," Jimmy says. He grabs his shoes and rises to his feet. "We keep having really good moments, and you icing me out. And you fucking just came out to me. How many other people have you told?"

I chew on my lips. "I've told Kyle and Michael."

He folds his arms, revealing the deep cut of his hairy forearms. "That's it?"

"What?" he asks. "Who else am I supposed to tell?"

He sighs, exasperated. "There's no one you're supposed to tell. But this is who you are, man." He shakes his head. "Man, this is just like fucking Joe."

"Joe?" I ask, suddenly angered. Is there someone else in his life? Another man?

He swats his hand at me. "It's nothing," he says.

We both stand there, silent, while he keeps shaking his head. And, more than ever, I want to tell him everything—about my time at Miss U, how I really feel about him, what Chris is doing to me. But then I'd be tempted to fuck him, and I'm afraid that would be the point of no return. With Chris, nothing's gone beyond oral, so I don't feel like God has completely cast me out. But if I were to have full-on sex again after so many years, right when I'm supposed to be taking myself seriously and starting a family, then I fear that would be the last straw w ith God.

Our eyes lock, and for a moment—just a moment—I fear that if he asked me one more time, I would tell him.

"Well, if you wanna go, then let's just go," he says.

I sigh, relieved—or disappointed, I'm not sure. He makes his way toward my car, and I follow, kicking up sand with every step. He walks faster than me, so by the time I reach the car, he's already slumped against it, his hands in his pockets. But, for whatever reason, him brooding just makes him more handsome. His furry eyebrows are pointed inward, and he glares down at his phone, the side of his face from where I stand deadly gorgeous and manly.

I unlock the car, and he gets in without a word. I fear this might be the last time I have him in my car. Or this close to me at all. God, he's right. I keep pushing him away. What the fuck is wrong with me? Why can't I both please God and the people around me? Our drive home is painfully silent. I want to say something to break it, but I'm more afraid that he'll get upset with me. And I wouldn't blame him if he did.

"You know," he says, adjusting himself in the passenger seat. He seems slightly less angry now.

"What's that?" I ask, hoping this will start a conversation.

"You're not the first person to come out to me."

Anger courses throughout my body, and that's when I realize it isn't exactly anger that I'm feeling. It's jealousy. Jealousy that Jimmy's been with other people who've trusted him. Which is fucking stupid. Because of course he has. I even saw him with someone. He's a handsome guy, and he knows what he likes. Very kind, too. There's no reason for him not to have been with other people. So why does that make me want to pull over and go drown myself in the Pacific?

"Really?" I ask, not knowing if I want to hear more about this, but I do want to hear him talk, so I let my question hang.

He nods and sits taller. "I kinda have this thing," he says with a sharp laugh. "A few years back, I started hooking up with men pretty regularly."

My chest tightens. Now *there's* the jealousy.

"One of the first guys I ever slept with, I fucked him so good that he asked to stay the night."

I tighten my grip around the steering wheel. Fuck. Why is it that I want him both to shut up and finish his story? I'm not sure which want is stronger, so I just let him keep on doing what he's doing.

"The next morning, I fucked him again."

Jesus fucking Christ. Sorry, God, but seriously? Fuck. Is he *trying* to make me jealous?

"Afterwards, he just wanted to talk. I didn't have anything going on for a while, so I just let him. And that's when he came out to me. That I was the first guy he ever had sex with. And that he loved it."

That little story makes me so nauseous I'm afraid I'm gonna have to pull over. But we're only five minutes from home. After that, I can retreat into my bedroom and he can go back to his little bungalow as he calls it. Then I won't have to hear anymore about his goddamn exploits.

But then that means he'll probably go out and find someone.

And that's the last fucking thing I want to have happen.

"What's your point?" I ask, trying to guise the tension in my voice, but I don't know how successful I am. Because I am, to the highest degree, furious and terrified. And desirous for this beautiful man who I can't have.

"He wasn't the only one," he says.

And now I want to pass out.

"A few months later, it happened again. Someone else came out to me, saying I was their first. And then it happened again."

When we pull onto my street, I don't think I've ever been happier to see my house. Because now it's settled. I don't want to hear any more of what he has to say.

"The fourth time, I ended up dating the guy," he says. "Joe, the guy I mentioned earlier. My ex."

I run my tongue along my teeth, trying to calm myself down. At least they're not dating anymore. Not like I care. Because I don't.

"But as I first said, I seem to have this thing with men, especially ones that have just come out," he says, almost gloating. "I know how to make them feel comfortable and at ease, so much so that they let me take their virginity. So much so that they tell me their secrets."

As I pull into the driveway, I break into a sweat. If he's anything in the bedroom like he is in casual conversation, I don't doubt him in the slightest. Jimmy's thoughtful, attentive. Perceptive too. I have no idea how those traits translate to the bedroom, but with how sexy Jimmy's smirk is right now—the one in the corner of my eye that I'm trying to block out—I desperately, so desperately, want to find out.

"But it seems like any further discussion about your sexuality is off the table," he says as I take the keys out of the ignition.

"What?" I ask.

But he gets out of the car without answering.

"What do you mean, Jimmy?" I ask as he's walking out of the garage toward the path that leads to the guest house, not even bothering to come inside with me.

"You said you're bad news, so I'll take your word for it," he says. "After all, you said right when we first met that you're not interested."

"I just said that I wasn't gay," I say honestly. I don't want him to pull away from me. I don't.

He shrugs, standing at the end of the garage right next to the path. "Whatever your reason was, you still rejected my advances. I know I'm a handsome guy, but I know my limits. I don't go after men who clearly aren't interested."

I clench my fists, and I want to rush up to Jimmy and grab his shirt and shake sense into him. I want to tell him that I am indeed interested, that I want him more than anyone or anything. That I rejected him because I was afraid of how hot he was, and how I'm even more afraid now because of how much I like him as a person. How I'm afraid that I'll fall in love with him and lose my graces with God completely.

"I'll take that as my cue to go," he says, turning around.

"Wait," I say.

He stops and looks up at me. "Yes?"

"Do you—" I bite my lip. "Wanna play video games? We can continue Majora's Mask together."

He folds his arms and furrows his brow, thinking. Then he shakes his head. "I'm kinda tired," he says. "Had an early morning meditating with Yousef, and I think I might actually get some decent sleep tonight."

Yousef. He's fucking hanging out with Yousef? And all his gay boyfriends? Have they fucked? Will they fuck?

"I'll see you tomorrow for breakfast," he says, turning around again.

And there's nothing I can say to stop him as he disappears around the garage.

My knees weak, I lean against the car, unable to even think about what to do next.

What? Am I supposed to just go inside and do God knows what for the rest of the night? While Jimmy's probably gonna go find some hot closeted virgin to fuck? Just the image makes my blood boil. And something else: it makes the blood rush to my groin.

What does Jimmy look like shirtless? Naked? Judging by his full beard and the hair that pokes up from his shirt, I know he's hairy. And from what he's mentioned, he's the one who fucks. I'm a big guy, so in the few gay fantasies I've had, I've always imagined myself as the one who fucks. And in a straight relationship, that's obviously what I'd do.

But with Jimmy? Hell, I'd keep my body folded in half for him all day if it meant he'd be inside me.

What. The. Fuck am I saying?

I push myself off my car and storm inside my house. I stomp past the kitchen and go straight to my room. I may push myself past the point of no return by doing anything with Jimmy, but I'm allowed to have my fantasies. And jerking off to him might be the only thing to distract me from the fact that he's probably searching for some hot guy right now. Thank God I forbade him from having any guy over. Because if I saw some guy walking past my pool to my guest house, knowing that Jimmy's dick would soon be inside him, I'd quit my NFO career immediately and admit myself to a psych ward. Because I'd go fucking insane.

I throw myself on my bed and grab some lotion from my nightstand. I pull down my shorts, my dick already semi-hard from the thought of Jimmy naked, and I get to stroking. I picture his hairy ass tightening as he rams it into someone else.

Someone else.

I try to picture myself, but guilt eats me up with every fantasy I try to conjure up. God, please, just this once—can I have this? I know I fucked up with Chris, but can I have this?

But the guilt stays.

So I try to picture some other guy, but that's when the jealousy takes over. I imagine him, right this very moment, driving over to somebody else's place and giving them the time of his life, and now my chest is on fire.

I bolt up from my bed. There's only one thing I can think to do right now, and it's fucking crazy. I don't know if it's me or the fact that what Chris is doing to me makes is making me horny, but it doesn't matter. I jump up and slide my shorts back up, but then I hesitate. If I do what I'm about to do, does that really count me out of God's graces for good? Because with how strongly I want to do this, I don't feel like I have an option. It almost feels like, absurdly, this is where God wants me to go.

I wipe my reddening face, trying to steel myself.

Maybe God *has* actually abandoned me after all that's happened with Chris, and so doing what I'm about to do doesn't change Him being in my life at all.

So, either way, doing what I'm about to do won't change anything.

What the hell.

I take a deep breath, and then I walk out of my bedroom door. I'm headed straight to my guest house—the *bungalow* as one very handsome man calls it.

I walk out my back door and gingerly walk around my pool, afraid with how uneasy I feel that I'll accidentally trip and fall in. Then I might lose all the courage I have and give up on my plan entirely.

But, alas, I reach my guest house door, and I don't even stop to wonder if Jimmy's already gone to fuck someone else. I don't know if I could stomach that.

I knock on the door, and to my great relief, I hear him walk toward it inside. He opens it, and his furry brow handsomely furrows when he sees me.

"What's going on, Tanner?" he asks, his arm flexed holding the door open.

I don't know what it is about him—I can tell the man works out, but it's not like he's NFO fit. Yet I still find him irresistible.

Fuck it. There's no turning back now.

"I was wondering..."

"What?" he asks, and I note there's a hint of impatience in his voice. And I don't blame him there. I've been pretty much leading him on for the last two months he's been here.

I sigh. "Alright, I'm just gonna say it."

He folds his arms. "Say what?"

I blow a raspberry through my lips, combing my hand through my hair. Here goes nothing.

"Will you please fuck me?"

Chapter 18

Jimmy Dillon

"I beg your pardon?" I ask. I did not hear what I just think I did.

Tanner huffs a breath out. He's staring down at the concrete as he scratches his blonde stubble with his thick hand.

"I want you to fuck me," he says again.

I almost laugh, but I don't want to embarrass him. I wipe my face and start stroking my beard, my other hand on my hip. "You want me to fuck you?"

He nods.

I cross my arms and lean against the door frame. "I thought you weren't interested in me."

"Okay, well isn't it clear now that I am?" he asks. "Or do I need to keep explaining myself?"

"Excuse me," I say, putting my hand out to stop his tantrum in its place. "You do need to keep explaining yourself. Yeah, I heard you. You want me to fuck you. No surprise there. You rudely rejected me when we first met, which now I presume you did because you were afraid that I was everything you wanted."

He clenches his fists, then relaxes them, which tells me all I need to know. I'm right.

"And then you're constantly hot and cold with me. At first, it puzzles me, but on the way home from the beach, it makes perfect sense. It's the same as why you rejected me in the first place. You're terrified of me, Tanner—no, not of me. You're terrified that you want me."

His jaw tightens, and I think he's about to argue more. But then he loosens it and sighs. "You're pretty much right there."

I relax slightly. At least now we're having an open discussion.

"Tanner, I'm not going to lie. When I saw you, I thought you were one of the hottest men I've ever seen," I say. "Hence why I hit on you."

He smirks up at me, and I'm reminded what a handsome guy he is. Fuck, a lineman in the NFO just asked me to fuck him? I should go buy a lottery ticket with the luck I'm having right now.

"But one thing I didn't mention in the car," I say. "Is I don't fuck just anyone."

Now he's crossing his arms defensively. "Oh?"

I sigh and rub my forehead, feeling a headache coming on. In the car, everything about Tanner's behavior clicked, so I brought up the stories about my fucking men who were just coming out as a way to get him to admit his feelings for me. And when he kept beating around the bush, I just gave up. Clearly, he didn't know what he wanted, and I wasn't going to waste my time any longer. I just threw in the playful tone to make him squirm a bit.

But then he shows up on my doorstep asking for me to fuck him? Holy hell. Truthfully, I never thought he would admit his feelings. So now that we're here talking about it, I'm struggling with how to approach this.

"These guys—they were just a quick fuck," I say. "I had no intention of continuing a relationship with them. But you? I work for you and will be for the next few months. You're in the NFO, which complicates things. And..."

"What?" Tanner asks, raising an eyebrow, which is tantalizing on him. I love how eyebrows are the same color as his dirty blonde hair.

"What were you about to say, Jimmy?" he asks.

I shake my head and look away from him. *And I like you*, I want to say. *You're interesting, thoughtful. You're not just a quick fuck—I'd want to get to know you. Which is fucking crazy. Because I haven't wanted to get to know someone like this since Joe, and we all know how that turned out. Cheating bastard.*

"And we have an existing friendship," I say. Yeah, that works.

"So what?" he asks. "The only way you'd fuck me is if we were strangers? Seems kinda backward to me."

I recoil, almost offended. "Backward?"

He shrugs. "You meet a stranger, and the first thing you do is fuck? But when someone you know decently well wants to fuck, you reject him? Just because you know him? I thought sex was supposed to be intimate."

"It—it is," I stammer.

"Then wouldn't it be more intimate to have sex with a friend rather than a stranger?"

I start grinding my teeth, a tightness forming in my chest. For a man who just came out, his reasoning around sex and hookups is remarkably sound. And it hurts because now I feel called out.

"Well, sometimes I don't like the emotional baggage that comes with sex."

He squints at me. "You don't want the emotional baggage that comes with sex, and yet you were just bragging to me that a bunch of different men have officially come out to you in a hookup situation. I'm no therapist, but that sounds like emotional baggage."

I feel my forehead begin to sweat. "Yeah, but then I don't see them again usually. So I don't have to hold on to the baggage."

"Ah," Tanner says, tapping a finger against his temple. "So a man just unloads his emotional baggage on you, you unload in him, and then you never see each other again. Like a cold a transaction."

I rub my chest that's aching now. Christ, when he puts it this way, he makes me look like an asshole. Having sex lifts me up emotionally in ways that I never got as a kid. And if it's two consenting parties, how is that so bad?

"You a cop or something? Jeez. I like sex because it's something to do, alright? I just like to do it with no strings attached. Is that so bad?"

"It's not," he says. "I just think that, by your reasoning alone, you should have no reason to not want to fuck me. Unless you're just not interested in me."

I look the man up and down. He's a wall of pure meat. He's my ideal body type: muscled and chubby, the kind of man that I could get off from him sitting on my face alone. It's just that he's more than just a body to me at this point.

He's intriguing and fun. But he's also remarkably similar to my mom. I can't forget that.

"I'm not *not* interested," I say, still leaning against the door frame.

Tanner closes the distance between us. He reaches out, I presume to touch or stroke my arm, but he retracts it just as quickly as he extended it.

"Sorry," he says. "I don't know—"

"Here," I say, grabbing his arm. "Come in here."

I pull him into the house and shut the door. I have my own personal kitchen windows open, so we can hear the gentle hum of the ocean. Besides that, it's quiet. Usually, I'd be taking off my hookup's clothes right now. But this is Tanner. He's not unlike any of the other men who've come out to me: fragile and vulnerable. We need to talk about things before we jump into sex. He may be an ass, but I want this to be a good experience for him.

"So," he says, looking around. "Do we..."

"Let's sit down," I say, gesturing to the couch. "Let's get comfortable before we do anything."

"Alright," he says, sounding his least confident yet. He sits down on one end, and I sit at the other.

This is just fucking, I remind myself. Sure, Tanner may be a friend that I think is sort of special, but this is just sex. As long as I keep my mind focused on that fact, this will be fine. I'll be fine.

I scooch over until our legs are touching. "So usually," I say, reaching out to stroke his arm. He bristles at my touch, then relaxes.

"Before I meet up with a guy I've never met before, I get to know a little bit about him just to make sure there aren't any big incompatibilities. Then, we talk about what we like sexually."

He nods, watching my fingers trace the tattoos on his skin.

"Have you ever had sex with a man?" I ask.

He nods immediately, and that's when I remember Kyle telling me about that little gay club at Miss U.

"At Miss U I'm assuming?"

He tilts his head. "How'd you know?"

"Kyle's told me before," I say. "He's never mentioned you though. I just put two and two together."

"Alright," he says. He reaches out with his big hand and starts stroking my leg. His hand trails up my thigh near my crotch, and he keeps it there, stroking back and forth. He's already so close to my dick.

"You said you wanted me to fuck you," I say, reaching out to touch the tattoo of hearts on his arm. I trail my hand up his arm, onto his shirt, and down his chest. I move my palm down his pec, slowing down at his nipple. He jumps a b it.

"Easy," I say. "Just getting to know your body."

He relaxes, and I continue trailing my hand down his pec to his belly, and it's firmer than I'd expect. I guess that's what an NFO workout regimen does to your body.

He sighs, and I can tell he's trying to put himself at ease. I already know I'm gonna love this. I love turning a walking ball of nerves into a mess of pleasure and relief. I can't wait to do that to Tanner.

And then we'll have to go on like nothing's happened. But will this be the only time? Since we live so close, will we do this again? Worse—will I want to do this again?

I bite my lip. I can't think about this right now. I just need to be in the moment and enjoy myself.

"Yes," Tanner says, his hand exploring my thigh. "I do want you to fuck me."

"Have you ever bottomed before?"

He squints at me, then nods once in recognition. "Bottoming is taking it from behind, right?"

I nod.

"No, I haven't."

Butterflies flutter in my stomach. I love being the one to top a man for his first bottoming experience. So much trust goes into it. I know some guys have gotten too attached after I fucked them for the first time, asking for a relationship. I hope that's not what Tanner does.

"So you probably don't know what douching is," I say.

His face hardens. "What'd you call me?"

I laugh. "I'm not calling you a douche. I'm talking about douching. It's where you clean your ass out so there are no surprises during sex."

He frowns, probably feeling stupid.

I pat his shoulder. "Don't worry. It's simple."

I get up from the couch and go into my room. I retrieve the bulb from a small box in my open suitcase on the floor. I come back into my living room to see Tanner fumbling with his fingers.

"This is a douche bulb," I say, presenting it to him as I sit down. "Just out of the box."

He takes it in his hand and observes it like it's an alien artifact.

"You fill this bulb with water, then you stick this nozzle on and shoot it up your butt."

He grimaces, almost laughing. "Really? That seems silly."

"It'll feel silly too," I say, trying not to smile, but his laughter is deep, boyish laughter is contagious.

He stares at it, his arms slightly extended, as if he's scared to have it too close to him.

"Let me show you how it's done," I say. I take the bulb and gesture for him to follow me into the bathroom. He does so shyly, and I start filling up the sink with water.

"Take the bulb and suck up some water," I say, doing so in the sink. "Stick the nozzle in. And then, once you're ready, stick the nozzle into your butt, shoot up the water, and then wait."

He looks at me with wide eyes. "Wait for what?"

I frown and suck on my lip. "The urge. You'll know. Just make sure you're on the toilet when you get it."

He stares down at the full bulb, this time slightly less uneasy. He then takes it from me.

"You sure you want to do this?" I say, leaning against the doorframe of the bathroom.

He looks up at me and gives a nod so solemn that I get butterflies. Damn, this man really wants me to fuck him. Hell yeah.

"I'll leave you to it," I say, putting my hand on the edge of the door. "Feel free to shower once you're done. Then after we can…"

"Sounds good," he says, as if me saying the words will jinx the whole thing.

I shut the door, then make my way to my kitchen and prop myself up on the counter, so uneasy I can't stand without assistance.

I can't believe it. I'm about to fuck Tanner Bash.

Chapter 19

Jimmy Dillon

WHEN THE SHOWER STOPS running, I get a knot in my stomach. As soon as Tanner comes out that door, we're having sex.

While I waited, I had to do what felt like a thousand things to keep my mind busy. I wiped up the counters in the kitchen, which I hardly needed to do since I never cook in the guest house. I finally unpacked the rest of my suitcase, which is crazy since I've been here for over two months. I refreshed my messages on the hookup app and, to my ego's delight, I did get some more messages, but none of these guys hold a candle to Tanner Bash.

Tanner Bash. NFO lineman. Hot, sweet, shy—unpredictable.

This might be a mistake. After all, his little emotional ups and downs are eerily reminiscent of my mother's. Could this be because, just like her, he's a narcissist? Someone prone to emotional manipulation? This could be why he asked me to fuck him. He felt me pulling away again, so now he's pulling the trump card and getting me to fuck him so then I'll be really attached. Well, Tanner, I'm two steps ahead. I don't plan on getting attached at all.

My bathroom door clicks, and I watch the door swing open as I sit on my bed. Steam pours out of the door, and out walks Tanner Bash.

And he's wearing only a towel.

I sit up, gawking at him, and I'm temporarily at a loss for words. His pecs are muscular and plump, and some light, blonde hair dusts his pecs, meets at his sternum, then travels in a straight line all the way down his belly. I couldn't see this when he was swimming, but I'm glad I see it now. There's a smattering of freckles along his shoulders that gradually disappear down his arms. His biceps look even bigger shirtless, and the man's torso is so large I'm afraid that I'll have to look away from it when we fuck. Because if I stare at those muscles for too long, I'll cum way too quickly. And as he steps out, the towel splits in such a way where I can the upper edges of his thick thighs.

"I figured..." he says, gesturing to himself. "You know, since we're... well..." Now he's at a loss for words.

I catch the side of my mouth twitching upward. "Come here, big guy," I say. "Let's get you taken care of."

He plods into my room. He puts a knee on the bed, and it lets out a loud groan. And then I get worried. I'm not sure if it can handle 500+ pounds.

"We're good," Tanner says, noticing my distress, now fully sitting on the bed. "I know this bedframe can take a lot."

I blush, knowing this 'a lot' that he's referring to will mean my dick in his ass. Fuck.

He sits closer to me, and our legs touch. "So how do we...?" he asks, sheepishly reaching out his arm to stroke my leg.

He's shaking, and I suddenly go into the mode I always do in these sorts of situations, ones where I'm the more experienced one and my partner is the nervous one—where they make up for their little experience with enthusiasm and desire, and I take them on the ride of their life, gently giving them as much pleasure as they can possibly take and not stopping until I can see on their faces just how much joy I've helped them discover.

"Don't worry," I say. I run my hands up his arms, over his tattoo, past his freckled shoulders, and then down his smooth, muscular back. "I'll take it from here."

I close the distance between us, and when our lips touch, electricity dances down my spine. I've had good kisses, many of them in hookup situations, but I could already tell the first time with Tanner that it was something special. Which worries me. Because it isn't supposed to be that way. But I won't think about that now. I'll let myself enjoy this so Tanner can, too.

I move my tongue between his lips, and, though reluctantly at first, he gradually lets me in, soon letting his tongue dance with mine. I get a little more aggressive with my kissing, and to my surprise, Tanner meets it with the same fervor. Then, his hand cups the back of my head, and he's pressing me into him greedily, as if he's wanted to do this for weeks and he's worried this is the only chance he'll get.

"Greedy boy," I say when I get a moment to breathe.

"Just please keep fucking kissing me," he says. And let him pull me back into him. With one hand behind his head, his other hand searches my body thirstily, like my body is sand and he's searching for buried treasure. He runs his roaming hand under my shirt and runs his fingers through my thick body hair, closing his fingers together to gently, but hungrily, pull on them.

I smile as we kiss. I know exactly what he wants.

I manage to pull myself away from him long enough to grab hold of the collar of my shirt and take it off. When I do, he pulls away and looks at me, his eyes searching me like I'm some long-lost tablet written in an ancient language that only he can decipher.

"Goddamn," he says, running both of his hands through my chest hair. "You're so fucking sexy."

Partly because I want to, but mostly because he's pushing me into it, I'm leaning against the headboard, slightly propped up. Unable to take his eyes off me, Tanner inserts himself between my legs, his hands still greedily searching the hair covering my belly and chest.

I smirk up at him. "Can't get enough, can you?"

He shakes head, his whole body almost shaking with it, while he fondles me. "No." His mouth hangs open as he fucks me with his eyes, and then he bites his lips, obviously trying to contain himself. But I've seen this look a number of times before. I'll save him the trouble and give him what he wants.

I put my hand on his neck, and he looks up at me, startled.

"I know what you're thinking," I say, low. With my bedroom window open, I can hear the gentle roar of the waves accompanying us.

"What?" he asks. But when I gradually lower his face down to my torso, his face no more than in inch from my pecs, it dawns on him.

He licks his lips. "Can I?"

I nod. "I want you to."

Afraid—I can tell by his shaking—Tanner extends his tongue and gently flicks it against the edge of my pec.

"Come on," I say, rubbing his back. "I know you want a lot more than that."

He extends his tongue further, then runs it along the edge of my pec, wetting the hair that adorns it.

"That's better," I say. "But I know you're still holding yourself back."

His tongue reaches my nipple, and then he holds himself there, sucking.

"There we go," I say, cradling his head with my hands. He looks up at me, my nipple still in his mouth, making my dick twitch—which, by the way, is about to burst out of my jeans.

His eyes linger on mine, and I stroke a loose hair—probably one of my chest hairs, off his face. And, looking this deeply into his ice blue eyes, I feel a tingling in my chest.

He's looking at me the same way I see him talking about the things he cares about—football, childhood video games. His eyes light up, and there's an energy he carries with him that I hardly ever see anywhere else. And knowing I'm the source of such energy in him fills me with pure, radiant joy.

His brow furrows slightly as he runs his warm tongue around my nipple, telling me he has a question. But he doesn't need to verbalize it.

I nod. "Just like that," I say, answering his silent question. "But I know you can do better. Worship my body like you really fucking mean it."

And boy does he not fucking disappoint.

He starts greedily sucking on my nipple, making desperate, slurping sounds. He releases the suction of his lips to lap up the wet hairs around my nipple like a dog, his entire body flexing as he holds himself level with my chest. Then he goes to my other, giving it just as much attention. I have to bite my lip and stare at the ceiling while I let out involuntary moans. I can tell that Tanner definitely doesn't have a ton of experience, but his enthusiasm towards worshipping my body actually makes this so much hotter. Because I know that all of this enthusiasm is genuinely for me.

I've described Tanner as a childhood bully but aged up. Now, I thought that I'd have wanted to be the submissive one in this scenario. But no. Because the more Tanner worships me, the more I want to get him on his back and make him beg.

He rests his huge body in between my legs as he laps up my nipple, putting an obscene amount of pleasurable pressure on my bulge. I peer back at his lower half, and his towel is so loose that I'm surprised it hasn't fallen off yet. I'll take care of that.

While he's going to town on my nipple, licking it like a desperate dog, I tear the towel off, revealing his lower half to the room.

And just when I thought Tanner Bash couldn't get more gorgeous.

I can see tan lines from his football pants just above the mountains of his ass cheeks and his knees. His ass is pale and hairless, and that's when I remember that no one has ever been inside there before. Hell, he probably hasn't even been rimmed. Hot fucking damn did God bless me today.

I grab hold of Tanner's head and lift him from my pec, and he looks at me like he's a dog that's had his dinner interrupted.

"You can have more later," I say. "But I think it's my turn."

"Your turn?" he asks, puzzled. And then his brows rise. "Oh, so you want—"

"Hey, sh," I say, stroking his back. "I got you, okay? I just want you to stay where you are."

"Where I am?" he asks as I move out from under him.

He gets up on his elbows, but I stroke his back again.

"Relax," I say, now standing. And from here, I swear his ass is taller than the mountains I flew over on my way to San Diego. This man has been doing a world a disservice by not letting anything be done to it until now. Well, I can't complain. Much more for me.

"What do you want me to do?" Tanner asks, looking up at me. The position makes the sides of his torso fold over itself like an accordion, which only makes his back and ass look more muscular.

"Face the other wall," I say, pointing toward my bedroom window.

He rotates to face the wall, and he's so tall that both his head and legs hang far off the bed.

"Here," I say, putting my hands on his huge thighs. "Put your knees on the bed and come toward my edge."

He gets into position, but he looks uncomfortable. His ass looks great, but his back is curved upward, and he holds his arms rigid.

"Sit back like a frog," I say. "Rest your ass on your knees and prop yourself up with your arms."

He obeys, and I nearly pass out at the sight. His back is now arched, showing just how muscular he is, and he's presenting his perfect asshole right in front of my face.

"Like this?" he says.

I nod even though he can't see me, my mouth watering at the sight of his hole. It's pink—hallefuckinglujah—with a light touch of hair. I'm going to fucking destroy this man.

"Uh, Jimmy?" he says. There's worry in his voice.

I stand up and press against the edge of the bed. He turns his head to look up at me, still in position.

"Everything okay?" I ask, putting my hand on his freckled shoulder, and damn is it thick.

"Yeah," he says, nodding. "But you're not gonna—" he pauses.

Oh no. Does he not want to be rimmed? Maybe he thinks it's weird for me to put my face in his ass. I guess that would make sense.

He clears his throat. "You're not gonna put it in yet, are you? I don't know if I'm ready."

I relax, then run my hand down his spine, gently pressing into the muscles around it. He curls his neck upward like a cat, and I can see him relax as pleasure floods into his face.

"Don't worry," I say. "We'll ease into it."

He nods.

I lower myself and kiss his shoulder, then down his muscular back all the way to the top of his ass. I gently kiss one cheek, then the other.

"We don't have to do anything you don't want to do," I say, kneeling on the ground. "But I'd like to eat you out."

He turns his head sideways. "You wanna eat my ass?"

"I do," I say. "Never had that done before?"

"Never, actually," he says shaking his head. "I've never done it to another guy either."

"Are you okay with me rimming you?" I ask, moving out from behind him so he can see me better.

"I want you inside me," he says firmly. "Whether it's your tongue or your dick."

His words light up my chest in excitement. "Then let's not delay it any longer."

But I don't dive right in. No. I want to build up the pleasure.

I move closer to his hole, salivating at how pink and soft it is. I pucker my lips, then I blow. His whole body shakes.

"You good?" I ask.

"Yeah," he says, shifting slightly. "I think so."

"Can I continue?" I ask.

"Please."

Galvanized, I lick my lips, and this time I exhale a warm breath onto his hole.

"Oh," Tanner says.

I blow on his hole again, and I smirk as I watch it pucker. I alternate between cool and warm breaths and watch as his hole gradually relaxes. And then I introduce my beard.

Tanner lowers his upper body to the bed as I gently, but firmly, rub my bearded chin across his now less tight pink hole.

"Fuck," Tanner moans.

"Feel good?" I ask.

"Your beard," he says. "Fuck, Jimmy. You're such a man."

I chuckle, and he widens his legs, which opens up his cheeks wider for me. "There we go," I say. "Good boy."

"Please keep calling me that," he says.

"What?" I ask, my smile wide. "You like being called boy?"

He nods enthusiastically, his entire body moving with it.

"Then you need to call me Daddy."

"Yes, Daddy," he says without pause, and hearing it in his deep voice nearly makes me go feral. It takes all my strength to hold myself back from sticking it inside him right now.

This time, I start with my nose in his asshole, then move up to rub it with my mustache.

"Oh, Jeez," he says, one of his hands clutching the bedsheets. The other is dangling off the bed precariously close to me. It's almost as if he's reaching out to me, like he wants me to hold it.

When my lips reach his hole, I kiss it, and he lets out a sharp cry of pleasure. But I don't linger there long. I immediately rub my bearded chin into him again, this time more aggressively, and he lets out a plaintive whine.

"Why does that feel so good?" he asks, and I swear he sounds a bit Southern there. It must come out when he's more raw.

I rub my bearded cheeks into his hole, loving the way he sings his moans to me with each movement. I have him wrapped around my finger now, so it's time to show him what I really got. Without warning, I put my tongue against his hole and flick it.

He gasps like a little girl, and I can't help but laugh.

"You good?" I ask, still laughing.

"Not funny," he says, but he's laughing too now. He's being a good sport about it.

"What's wrong?" I ask more seriously, but still smiling.

"That just—wow," he says, his head lifted. "I've never felt anything like that."

"Feel good?" I ask.

"Oh yeah."

"Then let me give you more of it."

He nods and lowers his head. I press my tongue into his hole and flick it again. When I pull it away, I see his free hand curled into a fist. When I flick his hole again with my tongue, his hand clenches even tighter, so tight I'm afraid he'll hurt himself. So, without giving it another thought, I reach my hand up to his, uncurl his tight fist, and slither my fingers in between his. His hand freezes up for a minute, but then it melts into mine, firmly gripping my fingers.

And I take that as permission to continue. This time, I let my tongue search the rim of his hole, only gently touching the hole itself every now and then. Every time I do, his body shutters, and his hole twitches. And soon, it'll be twitching around my dick.

I pull away. "You doing good?"

"I am actually," he says. He's collapsed into the bed facing the headboard.

"Good," I say, squeezing his hand. And he squeezes back. Which feels a lot more intimate than a typical hookup. But the thing is—it feels right. If any other man squeezed my hand like this while I was going down on him, I'd have to politely remind him after it's all over that I'm not a relationship guy. And then we'd never see each other again. But while I don't know if I'll have sex with Tanner again, I know I will, and want to, see him again. I just don't know if feelings are catching.

Tired of teasing him, I decide to press my tongue fully inside him. He hisses and holds my hands tighter as I pulse my tongue, pressing against the sides of his hole and coaxing it to relax.

"Don't stop, Jimmy," Tanner says when I'm about to pull away. "That feels really good."

"Call me 'Daddy'," I say, which is what I tell most younger guys to call me, even though I like hearing my name on his lips.

"Yes, Daddy," he moans.

And that just makes me go feral for his hole. I press into him, harder each time, and I can feel his body relax around my face, opening up to my touch and preparing for my dick to be inside him. As I continue to tongue-fuck him, saliva pools in my mouth, dripping down his ass, then onto my jeans. That's when I unbutton them and pull my throbbing dick out, and I use my excess saliva to lube myself up.

Then I lose all my technique. I let my tongue sloppily lap his whole, eating him up like the delicious meal he is. He loosens his grip as he moans deeply, but when I squeeze his hand, he grasps me firmly again, as if that's what he's supposed to be doing. Which it isn't, nor should it be. But I like it all the same.

"Daddy," he says. "Please, can you please fuck me."

"Yes," I say, muffled as my tongue probes his hole. My dick slick with precum, I stand up, and Tanner turns to face me.

"Christ almighty," he says, looking down at my cock. And that's when I really see his for the first time too. Even though he's a good few inches taller than me, our dicks are roughly the same size, except mine's a little thicker, and I have a smattering of thick pubic hair while he just a patch of thin blonde hairs.

"You sure you still want this?" I ask even though I damn well know the answer. It just feels like I'm delaying it at this point, even when I know it's the only thing I want. Which makes no sense at all. When I fuck randos, I'm eager to get to the point. But with Tanner, I want to drag it out.

He looks up at me like I'm crazy. "Of course I do," he says, sounding truly Southern now. Different than my Mississippi accent, but Southern all the same.

"Alright," I say, somewhat uneasy. "Let me grab some lube."

I walk to the nightstand where I just moved the lube from my suitcase, and I feel my heart begin to race.

I'm conflicted. There's a loud voice in my head saying I need to stop this right now—that I better stop now before I have a repeat of the Joe situation. Because how is this any different? Joe and I met during a hookup, and then we just kept seeing each other. But the difference with Tanner is that he feels so alive. He responds to my touch, and he asks for more. Joe just asked that I fuck him while he laid helplessly there. Which, sometimes, can be hot. But I think what I want more than anything is for someone who can meet me where I'm at, who warms to my touch just like I do theirs, and so far, Tanner is doing exactly that.

So why the hell am I scared out of my mind?

I find the lube which somehow buried itself underneath all the other random things I stuffed in here from my suitcase, then turn around. I'm hoping to find Tanner on his hands and knees, facing away from me, like how most men position themselves when we hookup. I fuck them, we both cum, I feel good about myself, and then we both go on our way. Even though I always try to be kind and thoughtful toward the men I'm fucking, it is purely transactional, not unlike Tanner what was saying.

But instead I find Tanner laying at the head of the bed slightly propped up under some pillows. He's holding his legs spread, pressing one of his fingers against his hole, as if trying to replicate what I was doing to him earlier. He's waiting for me.

"You still good?" I ask, crawling onto the bed.

"Yeah, man," he says, lowering his legs on either side of me. "Why do you keep asking? Do you not want to do this?"

Both of us happen to look down at my dick which has shrunk since the last time he saw it.

"No, I do," I say honestly. I pour lube on my dick and start rubbing it to get back to full hardness.

"Then what is it?" he asks.

That all this is confirming I really like you, I want to say. *And that if we go all the way, I'm afraid I'll truly catch feelings for you, ones that can't be ignored or wished away.*

But that makes no fucking sense. This is just sex, and sex doesn't magically tie you to someone else. That's some Christian bullshit. Sex is just sex. I want to go all the way tonight because it will feel good for both of us, and I'll feel good about myself having Tanner bottom for the first time. Feelings won't be caught. I'll be fine.

"Nothing, boy," I say, trying to invoke the daddy-boy dynamic we had going earlier, but it just feels stilted and wrong. "Let's do this."

Hard again, I alternate between pressing the head against his hole and lubing it up with my hand, slowly but steadily inserting my pinky inside him.

Tanner hisses when I get one knuckle of my pinky inside him. I pull it out.

"That's... wow," he says.

"You're tight," I say, trying to just be matter-of-fact, but I feel like I'm coming off more tender than I intend.

"Is that a good or bad thing?" Tanner asks.

I open my mouth to answer, but then I pause.

"Well," I manage to say. "We gotta loosen you up first so I can get my dick inside you. Too loose and it's difficult to feel good for either party. There's that sweet spot in the middle."

"Didn't realize it was this complicated," Tanner says holding his dick. "But I guess back in college we didn't really know what we were doing."

I thin my lips. He's got a point. With nearly every man that I've hooked up with—including Joe—we'd just jerk off while kissing or blow each other to get off if anal sex proved to be too complicated or messy. It required too much patience to do more than that. But seeing Tanner here laying like this, his eager eyes staring up at me, settling for what I see as a lesser sexual experience is the last thing I want right now.

"We can build up to it," I say. "I can help open you up. We can take our time."

"You sure?" he asks. "I don't want to—"

"I'm absolutely sure," I say.

And so we do it. I lube up my pinky more, and we continue opening Tanner up. And to my relief, we start to make progress. But by the time we get to my ring finger, I remember another reason why I choose to settle for mutual masturbation with randos: the awkward downtime that comes with opening someone up. With Joe, I never had this because he hated the stillness of it. I don't like it much either because it gives me chance to let my thoughts run wild, which I obviously hate. But with Tanner, it doesn't feel so bad. Because it gives me a chance to talk to the man.

"So you're a big video game guy," I say. He winces as I stick my ring finger in him further, but then he relaxes once it's all the way inside. "Tell me some other games you like."

His face gets all serious as he considers my question, which is good because he doesn't even wince when I pull my finger out.

"You ever played Paper Mario?" he asks as I slide my middle finger inside.

"You know, I never played that. Any good?"

He rolls his eyes, a smile coming on his face, and I get a little jump in my stomach. I'm excited to hear him talk.

"Is it any good? Jimmy, that's one of the best games Nintendo ever put out."

"Okay," I say with a smile, my middle finger now fully inside him. Man, he's taking me like a champ. "Tell me more about it."

"Well, the first thing you gotta know is that there are two that are really good," he says. "There's the first one for the Nintendo 64. It started the legacy. It was this RPG where you played as Mario, and you collected partners along your adventure."

As he continues talking, I realize that I've now stuck my thumb, which isn't small mind you, fully inside him, and Tanner hasn't even batted an eye. He's just going on about how the first Paper Mario revolutionized RPGs for all games afterward.

"Well look at that," I say, retracting my thumb once he's done talking. "Paper Mario saved the day. I think you might be ready to take my dick."

"What?" he asks. "I'm ready? Already?"

"I think so," I say with a smirk. "That is, unless..."

"Of course I still want to," he says.

"Okay," I say. "Then kiss me so I can get hard again."

He pulls me in, and his tongue searches my mouth eagerly. I don't know if this makes sense, but he kisses me the same way he talks—enthusiastically, sometimes long-winded, but nonetheless aware and present. And I can't get enough of him.

"Alright," I say, reluctantly pulling away, but at least my dick is rock-hard now. "I'm ready."

He nods and holds his legs open for me. I press my lubed head against his hole, and then I gradually press it in. He gasps and holds his breath as I press it deeper.

"You gotta breathe, Tanner," I say. "That'll make it easier."

He exhales abruptly. "Yes, Daddy."

I bristle at him calling me that, but he's doing as I say. I want him to call me by name, especially when I'm inside him, but I gotta keep us distant. We can't catch feelings.

I slowly continue to push myself inside him until, finally, I'm as deep as I can go. Tanner has his eyes closed, his hands behind his back, and he's breathing in and out audibly.

"So you told me about that first Paper Mario," I say. "You say there are more?"

His eyes shoot open, and there's a fire there. "Oh my God," he says as I slowly pull out, my arms propping me up on either side of him. "You mean the best game to ever be released on the GameCube?"

I chuckle. "That's a bold claim. Even better than Melee?"

"Better than Melee?" he asks when I'm finally out. "Any game is better than Melee."

"Now those are fighting words," I say. And I 'fight' by pressing my dick slowly back into him.

Tanner gasps again, but this time he's able to take it with slower breaths.

"Yeah," he says, his voice shaky from the pleasure. And I know it's from the pleasure because I feel just as damn good.

"And why is it so good?" I ask, inserting myself at a faster pace.

"Because," he says, biting his lip. "That was the game that made me happiest as a kid."

I pull out a second time, then put myself back in. And this time, Tanner doesn't as much take a breath. He just stares into me with those deep blue eyes.

"That was the game, more than anything, that gave me hope in a brighter future," he says. "Majora's Mask helped me feel seen, but Paper Mario: The Thousand Year Door gave me hope. I don't know why exactly—it just did."

Now I stare hungrily into his eyes, thrusting steadily now, and the big tank of a man just fucking takes it like the handsome stud he is. Fuck, he feels good.

"I'm glad you found it," I say, biting my lip from the pleasure lighting up my groin.

"Yeah," he says, wrapping his huge arms around my back, pulling me closer to him. "It helped me, at the very least, have a little happiness as a kid."

His arms around me, I lower myself until my hairy torso is pressed against his while I fuck him. Since he's taller than me, my lips only meet his collar bone, which is good. Kissing during sex is my weakness. So, of course, Tanner raises his head so our lips can meet. And I kiss him greedily, pounding him faster as I do.

I pull my lips away, still fucking him strong, our foreheads pressed together.

"And are you happy now, Tanner?" I say, staggered because of my thrusting. "Today? Right now?"

He nods quickly. "Yes, Daddy. I'm close. I'm not even touching myself, and I'm close."

My groin hot with pleasure to an immeasurable degree, nearly puts me over the edge. But what he calls me staves me off. "Tanner, please don't call me that," I say. "Say my name when I fuck you."

"Yes, Jimmy," he says without pause as I fuck him harder. "You make me so happy."

"Fuck," I say, wrapping my arms around his huge, tight, sweaty body. "I'm gonna fucking cum."

"Oh, me too—"

I let out a growl so deep I fear I've shredded my vocal cords, but I don't care. I spill my seed into Tanner and watch as he helplessly shoots his load all over his sweaty torso, his face contorted in pained ecstasy.

He looks up at me panting, his boyishly handsome face turning upward into a smile, and that's when all the pleasure in my body immediately turns to clarity. I fall onto the man and press his lips against mine, hungrily searching his mouth for something to turn back all that I just did, knowing full well that this is the last place I'll find it but searching for it just as desperately all the same.

Because I, Jimmy Dillon—the man who has sworn never to fall for the people he has sex with—have fallen for Tanner Bash.

Chapter 20

Tanner Bash

AFTER BOTH JIMMY AND I came—after he got me to cum without touching myself—the whole world was a blur. Up until then, I kept getting little flashes of guilt, thinking how God would disapprove. But I just kept looking at Jimmy to pull me out of that. And once he got me talking about Paper Mario, the doubt pretty much vanished completely. Now, we're laying in his bed—my guest bed—together. He's holding me in his arms, stroking my hair, and I'm burying my back into him, even though by size alone I'm definitely not the little spoon. But it just feels so good to be held.

"I can show you the Paper Mario game if you want," I say shyly, like a little kid wanting to show an adult their favorite rock.

Jimmy kisses the back of my neck, and his beard tickles my spine, sending warm chills throughout my body. "I would want nothing more."

The thought of us spending the rest of the evening playing video games makes my stomach flutter. But then my it growls, and I realize it isn't just the butterflies.

"Is it normal to have stomach trouble after bottoming?" I say.

"It can be," he says. "And I did fuck you pretty hard, not to brag. So I wouldn't be surprised if your tummy gives you a little trouble."

I laugh, turned on by his brash confidence. But when my stomach grumbles again I realize he may be right.

"Give me a minute," I say, getting up, sad to leave his arms.

"Of course," he says. "I'll be right here."

I make my way to the bathroom and sit myself down on the toilet. That's when I realize I left my phone in here too. I pick it up to scroll through social media, but that's when I see a text that makes me feel like I'll vomit as well.

"I want some action after practice tomorrow," a text from Chris says. "Meet me in the showers then."

I want to throw my phone into the wall so hard that it breaks and shatters Chris with it. But the solution wouldn't be that easy. God wouldn't make it that way, especially now that I've officially fornicated. That I let myself be sodomized.

But it felt so wonderful. I didn't even know I could get off without touching myself. And watching Jimmy's muscular, beefy body bounce as he thrusted inside of me was, in all senses of the word, a dream come true.

I open the text to respond, but then my heart begins to race. I have no idea what to say.

I asked Jimmy to fuck me, and it was damn near perfect. And I don't just want to do it again. I want to lay out a blanket in front of my TV and play video games with him all night. I want him to talk to me in that buttery Mississippi accent and make me feel like I'm the goddamn handsomest and most important man to walk the earth.

But if I were to turn around and let Chris do whatever he wanted to me, wouldn't I be betraying Jimmy? It would be cheating, in a way, even though I very much do not want anything to do with Chris. Yet I don't have a choice. Sure, I've distanced myself even further from God by letting Jimmy plow me, which, at this point, I don't really regret. Even if I don't go to heaven, at least I got a taste of it when he got me to orgasm without touching myself.

Yet if I were to let a video of me leak into the world—one where I'm very clearly fucking the face of a man—my sins would no longer be just between me and God. The whole world would know. And if I were to ever want to repent of my ways and go back to God after such a scandal—specifically by marrying a woman and starting a family—no one would want me. I'd be a scandal at best, a moral reprobate at worst. What woman would want to date a former NFO player who was caught having sex with a man? Surely not a woman of God. So, if I were to let Chris go ahead and post this video, I'd go off the path and forever bar myself from the straight and narrow. I'd never get the peace and happiness that comes from following God's divine compass again.

My thumb hovers over the keyboard while I think about what to say, and then there's a knock at the door.

"Everything okay?" Jimmy asks on the other end. "Just want to make sure I didn't kill you or anything."

I immediately close my phone and set it face down on the counter. "Yeah, all good," I say. Damnit. Why does he have to be so thoughtful? I finish up and open the bathroom door. Jimmy's wearing gym shorts with his arms crossed leaning against the wall, and he looks even more like a man than did before. I love how hairy his arms are, specifically his upper arms. Makes it look like he has wings or something—like an angel.

"You wanna get your game booted up?" he asks. "I can get some dinner prepared for us."

Outside, the sun is setting, and I get a warm feeling in my chest. Spending an evening with a charismatic, handsome man sounds ideal.

"I'd like that," I say, my accent stronger than usual. I don't know what it is, but being around Jimmy relaxes me, makes me more casual. When I'm most comfortable, my Georgia accent comes through—and it's come through a lot with him. Sure, I could say it's because he's a fellow Southern boy, but I like to say it's a little more than that.

He saunters by and claps me on my bare shoulder as he passes, and I melt into his touch.

"Good deal," he says. "Can't wait to see it."

I throw my clothes on and cross the pool area into my own home. I hurry on into my living room, feeling giddier than I have reason to be. This is the first time I've really just let myself fall into Jimmy, and I absolutely love it. It feels like home. I don't know what to do about my relationship with God, but maybe I can go solo for a while. As long as I have Jimmy, maybe I'll be okay.

By the time I get the game all up and running, Jimmy comes in with two big steaming bowls. He sets one down in front of me on blanket I've laid out, and the smell alone makes me want to gobble the thing whole. And to think months ago I was having trouble eating.

I pick up and put some of the dish on my fork. It looks like it's some pasta tomato dish with chicken, but that's where my knowledge ends.

"What'd you make this time?" I ask. "I haven't seen this before."

"It's called 'Marry Me Chicken Pasta'," he says with a smirk.

"'Marry me'?" I ask.

"I know we just had sex—pretty good sex too—but I think that's a little fast, don't you think?"

I blush redder than a goddamn sunburn.

He pats my back. "I'm kidding, big guy. It's a high-protein pasta dish with lots of flavor. I'm sure you'll like it."

Still blushing, I laugh. I fucking love that he just called me his 'big guy', the way he jokes around me with me like I'm one of his bros even though I'm still carrying his DNA in my fucking ass.

I put a forkful of his pasta in my mouth, and my face hardens. Holy shit. This does make me want to marry Jimmy. It helps that he's like the hottest guy I've ever seen and just rearranged my guts with his perfect dick, too.

"You like?" I ask.

"Yeah," I say, a little too desperately. Chewing, I glance up at him, and his gaze hangs on me while he wears a slight smile. There's a tug on my stomach, and I have to look away quickly.

That's the face I pictured when Chris forced me to let him suck my dick. That's the face that I stared into when I came with no hands. That's the face that, if I let fully into my life, will prevent me from having a full relationship with God. But it's the face that I want to be with right in this very moment.

So I'm gonna stay put.

"Wanna start?" I ask, setting down the bowl.

"Let's do it," he says, continuing to eat.

I start a fresh save file of Paper Mario: The Thousand Year Door, and I'm immediately regaled by the catchy tune of Rogueport, charmed by the quirky characters, and compelled by the gameplay and story. Occasionally, I'll glance back at Jimmy, afraid that he'll be on his phone or be otherwise checked out. But he's fixed on the TV, his fist propping up his chin.

"You like it so far?" I ask.

"How have I not known about this?" he asks. "I can already tell it's a masterpiece."

My chest warms, and his praise of the game feels personal, like he's calling me a masterpiece.

"It is," I say, wishing I had more words to say.

Without thinking, I scooch closer to him, wanting to touch him as I play, to cuddle in some way. But just when I'm no more than an inch away, I stop. This feels weird. Jimmy said this was just sex after all. Maybe I'm reading too much into this. It's probably too intimate to touch him.

But I'm dead wrong. Because that's when Jimmy sticks his arms under mine and pulls me toward him. He lays me down on my side right in front of him, and then he spoons me from behind. Instinctively, I remove my clothes, and he grabs hold of a nearby blanket and lays it on top of us. I nuzzle my ass into him, and then he slides his shorts off so his perfect dick is sandwiched right between my cheeks. He puts a pillow just below my head so I can lay down and play at the same time, and then he kisses the back of my neck, sending my entire body to heaven as he keeps his lips there.

I continue on with the game, finally finishing up the prologue.

"On to Chapter One," I say. When the little Paper Mario and his goomba friend appear on the other side of the pipe, we're introduced to Petal Meadows, a bright and cheerful place. But as soon as I hear the music, I freeze up.

Suddenly, I'm back in my basement. I'm slightly older than my last flashback—thirteen I think—but I'm so much more scared. I hear my parents stomping upstairs, which always makes me quiet up so I can listen for if they're coming down the stairs. So when I hear the steps approach the top of the stairs, my entire body clenches. My dad storms down the stairs.

"Tanner Patrick Bash," he yells, each syllable cutting into me.

I pause my game and turn to him, but I can still hear the Petal Meadows soundtrack in the background.

"Where the fuck is your brother?"

"I don't know," I say honestly. "I just got home from school and—"

He growls and shakes his head, cutting me off. "What is that goddamn church teaching you? You're your brother's keeper. You gotta keep track of him. You sleep in the same room as him, for fuck's sake. Yet here you are playing your stupid fucking game. Where is he?"

I try to hold it in, but I can't. The tears just start flowing. "I don't know. He wasn't there when I woke up."

His eyes bug out. "He wasn't there?" He takes an empty glass off a nearby coffee table and hurls it at the wall. I flinch raise my arms to block the flying glass.

"Heather!" he shouts, turning around and heading to the stairs. "He snuck out again." And without another word to me, he races up the stairs, two at a time, leaving me alone, curled up, in my tears in front of the TV, the Petal Meadows song blaring.

Just like it is now.

"Tanner," Jimmy says.

I sniffle.

"Tanner, what's going on bud?" he rolls me onto my back, and my eyes meet his, I just lose it. Tears stream down my cheeks, and I quickly raise my hands to my eyes to shield them.

Jimmy grabs my arms and lowers them. "Tanner, it's okay. I'm here." He gently shushes me and takes both my hands in his. He starts massaging the palms, and by focusing on my touch, I'm able to slow the flow of the tears.

"Hey," Jimmy says once I've let most of the tears out, still rubbing my hands. "Can you tell me what that was about?"

I bite on my dry lips.

"Here," he says. He gets up, and heatless void he leaves me threatens to suck me into nothingness. But he returns just in time with one of my bottles of water from the fridge.

"Drink this," he says, pushing me to sit up. "Helps replenish the liquids you lose when you cry."

I unscrew the lid and lift the bottle to my lips. I throw back the contents of the bottle and gulp my heart away. And for a minute, I feel bliss, just focusing on this one little task, like I'm in the eye of a hurricane.

I lower the bottle, and Jimmy reaches out to rub my back.

"You good?" he asks.

"I think," I say. "Thanks for the water."

"Tanner," he says, making my stomach lurch. He has me wrapped around his finger when he says my name so thoughtfully.

I look up at him. "What?"

"This isn't the first time this has happened," he says. "Mind sharing what's going on?"

I sigh. He's right. I flipped out like this when we played Mario Kart together. I ran away then so he wouldn't have to deal with me and so I could keep him distant. But I don't wanna be so distant from him anymore.

"Growing up for me was hard," I say, just deciding to spill it. I explain my addict brothers, my frazzled parents, and how I was caught up right in the middle.

"And the worst part," I continue, eyes puffy and out of tears. "Is that I continue to hold on to this. It's like I hear music that I used to hear a lot back then and it puts me right back in that place."

Without a word, Jimmy reaches for the remote and mutes the TV so I no longer have to hear the music. Goddamn, he's wonderful.

"Thanks," I say.

He nods. "Continue."

I sniffle. "It just fucking sucks because it's music from games that I love. Games that mark my childhood. That got me *through* my childhood. Shouldn't

I be able to enjoy them? Or does God hate me so much that he can't even give me that?"

"Woah," Jimmy says, putting his hand on my arm. "What's God hating you have to do with all this?"

I let out a sharp laugh. "Besides video games, church and football were the only things keeping me sane at this time," I say. "They kept the chaos at bay. But now that I keep reliving these memories, it's like I've lost God's peace. He's punished me. Which makes sense because I fucking deserve it."

"Tanner, what makes you think you deserve to be punished by God?"

I freeze up again, remembering Chris's lips on my dick. And dread pools in my chest as I imagine all the other things that he's gonna make me do.

"Is it because you're gay?" Jimmy asks.

"Not exactly," I say honestly. "It's more complicated than that."

Jimmy sighs and shifts in his seat. "Then what is it? I want to help you, man. I can see you're suffering."

I frown down at the carpet, running my fingers through the microfiber blanket we're laying on. I glance at my unfinished bowl of pasta. Before we started playing, I could have eaten the whole thing. But now my appetite is completely gone.

Tomorrow, in order to keep my reputation in check and to make sure I don't completely shut myself off from God, I have to give myself to Chris. If I let Jimmy all the way in right now, then I'll want him all the way, too. Like as a partner. As a boyfriend. And I may have given myself over to homosexuality, but I'm still monogamous, and I'm definitely no cheater. I couldn't date Jimmy while letting Chris abuse me in secret. That wouldn't be fair to him.

"Tanner, I—" he thins his lips and sighs through his nose. "Please, don't pull away from me again. I wanna be there for you. I—"

Hearing the desperation in his voice, I whip my head up to him. "What?"

"I fucking like you," he says with a sigh. "Alright? And that isn't like me. I fuck around a lot. Like *a lot* a lot. Ever since my ex, Joe, cheated on me, I haven't wanted to settle down. Like at all."

I clench my fists, and it feels like the room is starting to spin around me. I'm over the moon hearing his admission that he likes me, but hearing about all the sex he's had? And about his ex? Makes me want to run and jump into the Pacific to cool myself off.

"But with you man, I don't know. You got this liveliness about you, and you're so fun to talk to. You're so fucking handsome too. Before, when you would push me away, I would brush it off. But I couldn't really get over it. And now that I know I like you, it'd break my heart. So please. I really want to know what's going on with you. I want to be there for you, man. So let me."

I shake my head, tears warming my eyes again. *I like you, too,* I want to say. But what would that mean? Falling into him? Jimmy's not like the pool between our houses. He's like the fucking ocean outside, and I know if I were to swim too far into him, I'd never get back to shore. And I can't let myself do that with Chris in the way—especially if I want to keep a path open in the future for me to come back to God.

"I like you, too," I say. "But we have to stay friends."

His face puckers like he's tasted something sour, and I swear I can see his eyes watering now too. "Friends?" he asks. "Are you telling me you don't feel anything for me?"

I look away, unable to bear the hurt in his beautiful brown eyes. If I told him the truth, I wouldn't be able to save either of us. So I muster up all the strength I have to say what I'm about to say.

"I wanna be friends, Jimmy," I say. "Just friends."

He frowns and lets out a shaky breath. He wipes the single tear falling down his cheek and sniffles. "Alright," he says. "You seem to know what you want."

He collects his clothes that he took off while cuddling and quickly puts them on. I just stare at the ground, holding a blanket tight to my body. On the TV, Paper Mario's paused. But, at the very least, thanks to Jimmy, the music isn't playing. At least I can't add another bad memory to the sound.

Fully clothed, he stops to look at me. He opens his mouth to say something. Then he closes it, and I'm both relieved and incredibly disappointed. I want him to say more, but he and I both know it will make this harder.

He walks out my back door, and I collapse into the blankets on the floor.
And I weep.

Chapter 21

Jimmy Dillon

"Are you excited to see your family again?" Yousef asks me as he drives me to the San Diego airport. It's early, but I can see hints of the sun's rise in the horizon.

"Yeah. We always spend Thanksgiving together," I say, referring to my chosen family back in Glamour Springs. "And I've been away for a few months. It'll be good to see them."

"Certainly," he says as we pull into the airport.

Once we reach my terminal, we get out, and he helps me collect my bags.

"Oh, I almost forgot," Yousef says. He rushes to the back seat of his car. He returns with a small paper bag and hands it to me.

I grab hold of it, and I nearly drop it. It's heavier than I would expect. "What's this?" I say, letting go of my travel bag to open it. I reach in to pull out an ornate little metal bowl with a mallet inside. It looks like the one Maria uses for our meditation sessions.

"It's a meditation bowl," he says. "Your very own."

I look up at my new Iranian friend, a wide smile forming on my face. "You didn't have to do this."

He shrugs. "You're right, but Chewy in particular noticed how glum you have been at our meditation practices the last few weeks. So he decided to give you his Christmas present early."

I move the bowl around in my hands, enjoying the way the cold metal feels against my fingers. These past few weeks, I've been going to every meditation session that Yousef and his friends have been holding. It's really been the only thing keeping me sane since Tanner told me he'd rather be friends. Since we had some of the best sex of my life. From the moment I confessed my feelings for him and he rejected me.

I reach out and give Yousef a hug. "Thanks for everything."

"You talk like it's goodbye," he says. "I'll see you in a few days, right?"

"Yeah," I say, pulling away. "Once Tanner's back in town from his away game, I'm back to cooking for him."

"Lucky us. We get to keep you in San Diego for a couple months longer."

I nod. And then once the football season's over, I'm back to Glamour Springs for good, and then Tanner Bash will be a distant memory. I don't know how to feel about that.

"I better catch my flight," I say, putting the meditation bowl in my bag.

"Meditate while you're away," Yousef says, shutting his trunk.

"I definitely will," I say. "Thanks again for the ride!" And then I rush to make my flight.

Once I'm on the plane, I panic when I realize that I forgot my cold medicine to knock me out. But then I calm myself down. Yousef recommended some sleep meditation podcasts to help me get to rest, and this has especially helped when Tanner's been on my mind. So, once we're up in the air, I plug in the podcast, close my eyes, and before I know it, I've landed in Memphis.

When I get outside, I grimace as I'm assaulted by the humid Tennessee air. I've been spoiled by California weather. But the grimace turns into a wide grin when I see two of my best friends waiting to pick me up.

"Jimmy Dillon!" Kyle Weaver, former legendary linebacker, shouts.

I rush to hug the huge man, and then I quickly let go to hug my other best friend, Silas. I nearly knock off his cowboy hat in the process.

"Thanks again for picking me up," I say to them.

"Anytime," Silas says as Kyle loads my bags into the car. "It's quieter in Glamour Springs without you."

We all get in the car, and then we set forth to my home.

"I know the boys miss you too," Kyle says.

"Hush," I say, turning around to whack his arm as he sits in the back seat. Since my breakup with Joe, I've rightfully earned the reputation as the group slut. But since Tanner rejected me, I don't know. Sure, I've slept with a handful of guys, but it hasn't felt the same. And now that I'm meditating more, I don't feel the need to do it so much. I don't know, but it feels like my brain's a little q uieter.

When we finally get to Glamour Springs, I breathe a sigh of relief. California is nice, but it's nicer to be in a place where people walk, talk, and look like you. If I see another man with perfectly sculpted abs, I might think I need to lose my belly and shave my body hair altogether—kidding, of course, but the feeling is th ere.

"For Thanksgiving this year," Kyle says, "My ma got us all a cabin."

"You're kidding," I say.

"Nope," Silas says. "Ms. Higgins has surpassed our expectations once again."

"Who'll be eating with us?" I ask.

"The usuals," Kyle says as we make our way to Glamour Springs Lake where all the cabins are located. "Me, Michael, Silas, you, ma. And then we got Martha and Llewellyn."

"Oh, sweets," I say, pressing my hand against my chest. I miss my lesbian bookstore owners like crazy.

"And you're gonna love this," Silas says. "Marissa and Lilah."

I make a grand gesture of falling back into the passenger seat and passing out. "My girls?" I ask. "Are eating with us?"

"Per invitation of Ms. Higgins," Silas says.

"Christ," I say, shaking my head. "They're gonna yell at me if I try to help Kyle's mom out at all."

"As if she'd let you," Kyle says.

I laugh. "*You need to take a sabbatical,*" I mimic my assistant managers saying. I hiss, but a wide smile is forming on my face. "Those girls will be the death of me." And I couldn't be happier that I'm spending Thanksgiving with them.

Funny how their little suggestion led me to a place where my life would change in more ways than one. Heartbreak, sure. But at least I've met cool people and learned some meditation tricks.

We pull into the driveway of one of the biggest cabins on the lake.

"Think this'll fit all of us?" I ask.

Kyle exits the car and starts unloading my stuff from the trunk.

"Wait 'til you see the inside," Silas says. "It's gorgeous."

When the three of us walk in, I swear I have to pick my jaw up off the floor.

We stand at the precipice of a large room with several skylights, and a huge chandelier hangs perfectly between them all. In the center of the room, there's a giant, circular couch facing a fireplace, and just behind that wall is a huge deck that leads straight in the lake. To the right, the kitchen is bustling with several people.

"Has Linda Higgins finally allowed more than one cook in the kitchen?"

Kyle's mom, a woman I'd say I've adopted as my own mother, strolls out of the kitchen and fake pouts. "Don't you start anything with me," she says, wrapping her arms around me and giving me the strongest hug a woman her age can give. "It isn't even Thanksgiving yet."

"Just keeping you young," I say, rubbing her back.

"More like making me die young," she says. But then she kisses me on the cheek. "It's good to have you back."

"Good to be back."

"And yes," she says, her hands on my back. "We do have one other cook in the kitchen."

"Jimmy!" Michael, Kyle's fiancé, comes rushing out of the kitchen. He's wearing a dirty orange apron with a cartoon drawing of a turkey, and his hands are covered in flour.

I hug him anyways. "How's the world's best author?"

"Oh, you know," he says. "Planning a trilogy right now."

"No way," I say. "You gotta tell me more."

But I don't get long with him before Linda takes him back to the kitchen.

"You all can catch up later," she says. "We are on strict deadlines."

"Alright," I say with a laugh.

After the entire house takes a nap, we get together for some chili that Linda made, and it's much better than the deer chili I was experimenting with a few months back. By the time I'm finished, I lay down on the gorgeous circular couch.

"Isn't even Thanksgiving yet," Kyle says. "And you're already passed out?"

"Oh I know," I say. "I'm just preparing myself."

The five of us—me, Kyle, Silas, Linda, and Michael—all play some board games to Christmas music, and I feel right at home. There are moments where Tanner flashes across my mind, but I banish the thoughts quickly. I don't need to be thinking about him right now, especially when I've still got a couple more months with him. I'll have plenty of time to feel heartbroken in the future.

The next day, Martha and Llewellyn, the lesbian bookshop owners, arrive early in the morning and set their stuff down in their room. I go and get brunch with them, Silas, and Michael.

"So, we have some good news," Martha, the redhead, says.

"We're finally adopting!" Llewellyn says, her dreads bouncing with excitement.

"I'll be," I say, leaning onto the table. "I'm finally gonna be an uncle!"

"Congrats, guys," Michael says.

"Well, I wouldn't congratulate us yet," Martha says. "We're still going through all the paperwork. But based on what the social worker is telling us, it's promising."

They go on to explain the logistics, and I just smile as they do. Early on in their relationship, they decided they wanted to eventually have children. But they didn't want children of their own—they wanted to adopt and help a child already born on this earth, which I think is sweet.

"But we can't forget about you," Llewellyn says to Michael. "You and Kyle have finally set the big day?"

"We have," he says, beaming. "Around next Thanksgiving."

Both Martha and Llewellyn squeal, and on the outside, I express my enthusiasm for my good friend. He and Kyle deserve it after all they've been through.

But I can't help but feel a little bit empty hearing the news. Not because I'm not happy for them, but I think because I feel a little bit sorry for myself. I wish I could share some good news and say that I have a boyfriend in the NFO. But I can't.

"And what about you all?" Martha asks me and Silas sitting right next to each other.

We both glance at each other, then chuckle to ourselves. Ever since Joe's breakup, we've been the perennially single ones.

"You know me," Silas says. "Just focusing on PT school."

"And me?" I decide to say now so I won't accidentally drop the truth later. "Just sleeping around. Nothing serious." But I swear I don't come off as convincing. Because while Martha, Llewellyn and Michael acknowledge my answer, Silas just squints at me.

After brunch, we all go about the town, stopping by to see what the various stores have for the holidays.

"What was that about?" Silas asks when the others are distracted inside a new chic office supplies store.

"What was what about?" I ask, folding my arms.

"You know," he says, taking off his cowboy hat to scratch his head. "You're acting all quiet and weird."

I sigh. Silas can read me like a children's book. "You're not gonna believe this."

"Oh my God," Silas says, pulling on the hairs of his mustache. "You and that Tanner guy are fucking."

I drop my arms. "Don't say it so loud."

We step to the side of the sidewalk to let others pass by.

"How the fuck did you guess it so fast?" I hiss.

"I mean, isn't it obvious? He's your type, and you're living with him."

"In a guest house," I say.

"What difference is that?"

I shrug.

"And you have that pensive, broody Jimmy look."

I stare at him, deadpan. "Now what the hell is that?"

"Most of the time, you're carefree. Funny, gregarious, outgoing."

"Am I not funny anymore?"

"That's not the point," he says, swatting his hand at me. "It looks like something's holding you back. And I've known you long enough to see that it's boy related. You had the same look when you were going through it with Joe."

I fold my arms and lean against the brick wall of the shop. "I don't know what to do, man."

"What's going on? Is he closeted?"

"No," I say, stepping away from the wall. "And that's the weird part. We've been living together for a while. He even came out to me. He'll invite me in, push me away, then invite me in again."

"Sounds like your mom."

"Right?" I say, gesturing to him. "And I caught him sniffing my fucking laundry."

His eyes widen. "Is it weird that I think that's hot?"

"I sure thought it was," I admit. "But it was weird because up until then I thought the dude was straight."

"Is this when y'all fucked?"

"No," I say, shaking my head. "Now that was even weirder. After the laundry incident, he asks for us to go out for ice cream."

Tanner furrows his brow so fast his cowboy hat moves with it. "Seriously?"

"I know," I say. "But then he pushes me away. And just when I had enough, he knocks on my door. And you know what he asks?"

Silas shrugs. "For sex?"

I half scoff and half laugh. "Goddamnit, are you fucking psychic or something?"

"Honestly, that was just a guess."

"Well, yes," I say. "He asked to fuck. And holy hell, Silas. That was some of the best sex of my life."

"That's saying something."

"Hey."

"You're a self-described slut," he says, shrugging. "So I'm guessing you caught feelings?"

"Kinda. I had been catching feelings the whole time. See, he's real nerdy, loves video games. We'd play Nintendo games together, and he'd get all animated talking about them. Had a real hard childhood growing up, and sports and video games seemed to be his only refuge. Oh, and religion."

"Right," Silas says. "I was wondering where the baggage was. You answered that for me just now. He's religious."

I swat my hand at that like it's nothing. "But I love hearing him talk, Silas. He's got this real pure nature. So genuine. And he's so goddamn handsome. The sex was what confirmed to me that I liked him. But when I said I wanted him to open up to me, for us to have something more serious, he just pushed me away again. Said he wanted to be friends only."

"Could it be because of his religion?"

I shrug helplessly, this whole conversation bringing up the emotional muck from my time with Tanner.

Silas furrows his brow. "Maybe you could—"

But then our three friends come out of the shop with some new trinkets—pens, journals, and the like, so I shut up. I trust these folks, but I'm not ready to talk about my unrequited love with an NFO player just yet—especially one that's closeted.

As we head back to the house, Silas manages to isolate me so we can talk in private for a brief moment.

"I was gonna say you should talk to Michael," he says. "If anyone knows how to handle a relationship with a closeted NFO player, it's the guy who's about to be married to one. Well, Kyle's not closeted now, but you get what I'm saying."

I nod as we walk. "You're right. Maybe I'll talk to him."

Back home, we rest up a bit. And by the time we gotta start really cooking, my assistant managers show up.

"Well if it isn't the girls who ran me outta town," I say as I saunter over to them.

"Jimmy!" Lilah says, wrapping her arms around me. She's wearing a shirt with Kirby on it, and he's dressed like a turkey.

"I love that," I say, pointing to her shirt as I pull away.

"Missed you," Marissa says, giving me a side hug.

"She feels after all," I say.

"Don't make me take it back," she says. "But I guess having you away made me miss ya."

I squeeze her arm. "Missed you too, girl."

"How's your sabbatical going?" Lilah asked. "Picked up any hobbies?"

"You know," I say a little smugly, my hands on my hips. "I've been meditating, actually."

Lilah brightens, and Marissa rolls her eyes.

"You better not go all 'new-age spirituality' on me," Marissa says.

Lilah playfully whacks her arm. "That's cool, Jimmy. Sounds peaceful."

"It is," I admit, folding my arms. "Hope the diner's doing okay?"

"Better than okay," Lilah says. "We're doing great. Lots of business. But people keep asking for you. It's not the same with you gone."

I sigh, thinking about how a few months ago, I was just working in a diner and fucking whoever I wanted in my free time. Now I'm the personal chef for an NFO player, living on the beach in San Diego, and I don't really even want to fuck anyone anymore. What the hell's happened to me?

"Alright," Linda says, storming out of the kitchen. "I concede. I am defeated."

"What's going on?" Silas asks.

"Are you alright, Linda?" I ask.

"She is," Kyle says, coming out of the kitchen and rubbing her back and she rests with her hands on her knees. "She just needs a lot more help than she expected."

"It's just so embarrassing," she says, wiping her gray hair from her face. "I used to make so much food for everyone. But I'm getting old and tired."

Marissa puts on one of her rare smiles. "We'll help you out, Ms. H.," she says, rolling up her sweater sleeves.

"We will," I say. "And I'll finally get a chance to cook with my girls again."

So, while Kyle, Martha, and Llewellyn keep Linda rested on the couch, the rest of us get busy in the kitchen preparing the rest of the food. Whoever said it's bad to have too many cooks in the kitchen clearly just didn't have a big enough kitchen. Because we're doing just fine. By the time everything's prepared, the sun is setting over the lake and shining through the brown, orange, and red leaves, giving the cabin a wonderfully autumnal feeling.

As we eat, I remember why I call these folks my family. They love me for who I am, and they support me in all the ways they can. I may not be close with my biological family, but I feel close with the people in this room. And this Thanksgiving, that's who I'm grateful for.

"Oh, isn't there an NFO game right now?" Linda asks. We're mostly done with our main course, and Silas is walking to the dining table with some pies.

"There is," Kyle says, his hand over Michael's chair. He looks to me. "And your guy is playing in it."

My heart picks up speed. "My guy?"

"Tanner Bash," he says. "Your 'boss', technically. The seals are playing against the Montana Mountaineers."

"Right," I say, my forehead itching from the sweat that's breaking out there. I'm just his personal chef and nothing more. I definitely haven't injected my DNA into his asshole, and I most certainly do not have any feelings for him.

"Well let's watch!" Linda says. "I miss watching my boy play. It gave me an excuse to enjoy the football season more."

"Let's turn it on," Lilah says. "I'd love to watch some football."

I want to protest, mostly because I don't want to see Tanner Bash in his football uniform, but it's what the group wants to do, so I'll suffer through it.

"But we can't watch the entire thing," Linda says. "Because we have the annual Thanksgiving lantern festival, and we don't want to miss that."

At this moment, all the couples in the room eye each other, and Silas and I just give each other an all-knowing glare that only single people understand. If Tanner hadn't rejected me, maybe I would be able to enjoy the festival with someone, too.

We watch the game, and it's hard to keep my eyes away from the screen. Sometimes, the camera zooms in on the players, and I catch glimpses of Tanner. With his helmet off, his blonde hair is matted, and his face is pink from exertion—the exact same shade as his hole.

I have to look away before my dick gets any ideas. Because, if I remember correctly, his face was also that flush when I made him cum handsfree.

Everyone's sort of lounging around on the couch watching the game, but Michael's still sitting at the table, nibbling on a piece of pie and reading a novel. This might be my chance to get his thoughts like Silas suggested.

I come over and sit next to him.

"Hey you," he says, setting his book down. "How's San Diego?"

"Wild," I say with a sigh. "Got a minute to chat?"

His eyes shine. He's almost as earnest as Tanner. "Sure," he says.

I nod to the kitchen, and both of us get up without anyone else noticing. The kitchen is a mess, so Michael and I decide to do some cleanup while we chat.

"So, I got a question about when you and Kyle were seeing each other. I know you've explained to us how you all met before, but I wanna know how it really was. What you don't tell people."

I expect Michael to bristle, but he just chuckles. "Alright, sure."

I set down a dish towel and lean against the counter with my arms folded. "Give it to me straight," I say. "Did you really think you and Kyle would get together?"

Michael mirrors my position against the counter across from me. "Honestly? No. I was insecure, Jimmy. I thought that I was cursed to always be attracted to men who could never love me back. So when Kyle just fell into my lap, I only felt like this curse was confirmed. After all, what closeted NFO player is ready to be in a healthy gay relationship?"

My stomach twists, and I adjust my stance. "Then how did it end up working out? You guys look happy, and from the outside it looks pretty healthy."

"I'd say it is pretty healthy, and that's to do with both of us working on ourselves."

I furrow my brow.

"You know," he says. "You're in AA. You're trying to improve yourself. I go to Al-Anon, and Kyle really takes therapy seriously. We're both on journeys of self-improvement, and that makes our relationship work in the way that it does. If Kyle had never gone to therapy when we first met, he might not have come to terms with his sexuality and his relationship with his dad, which would have made committing to me so much more difficult. And I wouldn't have been able to make it work if I was still insecure over my alcoholic ex.

"Both partners have to face their demons and work on them constantly or else they'll rear their ugly heads and wreak havoc on the relationship."

I nod, sucking on some of my beard hairs. "I can see why you're a writer," I say. "Because you explain things damn well."

He laughs. "Thanks. And it was you who inspired me to open myself up again, don't forget that."

My chest warms as I remember that phone call with him on a cold winter's day. He and Kyle were going through a rough patch, and I gave him some words of encouragement.

"Didn't know it helped you that much," I admit.

"Oh, Jimmy, if I haven't said how wonderful you were, then I'm sorry. Because you really brought me out of my funk that day. Thank you."

"Of course, man," I say. "Any time."

Both of us sit there as the folks in the other room cheer. Sounds like the Seals have scored.

"So, my turn for a question," Michael says, taking a roll from the counter.

I perk up.

"Are you asking me about this because there's a certain football player in your life?"

My chest tightens, and I cross my arms tighter. "Don't see a reason to hide it," I say with a sigh. "It's Tanner."

Michael nods. "He's cute, I'll give you that."

"You have no fucking idea, man."

"Do you think you guys have a chance?"

I groan. "Now that's the million-dollar question. I can really tell he wants it, man. That he wants me. But he keeps pulling away. He's had a rough past—siblings with drug problems and abusive parents—so I get it. But every time I ask him to get closer, he pulls away. And now he's said we can only be friends. And of course this is after we had life-changing sex."

Michael winces and hisses through his teeth.

"I don't know what to do. Do I push him for more? Do I try to fucking seduce him? Lord knows I could."

Michael laughs. "Lord knows that's true."

"But that doesn't feel right. I want to give him a choice. But I want him to know that I want him."

Michael frowns and chews on his lips. "I can relate there," he says after some silence. "But there's more than just wanting him. Because you want all of him. In other words, you don't want to have him one day and then have him slip away another."

"Exactly," I say, exasperated. "But how do we get there?"

He narrows his eyes at me. "I think a more important question is why you want him so badly."

My chest tightens further, and my palms begin to sweat. "What do you mean?"

"You go from not wanting any commitments, fucking several guys a week, to wanting to lock down a man who's unavailable."

I pull at my collar, feeling hot. "What's your point?"

"Forgive me," Michael says, standing up straighter as if wrapping up the conversation. "I don't want to make uncomfortable."

"No," I say, nevertheless feeling my face burn from how much I don't like this conversation already. "I want you to say it."

He sighs. "There's a pattern here. You keep wanting things outside yourself to feel better. But I don't think that's how it works. It's not how it works for me, at least. In order for a relationship to work, you both need to be 100% dedicated to yourselves for the relationship to be 100% successful."

My face hardens. "What? So I have to be a guru before I get in a relationship?"

"Come on, Jimmy," Michael says. "You know that's not what I mean. I mean that you need to be filled up before you can give to others."

Suddenly, I hear my mother's voice again, ridiculing me for being needy and emotionally dependent when I asked for her support as a mother. That's why having casual sex has been so nice. I can easily quiet her voice and feel good about myself. But now that I'm interested in someone who's hard to get, quieting her voice has become so much harder.

"Boys," Linda yells from the couch. "The lantern festival is starting soon."

"Coming," Michael says. Then he pushes himself off the counter and approaches me. He puts a hand on my shoulder. "All I'm saying is that for your relationship to really work—like for both of you to be fulfilled in the long run—you gotta first answer why you think you so desperately need someone else to make you feel better and then learn how to feel better on your own. Then a relationship can work."

As he pulls his hand away, tears form in my eyes, and I sniffle and wipe them. I wrap my arms around my friend.

"Thank you," I say, patting his back.

"Anytime," he says. "Now let's go light some lanterns."

Out on the back porch, the string quartet at the community center is already playing, and there are several lanterns covering the surface of the water. Linda makes a wish to herself, then lights her own and sets it off into the water, followed by Martha and Llewellyn. Kyle and Michael kiss and then release theirs, followed by Lilah and Marissa.

Silas and I decide to release one together.

"Whatcha wishing for?" Silas asks, taking off his cowboy hat to light the lantern.

I pause and think. "If I told, wouldn't that ruin it?"

Silas shrugs. "Fair enough."

As we release our lantern into the water, I wish, for the first time, to understand why I do the things I do—why I'm always in a rush, why I have to stay busy, why I always have to be fucking someone. Sure, I tell myself it's to avoid the racing thoughts, but they're my thoughts. The call is coming from inside the house, in other words. I've always believed that my thoughts just were, that I couldn't change them. But after talking to Michael, I think I'm starting to see that this is wrong. Maybe, instead of looking for outside things to quiet my mind, I can quiet it from the inside. This way, I won't have to be a victim of my mother's harsh words anymore.

We watch as all our lanterns drift off into the water, and the couples hold each other in their arms. Silas goes and sits down next to Linda, and suddenly I find myself all alone. But I get the feeling that this is just what I need right now.

"Hey, all," I say. "Feeling kinda sluggish. Think I'm gonna retire early."

"Alright," Linda says. "Sleep well. We'll see you in the morning."

"Thanks," I say, and I wish everyone else a good night. I make my way up to my room and sit down on my bed. My bedroom window has a perfect vantage point of the lake, and I can see all the lanterns drifting about from here. In fact, it's almost prettier up here than it is down at the lake. Habitually, I pull my phone out and check my hookup app. I've gotten some messages from some fellas visiting for the holidays, and they're pretty good-looking, too. If I wanted, I could find myself at someone else's place tonight. But I'm not feeling that right now. And it isn't just because I've caught feelings for someone else. It's 'cause I want to be my own company tonight. And, for the first time, I'm okay with that.

I stand up and walk to my travel bag. I pull out the small paper bag from inside and take the small metal bowl out. I make my way over to the desk in the room and pull out the chair, then set it right in front of the window. I close my door, then sit down on the chair and look down at the bowl.

"Maria taught me how to do it," I say, picking up the mallet. "Here goes nothing."

I tap the mallet against the bowl, and then I circle the mallet around the rim. A forceful, yet steady ringing sound fills the room, and it calms my mind. Just like I've done on that San Diego beach several times now, I close my eyes and let my body go into a meditative state.

Sitting still like this, the only thing to distract me the singing bowl, my thoughts naturally go haywire. I think about what I'm cooking for Tanner when

I get back, what the meth really would have felt like had I taken it. I think about Yousef and his boyfriends and all the other people in meditation group and what they may be up to this Thanksgiving.

I hear my mother's voice, too. I mean, I always do, but I hear it really loud right now. Telling me that I'm a loner, that I should be with my friends down on the dock. And that because they aren't asking for me, I'm a lonely loser who will never find friends. I'm tempted to stop ringing the bowl, but it's the only thing that's keeping me grounded.

I take a deep breath as I continue ringing the bowl, and the thoughts only grow louder. And that's when, with my eyes still closed, I see a vision of myself down on the dock, alone, staring out at the lanterns in the water.

My mother's there, too. She stands amidst the lanterns on the water, staring at me with a hateful glare. But as the window blows by—as I continue to meditate and let her voice run freely in my head—part of her arm blows away with it like dust. Then, another gust comes by, sounding like the ringing of the bowl. It makes the rest of her arm flow away. Gradually, the wind blows more and more parts of her away until it's just her head that remains. Her voice still persists, but when that final gust comes—marked by completing a full circle on the singing bowl—she finally disappears. And her voice quiets with it.

When I open my eyes, I find myself in my room, the bowl in hand, the echo from my last circuit still ringing through the room. And, as I sit in the chair, my mind blissfully devoid of my mother's voice, I realize that I'm okay sitting here alone.

In fact, I just might be happy.

Chapter 22

Tanner Bash

WE MAY HAVE JUST scored, but this game is far from over. We're in the bottom half of the game, and it's still 19 - 21 with us losing against the Mountaineers.

We get into position as snow falls steadily to the ground. Man, it's cold as hell up in Montana. I'm glad I live in San Diego.

I grab hold of the football and take a deep breath, kicking myself for my stupidity.

I've been neglecting my diet again. And while I didn't know exactly why before, the reasons are clear now: I'm being sexually abused by my teammate, and I pushed away the man I want to be with. So, I'm exhausted to say the least, and I just know coach is gonna be on my ass about it after the game.

I snap the ball and rush out to block the linebacker from advancing to our quarterback. But I'm sluggish, and he manages to push me aside and advance right to him. Luckily, our quarterback already threw the ball out to the tight end, and he's running to the end zone. When he scores, I'm relieved. That means that my poor playing won't be so scrutinized.

Miraculously, we win the game by scoring a touchdown in the final two minutes, and I'm just glad that it wasn't my shitty eating habits that led us to lose. In the locker rooms, Carter pulls me aside.

"Hey man, you doing okay?"

I throw my sweaty, dirty undershirt into my bag. Something catches my eye, and I glance up to see Chris glaring at me. The fucking disgusting man.

"I'm alright," I say quickly.

Carter sits down next to me. "You sure?" he asks more quietly. "Because it looks like—"

"Hey man," I spit out. "I'm good, okay? Just need some space right now."

"Alright," he says, sliding away. "I'll leave you to it."

I shake my head and get to taking off the rest of my clothes.

I fucking hate this. I don't want to be a dick to Carter. Hell, I don't want to be a dick to anyone, but it seems like that's all I am as of late. Ever since I had to tell Jimmy that we're just friends, everything's felt so off. In that moment, it felt like I denied a key part of who I was. And what only makes it worse is Chris will hit me up at the most random, inconvenient times demanding something sexual. The anticipation of his requests is keeping me up at night, and I don't need another thing suppressing my appetite on top of my heartbreak for Jimmy. I'm just fucking sick of everything.

Carter pats my shoulder lightly just before he hits the shower, and his touch calms me a bit. I'm hoping I can apologize to him some time soon. Tonight, we're all staying in a hotel since the flight back to San Diego would go too late in the night. We have another game a couple days from now, and Coach Larson wants to make sure we get as much rest as possible before then. This is why I told Jimmy he could go home for the holiday—I'll hardly be in San Deigo. But it's left me wondering what he's up to. Is he sleeping with someone else? Taking someone else's gay virginity and making them fall in love with him?

I manage to shower and change before Chris can catch me alone in the locker room. And by the time we make it to the Billings hotel, I make it to my room without even a text from him. I might get my body to myself tonight, thank God.

But just as I'm drifting off to sleep, there's a knock at my door, and dread pools in my stomach. I already know who it is. When I open the door, I hardly even react when he just strolls in. I only pray to God, who I hope still listens, that tonight will be quick. Luckily, Chris hasn't asked that we do any penetrative sex. It's just been blowjobs and handjobs. But it feels like violation all the same. And it makes me feel small inside. Disgusting. Forgotten. After he leaves, I cry myself to sleep.

On my flight home to San Diego the next morning, I keep pulling on my fingers as my heart races, but I don't know why. There could be a million reasons why I feel distressed. But when my mind drifts to Jimmy, it makes a little more sense.

For the last month, we've done a good job at ignoring each other, letting the other do their thing. There've been a couple times where he's asked to play some of my video games. I even sat in and watched him play Majora's Mask for a little bit. Sometimes, we got it where we could be really just be friends.

But when he would go off to hangout with Yousef and his meditation friends, or he'd leave to go meetup with a discreet nobody, my chest would get all twisted, and I'd get uncontrollably angry—so angry that I'd go to the Seal's facility and work out, no matter the hour. Or I'd go out and get fast food, only to throw it away when I got home because I have no appetite. I just gotta force myself to eat to get through the rest of the season. At the very least, I'll get Jimmy's cooking again. It may be difficult to eat, but his food makes it slightly easier.

After Girish drops me off at home, I have to run some errands, and once the evening rolls around, Yousef's dropped Jimmy off at the front of my house. I watch through the front window as he carries his bags around back. I walk to the other side of the house and watch him enter my pool area. I muster up the courage and decide to say hello.

"Have a good time visiting home?" I ask, standing at my open back door.

He looks up and gives me a half-smile, surprised to see me. Even after everything, he's still kind, which is a testament to his character. He has his bag slung over his shoulder, which makes his thick, hairy arm all the hotter. Fuck. What Chris is doing to me still has me horny as hell.

"It was exactly what I needed," he says, walking to his door. "How was your game? Congrats on the win."

My stomach clenches at his response. What does he mean he needed it? Is he not enjoying his stay here? With me? Does he not like me or something?"

"Thanks," I say, kicking the concrete. He gets to his door and reaches into his pocket for the keys.

Goddamnit. Being this close to him makes me realize just how much I miss him. And it isn't just his looks that I miss. It's his words, our conversations, even when they're just friendly. His presence also calms me down. Whenever he's cooking, I try to stay nearby, usually in the living room, so I can just feel the presence of a warm body. Truth be told, I'm relieved we're both back. But I want more than just a casual conversation.

"Hey, uh," I say, scratching my chin. "You maybe wanna play some video games tonight? I could continue Paper Mario."

His door clicks open, and he sets his bag down inside. He then looks back at me with a skeptical look, one I can already translate. Video games, when we've played together, are where things have either gone intimate or where I'm pushed him away.

"I've actually got plans," he says, turning to step inside.

"Plans?" I say, my stomach tightening so hard I'll be surprised if I can ever eat again. I make my way over to his door so we can talk closer.

"Yeah," he says. "Yousef's potluck."

I grit my teeth. Mostly gay guys attend those. Has he met someone else there? I want to ask, but I have no right knowing. But my eyes heat up just thinking about him with someone that isn't me.

"Oh," I say, scratching the back of my head.

"Yeah," he says, stepping inside. He puts the hand on his door. God, how did we become so distant? Right, because of me. It's all because of me. Tanner's the one who wanted more, and I just fucking pushed him away. Fuck me.

He's about to shut the door, but then it's like something possesses me.

"Wait," I shout louder than I intend.

Jimmy holds the door open, but he stares at me warily. "What's up?"

I swallow the saliva that feels like concrete in my throat. "Maybe we could go get Zhao cream again?"

Jimmy's hardened face softens a bit, and I feel hope for the first time in weeks.

"I still got plans," Jimmy says.

And that's when I clench my fists. I step closer to the door, but Jimmy doesn't close it. In fact, he opens it more and leans against the frame. I stand right of his door looking down at him, so close I swear I can smell his signature earthy, sweet scent.

"What?" Jimmy asks. "What do you really want, Tanner?"

Do I tell him what that is? Do I risk his dignity and my own with all that Chris is doing to me? Do I throw away any potential relationship I could have with God with this confession? I don't see any other choice.

"Isn't it obvious?" I ask, my voice cracking. "I want you, Jimmy. I want you to fuck me again. I'll do anything for you to fuck me again."

It feels like my entire body shatters. I break into a sob, and I crumple to my knees, my face in my hands. I look up at him, pleading, and he stares down at me like I'm the most pitiful creature in the world. Because I fucking am.

"I'm sorry I keep fucking up and pushing you away," I say. "I just really fucking need you right now."

Chapter 23

Jimmy Dillon

"I JUST REALLY FUCKING need you right now," Tanner says, crumpled on the ground.

It's a sight to see a hulking man of 6'4" confess that he wants you to blow his back out. And it's a whole other thing to have him confess, while weeping, that he needs you.

"Tanner, I—"

"You know what?" Tanner says, standing up and dusting himself off. "I'm sorry. Let's pretend like this never happened." And then he makes his way back to his house.

And that's when I know I've had enough.

"Tanner Bash," I say in the lowest, meanest voice I can.

He stops and turns to me, tears fresh in his eyes.

I snap and point to the ground in front of me. "You get over here right now."

He nods and walks over to me, his blonde-stubbled face lowered in shame. I stand up in front of him with my arms tightly folded against my chest like I'm a fucking drill sergeant. Which sounds silly, but I don't know any other way to get to this man.

He looks up at me meekly. "Yes?" He holds out the 's' like he's about to say sir, and on any other day with any other person, that would be my breaking point—the moment where I would decide to take them into my room and fuck the living daylights out of them.

But today's different. Tanner's different. And most importantly, I'm different, too.

I'm not sure what's exactly changed, but I don't want to get over my own feelings by getting Tanner under me. That's unfair to him and unfair to me. Besides, it doesn't just seem like he really wants sex. He wants emotional help.

"I'm not going to fuck you," I say firmly. "But you and I are going to take a nice little stroll down to the beach. And we're gonna talk. You don't have to share what you don't want to. But we're going to have a conversation. And that's where you and I end tonight, okay? I'll go to Yousef's potluck, and you'll go your way. You understand me?"

Tanner bites his lip and nods at the ground.

"Good," I say. "Grab your sandals."

* * *

Tanner and I walk along the shore, and the cold water tickles my feet. I'm wearing flip-flops, some cargo shorts, and a hoodie, while Tanner's wearing similar flip-flops, gym shorts, and a zip-up. The sun is setting now, and there's a slight chill in the air. But it's comfortable.

"Thanks," Tanner says, breaking the silence. We haven't spoken since I told him to grab his sandals. "Thanks for uh... spending time with me."

"No problem," I say.

Some sand gets in my flip-flops, so I just decide to ditch them entirely and hold them in my hand as I walk. Pretty soon, Tanner does the same.

"I don't know why I keep doing that," Tanner says.

"What?" I ask.

"Exploding," he says, almost with gritted teeth. "It's like I have all this pressure inside, and then it just explodes. And It's always around you when it explodes."

He stops and picks up a small, flat rock. He walks out further into the water, extends his arm backward, then hurls it into the water. It skips a good five times before an incoming wave swallows it whole.

"That was pretty good," I say.

"Thanks," he says with a shrug.

When he gets back to me, I'm tempted to reach out and hold his hand. Because that just feels like what we are. But I think that would just complicate everything further. We're not together, and we certainly won't be after this conversation. I'm not even sure why I asked him to walk out here with me. I just felt like it was going to be the only thing to diffuse the tension between us.

Then I remember what he told me about his childhood: his rowdy brothers, his crazy parents.

"Tanner," I say. "You said yourself you still relive parts of your childhood."

He stops to pick up another rock. "I did," he says.

I look out into the waves and think. What I'm about to say feel remarkably similar to the advice I've needed about my mom. "You ever stop to wonder why?"

He stops to watch as his rock gets seven skips this time. But then he just stands there, his fists clenched.

"Tan—"

"Of course I wonder why," he says over his shoulder.

I pause. I feel like he's got more to say.

"All those times we've been playing video games and I freeze up? It's because I'm back in my childhood home getting yelled at, or worse. I would like to figure out why I still linger on these memories, but what's the point? It's not like that'll solve the problem. It's just something I gotta deal with."

"But what if it wasn't?"

He turns and looks back at me like I'm crazy. But I have to say he looks really good at this angle, his muscular body twisted toward me. His ass looks perfect, and his stubble is a little longer today—

Stop it, Jimmy. You're not here to sleep with him.

I walk into the water until I'm standing right next to him, the water lapping against our legs. It's times like these where I'm reminded why people spend all this money to live in places like this. This is heaven.

"I've had moments from my childhood that still hurt me, too," I say. I want to put my hand on his back, but I feel like it's best to not be physical. At least in this very moment.

He looks up at me, not saying anything, but he asks me to go on with his eyes.

"My mother was a narcissist," I say.

"Narcissist?"

I sigh. "Think of it like a person who only sees other people for what they can gain from them," I say. "Even their own children."

He grimaces. "Think I know one or two people like that." He extends his huge body and throws another rock into the ocean. Three skips. Not his best, but not bad either.

"She would constantly put me down," I say. "And use me to make her feel better about herself. My entire life, I've heard her voice repeating back to me all the shit I think about myself."

He tilts his head toward me. "What kinda shit is that?"

I trill my lips. "The message changes depending on the situation, but it's always something like: I'm a loser. I'm fat. No one likes me. I'm ugly. I'll never amount to anything."

He winces and throws another rock, but this one just plops in the water. "That's harsh."

"Right?" I say. "But I've realized, especially lately, that I can let that voice go. I don't need to hold to what she thinks of me anymore."

He's scraping off some sand from a rock, staring at it intently, but I think he's listening.

"Maybe you can let go of some of your childhood, too," I say. "I can see how it hurts you."

He huffs out a sharp laugh. "Sure. Sad part is that's not the only thing stressing me out right now."

"What else is going on?" I ask.

He bites his lip and throws out his second to last rock. It also just clunks into the water.

"You said I don't have to share everything. That's something I won't share."

"Fair enough."

We both sit there in silence. I have my hands thrust into my pockets, and the breeze feels nice blowing through my beard. I wasn't exactly sure where this conversation would go, but it feels good to connect with Tanner this way, even if we aren't dating.

"So how can I let go of my childhood like you have?" he asks, fondling the last rock in his hands.

I laugh. "I haven't fully let go of my childhood. In some ways, I'm just starting. But meditating has really helped. AA has given some tools of awareness that help me see my childhood for what it really is: the past. And how I don't need to carry it with me."

"One of my brothers tried AA once," he says. "Should I?"

"You don't have a drinking problem, do you?"

He shakes his head.

"I think you would be better in Al-Anon."

He looks at me funny. "Isn't that the same thing?"

I shake my head. "It's for loved ones of alcoholics. Like their families and stuff. Because apparently loving an alcoholic can make you just as crazy as drinking alcohol can. I bring it up because of your brothers."

"Huh," he says, nodding, looking into the ocean.

"One of my friends in the meditation group—Maria—she's in Al-Anon. I could recommend you go with her."

He sighs. "But I don't talk with my brothers anymore. I don't see a point."

"You can take it or leave it," I say. "But you have admitted that you still carry this past with you. So it's not like it isn't a present-day issue."

"True," Tanner says.

"Also," I say. "It might help you with whatever else you're dealing with."

Tanner extends his arm, then tosses the rock onto the surface of the water. It bounces one, two, three, four, five, six, seven—eight times!

"That's a record," he says, a small smile forming on his face. It's good to see him amused.

"Good job," I say, genuinely impressed.

We both stand there, and it takes all my strength to not reach out and hold his hand. We're just not there yet, and I don't know if we'll ever be.

He turns to me. "Could you talk to Maria?" he asks. "I think I'll do it."

I resist the impulse to put my hand on his back, but this time it doesn't feel so wrong. So I put it there, and he doesn't soften against my touch. But he doesn't bristle, either.

"Sure, buddy," I say.

And then he wraps his arms around me. We stay hugging until the sun dips just below the horizon, and I'm tempted to pull away from Tanner. But it feels better to be this close.

Chapter 24

Tanner Bash

"How come Yousef never told me that he lived next to an NFO player?" Maria, Jimmy's meditation friend, asks.

I chuckle in the passenger seat as she drives me to my very first Al-Anon meeting. She keeps diverting her eyes from the road to me as we drive, and I'm worried she'll get us in an accident. But we've stayed in our lane so far. We'll probably be fine.

"I mean, I do prefer my privacy," I say.

"That's true," she says, the 'tr' coming out with a roll of her tongue. Maria is from Michoacan, Mexico, and came to the states a good twenty years ago. She married a lawyer and has spent most of her life raising her kids, and now that she's an empty nester, she likes to experiment with a lot of spiritual stuff.

"Well, lucky for you, we like to stay anonymous at Al-Anon, so nobody will give you trouble," she says.

I let out a sharp laugh, remembering how Jimmy reacted to me saying I'm a celebrity. "That's good, but I think I'll be fine. I doubt anyone will recognize me anyways."

We pull up to a church, and my hackles are immediately up. Sure, following God's compass got me through my childhood, but I'm not in such good graces with God at the moment. So I don't know how comfortable I feel being inside a church.

She leads me through the front doors, and then we go to one of the side conference rooms. Inside, there are several other Hispanic women, mostly middle-aged, and one Asian woman—Vietnamese I'd guess. There are two white women and then one lone Hispanic man. And they're all at least ten years older than me.

A woman reaches out to touch my shoulder to introduce herself, and I tense up at her touch. Ever since Chris and I started regularly doing things—well, him doing things to me—I don't really like to touch unless I'm initiating it. After she walks away, I hunch over and hope no one else will talk to me.

The meeting starts, and there's a lot of words and phrases I don't understand. Maria just told me to listen and not worry if I don't understand something, so that's what I try to do. She said I could ask her any questions afterwards as well. They welcome me as a newcomer, and I shyly introduce myself, and I'm relieved once all the attention is off me. Eventually, we get past what sounds like the business part of the meeting and we start reading from this book that Maria and I share.

"The topic for today is Higher Power," she says. "Which some of us call God or whatever we may choose. I've selected a number of readings from this book to read and then share about."

So that's what we do. We read a section on one page, then we skip ahead twenty or so and read another. It's hard to keep track of what's going on, but I catch a couple sentences that confuse me. The book says that we all come to have a relationship with a God of our own understanding, which is wrong, because there's really only one God. And He hates me right now.

"Alright," the chair says when we're done with the reading, and I'm relieved because I'm done talking about God. But then we do something that's even more uncomfortable: people start talking about themselves.

The white lady who touched me starts sharing about how she dropped off her husband in an expensive rehab facility, and she's hoping that this fourth time will be the time he gets sober. A Hispanic woman shares about her husband who she just divorced because of his drinking but can't stop thinking about. And then this petite Hispanic woman, probably no more than four feet tall, starts talking, and she sounds so emotional and genuine that I can't help but listen closely.

"Growing up," she says. "My home was really chaotic. But that's when I went to the Catholic Church and found a lot of stability. Yet as I got older, the more I drew on my faith to cope with my problems, the more sad I became. Because I believed that by faithfulness I was going to be blessed, but my life was only getting worse. I thought God hated me. And then, when I came to Al-Anon, I learned to develop a relationship with a Higher Power who is understanding and loving and doesn't give suffering to those he doesn't like. Suffering just happens, and we all have to deal with it. Now I use my Higher Power to learn how to grow from suffering. I no longer use my God to make myself more miserable when life is going bad."

She continues on with some specific things happening in her life with her daughter, but I can't stop thinking about what she just said. You can't pick and choose who God is. That defeats the whole purpose. God is truth. God is righteousness. God is not who we choose Him to be.

Yet the way this woman is talking, she sounds happy. Like she's found peace with herself, as if she's found God's compass, the one that I've lost.

Other people chime in to discuss the topic, but I feel myself getting all hot, and I'm starting to feel dizzy. I don't know if it's because I didn't eat after practice this morning or if it's due to the topic, but either way I don't feel good.

Once the meeting's over, I'm bouncing my leg under the table. I want to get up and go somewhere, but I don't know where the hell to go. I didn't drive myself here, and it feels weird just to get up and leave now.

Soon, the chair starts reading from a script to wrap the meeting up, and I can finally be out of here. How does God feel about people discussing in His house their worship of other gods that aren't Him? It's ridiculous. It's blasphemy, idolatry. I don't want any part of it.

She reads this paragraph about violence, and I curl into myself. She says that if any of us are struggling with physical or sexual abuse, we have a right to seek safety and that we should talk to the appropriate parties to ensure this safety. But I just tune it out. At this point, there's nothing I can do with Chris. He'll ruin my whole reputation if I don't do what he says. Plus, if God wanted it to stop, wouldn't he stop it? If he hasn't, it's probably because I deserve it. And after all I've done to deserve his ire, that only makes sense.

The whole room says the serenity prayer in unison, and I keep my lips fucking zipped. Then, we're all free to mingle. And I know I should jump out of my seat like it has hot coals on it, but I feel stuck here, frozen. Because I don't know where else I would go.

"So what did you think?" Maria asks.

My shoulders tense, and I sit up straighter in my seat. "I, uhh."

"Maria!"

The petite Hispanic lady who shared about choosing her own God comes over and hugs Maria from behind.

"Lupita," she says. "How are things? I loved your share."

I grumble to myself as they talk, but I can't help but listen. After her share, I want to know more about her relationship with this 'God' she 'created'. I want to understand how the hell she thinks she's justified in such idolatry. Insanity is the only explanation.

But, listening to her talk to Maria, she seems remarkably normal. Almost boring. She asks Maria how her kids are doing at USC, and Maria asks how Lupita's embroidery is going. The lone man in the room is standing off to the side, and I assume him to be Lupita's husband.

"See you at Zhao's?" Lupita asks, her hand on Maria's shoulder. She's remarkably affectionate.

"Yes, see you soon," Maria says. She quickly turns to me. "I'm so sorry, I forgot about getting ice cream after. Some folks from the meeting like to meet up and chat. If you'd like, you can come, or I can drop you off back at home.

I watch as Lupita and her husband walk out of the room. Like I said, I don't really want to be here around these blaspheming people anymore, but I don't want to go home either. If I do, I'll be tempted to either see what Jimmy's up to and inevitably be told he's busy. And then, when I'm alone, I'll either be wondering what he's up to, or what this Lupita woman said will bounce around in my head and keep me up all night.

So I begrudgingly decide to get some Zhao cream with these blasphemers.

"I can come," I manage to choke out, but my throat's all gunky.

"Wonderful," she says. "Do you have any questions?"

How do you all have the audacity to go against the true God? I want to ask. *In His own house?*

"I'm good," I say, my teeth gritted.

On the way over, I keep thinking about what Lupita said. Choosing God. Ridiculous. But I should say that the first God she believed in, whatever that means, was really similar to mine. Just like me, she felt she needed to obey all of God's commandments in order to be happy. And then she said she somehow discovered this other 'Higher Power', and then that led her to feel more comfortable in herself.

I definitely want to feel more comfortable in myself. But that's done through obeying his laws, not making them up.

Right?

Because, if I'm not mistaken, Lupita looks a lot happier than I feel right now.

But maybe that's just because that's what sin does. It makes the sinner look happy. Yeah, that has to be it. But when we get to Zhao's, I plan on confronting this woman regardless and asking where in the hell she got the gall to try and redefine God.

When we arrive, there aren't a lot of people around. I guess the beginning of December isn't a great time to get a frozen treat, even in San Diego. But apparently they have new Christmas flavors, mint and red velvet, so I'm looking forward to giving those a try.

About half of the people at the meeting arrive, and they all talk to each other, leaving me the hell alone, which is good. This is what I prefer. But then, as if the devil himself prodded her, Lupita comes up to me and strikes a conversation.

"So this was your first Al-Anon meeting?" she asks. "Welcome. It's so good to have you."

She reaches out her hand to shake mine, and if I had the strength, I wouldn't dare touch her hand. But she's proven to be nothing but stupid nice, and I do believe I should be a gentleman, especially to an older woman, even if she's committed sacrilege. So I extend my hand reluctantly, and we shake all the same.

"So are you from around here?" she asks as we move up in the line. I bet us standing next to each other looks real funny. I probably look twice her size, and that's my height alone. I wouldn't be surprised if I was two-hundred pounds heavier than this woman. Well, maybe if I was eating how I'm supposed to be.

"From Georgia," I say shortly.

"Georgia!" she exclaims, her Mexican accent coming through. "And what's brought you here?"

I chuckle to myself as I remember Jimmy saying that nobody knows who I really am. I'm definitely no Sexiest Man Alive like Kyle Weaver.

"I play for the San Diego Seals," I say. "I'm their center."

She grabs my wrist, and I almost keel over. "Shut up. Are you serious? How have I not recognized you?"I nod. "I mean—"

"Juan Carlos," she says, turning to her husband sitting at one of the mesh tables. "Vente. El juega con los Seals!"

Her husband Juan squints at me, and then his face breaks into surprise. He jumps up from the table and joins us.

"You are Tanner Bash?" he asks.

I look away, blushing. "That's me."

"Ay, Dios," he says. "I thought I recognized you, but I just assumed you were someone else. I didn't think an NFO player would come to an Al-Anon meeting."

I let out a sharp laugh. "Me either." And I'm definitely not coming back after seeing what blasphemers they are.

"We love the Seals," Lupita says. "We've been fans ever since..."

"Forever," Juan says.

My chest warms at their genuine enthusiasm. "Thanks. They're a great team."

"And you're a great player," she says, tapping my arm. "You really held us up against the Mountaineers."

I look at her funny. I definitely do not agree with that, but I guess I had some important blocks that kept the game going in our favor.

"Y'all think so?"

They both nod eagerly.

"This is so cool," Lupita says.

"So, can I ask," Juan says. "Are we destined for the playoffs?"

I let a laugh, much more comfortable with this conversation than the one about making our own God. And so I talk to them, almost forgetting that earlier I was stewing toward Lupita especially. We order our Zhao cream, and I end up getting a mix of both the mint and red velvet. When I put it in my mouth, I have to force myself not to moan. It's divine.

"Well, you probably get enough questions about football," Lupita says after we've been eating our ice cream at the table for a while. I've been telling them what I can: our stats, our general strategy, how hard we've been working for the playoffs, what we're worried about. And they've been eating it up.

"It's all good," I say. "I don't get asked as much as you think."

Which is true. When I got drafted, I knew my brothers wouldn't have cared. They were either homeless or wasted or both. My parents, on the other hand, I hoped would be proud of me. But they were too frazzled by my siblings to care. And when they finally did come around to acknowledge my playing, they weren't impressed. In fact, all my dad said was that I better think about what to do after I retire because not working after thirty will be a very boring life. And that was when I pretty much stopped talking to my family altogether.

"So," Lupita says, thumbing her empty Zhao cream container. "What's brings you to Al-Anon?"

I think back to that conversation with Jimmy on the beach.

"I had a friend who was concerned for me," I say. "So he said I should come. I grew up with addict brothers, but I don't talk to them anymore, so I'm not really sure if Al-Anon is for me."

"Oh," Lupita says, and there's some sadness there. "Well, I shared about our alcoholic daughter," she says, gesturing to husband. "But we actually lost her a few years ago. To suicide."

My chest tightens, and I lean forward in my chair, briefly forgetting that just a while ago I wanted to confront this woman for her idolatry. "I'm so sorry," I say.

"It's alright," Juan says. "Well, it isn't, but we make our peace with it every day. "

"My Higher Power really gets me through," Lupita says. "I don't know what I would do without him."

And that's when fury rushes through me. But also just as much confusion. She said she was Catholic. I know the views toward anyone who has taken their life is complicated, but my experience tells me that Catholics don't tend to view the suicide victim favorably. That is, the Catholic God doesn't. So how has she made her peace with it?

Gah, why am I saying the Catholic God? There's one God, and He's truth. But this woman is genuinely peaceful and happy, so clearly she's moved on from her old God, whatever the hell that means. And I need to find out how.

"I'm sorry," I say. "But what the hell do you mean your Higher Power gets you through?"

Juan recoils, but Lupita doesn't bat an eye.

"It's okay," she says to her husband. Then she turns to me. "Al-Anon helped me come to find a God who loved me."

"But that doesn't make sense," I say. "There's one God. There has to be. There's one truth. There can't be multiple truths, so there can't be multiple gods. If there were, there'd be chaos. There would be."

My heart starts to race as I picture what my childhood would have been like without Church. I would have been stuck at home, permanently sandwiched between the erratic brothers and punished just like them. I'd be alone, isolated. Church helped me find solace in the fact that there was a path to happiness. That there was a way to leave the chaos of my home. If there isn't one God, then isn't this all a lie?

"You make a good point," Lupita says. "But let's talk about that. You say you had alcoholic brothers, right?"

I nod, my jaw so tight I'm afraid I'll crack my teeth.

"Let's say your brother has vodka hidden under his bed. You threaten to tell your parents. So what does he do? He puts it under your bed and then blames you."

I feel myself breaking into a sweat at just how accurate this little hypothetical is.

"Then your parents punish you. But you try to tell them the 'truth'—that you didn't do that. That it was your brother. Yet your parents refuse to believe you. So you get grounded, and your brother can continue on drinking as he always does."

I fold my arms tightly just like I see Jimmy do so often when he gets defensive. "What's your point?"

"To you, the truth is that your brother framed you. To your parents, you were hiding alcohol under your bed. And there's was nothing you could do to convince them otherwise. So this is their truth."

I huff out a breath through my nose.

"And your brother? His truth is that he can continue drinking by creating diversions."

"Okay," I say, letting my hands fall into my lap. "What's this have to do with God?"

"I don't believe in multiple Gods like you think I do," she says. "I, too, believe in one God."

"Then why are you talking as if you discovered another God? That doesn't make sense."

"Because," she says. "The God I had growing up was the God I was able to understand at the time. As I grew older and saw the need for a God who was more loving, that's what my understanding of God developed into. As I changed, my understanding of God changed. And as my understanding of God changed, so did I."

I shake my head, still confused as hell. "But the God I grew up with," I say. "He got me through the chaos of my home. If I were to give up on that God now, wouldn't I lose out on all the same blessings of peace I had as a kid?"

"Have you changed since you were a kid?"

I scoff. "Well, yeah."

"Then why wouldn't your understanding of God change?"

"Because God is unchangeable."

"But you aren't unchangeable," she says. "You change all the time. As I grew and started attending Al-Anon, I saw how, maybe, the true God was much more kind than I had grown up to believe. So, I leaned into this new understanding of God. And I came to see how loving He truly was. You can do the same."

I look away and stare out into the ocean. If, as I grow, I just come to a new understanding of God, that makes sense. It's not like I'm coming to believe in a new God. It's just seeing the true God more clearly.

"I think God meets us where we're at," Lupita says. "That He gives us people and experiences that give us the opportunity to grow into people who have a better understanding of him."

My mind immediately goes to Jimmy. I think about how, before meeting him, I just saw men as a way to get off, that eventually I would find real love with a woman and obey God's commandments that way. But according to what Lupita is saying, the people and experiences introduced into my life can change the way I see God. So, if I happen to meet a man who I think is hotter than the sun, who is charming and kind, who's willing to talk with me rather than just fuck me, isn't that, kinda sorta, like a person sent from God? One to help me understand Him better?

"And who knows," she says. "Maybe it wasn't just the religion you grew up with that helped you. Maybe there were other things that got you through."

My eyes widen. Other things that got me through. Of course. It wasn't just going to church on Sundays that made me feel better. It was video games, too. All those days playing Paper Mario and Majora's Mask—playing those felt like shelter from a storm, the same way church did. If I expand my definition of God, that was Him helping me, too. And if I expand it even further, maybe God hasn't abandoned me after all. Maybe he's shown his love for me in the form of a very attractive man who cares about me.

"That make sense?" Lupita asks me.

I turn back to her, my eyes slightly wet. "I think so," I say.

Maria walks up from another table and puts her hand on my shoulder. "I have to get going," she says. "Are you okay if we leave?"

I nod and push my chair out. I say goodbye to Juan with a handshake, but Lupita doesn't even extend her hand to me.

"Can I give you a hug?" she asks.

I freeze up, not knowing if I want to be touched. Because of Chris, my body doesn't feel like my own, so I feel so discombobulated all the time. I fucking hate i
t.

Lupita extends her hand. "Handshake is fine too."

But I brush her hand out of the way and wrap my big arms around her, careful not to crush her. Because, seeing how kind and thoughtful she really is, I do want to hug her. She hugs me tightly in return, and we hold each other there for a minute, the sound of crashing waves our accompaniment.

"I hope you come back," she says, pulling away. "To the meeting."

I nod and thank her, wiping my running nose. I say my goodbyes, then I follow Maria to her car, and she takes me home.

I stare out at the beach through the houses as we drive, feeling slightly more contented than I did before I came to the meeting. So God hasn't abandoned me. He was just showing his presence in different ways—through the forms of Jimmy and Lupita, for example. And He's inviting me to grow into a bigger person to see these different ways. I just have to accept the invitation.

"Can we do that again?" I say, breaking the silence.

"You want to keep coming back to the meetings?" Maria asks me, smiling.

I nod. "I do."

Chapter 25

Jimmy Dillon

I saunter into Tanner's kitchen early on Christmas Eve morning. The sun has just peeked over the horizon, and I'm feeling good. I actually got a full night's sleep. I've been listening to the sleep meditation podcast that Yousef recommended, and it knocks me out like alcohol used to do. Except this time, I stay asleep, which is pretty cool.

After I start my coffee, I pull out the all ingredients that I need and set them on the counter: sugar, brown sugar, powdered sugar, butter, vanilla, eggs, baking powder, baking soda, flour, salt, and all the utensils I need.

Today, I'm exploring a hobby I enjoy but have neglected for a while now.

I'm making cookies.

Tanner said that I could go home for Christmas if I wanted. He has a stretch of several days with no games over the holiday, so he said he didn't need any meals. But at the last minute, I cancelled my flight. I'm really enjoying the meditation sessions that I'm doing with Yousef and my other friends, along with the potlucks. I really feel like I'm coming to let my mom go. Plus, Tanner's been letting me play on his Nintendo consoles, and that's been fun as hell. My time in San Diego is coming to a close in either January or February, depending on how far the Seals go into the playoffs, so I want to make my time here count. I've really come to love San Diego. And it's not because of the men like I thought it would be. In fact, I haven't slept with another guy in a couple weeks. That's a record since before Joe.

I put on the 'Kiss the Hot Chef' apron, turn on some Christmas music on my phone, preheat the oven, and then get to work. Baking is something I never really did a whole lot before, even though I always wanted to. Too much waiting and time for my thoughts to go rampant, I reasoned. But now I feel like I have the patience to go through with it.

I hear a door shut in the other room and steps leading into the kitchen. I take a deep breath and brace myself for the man of the hour.

Tanner walks into the kitchen wiping his face. He gives me a puzzled look when he notices me.

"I thought I heard something," he says, sitting down at the table. "What are you doing here? I thought you were going back home to Mississippi for Christmas."

My chest warms a bit as I turn down the volume during 'All I Want for Christmas Is You'. Whenever Tanner sits down at the table, that means were in for a conversation, and truth be told, I always enjoy talking to him. Especially the last few weeks. Ever since Maria took him to that one Al-Anon meeting, he's been going consistently, and he's a lot more subdued than he used to be. I can't believe he grabbed me by the collar that one time. Things have changed.

"Slight change of plans," I say. "I decided to stay here. I saw my folks last month anyways. I want to spend time in San Diego while I can."

He nods and looks down at some mail on the kitchen table, but I swear there's a smile on his face. Is Tanner Bash happy to have me around? Sure, he's been easier to interact with lately, but he's still kept his distance. I figured it was 'cause he resolved himself that he's fully straight now or something. But here he is, happy to see me.

"Whatcha making?" he asks. "Smells real good."

"Thought I'd try my hand at baking," I say, pouring some vanilla into the mixing bowl. "'Tis the season, after all. I'm gonna make a bunch of different kinds of cookies. Thinking I'll give some of them away to Yousef and my meditation friends."

He stands up and approaches the counter. He's wearing a sleeveless tee and short gym shorts that show off how thick his thighs are—the thighs that I once spread to fuck his hole. He's also got some morning musk on him, which I like. It's like his natural smell. And part of me just wants to tear all his clothes off and breathe him in. But after our conversation on the beach, that feels like I'm taking advantage of him. Besides, he was probably just horny then. I don't know if he still thinks of me the same way now that he's addressing his issues.

After he serves himself some coffee, he leans over the counter, and we're so close that I can see the little blonde hairs on his huge upper arms. "Can I help out?" he asks.

I start mixing. "You really wanna help?"

He sticks his finger into the batter and then puts it into his mouth. He eyes me as he sucks his finger clean, and heat immediately rushes to my groin.

"As long as I can eat some of the dough," he says.

I smirk. "Fine. But just not too much."

He manages to find the other apron from the pantry—a plain one unfortunately—and then we get right to it. While I'm putting balls of sugar cookie dough on the baking rack, I instruct him to make the dough for some chocolate chip cookies. And once I'm done, I turn the stove on while some Charlie Brown is playing on my phone. It's time to brown some butter and make some caramel.

"Are you used to it being this warm on Christmas?" Tanner asks me. Before, he was working on the other counter, but he's moved over right next to me. He's folding the chocolate chips into the dough.

I gradually pour heavy cream into the melted butter and relish the satisfying sizzle. "It's actually pretty warm down in Mississippi, too," I say. "Not as consistent as here. But I don't think I've ever had a white Christmas."

"God," he says, looking up from the bowl. "I had a white Christmas in Georgia once. Felt like the entire state was in a tiffy. But it was awesome." He starts stirring again. "One of the better Christmases I had."

I throw some salt and vanilla to the caramel, and I start stirring until it gets to the ideal consistency. This gives the time to reflect on what he's told me about his rough childhood.

I look up at him. "I'm real sorry about what you had to go through as a kid," I say. "Don't know if I ever got a chance to tell you."

He nods. "Thanks, Jimmy. Means a lot. But I feel like I'm actually starting to heal from it." He smiles as he folds in the last of the chocolate chips. "I actually asked Lupita to be my sponsor."

I grin wide. "That's so awesome, man," I say, patting him on the back. "Having a sponsor's a big deal. They really help."

"Thanks," he says, his cheeks slightly going red. "It's been really good so far." He looks up at me. "Thanks for suggesting I go. Turns out Al-Anon was right for me."

I have to look away from his boyishly handsome face before I get any ideas. I'm tired of jumping straight to sex. I wanna have a moment with Tanner. An emotional one. And whether or not it leads to sex, who cares. I just want to enjoy Tanner as a person and not a body.

"But enough of the sad stuff," he says, starting to roll the dough into balls like I asked him. It took me all my strength to not make an innuendo in my request.

"What about you?" he asks. "What's your favorite Christmas?"

And we get into a flow. While old Christmas classics play out of my phone, I tell him about a Christmas I spent with Silas, Martha, and Llewellyn where we just played board games through the night and into Christmas morning. This gets us into talking about the all-nighters we've done in our lives. Turns out Tanner was a pretty studious guy back at Miss U. He actually chose to be a history major because he wanted to learn more about Christianity through the ages, which is like super nerdy and cute even though it's Christianity. He pulled some all-nighters for papers he neglected until the very last day. I never went to college, so most of my all-nighters were sex or party related, usually both. One in particular I met this really hot guy who was visiting town, and we got super drunk and fucked all night. It was awesome. Tanner gets all quiet when I tell that story, and I can tell by the way he's holding his jaw tight that he's jealous. And I just think that's the cutest thing.

"Don't worry," I say. "I don't really sleep around a whole lot now."

That's when he sighs, and it looks like a ton's been lifted off his shoulders. He really wanted to hear that. Damn, he *was* jealous. And that means he probably still likes me.

"Alright," he says after he's replaced the sugar cookies with the chocolate chip ones in the oven. "What's next?"

While I was stirring the caramel, I started browning some butter on another stove plate. I stick the caramel in the fridge to cool, and then I stir the browning butter.

"This next one is a little complicated based on the recipe," I say. "You ready for it?"

He folds his arms and leans against the counter, and I have to look away so I'm not staring at his hulking arms. "I'm ready."

I pour the perfectly browned butter into a glass dish, and then I place that next to the caramel in the fridge. "Alright," I say, sliding my phone to him. "I need you to put this much dry ingredients in that big bowl over there."

"Got it," he says, looking at the directions on my phone.

As go about preparing the frosting for the sugar cookies, I get a warm feeling in my stomach. When Tanner's not talking about his passions, he's not the most verbose guy, but his presence is calming. Before, when he seemed more stressed and flaky, he sometimes had this calming presence, but it flickered on and off like a faulty lightbulb. Now, it feels like his calming presence is shining brightly.

"So you say you used to have sex a lot," he says.

I blush. Is a man a day a lot? "You could say that," I say.

"But you also had an ex?" he asks. "Joe, right?"

Hearing that name come out of Tanner's mouth does a funny thing to my stomach.

"Yeah," I say. "That ended badly."

"How so?" he asks. "Of course, you don't have talk about it."

I sigh. "No, it's fine. It's been a while. I'm mostly over it. Joe and I met on a hookup app. We had sex one night, but like I mentioned to you a while back, he was one of those closeted men I gave a really good experience so they came out to me."

He lets out a sharp laugh. "Still surprises me how many guys you've done that to."

"Does it really surprise you?" I ask, smirking at him. And then I wipe it from my face. Maybe let's keep it friendly right now. Not flirty.

"I mean," Tanner says, starting to mix the dry ingredients. "Not so much."

My whole body electrifies at that. Is Tanner Bash flirting with me, too? Is this going somewhere?

"You were saying?" Tanner says, whisking the bowl while Ariana Grande's Christmas music starts playing.

"Right," I say, "Joe. After he came out to me, we started dating, but it was kinda secret. In the dark. He didn't want his family knowing, which was fine because he wasn't close with his family, but he didn't want a whole lot of other people knowing either. He didn't want to be affectionate in public, and he was always nervous, even when we were alone. So nervous that he made me nervous, too."

"Why'd you stay with him?" Tanner asks.

I suck on my teeth. "I guess I didn't know better. He was hot as hell. Kinda looked like you, honestly."

He grins at me, and I look away.

"But you're obviously different—you look different, that is," I say.

"So I'm uglier?"

"No, no," I say, reaching out to touch his arm. And I swear he's got voltage in him or something because it feels like my entire body is vibrating.

"You look good, too," I say, looking into his eyes.

It feels like the whole world stops here, and I just let the both of us be for a moment. Tanner drops what he's doing and turns to face me fully. He moves my arm and pulls me into him until we're flush. We're so close that I can see the full length of his blonde stubble. I breathe in his musk and let out a shaky breath. I run my fingers along the tattoo on his forearm, remembering what he told me about it—that it's a reminder that we, just like video game characters, can heal from anything. He puts his arms around my back and rubs it, taking my breath away.

I don't know what the fuck this is. I feel like a little girl. I feel like I've never even had sex before. But my stomach's all in knots—the good kind—and my hearts racing like I just got done with a fucking work out. What is Tanner Bash doing to me? And why now? I've had plenty of sex before, and I've even fucked Tanner before. So why, now, does it feel like the first time we've ever been this close? Like the first time I've been close with anyone?I look up at him, and his lips are dangerously close to mine. His dick is hardening against my stomach, and I feel mine hardening against his leg. He closes the distance between our lips, and then—

The over timer goes off.

I push myself away to get the chocolate chip cookies out of the oven. Tanner wipes his face and adjusts his shorts as I set the cookie sheets down on some oven mitts on the other counter.

"So what's next?" Tanner asks, wiping his nose.

I turn away to adjust my dick in my jeans and clear my throat. "Well," I say, making my way to fridge. I open the door and pull out the brown butter. I know it's definitely not that cool yet, but I don't want to wait around—and that's not because I can't. It's because I don't know what I'd do with myself next to Tanner if we had downtime.

"Now if you could put these eggs and this vanilla I've measured out in the brown butter, that'd be wonderful," I say, sliding the things to him. He takes it without question. Sorta how he took my dick when I fucked him.

Goddamnit.

"So," Tanner says as he stirs the wet ingredients together. "You were saying about Joe?"

"Right," I say, scooping up the frosting with my spatula to see if it's got a good consistency. And it is—because I'm a fucking good baker. Don't really know why I delayed doing this so long.

"As I said, Joe was really insecure about his sexuality. And so when his family discovered us—that he was dating a man—he tossed me aside like I was garbage. And you wanna know what the worst part is?"

"That's not the worst part?" Tanner asks as he sets the mixed wet ingredients aside.

I plop the spatula down in the frosting and look at him. "You would think, right? But no. Turns out he was dating another man the whole time. But he breaks up with me and keeps the other guy."

"No fucking way," Tanner says. "That's cold."

"And then they went public. Like he was never afraid of his sexuality to begin with."

Tanner sucks air through his teeth and winces. "Fuck, man. I'm sorry."

I let out a bitter laugh. "Thanks. I swear, after that I just wrote off relationships altogether. I couldn't help but wonder what it was about me that led a man to want to hide me but be open with someone else."

Tanner furrows his brow. "You think it's your fault?"

I huff air out my nose. "Why wouldn't it be? Joe couldn't be seen with me. And yet he flaunted his new boyfriend around like it was nothing."

"I don't know, Jimmy," Tanner says, looking back down at the bowls. "It sounds like it was this guy who had a problem, not you. You seem like a cool guy. I definitely wouldn't be ashamed to show you around."

I lean forward onto the counter and tilt my head up at him. "You sure you mean that?"

"I do," he says, looking me right in the eyes.

I swear there's an electrical current running between us. But I don't know how comfortable I am with it. If Tanner really is flirting with me, does he mean what he says? Would he really not be ashamed to be openly gay?

"Then help me finish up these cookies," I say, breaking the spell between us. I'm not ready to think about if he's serious.

"Tell me what to do, boss," he says.

I instruct him to pour the fractions of the dry ingredients into the wet and gradually mix until it's incorporated into a dough. Meanwhile, I start frosting the cooled sugar cookies. Once we're both done, I pull the cooled caramel out of the fridge.

"Now for the best part," I say, setting the caramel out between us. "We get to stuff 'em."

"Stuff what?" he asks.

Your asshole, I want to say. But I *obviously* can't.

"We're gonna take a spoonful of the caramel, like so," I say, scooping up some of the caramel. It's hard enough to keep its shape but warm enough to where it's malleable. "We're gonna take this much dough." I grab a small fistful. "And then insert the caramel inside. Then we cover it up with the excess dough, and we're good," I say, setting the ball of dough and caramel down on the cookie sheet.

"Seems easy enough," he says.

And so we both get to it. I watch patiently, my hands clasped in front of me, as Tanner scoops his caramel and dough out of their bowls, and I'm not holding myself this way because I'm trying to show patience with his lack of baking skills. It's because I don't want our hands to touch.

"Sorry," he says, struggling to enclose the caramel as some of it slowly oozes down his wrist.

I laugh. "It's all good. It'll all taste the same."

He looks up at me with a shy smile, and this time I just decide to meet it with my own. And it makes me all tingly inside. Eventually, we cobble together twelve cookies between two cookie sheets. The four that Tanner managed to make are very distinguishable. Mine are near perfect spheres, while his look like deflated soccer balls, caramel oozing out the sides.

I toss both sheets into the oven, set a timer, and lean back against the counter. And then dread pools in my chest.

It's time to wait.

I've already managed to clean everything up and put the necessary dishes in the dishwasher. The chocolate chip cookies are done, and the cookies are frosted. All we're waiting on are the caramel cookies.

"Alright, moment of truth," he says, walking over to the freshly baked cookies. "Can I try?"

"'Course," I say, turning to watch him.

He takes a bite of the chocolate chip cookie and then nods silently at me with a thumb up.

"Good?" I ask.

"Good doesn't cut it," he says, taking another bite. "These are excellent."

My chest warms. "Thank you."

"You want one?" he asks.

"I'll have a sugar cookie," I say, walking over to the other counter. I make sure to stand a couple feet away. Yes, he's flirting with me, and I'm flirting with him. But I don't know what we are right now. He's still probably emotionally unstable, and I don't really want casual sex. Christ, I can't believe I'm saying that. But it's true.

He finishes off his chocolate chip cookie, then hands me a sugar cookie. He takes one for himself as well.

We both take a bite of ours at the same time, we moan as if we were giving each other the pleasure.

"Damn," I say, taking another bite. "I knew I hadn't made something like this in a while, so I wasn't expecting it to taste that good."

That's when Tanner inserts the entire thing into his mouth, and I swear my dick twitches at the sight.

"The cookie," he says, his mouth full. "And the frosting. That frosting is so damn good."

I laugh. "You know, that's not the only thing I know how to frost," I say.

That's when he looks at me, deadpan.

What the fuck is wrong with me? I didn't even *mean* to make that innuendo. But now all I can picture is Tanner's cum sloppy hole as I pulled out, still hard.

"I mean that I've frosted other things, like cakes and donuts," I say.

Tanner swallows and clears his throat, a mischievous smile forming on his face. "Sure," he says.

"Tanner, I swear," I say, wiping my sweaty forehead. "I didn't mean for that to come out."

Tanner closes the distance us so that our bodies are touching again, and I feel my heart pick up. Fuck, he is such a man.

He puts his huge hand on the back of my neck and rubs it, and I melt into his touch.

"Tanner," I say, finally just deciding to say what's on my mind. "Are you sure this is a good idea? We've done this before, and it's not ended well."

His face gets more serious, but he doesn't stop rubbing my neck. "I know that I've been flaky," he says. "Always running away from you when we get close. But I don't want to do that anymore. I've always been a Christian man, but I've also been learning what it means to have a good relationship with God. And right now, that means accepting that I'm gay."

I blink twice after hearing the gay word.

"Yes, you heard me right," he says.

"Just didn't think you'd say it so confidently."

With his other hand, he uses his thumb to brush my cheek, and warm shivers rush down my spine.

"I'm kinda surprised, too," he says. "But I just think you make me so sure of myself."

I blush, my chest warming again. "You little fucking flirt," I say, a smile forming on my face.

Tanner closes the distance until our foreheads are touching, our noses nuzzling.

So, it turns out that something's gonna happen after all. Except now it feels like it should. Tanner seems like he's accepted himself, and it doesn't feel like I'm trying to use his body to feel better about myself. It genuinely feels like we just want to be closer with each other because we like each other. That must be why all of this feels so new and exciting. I'm actually being vulnerable with someone.

The oven timer goes off, but neither of us startle.

"I'll get it," Tanner says. "Stay right there."

He takes one of my oven mitts and opens the oven. He puts both cookie sheets on the stove to cool, and I laugh at the clear difference between our cookies. Mine are pristine and round, while his have oozed caramel all over the pan.

"I hope you're right about the cookies tasting the same," he says, turning off the oven. "Because if they taste how they look, then mine'll taste real ugly."

I laugh, leaning against the counter. "Come here, big guy," I say, gesturing to myself.

He closes the distance faster than I would expect and presses his body against me. "I fucking love it when you call me that."

"Big guy?" I ask.

He nods, clasping one on his hands in mine. "You're just so fucking confident and sure of yourself and it makes you so fucking hot," he says, almost out of breath. "I just want to worship you like the man that you are."

His lips brush mine, and I pull away. Not because I don't want to kiss him. But because I want to tease him.

"Then what's fucking stopping you?" I whisper.

He groans, pressing his hard cock against me. "Jimmy," he says, low and hungry. "Will you please fuck me?"

I smile. "Worship my body," I say. "And I'll decide when you earn it."

He lets out a shaky breath, then smiles. "Yes, Daddy."

"Call me Daddy when you worship me," I say, knowing exactly what I want from him. "But when I'm inside you, you call me Jimmy. Understand?"

He nods eagerly.

"So fucking kiss me already," I say.

Chapter 26

Tanner Bash

I KISS JIMMY LIKE I'm afraid he'll disappear if my lips aren't touching his. And even though he's shorter and smaller than me, he commands my body with a confidence that could make me do anything and everything he wanted me to. My tongue thirstily searches his mouth, but he kisses me back leisurely, like he has all the time in the world. And it only makes me more desperate.

"Come to the couch?" I ask.

He nods, and I take him by the hand, afraid that if I let go of him, he'll vanish.

Standing in front of the couch, I wrap my arms around him and untie his apron. Then I take his shirt off. I can smell his earthy cologne mixed with the sweat he's worked up cooking in the kitchen, and I'm afraid I'll faint from pleasure.

I unbuckle his belt and gradually pull his pants down. His huge dick, still in his underwear, bounces up when I pull his jeans past it. I gesture for him to sit down, and he falls back into the couch, his body splayed out and relaxed.

"For all the times I kept you hanging," I say, kissing his hairy leg.

"Don't worry about the past," he says, stroking my hair. "Just focus on this moment. And remember what you're calling me."

"Yes, Daddy," I say, kissing his leg again.

I raise myself to his underwear—he's wearing black briefs—and I press my nose against his shaft. I want to breathe in his scent, but it feels weird, so I just kiss it instead. Slowly, I pull on his waist band until his dick bounces up into his thick, black pubes. And I don't even leave a second to waste. I put that holy rod right in my mouth.

And I worship Jimmy like the man he is.

Before, such an act would have made me profoundly uncomfortable. Worshipping a body like this would be something like idolatry, right? But I've been learning that as I grow, there are so many ways to have a relationship with God. And one of these ways, I believe, is through sex. After all, Lupita has shown me that God gives us more opportunities to be closer to him, and sex is amazing. Why wouldn't I feel closer to the divine when I'm doing something that feels so g ood?

"Fuck, boy," Jimmy says, as I go up and down his shaft. I'm fucking slurping it up like he's a lollipop.

I take a breath. "Call me 'big guy'," I say. "Or big boy as well, please Daddy."

"Alright, big guy," he says as I get back to sucking, which only makes me go more wild.

I get my hands involved as I'm sucking, but I feel like I'm bad at it. Because I want his dick in my mouth so badly that every time I get my hand involved, I get greedy and just want the whole thing in my mouth again.

"That feels so good, big boy," he says, which sends warmth down my back. I fucking love pleasing this man, and I'm glad that my desperate, crude attempts at it are working.

I look at him, and his perfect pecs almost smile down at me, so I decide it's time to worship other parts of his body. I quickly discard my clothes and kiss up his hairy stomach, occasionally using my whole tongue to lick, until I reach his nipple.

"There we go, big guy," he says as my lips enclose it. He uses one of his hands to cradle the back of my head, the other to stroke himself. "That's it. There we go."

I greedily suck it like I'm fucking nursing him myself, and he tastes so good. Like sweat and salt and skin. I move to the other pec and give it just as much attention. I move his hand from his dick and start jerking him off myself.

"I don't want you lifting a muscle," I say. "I want to be the root of your pleasure."

"Have at it then, boy," he says with a smirk. And I wipe that smirk off his face with a kiss. I get up onto the couch and mount him, reaching behind me while we kiss to situate his dick against my asshole.

I run one hand through his hair as we kiss, the other through his beard. I grind back on his dick, my own dick swallowed up by the hair on his stomach. But I don't give a shit about my own dick. All that matters is my hole and that he fucks it.

"I want it in me, Daddy," I say, one of my hands stroking his firm pecs.

He reaches around me and slaps the head of his dick against my hole, and I let out an almost feminine moan.

"You want this dick, boy?"

I kiss him and nod. God, I swear there's nothing that could tear me away from this man. I want to taste every inch of him.

"I want you to fill me to the brim," I say. "Fuck, I want you to cum in my ass in the morning and I wanna walk around with it all day. Hell, I want you to cum inside me before a game, and I want you to watch me and know that I'm playing on the field with your DNA in my ass."

Jimmy smirks and slaps both of my thighs, flexing his chest in the process and showing just how wide, muscular, and hairy it is. God, I want to bury my face in it when he cums inside me.

"I don't think I believe you," he says.

I groan, pushing myself back onto his dick. "I'll do anything to prove it to you. I've been holding myself back for two long. I want to fucking drown in you, Jimmy. I want you to fucking suffocate me and bring me back to life."

He strokes my arms gently, and my dick is so hard that I'm afraid this act alone will get me to cum.

"Easy, big guy," he says, touching me so softly he could make me fall asleep. If I wasn't so horny for him. "I'm not going anywhere."

I whimper at that and press myself so hard into him he grunts.

"I assume you're not douched?" he asks me.

I pause for a second, remembering that means. "I'm not."

He moves his head back and forth for a minute, then shrugs. "I'm good to just fuck you if you are."

I take a moment to think, my hands on his shoulders. I don't want to have any accidents, and I definitely don't want to worry about accidents while we're fucking.

"Do you still have the bulb?"

"'Course I do," he says. "Mind setting me free so I can go grab it?"

"Yes, yes, sorry," I say, getting off him. "No worries," he says, patting me on the knees. He slips on his shorts and jogs out the back door while I sit on my couch naked.

I feel like I should be nervous right now, or guilty. But I just feel eager and excited. This is me accepting God's invitation to get closer with him. By allowing myself to be gay—by accepting who I am—I'm opening myself to a whole new level of God's love. And it's amazing.

I hear my phone buzz in my shorts' pocket, but then I'm distracted by Jimmy coming in through my back door. My heart skips a beat when I see him wearing just his jeans. I'm not nervous or anything. He's just so damn hot, and seeing him just means we're one step closer to making love.

"Here," he says, handing the bulb to me. "It's clean, and it hasn't been used since you used it."

I take it and stand up, relieved Jimmy hasn't let any other hot man use the bulb and then taken their virginity. I grab my phone from my shorts and make my way to the bathroom so I have a way to entertain myself while I clean up.

"Meet me on my bed?" I ask, standing at the bathroom door.

Jimmy comes to me. He kisses me on the cheek and pats me on the back. "I'll be there," he says, and my entire body tingles.

I close the bathroom door, a wide grin on my face, and I set my phone down and get the douching started. While I'm filling it up, my phone buzzes again, but I hardly notice now that I'm so excited for Jimmy to fuck me. The first time he did doesn't even feel real. It feels like this is the first legitimate time we're having sex. Like, we're both approaching it from a more mature perspective. And I can tell he feels how much better this will be, too.

I plop down on the toilet and get to it, and that's when my phone buzzes again. Who is texting me this much? Did I forget a phone check-in with Lupita or something? But when I pick up my phone and read the texts, my entire body goes cold.

"I wanna fuck this time," the first text says.

"Before the game tomorrow," the second reads.

"Hello?"

My hand's shaking so bad I'm afraid I'll drop the phone.

No. Chris can't do this to me. Not when I'm about to have legitimately perfect sex with a man I think I love.

Fuck. Did I just say I love Jimmy? I mean, I think I do, but this realization could not come at a worst time. Fuck. Fuck. Fuck.

My phone buzzes again.

"Are you there or what?" Chris says. "Or do you want me to post the video?"

Three dots appear, and I'm afraid he'll jump and do something if I don't reply or something.

"Yes, I'm here," I type and send quickly.

"Good," he replies. "So I take that as a yes?"

I feel a headache come on, and now I'm starting to sweat.

Fuck, man. Tonight, I was going to give my entire self to Jimmy. We were gonna have sex for real this time, both of us fully present. But now I can't because of Chris.

And you know what? I don't even give a fuck about what the public may think of me being gay anymore. I don't want a wife, and I sure as hell don't care what people may think about what I do with my dick.

But I care now what Jimmy thinks. Earlier, he's telling me about all the escapades he's been on but how now he's not much into casual sex. If he knows that I've had casual sex—that I'm having casual sex with Chris—will he think of me differently? Surely. I can't let him know about me and Chris, which means that video can't leak.

"Fine," I say.

"Alright," he says immediately. "I'll send where we're meeting later."

Exasperated, I put the phone face down on the counter and get to the rest of my douching. By now, my libido's been compromised, and I'll be surprised if I can get hard again. Fucking Chris. I hate that son of a bitch.

When I'm done, I take a shower and dry off. Then, I wrap up my bottom half with a towel and walk out of the bathroom into my bedroom. Jimmy's laying sideways on my bed in his jeans reading one of the Al-Anon books I had on my nightstand.

"Man, you look good," he says, as I walk into the room. He has the window open, and a nice cool breeze is blowing in. The sun is shining outside, and the waves provide a nice, soothing background sound.

"You do too," I say, approaching the bed.

I stand between his spread legs, and he kisses up my belly. Guilt twists inside my chest knowing that tomorrow I'll be doing the deed with the man I hate the most, but it's not like I have any feelings for him at all. My heart belongs to Jimmy. I just have to keep this hidden so he doesn't get hurt.

"You okay?" he asks, grabbing my hands. "You seem tense."

I have to resist pulling them away from him. "Yeah," I lie. "Just nervous." Which isn't exactly a lie. I'm nervous, just not for the sex.

"Well," Jimmy says, standing up. I expect him to kiss me, but instead his lips meet my collar bone. Then, he rubs his beard lightly all across my pecs, and I shiver at the touch. But in a way that melts and eases the tension in my body.

"You like that, big guy?"

I practically melt into goo when he calls me that. I nod.

"Here," he says, grabbing my elbows. He turns us around and then sets me down on the bed. "You lay down and stretch out."

I do, and he removes my towel.

"Now it's your turn to relax," he says. "Let me worship you."

"Are you sure?" I ask. "I want to—ah."

He's blowing air around my dick—not on my dick, but around it—on my crotch and the crevices between my legs. Then he switches it with his warm breath, and I feel like I'm ice cream melting on a hot day.

"Fuck," I say.

He seamlessly takes hold of my dick, but he doesn't go hard like I was to him earlier. He's going soft, as delicate as butterfly wings and the mist that rolls off the ocean waves. He's real quiet, too, which makes this more intimate.

He manages to get me rock hard in only a few seconds, which I think is a record. And every time he takes it all the way, his thick beard tickles my balls, making my whole body shiver. Which reminds me that I'm no different than fucking cookie dough in his hands.

He releases hold of my dick and comes up to kiss me, his hairy body grazing mine. He collapses all of his weight onto me, and I wrap my arms around him.

I love you, I want to say. I want to tell it to him. But I can't, right? Not with the Chris stuff? But if the Chris stuff never stops, will I regret not telling him now?

He rolls off my body to the side, then moves my arm above my head.

"What are you doing?" I ask.

He sticks his face into my hairy, sweaty armpit—the one I didn't even wash when I was showering—and takes a big whiff.

"Fuck, I'm so glad you didn't wash this," he says, rubbing his nose into it. "I was smelling you in the kitchen earlier and couldn't get enough."

I let out a nervous laugh. I mean, I like the way Jimmy smells, but smelling his armpit? Okay, the thought does arouse me, but isn't that kinda fucking weird?"It really smells good?" I ask stupidly.

He smells again and gives me a firm nod.

I watch him, mesmerized, as he kisses from my armpit to my nipple and back, licking along the curves of my muscles. The sensation of his tongue, the air he's exhaling and the touch of his luscious beard, all make my dick twitch. And the way that he's smelling me up makes me wonder how he smells.

"Can I..." I trail off.

"Can you what, boy?" he asks.

I bite my lip, feeling silly and perverted for asking. But he's doing it, so why can't I?

"Will you..." I nod to my own armpit, then to his.

He squints at me, then his face melts into recognition. "Oh, I know what you want," he says.

He gets on the other side of me, then opens up the under of his arm to my face. "So we both can do it at the same time."

He lowers his armpit and keeps it hovering just above my face. I take in a tentative sniff, and then my entire body electrifies.

"Fuck," I say, taking another smell. I take some of the hair in my lips like I've done his chest hair and pull it, all while breathing him in. "You smell so good."

"You like that, big guy?"

I rub my face into him, loving the way his armpit hair almost cuts my face. He smells like coming in on a hot summer's day and relaxing on the couch. He smells like earth after it rains. He smells like home.

But it doesn't stop there. He continues worshiping my own armpit, I'll admit doing it a lot better than I am his. I'm like a big dog slurping up every inch of him I can, while he's being delicate, methodical, sensitive.

My dick throbs, and I don't know why. It's almost like Jimmy's slow, deliberate touches turn me on more than when we go rough. I know that sounds stupid and weird, but it's true. So I reach down to hold my dick. I don't want to stroke it, but I just need to hold it so it doesn't keep twitching out of control.

"You really like that, don't you boy?"

I take a big sniff of him, then lick his whole armpit with my tongue. "Yes, Daddy."

"You wanna cum this way?" he asks.

"Will you let me?" I ask.

"You still want me to fuck you after you cum?"

"I'd still want you to fuck me if the sky was falling," I say.

He chuckles, his whole body shaking, which makes me just worship him harder.

"Then, cum for me, big guy," he says. "Cum while you're eating Daddy's armpit."

I wrap my free arm around his body and press him into me until I can't breathe. My entire body contracts, then releases in one big beautiful orgasm. I shout into his armpit, but he just keeps it there, smothering me.

"Good boy," he says. "That's such a good boy."

As I come down, I kiss and lick him hungrily, unable to contain myself. Eventually, he gets up, and I'm able to take a full breath again. He looks down at me with the most genuine smile possible, and that's when it just comes out.

"I think I love you, Jimmy," I say.

He licks his lips as he stares down at me, and my chest gets all tight.

"Sorry, I know that's weird. I know we've been through a lot. It's probably too soon. I'll just—"

He puts a finger to my lips to shush me, and I just want to suck on it like it's his cock.

He lowers to lay next to me, then removes his fingers to kiss me on the lips. "I think I love you too," he says. "But you're right. It is early. I say we give the relationship time for this love to blossom. What do you think?"

I shift to look at him better as he lays next to me. "Are you saying that we be boyfriends?"

He shrugs. "I don't see what else we'd be."

"Like monogamous boyfriends? We couldn't sleep with anyone else?"

He nods. "You'd have my loyalty."

Guilt tugs on my heart, and I look up at the ceiling. If I say yes to this, I'd have to end things with Chris and suffer the consequences of the blackmail. Or I'd have to lie to Jimmy. I don't really want to do either, but I know what would cause a lot less damage.

"Alright," I say. "The NFO's more accepting of gay people now that Kyle's come out. So we could work." I let out a deep sigh. There's no one else I feel safer with, who I'd rather be with. "Let's do it."

He kisses me on the cheek. "Alright, boyfriend," he says, getting up. He inserts himself between my legs. "You still wanna get fucked?"

My entire body's buzzing with guilt now, but at least if I'm fucked I can distract myself.

"Please, Daddy," I say. "Fuck me."

He smiles as he grabs the lube he's set down on my nightstand. "And remember," he says, squirting some lube onto his dick. "You call me by my name when I'm fucking you."

"Yes, Daddy," I say.

And then he fucks me, and it feels like heaven. But when he cums inside me, as we're yelling each other's names, my lips burn from guilt.

I'm lying to Jimmy, and I don't think this will end well.

Chapter 27

Jimmy Dillon

As I hold Tanner in my arms, I couldn't feel happier.

I don't think I've ever had sex that nice.

And I didn't use Tanner for his body either. Instead, I feel like I'm getting to know the man organically. What we did with the cookies—that was almost like a date. Hell, it was a date. We talked and got to know each other, and it wasn't just to get him into bed. But when we did get in bed, it was all the more better because we cared about each other as people.

Tanner adjusts himself in my arms and kisses my shoulder. "Merry Christmas, Jimmy," he says. "Well, it's Christmas Eve still, but you know what I mean."

I kiss the top of his shaggy head. "Merry Christmas, handsome Tanner," I say. And he hugs me tighter.

But the pressure he puts on my belly makes me realize how badly I have to use the bathroom.

"Mind if I use the men's room?" I ask, untangling my arm from his body.

"Not at all," he says. "You wanna sleep here tonight?"

I stand up and look at his handsome, huge body splayed out and nearly taking up the entire king bed.

"I do," I say. "As long as you give me room."

"I'll think about it," he says, getting under the covers.

I laugh as I make my way to the bathroom. I feel a lot more comfortable with Tanner now. Before, he reminded me of my mom with his emotional volatility.

But unlike her, he actually wants to and is improving himself, and I can see it. It's easier for him to be himself and open up around me, and I think that's partially why the sex was so good. I think as we embark on a relationship, as long as we stay working on ourselves—him in Al-Anon and me in my meetings with meditation—we'll be good.

I make it to the bathroom to relieve myself. And the best part is this feels nothing like Joe. In fact, Tanner and Joe are opposites. In the beginning, Joe was the gregarious, talkative one, and that only lessened the more anxious he got. Tanner's just opened up more and more. Of course, Joe got more secretive because he was cheating on me. And with how new Tanner is to being gay, that's the last thing I'd expect from him.

As I'm washing my hands, I hear a buzz on the counter. I glance to see Tanner's phone. He must have left it in here when he was douching. I'll bring it to the bedroom for him. While I'm drying my hands, the phone buzzes again, and I get curious. Tanner isn't a very social guy, so I wonder who could be texting him. When the phone buzzes again, I let the curiosity get the best of me. I turn the phone over to see what the messages are.

And what. The. Actual. Fuck.

His phone is open to a chat history with some guy with the contact name 'Chris Seals'. Is this same Chris Whitacre that plays as a wide receiver for the Seals? That would be insane, because if I'm reading these texts correctly, then these guys are fucking.

"Let's meet in the extra locker room in the stadium tomorrow," the first message says.

"Bring lube," the second reads.

"I've got some pills for you to take," the last one reads. "I know how hard it is for you to keep it up."

My vision goes blurry, and my chest gets so tight I feel like I'm having a heart attack. Is this a heart attack? A panic attack? Cardiac arrest? I don't fucking know, but I have to lean against the bathroom counter to get my bearings.

I pull up the message history and start scrolling back in time. These messages have been happening for the past few months. Since September at the earliest.

So Tanner's been fucking some guy this entire time? All while he's been trying to get to me?

But that doesn't make any sense. Tanner's struggled to even accept his attraction to me, as far as I can tell. So how come he's just fucking someone on the side so easily?

A realization comes, and I have to grip the counter so I don't collapse.

It all makes sense.

I thought he and Joe were different, but it turns out they're exactly the same. Turns out it's too hard to just like a guy like me. With Joe, he was fucking someone on the side easily even though I struggled to have any semblance of a relationship with him. Apparently, I'm just not cut out for any kind of relationship.

And so it is with Tanner, too. He has someone else, and he's just using me to get to him—the reason? I don't care. But he is. There's no other explanation. Why else would he have a message history with someone showing that they've fucked? Fucking figures. This would happen to me. Sure, I sleep with lots of guys. But I don't hide it. And I definitely don't keep it secret when I ask someone else to be boyfriend.

Today was too good to be true. Tanner saying that he's no longer going to push me away? That he wouldn't be ashamed to go public with me? All a lie. He's had someone else hidden away side this entire time, and he's probably planning on dropping me just like Joe did. Which will be any moment now, considering how desperate he's been for me to fuck him and how I just gave in to that request. He's gotten what he wanted, so he can throw me away.

Well I'm gonna fucking beat him to it.

I walk out of the bathroom, Tanner's phone in hand, as a completely different man. I make my way to Tanner's bedroom doorway and just stand there, my fists clenched.

"What's wrong?" he asks, sitting up. "You look like—"

"You know, I wish I could say this didn't make sense," I say, tossing his phone onto the bed. "But it's crystal clear to me."

He looks at his phone, sees the messages, and then his face goes white.

"I still don't understand why guys always use me as a stepping stone to reach the guys they'd prefer, but who am I to try and understand lies and cheats."

"Jimmy," he says, sitting on the edge of the bed. "It's not what it—"

"What, Tanner?" I ask. "You've been sleeping with another guy this whole time, yet it's taken you a whole lot of courage and self-improvement to let yourself fuck me? Am I just a prude to you or something? Or is it that you were worried you wouldn't be able to secure me if you didn't improve yourself?"

Tanner's eyes start to water the same way Joe's did when I caught him. Like a fucking prophecy being re-fulfilled. I don't want to hear a word he has to say.

"Jimmy," he says, standing up, his voice shaky. "I promise you—"

"What worth is your promise?" I ask, leaning against the doorframe. "Because clearly you aren't the man I thought you were."

"Let's just talk about—"

"Oh, so now you want to talk?" I ask, wanting him to hurt like I hurt. "You get to run away from me whenever the conversation's hard, but now that I find definitive proof that you've been fucking someone else this whole time, I have to sit here and listen to more of your lies?"

"I'm not really lying," he says, tears now streaming down his face. "It's not like—"

"And if you've been fucking this guy as a closeted gay, I can assume that you probably weren't being safe about it, right?"

Tanner looks at me like I have two heads, and I just laugh.

"Of course as a baby gay you have no idea what I'm talking about," I say. "Fucking figures. Now I gotta go get tested to make sure you haven't given me anything."

He shakes his head, now understanding what I'm talking about. "No, no. We haven't—I haven't—it's not that simple, but no, he's just stroked me off and blown me a couple times. It's not that—"

"So he finally admits it!' I say with my arms widespread, feeling validated.

"Jimmy," he says, shaking his head. "I'm sorry. I just haven't known what to—"

"Shove your apology up your ass," I say, collecting my clothes from his bedroom floor. "Because it means nothing."

I expect him to grovel more, but he just weeps into his hands. Which is, I admit, very different from Joe. He kept trying to convince me that I was wrong, that I needed to hear him out. He never gave up like Tanner is. I collect my lube, then bulb from the bathroom, all while Tanner weeps into his hands, his shoulders shaking. For a second, I think that Tanner might be different than Joe, that I should hear him out. But then I think about all the times I gave my mom a second chance and how often that burned me. And with how much Tanner has lied, he's not that different from her either after all.

"I'll see you around, Tanner," I say, leaving the room. I collect my shirt from the living room and scoff at the apron that Tanner so eagerly removed from me earlier. I don't think I can ever wear that again.

I storm out of Tanner's back door and stomp over to my house, angry that the day feels so temperate and nice even though it's Christmas Eve. I fucking hate San Diego. The weather's too perfect.

I make my way to my room, slam my door, then throw myself under the covers and shut the world out. Mercifully, even though it's only the afternoon, I fall asleep quickly. That sex we had—as confusing and amazing as it was—wore me completely out.

Chapter 28

It's Christmas morning, and I'm alone.

I sit in my kitchen early in the morning, trying to force down the breakfast casserole Jimmy made for me. Of course, I haven't seen him since he discovered my texts from Chris last night. He stormed out faster than I could explain myself.

But the truth is I don't know what the hell I could say to him. Do I say that another football player on my team has forced me to do sexual things for the past few months? Would he even believe me? And even if he did, wouldn't he see me as complicit? That I allowed it to happen?

I'm fucking hopeless.

I gag down a piece of sausage. Honestly, this casserole is great. Jimmy's made it for me before. But I haven't wanted to eat a lick since he discovered the truth about Chris. Yet I know I need to or else coach will put me on the bench, and that's the last thing I want to do this close to the season being over. I want to play and help my team out. It feels like football's the last thing I have.

Speaking of which, I gotta make it to the stadium. Today we have an important game against Washington State, one that will help determine if we make the playoffs. But I don't know how well I'm gonna play because I'm exhausted, and that's not just 'cause I hardly got any sleep last night. It's also because food is repulsive, and I can't eat. I feel weak.

My phone buzzes, and my heart skips. Is that Jimmy? Does he actually want to hear me out?

But it's not his name on my phone I see. It's Chris.

"Where the hell are you?" it reads. "I said to be here early so we'd have time. I don't even see your stuff."

My stomach lurches, and I'm worried I'll throw up the little I've eaten. If I let him release that video, I may lose football, too. I can't let that happen.

"Sorry, slept in," I say. "Be right there."

I manage to collect my things and get to the stadium in remarkably little time, though I bet a look like a mess. I didn't even have time to shower. I park in the player's wing and take the secluded entryway down into the locker rooms—the same place where Chris is going to make me fuck him.

The last time I fucked a man was back at Miss U. And even though it wasn't heartfelt, at least I wanted to do it. And Chris is apparently gonna make me take one of those pills to keep me hard. This is a fucking nightmare. I have no idea how I'm gonna get out of this.

I pass by the glass wall that separates the coach's office from the rest of the locker rooms. Coach Larson is in there with the other coaches, and it looks like they're discussing strategy. Coach Larson lifts his head, and our eyes lock for a moment, but he then I pick up the pace so I'm out of eyesight. Luckily, I make it to the locker rooms without him trying to stop and tell me how I'm not heavy enough to play or whatever.

"There you are," Chris says from behind me when I open my locker. His icy voice makes my whole body shiver.

"Hi, Chris," I say flatly, setting my bag down.

He sits down on the bench beside me and rubs my leg, and it takes all my strength not to recoil or punch him in the face. Because if I do, he posts that video and everything's over.

"There's a part of the locker room with old equipment and stuff," he says quietly. "We can go there and not be noticed."

I don't say a word as I take off my street clothes and change into some sweats and a T-shirt. If we're really having sex, I at least want to be comfortable.

"Here," Chris says. He's holding out a small blue pill in his palm. "This'll keep you hard."

I reluctantly take it and slip it into my pocket. "Let's get this over with," I say.

He stands and I follow, and it doesn't even feel like I'm walking to my death. It feels like I've already died and I'm in hell. I'm in hell because God's abandoned me.

You know what? Fuck what I've been 'learning' in Al-Anon, from Lupita. This supposed new, more loving version of God who I'm supposed to be closer to now? It's a myth. Because if there was a God that was loving, he wouldn't let me be doing this right now. He wouldn't have let me be molested for months on end, all while teasing me with a man that I really do like—only to have this very man discover the molesting and blame me for it. If there is a God, he's the one I found as a child: a rigid, unyielding one. That's the only thing that can make sense, at least. Because how else can I explain all this? I've strayed from God's laws by letting my homosexuality get the best of me, and now I'm paying the price. And if this God doesn't exist, then there isn't one at all. So there's no point in praying now. Either God won't answer it because I'm already too far gone, or there's no God to answer me. I've been truly abandoned.

We reach an old section of the showers that's stuffed with old equipment, and it truly smells like ass in here. Chris starts stripping, and I guess the smell is fitting. Because what we're about to do is as foul as hell.

I take the pill out of my pocket, and Chris slides my pants down.

"Let me suck it first," he says.

And I nod, trying not to grimace. Just as he's about to put his lips on my cock, I lift the pill to my mouth.

And then I hear someone call my name.

"Who's that?" Chris says, rigid and pale as a ghost.

I hear it again, and this time I recognize his voice.

"That's coach," I say, almost relieved.

"Tanner Bash," he yells, clear now. "Where the hell are you?"

Chris quickly stands up, and I pull my pants up.

"You get out of here first," he says. "Since coach is looking for you. And then I'll leave later so no one suspects anything."

I nod absent-mindedly, not even caring that Coach Larson could catch us together like this. Because all that means is that I no longer have to fuck Chris.

I make my way out of the recesses of the showers first, and I see Coach standing among the benches of the locker room.

"Where the hell were you doing back there?" he asks.

I shrug, my brain in a haze. My hunger, combined with the anxiety about fucking Chris, is making me feel like a zombie.

"That doesn't matter," he says, turning around. "Come with me."

I follow him past the glass wall and into his private office. I sit down across in front of his desk and slouch in my chair. I know this meeting probably isn't a good thing, but it's much better than what was about to happen.

"What's going on?" I ask, my head low.

"I don't know what it is about you," he says, sitting down at his desk.

I perk up, worried. Does he know about me and Chris? The video?

"What about me?" I ask.

"You start out the season underweight," he says, stroking his salt and pepper beard. "Then you gain most of it back in a month, and but then a lot of it is lost a month later."

Right. Because right when Jimmy started cooking for me, I gained weight. And then I started losing it again after the whole thing with Chris started. Then I started attending Al-Anon, and my weight has been coming back. But it's still not up to where it should be. And now that Jimmy and I are done, with Chris more demanding of me than ever, my appetite is so shot I doubt I'll ever get my weight up again.

"Yeah," I say. "Sorry. I've just had trouble eating."

"Still?" he asks. "Where the hell is your chef?"

My stomach curdles, and I resist a grimace. "He's doing his job."

He sighs, rubbing his already sweaty forehead. "Tanner," he says. "We can't keep doing this. You're *still* not up to your ideal weight, and it's almost the end of the season. I've been holding out this long because we were seeing some progress. But seeing you all disheveled earlier and hearing you now, I'm worried that you'll never get up there."

My chest tightens, and my heart starts to race. "I promise I'm trying."

"Trying isn't good enough, Tanner," he says, tapping a pencil against the fake wood of his desk. "And I'm afraid it's too late."

My stomach sinks to the floor. "Too late? What do you mean?"

He rubs his temples like he has a headache. "Look, I don't want to have to do this, but these new few games are as important as ever if we want to get to the playoffs, and I need guys on the field that I can trust. That are consistent."

My stomach twists around itself so much I'll be surprised if I can eat again at all.

"So," he says, leaning back and looking me right in the eyes. "I'm gonna have to ask you to sit out this game."

I feel like a wet towel being rung out. "You're benching me?" I ask, my voice hardly sounding like my own.

He nods with a frown. "Brian, your backup, has been playing well. I'm gonna ask that he play as our center today."

I scoff at him, feeling my eyes heat up. This can't be happening. Football's been the only thing keeping me through all this. I can't lose it.

"But I need this, Coach. I need to play."

"What you need," he says. "Is to get your life in order. Don't worry. You don't have to sit the rest of the season out. Just get your shit together, Bash. Stop going back and forth with your weight and eating. Treat yourself right. Go get help if you need it. We can set you up with a shrink if you need one."

I shake my head, unable to process what's happening. If I don't have football—or Jimmy or anything else—then what am I? All I have is fucking Chris, and I doubt I could tell Coach about that. That would cause all sorts of problems.

He stands up, walks around the desk, and pats me on the shoulder. "You're a good guy," he says. "Go home and rest if you need. Just take care of yourself."

He leaves his office, letting me stew in silence with my loud thoughts. Sure, Coach says I'm not out the rest of the season, but that's only if I get my weight and food issues resolved. And I know that those are only going to be resolved if I can just stop being so anxious and upset all the time. Which can only happen if I somehow stop what Chris is doing to me and resolve things with Jimmy. Like either of those things will ever happen.

Eventually, I make my way out of Coach's office. By now, the guys are getting dressed to go practice out on the field for our game. Chris is getting dressed, but he won't even look me in the eye. Good. I'm so tired of looking at his fucking face. I sit down in front of my locker and put my face in my hands.

"Hey man," Carter says, putting a hand on my shoulder. "You doing okay?"

I look up at him, and when I see how concerned he is—even though I was such an ass to him a while back—that breaks whatever fortitude I had. And I just start crying.

"Hey," he says, looking around. But everyone's too busy getting ready to care.

"Sorry," I say. "I'm sorry I was such a jerk to you. You just cared about me."

He sits down on the bench and looks at me. "Hey, look at me."

I meet his gaze, tears still running down my face.

"You don't say a whole lot, but I know you're going through it with all your eating issues and such," he says, squeezing my arm. "I don't blame you. It's gonna be okay."

"Coach doesn't want me playing today," I say, my voice all groggy from the tears. "Says I'm too inconsistent with my weight and eating. Says I need to get my life in order."

"Well, he's not wrong," Carter says.

"I know," I say. "But I just feel so stupid for letting myself be so swayed by what's going on in my life. It's like things go well so I can eat easily. But then things go bad, and my stomach clamps up."

"Hey man, that's actually pretty normal," Carter says. "But what isn't is keeping it all those feelings stuffed inside. You gotta talk that shit out, man. You can't isolate even though I know it's what you like to do."

I sniffle, trying to process his words. But my brain's too fried.

"I agree with Coach," Carter says. "Sit this one out. You should go home. Figure your shit out. Talk to someone who can help. And then come back stronger than ever. You can do that."

I look at him, my face swollen and heart tired. At least if I go home that'll give Chris less chance to try and molest me after the game.

"Thanks, Carter," I say, tapping his shoulder as I stand up. Most of the guys are headed out to the field to practice before the game. "I think I'll head home."

"You know you can reach out to me if you need it," he says, standing up.

I nod. "You're a good friend, man."

He nods and makes his way with the others out onto the field. On my way out, I find Coach.

"I'm gonna head home," I say. "To take your advice."

"Good," he says, patting me on the back. I can tell he wants to be more affectionate with me but feels like he can't. "You take care."

I make my way out of the locker rooms and eventually back into the parking garage. I'm bummed I'm not playing, but I'm more relieved that Chris never got a hold of me. Maybe since we almost got caught by Coach I'll have a break for a little bit.

But as I get in my car and drive home, I notice how beautiful the sunset is, and my mind immediately turns to God. I want to feel anger toward the cold, perfect God who was clearly punishing me for my homosexuality. Hell, I'd even expect to feel nothing now that God could nonexistent altogether.

Instead, I feel gratitude.

The sunset is beautiful. I don't have to fuck Chris. And now I get a day to myself. I'm exhausted, and some of my appetite is coming back, so I'm hungry. In other words, I don't really feel like I'm being punished, and I feel like the kinder God—the one that Lupita was helping me believe in—is the one behind all this.

Coach said that I need to take care of myself. I think that means eating something and getting some rest after a long night of no sleep. But I also think God getting me out of fucking Chris means more than just that moment. If I really am to take care of myself, maybe that means I should end this shit with

Chris. For good. I know he's threatening me with that stupid fucking video he took without my consent, but I don't want that to hang over my head forever. Plus, his demands will only get worse as long as I cave in. It went from blowjobs to sex. Who's to say that it wouldn't turn into a relationship next? And, even if this doesn't happen, I'll never be able to have a real relationship with Chris still in my life.

On my way home, I pass by the exit that leads to the Zhao shack, and I smile to myself. That's where I first took Jimmy when I wanted to apologize to him for being so flaky. It's also where I went after my first Al-Anon meeting and where I got to talk to Lupita for the first time. During that meeting, and all the meetings I've attended since, I remember the little bit they say at the end about sexual assault—how the victims deserve to feel safe and get help.

I think I, Tanner Bash, am a victim of sexual assault. Even though I still cum when Chris sucks my dick and when I sometimes I enjoy it. I don't ask for it, and I don't want it to happen. So maybe I can get some help. And maybe this is just the kind of help that Coach was talking about.

When I pull into my driveway, I take out my phone. Once I'm inside, I rush to my room even though I know Jimmy's not here and won't be for the rest of the day. All my meals are made, so there's no other reason for him to be here. But I nevertheless want to ensure my privacy.

"Hello?" Lupita answers

"Hey, Lupita," I say, shutting my door. "Do you have time to meet? I got something I need to talk about."

"Sure, Tanner," she says. "When are you free?"

Chapter 29

Jimmy Dillon

AFTER I GET A message from the third guy sending his address for me to come over and fuck him, I think I should feel better right now. I should feel attractive, needed, hot. I should feel worthy.

But I just feel like absolute shit.

Unable to sleep, I got up at the ass-crack of dawn to finish Tanner's food for the day. And so I wouldn't run into him. That fucking asshole—fucking just like Joe. He was fucking someone else this whole time, so that's probably all he wanted from me. A nice fuck. Then he fucking asks me to be his boyfriend. Was he hoping to just keep this guy on the side the whole time? He fucking agreed to have sex with that Chris guy today—which they're probably doing right now—just before he agreed to be my boyfriend.

Before he fucking told me he loved me.

Why is it that I keep going for guys who find it so hard to just accept themselves with me? And yet they can so easily be gay with someone else? Am I just defective or something? Ugly? It makes no sense.

So that's why I'm back on the hookup apps again. I need my self-esteem back.

I pick the hottest guy ready to fuck. I plug in his address into my phone, and then I throw some clothes on. I just worked out and still haven't showered, and I feel like shit, but it doesn't matter. I'm topping anyways.

I walk past the pool and the garage to the driveway. The garage door is open, and Tanner's car is inside, which is weird. He's supposed to be at his game now.

Why do I fucking care? The man probably got his fix with that football player and decided to come home. Asshole. I get in the car and make my way to the stranger's house.

The sex is fine. I get him to cum in ten minutes, but I'm too lazy to get myself to cum. He asks to suck me off. I tell him I have to go. So then I get in my car and look for someone else to fuck. While I'm searching, I get a text.

"Missed you at Christmas morning meditation," Yousef says. "Everything okay?"

Right. Today's Christmas. Now that's fucking poetic.

I ignore his message and find someone else to fuck. When I show up to this couple's house, they both want me to fuck them. Fine with me. One kisses me while I fuck the other, and when we switch, the other eats my ass while I fuck his husband. All this should be enough to keep my thoughts from racing. But you know who I can't stop thinking about?

I can't stop thinking about Tanner and how thoughtful he is. How cool his mind works. How handsome he is. How electric he felt in bed. How much I wanted to call him my boyfriend. No one, besides Joe, has ever caught my attention like that. Caught my love and interest. And as much as I want to say he's exactly like Joe, he isn't. He's considerate. He's kind. He knows how to be present with me. He sees me. He told me he loved me first. So, it honestly makes no sense for him to cheat on me. It's out of his character.

The couple finally gets me to cum as they take turns sucking me off, and the orgasm sucks so much out of me I'm tempted to pass out on their bed. And seeing how nice this couple is, I bet they'd let me, but, even though my thoughts are all over the place, I'd rather just be alone. So I wish them well and head home.

Once I'm back in the bungalow, I get a text from the first guy I fucked this morning. He tells me that his boyfriend just tested positive for chlamydia, so I should get tested, too.

Fucking fantastic.

So then I gotta text the couple I just fucked and tell them the news. I want to text Tanner and tell him because we had sex recently, but then I remember that it's very likely he could have given me something too. I still can't believe he was sleeping with someone else while we were fucking. Sure, I was too, but I wasn't posing as some closeted football player. I was just myself. But Tanner was lying.

I curl into a ball on my couch, and just as my body begins to relax, I hear my mom's voice loud and clear.

Alone on Christmas, she says to me. *What kind of loser are you? How many years is this in a row? Too many. I bet Joe's happier than you right now, living it up with the boyfriend that he actually feels comfortable being gay with.*

"Shut up," I say out loud.

Almost forty, she says. *And you don't have a family. Or that many friends, let's be honest. And you're wasting your life cooking for an NFO player all while some other more competent managers take charge over your shitty diner.*

"Mom, please just shut up," I say. "Leave me alone."

And don't even get me started on Tanner, she says. *You prize yourself on men coming out to you. Have you ever thought it's 'cause you're easy?*

"Please, Mom, just—"

Have you ever thought that men find someone else to go steady with because you're an easy lay? They use you as a steppingstone into better relationships and better men? That your whole purpose is to be used and discarded? That you'll never be enough to be in a true, lasting relationship? That you're not enough to be loved?

"Shut up!" I scream. I throw the pillows from the couch across the room. "Shut up, shut up, shut up!" I bang my fists into the couch and curl into a ball, trying unsuccessfully to hold back my tears.

My mom's voice persists, repeating these messages over and over again.

Maybe I could drown myself in the ocean. If I went far enough, the tide would take me out. Or I could find that crystal meth guy again on the hookup app. Because sex isn't enough to stop the thoughts at this point. I need something much, much stronger.

I pull out my phone, my tears almost blinding me. I'm about to open the app, but then I hear my mom's voice reminding me how ugly and unlovable I am. Crystal meth guy and his friends wouldn't want me over again. Not after I left having not joined their little orgy. They probably think I'm a freak or something.

I press my face into the couch, wishing I could just suffocate and die.

And then there's a knock at my door.

Thinking it's Tanner, I cover my ears and close my eyes, hoping that if I can't hear or see him, he'll go away.

But the knocking persists.

"Go away!" I shout.

"Jimmy?" Yousef says through the door. "Are you alright?"

Yousef. I wipe my eyes and get to my feet, not knowing which powers of the universe are giving me the strength to do this. But I don't want to leave Yousef hanging again, not like I did this morning. He's too nice.

I open the door to find my wiry Muslim, Persian friend smiling at me.

But then his smile falters.

"My friend," he says. "Are you alright?"

And, without thinking, I extend my arms like a childhood who's upset but has no words to say—because, let's be honest, that's exactly who I am right now.

Yousef sets down his rice dish on a nearby chair and wraps his arms around me. I sink us to the floor, unable to keep myself standing. And we sit there in my doorway, my face buried in his chest that smells like cumin and saffron, and I let myself be a little weeping kid again. Because Lord knows with my mother I never really had that opportunity.

I'm not sure how long we sit there. Seconds, minutes. Maybe even an hour if my tears put me into a dehydrated delirium. But it doesn't matter. Because I feel so safe in the arms of a friend who I know deeply cares about me. Finally, I pull away and wipe my eyes.

"Care to take a walk with me?" he asks.

"On the beach?" I ask.

He nods. "Doesn't it sound wonderful? A Christmas day walk by the water?"

I laugh at his goofy smile. It's like this man radiates joy.

"I think I'd like that," I say.

"Let's get you some water first," he says, standing up and brushing himself off. He picks up his rice dish. "And put this dish inside. Don't want the seagulls getting to it."

We walk into my bungalow. Yousef sets down his rice dish—Tahchin if I remember correctly—and then fills me up a glass of water. He hands it to me, and I gulp it down greedily.

"To replenish your fluids," he says, filling me up another glass. "You lost a lot in your tears."

"Damn right," I say after I clear my throat. I drink the rest of the water and feel substantially better. I'm reminded that I've done something similar with Tanner: comforted him in his tears, asked him to drink water to feel better. It's nice to have someone return this service.

Yousef claps his hand and rubs them together. "Now, our walk!"

Since it's Christmas, the beach is remarkably empty, which is nice considering how much I don't want to be around people. It's probably no more than sixty degrees, so it feels perfect wearing an over-sized hoody and old gym shorts.

"You are heartbroken?" he asks.

I chuckle. "How could you tell?"

He gestures to my whole outfit and red eyes. "This is usually what heartbreak does to you."

"That it does," I say.

"And it's Tanner, isn't it?"

I look up at him, surprised. "How did you—" But then guilt floods my chest as I realize that I'm probably outing him.

"I figured he was gay," Yousef says. "That's how a lot of those closeted, shameful men hold themselves. Quiet. Verbose at times, but most of the time quiet."

I nod. I fucking love it when Tanner's verbose.

"But you cracked his shell?"

"That I did," I say. Then I remember all that I imagined my mom saying about men like Joe using me for this and grimace.

"It's really cool to hold someone's trust like that," he says.

His words penetrate me like the sun shining through the clouds on a gloomy day.

"What do you mean?" I ask.

"For someone to come out to you—it requires a lot of trust. They need to feel safe with you."

I nod. "I guess."

He stops and looks at me. "You don't think so."

The waves lap against my ankles. "Well, if they did trust me, wouldn't at least one of them stick around?"

Yousef nods. "You have that ex, no? The one who really broke your heart?"

"Joe?" I ask. Though I hate to admit that he 'really' broke my heart. He just broke my heart. I don't want to give him *that* much power.

"Yes, that one. The one that was cheating on you and left you for him. The one who was closeted."

"Yep," I say with a sigh. And we continue walking.

"You don't see yourself as admirable for holding his trust enough for him to come out to you? Coming out is a scary thing, you know. Not a lot of people in this world get that opportunity. I would know."

"You're right," I say. "But—"

"So for him to see you that way—Jimmy, that's something really beautiful. Even if he did leave you. You ought to celebrate the good you have done. Not how things may have ended poorly."

I rub my eyes. "But then why did he run away?"

He stops again and looks at me squarely. "Do you really think that people need to fall in love with you to appreciate you?"

I scoff as my chest tightens. "No, that's ridiculous."

"That's what it sounds like."

I stand there, my whole body heating up, properly chastised. "I just want people to respect me the same way that I respect them."

"So tell me," Yousef says. "How do you think Tanner disrespected you so much that you break down in my arms?"

I fold my arms. "He did exactly what Joe did."

He crosses his arms behind his back. "Can you be specific?"

"I found out that he was hooking up with someone else," I say. "Just after he asked us to be boyfriends. After he told me he loved me."

A deep V forms on Yousef's face. "That is very strange."

"See?" I say. "And this is why I say he's like Joe. He was just using me as a steppingstone. He was coming out to me and then moving on to bigger and better things."

"But if he was using you as a steppingstone, why would he ask you to be in a relationship? Wouldn't he ask this other guy to be in a relationship if you were just a steppingstone?"

I furrow my brow, and I get an uneasy feeling in my stomach. "Well, I guess, but—"

"I don't think it's Tanner that using you as a steppingstone," he says. "I think it's you that sees yourself as a steppingstone."

"I beg your pardon?"

He sighs, digging one of his feet deep into the wet sand. "You are the one who thinks you are lesser, not bigger and better. That you are not worth it to be in a relationship. You picked up this message somewhere, and you went with it."

I think back to my mom hitting me over and over again with this message: in short, that I was never good enough for anything, let alone love.

"And if I'd guess, that's probably why you have so much sex. Because you think that's all you'll be good for."

"Woah, hey," I say, my chest tight, regretting for a moment opening up to him these past few months about my sexual escapades. But then I pause and think about it for a moment. "That's kinda right, actually."

"I know it is," he says. "So when this man Tanner says that he wants to be in a relationship, you look for a way to sabotage it. And you found one, it looks like—him supposedly cheating on you. So then you could say it was his fault and that it was over before it happened. And the message you tell yourself that you aren't worthy of love bears repeating."

"Okay," I say. "But that ignores the fact that I did find evidence that he was sleeping with someone else. Very clear evidence."

Yousef sucks on his lip and shakes his head. "Did he try to explain himself to you? Did you let him?"

I think back to the conversation, how I talked over every one of his attempts to explain the situation. And my face heats up with shame.

I shake my head.

"This makes sense," he says, nodding. "By focusing on what he did and not letting him redeem himself, you forced the relationship to end instead of letting it take its course. All because you were too afraid that the message you've told yourself your whole life—that you aren't worthy of love—would be proved true over the course of the relationship. So you ended it before that could happen!" He walks over to me and clasps my shoulder. "You, my friend, are a Grade A self-saboteur!"

I remove his hand from shoulder as he laughs, grimacing, but unable to hold back a smile. Because he's completely right. And honestly, I'm slightly relieved. If I'm partly to blame for this whole thing between me and Tanner, then that means I can do something to fix it. And I just really like Yousef. If there's anyone I want chastising me, it's him.

We both stare into the setting sun for a minute, mesmerized by the waves.

"Okay," I say, conceding. "So what now?"

He sighs and folds his arms. "You can keep doing what you've always done," he says. "Which, as we like to say in recovery, is insanity."

"Right," I say, nodding. "I don't think I wanna do that."

"Or," he says with the tilt of his head. "You could put yourself in a vulnerable position. You could go back to Tanner. Talk to him. See what's going on. And let the relationship play its course without you intervening to get what you're always used to: sex and a breakup. This time, maybe you could let the relationship succeed on its own terms."

I fold my arms, wincing at the uncomfortable feeling in my chest. "Or I could do the less scary thing and just keep fucking people until the day I die."

"But I don't think that's what you want," Yousef says. "At least not anymore."

I nod as a particularly big wave crashes against my shins. Going back to Tanner is scary. It means that I'm putting myself out there for rejection or heartbreak again, but this time not on my terms. I don't want to give up this control, but I think it's my only option if I want to come out a better person from this. And this means I can't just talk over Tanner. I have to listen to him. Which, I think, will be easier due to all the meditation I've been doing. I can handle silence and letting go of my racing thoughts a little easier now, so I should be able to be patient during conversation.

"Alright," I say. "I'll talk to him."

"Great," Yousef says, patting me on the back. "Oh, I ran into Tanner earlier when I dropped off his Tahchin. He was telling me you made us cookies?"

I widen my eyes. "I completely forgot! They're in Tanner's kitchen. I can give them to you. Let's head back."

"Great," Yousef says as we turn. "I love a good sugar cookie."

Chapter 30

Tanner Bash

"Let it out," Lupita says, rubbing my arm. "Just let it out."

We're the only patrons sitting at a table next to the Zhao shack. Our containers of Zhao cream are empty, and I've finished telling Lupita everything.

I don't know how this happened, but the second I opened my mouth about Chris, all of it came out like vomit. So many emotions came with it, too. I felt ashamed, then relieved, then angry, then so, so afraid that Lupita would judge or blame me for what happened.

But she's just listened and validated me the entire time.

So now that I'm finished, I'm letting out some tears of relief. Because, goddamn, I am so relieved.

"Tanner," she says, squeezing my wrist. She's remarkably strong for a woman literally half my size.

"This is not your fault," she says. "What Chris has been doing to you is awful. It is not okay. But it is not your doing."

"But I've done nothing to stop it. And—" I grimace and get closer to her. "I've climaxed every time. I've enjoyed it. That's not good."

She squeezes my wrist harder. "You can't control your bodily functions, Tanner," she says. "And besides, the brain does funny things when trying to protect you. It makes it seem better than it is so you can survive it, but then you start to feel guilty about it. Let me say it again: you are not at fault here. And

you are so brave for saying it out loud. You would be surprised how few people d
o."

I thank her with a pained smile. "But I don't know what do now," I say. "It's not like I can just tell him to stop. He has that video of me."

She sits back in her seat, disgust all over her face. "I know," she says. "That bastard."

I laugh. "Maybe I should send you to beat him up."

"I would!" she says with a straight face. "I'll kick his ass."

I exhale sharply through my nose. "I wish that would solve it."

"Me too. What about the authorities?"

"I don't know," I say, shaking my head.

"That's the only option."

"But we're in the NFO. Other players have gotten by doing much worse to their wives."

She grimaces. "Ay, Dios," she says.

"I know."

We both sit there in silence for a while, watching the ocean. Nearby, the Zhao's close up their shack for the night and thank us.

Lupita waves to them, then grabs my wrist again. "Look," she says. "I don't know how to handle this at the moment. But I want to do what you're comfortable with. This is happening to you. It's your body. So I can think of ways to resolve this, but at the end of the day, it's your decision how we do it. Whether it's authorities or not."

I put my hand on hers and squeeze it. "Thank you," I say. "Honestly, saying it out loud has been relieving enough."

She points a finger at me. "But you do not keep letting this happen," she says. "Respect yourself by protecting yourself. This has to end somehow."

I nod.

"You promise me? You deserve to be safe, Tanner."

I blush and nod again. "I promise." I don't think anyone, not even my parents, has expressed this much concern for me. Out of anyone I could have told this to first, it had to be Lupita.

"But I need some time to think about what to do," I say.

"I understand," she says with a nod. "You call me if you need me, okay?"

I bite my lip, feeling my eyes sting. I just can't believe someone I almost chewed out for idolatry now loves me this much. And I truthfully love her back.

"I will," I say.

We wrap up our conversation, and I head home. I feel weird right now, but it's a good kind of weird. Even though I'm benched and Jimmy's no longer talking to me, it feels like an enormous weight's been taken off my shoulders. I finally came clean about what Chris has been doing to me. And Lupita affirmed to me that it's sexual assault—in other words, that I'm not to blame, even if Chris did get me to cum. If I didn't have her, I don't know how I would have survived this. I probably would have just kept it going until I pissed off Chris enough for him to post the video anyways.

Which leaves the only thing left to be taken care of. I'm still under Chris's thumb as long as he has that fucking video, and I won't have much peace until I know it's gone. But there's no way to guarantee that.

I pull into my garage nearly biting my fingernails off. Sure, it was nice to get all that happened off my chest, but I think the hardest part has yet to come. Somehow, I gotta stop this thing with Chris and prevent that video from getting out. Fuck. I need something to eat.

I lazily walk into my kitchen, exhausted from my conversation with Lupita. With all the emotions that went through my body from such a confession, it feels like I've played a full NFO game.

I open the fridge and stare into it lazily. Jimmy's food is good, but I don't even have the energy to put something in the microwave. I glance over at the table and see the rice dish that Yousef brought over yesterday for Christmas. That'll do.

I take some leftover caramel brown butter cookies from a container, grab a plate, and sit down next to the rice dish, whose name, for the life of me, I cannot recall. I cut some up and put it on my plate, the chicken and fruit spilling all over the place. And it is divine. I lift up a forkful to my mouth, and the second I taste it, my entire body curls in pleasure.

"Holy hell this is good," I say. I keep eating, surprised how fast I'm scarfing it down. When I'm finished, I take a big bite out of the cookie, and caramel oozes down my chin. Damn, Jimmy knows how to make a cookie. And Yousef really knows how to make a rice cake. I'm kicking myself that I've never had this before. After I finish my cookie, I get another big slice of the rice dish and gulp that down quickly. When I'm done, I pause and gawk at my empty plate. I just ate a shit ton of food, and it wasn't difficult at all. I guess being honest about my problems helps with my appetite.

There's a knock on my back door, and I nearly jump out of my chair. I look up to see Jimmy at the back window.

"Sorry," he mouths, and it takes me a minute to consider what he's sorry for. For walking out on me? For not letting me explain myself? But then I realize he's just apologizing for startling me.

Truth is, I don't know what to feel about Jimmy. I don't know if I should be angry with him, sad about us, or happy that he's here. It's all a jumbled mess. I get that he was angry, and I only made it worse by not what to say about Chris. I am sad that he walked off, but I see where he was coming from. I never really talked to Lupita about my relationship with Jimmy. I did come out to her, but I didn't say a word about him. And I honestly don't know how this conversation's gonna go. I mean, I wasn't really even able to process I was being sexually assaulted until I confided in Lupita. So, if he's still angry about all that happened, at least I'll be able to explain myself fully.

He puts his hand on the doorknob and cracks the door open just enough to stick his head inside. "Hey," he says.

"Hi," I say, leaning back in my chair. My belly's bulging from all the food, and I feel satisfied.

"Can you talk?" he asks.

I shift in my seat. "Sure," I say, gesturing to a chair.

He nods and shyly lets himself in. He shuts the door behind him and sits in the chair across from me. He glances at the rice dish that Yousef brought over and smirks.

"I see Yousef brought you one as well," he says.

I smile slightly. "Yeah," I say, looking at the dish, savoring the taste in my mouth. I look back at Jimmy. "He really liked your cookies too."

"S'what he told me," he says. "He came by for a visit yesterday."

I nod.

"I can tell you liked the cookies, too." He gestures to his own chin. "Because you got a little something."

"Oh," I say, standing up, embarrassed. I walk to my sink and grab a paper towel to wash it off. Meanwhile, Jimmy's swiveled himself halfway in the chair to face me.

"Look," he says. "I'm sorry for running out on you the other night." He sighs then looks up at me, I swear, with puppy dog eyes. That melts my heart. "I'm just gonna rip the bandage off. I wanna talk about what happened."

Suddenly, my chest gets tight. I remember him storming into my room, accusing me of cheating on him. And, I mean, I can definitely see where he was coming from. I had just asked him to be my boyfriend and just told him I loved him. It would be disorienting to find texts like that. But after opening up to Lupita, I'm angry that I didn't get a chance to say my two cents.

"Alright," I manage to say.

"What were those texts about?" he asks.

I take a deep breath, then exhale through my nose. "It's, uh..."

I find myself clamming up. Telling Lupita, in a way, was easier. She's a harmless older woman who's half my size. And most importantly, I know she loves and cares about me. But Jimmy? We've had an on-again off-again friendship-relationship for months now. And we've had sex twice. Our feelings for each other are probably all complicated. I'm afraid that if I share this, and he reacts poorly, I won't be able to handle it. I feel like I'll just end up taking on his hurt and blaming myself again.

"It's just—" Jimmy pauses and takes a breath. "Sorry. I'm trying not to jump the gun here and talk over you. You just gotta understand where I'm coming from. We've had such a strong connection, and I never felt closer to you on Christmas Eve. But then to see so clearly that you were fucking someone else..."

"I know," I say. "You musta been devastated."

"I was," he says with a nod. "But I was stupid to walk out without at least an explanation. So now I'm here. And I'm willing to listen."

"Okay," I say, pressing my lips together. I fold my arms and lean against the counter, sighing. I reach out and fumble with the container carrying the cookies. I open it up and stare down at the contents. I decide to pull out a sugar cookie and nibble on it. And Christ that's good.

Jimmy sits there patiently. In all honesty, I have my thoughts together. But I'm just trying to gather the courage to say them out loud.

"Of course, you don't have to do this," Jimmy says, sitting up in his chair. "If you'd rather not explain yourself, that's fine. We can just go on as friends. I can finish out being your personal chef, and we can go our separate ways."

There's a sharp tightening in my chest. I don't want Jimmy to leave. I like him. And I think I still love him.

His words are followed by more silence.

So he stands up.

"I don't want to keep you," he says. "I'll be back in a bit to start cooking some of your next meals." He walks to the door and puts his hand on the doorknob, and just as he's opening it up—as a fire of shame and fear burns in my chest—I decide to say it.

"I was being sexually assaulted," I say.

He freezes and glares at me. "You were what?"

I falter, feeling my entire body heat up. My throat gets tight, and I feel myself get dizzy.

Jimmy shuts the door, and his face is deadly serious.

Tears well in my eyes, and my breath gets short. I have to remind myself what Lupita said: that I am not at fault. That I'm a victim, not a perpetrator. But I'm afraid that Jimmy will get even angrier with me, that he'll say a man as big as me can't be sexually assaulted. That I'm making up lies just so I can get away with sleeping with someone else.

Jimmy slowly walks around the kitchen counter and stands right in front of me. I look down at the container of cookies, tears leaking out of my eyes. He reaches out, about to put his hand on mine. But then he hesitates and sets it right next to it. Which is good. Because I don't know if I want touch right now.

"Tanner," he says, low and serious. "I—" His voice falters.

I look up, afraid he'll yell at me just like my parents did even though I always tried to do the right thing.

But he doesn't. His lips quiver, and he looks me in the eyes. His bearded face and body are tensed in such a way that makes me think he could pick up a kitchen chair and tear it in half.

"I am so fucking sorry," he says. "Goddamnit, I was so fucking stupid."

Cool relief floods my hot body. He's not angry with me.

"Jimmy, it's ok—"

"No, it's—" He tenses his hands, then lowers them to his sides. "I'm trying to do better about talking over you and avoiding silence," he says.

"I wanted to say that it's okay," I say. "I understand your reaction."

He shakes his head and looks at me. "But I don't think it's okay. I steamrolled you all because I was afraid you would be the first one to reject me. I wanted to do it first. But it turns out I had the entire situation misunderstood." He shakes his head again, his eyes on the stove. "You were being fucking violated."

I nod, but my heart is racing now that we're really talking. "His name is Chris," I say, my voice slightly wobbly. Lupita said I don't need to always talk about it but that I should share with others when I feel it's necessary. And this feels necessary.

"I saw his name on your phone," Jimmy says. "Is he on your team?"

I nod. "He joined the team a couple years back. When we both lingered in the locker rooms after a practice, that's when we fooled around for the first time. And we did for a while after that. It was consensual then. Eventually, I got tired of it happening, but I didn't do much to end it. Until one day, I put my foot down."

"Good for you," Jimmy says, leaning against the stove with his arms crossed. It's nerve-wracking telling him this story, but in all honesty, I'm so glad he's here. He's like being covered with a big, warm blanket on a cold day.

"But that's when things started getting bad. Turns out, during one of the times we hooked up, he filmed us."

Jimmy scoffs. "That fucking creep."

"And in the video, you can clearly see me and my heart tattoos, but you can't see him."

Jimmy lowers his arms. "No."

I nod, knowing exactly what he's thinking. "Yep. So he blackmailed me. Saying that if I didn't do what he wanted, he'd leak the video."

Jimmy's jaw goes rigid, and he turns around to put his hands on the stove, his wide shoulders tense. "And so you did what he said."

I sighed. "I did what he said. And I have been for months."

Jimmy stares at the wall, and his eyes gloss over. Suddenly, I start to panic again. Maybe he's piecing together in his head how crazy it is that a fucking center in the NFO is getting sexually assaulted. Maybe he thinks I'm lying. But when he turns to me, there is such a soft tenderness in his eyes that all doubts are dashed from me. He extends his hand to mine on the counter, then pauses.

"Can I—" He clears his throat. "I've never been violated like that, but I know what it can do to a person. So can I touch you?"

I look down at his hand, and I don't know why, but it feels like the distance between us is greater than a thousand miles. But I nod, because after talking, I do think I want him to touch me.

His fingers touch the top of my hand, and I flinch. He pulls away.

"Sorry," he says.

"No, it's—" I sigh. "It's fine. Please."

He puts his hand back on mine, and I try to keep my breath steady. I don't know what it is. Back when things first started happening with Chris, I was mad horny. I wanted Jimmy to fuck me like crazy. But now any sort of touch feels like a violation. Which makes no sense. I opened up about all that happened. It should be the other way around. I should have been afraid then but horny now.

"Hey," Jimmy says. And that's when I realize that my face is wet from my own tears.

I look away.

Jimmy gets closer and raises his hand, but then he hesitates and lowers it.

"Tanner," he says. "I... I've said it so many times before. But I want to say it again: I want to be here for you. I'm so honored that you decided to tell me the truth. I know how hard it can be. And..."

I look up at him as his voice falters. "I really like you. I don't think I've ever felt this way about anyone before. Not even Joe. Because with Joe, there were red flags along the way. But with you—I feel like we've been growing together in our own ways. And that feels really healthy. But I want to give you space, especially after all that you went through."

I let out a shaky breath. "And still going through."

Jimmy widens his eyes. "What?"

"All I've done is admitted it to my Al-Anon sponsor, Lupita, and you. Chris could still text me right now and expect something from me."

Jimmy squeezes my hand, and I let him keep it there.

"Tanner, you—" he shakes his head. "You gotta do something."

I pull my hand away from his, and I have to look away so I don't see the hurt on his face.

"It's not that simple, alright? I can't just tell him 'no', or else there'll be a sex tape of me all over the internet."

"So you're just gonna let him keep hurting you like this?"

I groan and drop my face into my hands. "I don't know, okay? I don't fucking know."

Both of us sit there in silence, the words we've thrown at each other feeling no different than shattered plates thrown across the kitchen.

He rubs the bridge of his nose, then looks at me, his eyes red. "I know you don't know. But can you, at the very least, let me be there with you?"

I fold my arms. "What do you mean?"

"So often, you've pushed me away just when things have gotten hard. I'm asking that you don't do that now."

I look down at the container of cookies we made and suck on my lips.

"I know this is the hardest it's ever been," he says. "And I meant every word that I said when I told you I still liked you. But it aches to not have you let me in.

I want to be there for you. Hopefully as a partner, but I'll take you in any way I can get right now. But if you push me away, I don't know if I can go through all this again."

His words hang heavy in the air, and I take the time to pull each one and hold it in my mind. I know it's not good to go through this alone, and it's clear that Jimmy won't judge me for what's happened. And I really do miss being so close to him. Even though I don't know what to do about Chris—let alone know what I want romantically—I think it would be good for me to be vulnerable with him.

"Alright," I say. "I'll do my best to keep you close."

Jimmy sighs, and his lips form a smile. "Thank you," he says.

"I can't make any promises about us," I say.

"Understood," Jimmy says.

We both sit there for a minute, but the silence this time feels whole, like we've reached the end of some long video game or orchestral piece and everything feels complete.

"Well," Jimmy says. "I should probably get your meals for the day started."

I wipe my nose and the last of the tears from my face. "And I should probably get going to practice," I say. Then I sigh. "Even though I'm technically on the bench now."

"You are?" Jimmy asks.

"Long story," I say. "But it has to do with my tendency to not eat."

"Ah," Jimmy says with a nod. "Well I'm making more of that breakfast casserole you always like and burgers for dinner. Maybe that'll make it easier."

I can practically feel my stomach growl. "Sounds delicious," I say. "Now that I've opened up about what's going on, it's a little bit easier to eat."

Jimmy puts on the biggest, genuine smile ever. "That's wonderful," he says, and I remember why I've fallen for the man. He's kind, paternal, and so god-damn handsome.

I give him a lukewarm smile and then turn to head to my room. I gotta gather my things and head out. But if I leave now, I feel like something would be undone. And there's only one thing I think to do to satisfy this feeling.

My heart racing, I turn around and make my way behind the stove where Jimmy's just putting on that ridiculously cute apron. He's tying a knot behind his back.

I make my way to him.

He looks at me funny. "What's—"

And that's when I wrap my arms around him. I press my nose into his shoulder, taking in the scent of my laundry detergent and his natural odor. When he wraps his arms around me, I can already feel my heartrate slowing.

"Thank you for being so kind," I say. "And forgiving. I really needed it."

After we squeeze each other, we pull away from each other, and he puts a hand on my shoulder.

"Anytime," he says with more warmth than the sun. "I'm here for you."

I'm tempted to lean down and kiss his bearded, handsome face, but now I feel like the conversation ended at the perfect moment. And I want to keep it there.

"Be back later," I say. "Can't wait to eat the sliders."

"They'll be waiting for you," he says.

And as I grab my things and walk out the door, I'm consoled by the fact that he'll be waiting for me, too.

Chapter 31

Jimmy Dillon

IN THE EARLY MORNING after my workout, I cross the pool area over to Tanner's to cook for the day, and I'm feeling conflicted. Last night, I got a full eight hours of sleep, and I can't remember the last time that's happened. Physically, I feel wonderful, and I know a lot of that is due to my meditation practice calming my mind. I've even been able to spend some time with Yousef and his polycule for their post-meditation potlucks, which has been some good socializing. And to think I almost did crystal meth. Who knows what path I woulda went down with that.

But on the other hand, I feel horrible for Tanner. A few days ago, he confessed to me that he's being blackmailed and repeatedly sexually assaulted. And there's nothing either of us can do. I've racked my brain as to how to get him out of this, but I've got nothing. And the few times I've seen him, he's looked morose as ever, and it's only getting worse. I don't know what to do.

When I open the door to the kitchen, I'm startled to see Tanner sitting at the kitchen table in his robe. He's playing on his Nintendo Switch, but he's got various books scattered around him—Al-Anon literature, by the looks of it—and an open journal.

"Hey, big guy," I say, shutting the door.

He perks up, adjusting himself in his seat. I could say that I forgot how much he likes me calling him that, but then I'd be lying. I like making him feel good any chance I can get.

"Hey," he says flatly. He's wearing an oversized hoodie, and his stubble is almost the length of a full beard, which is unlike him.

I make my way around the counter to start some coffee, and that's when I realize Tanner already got some going. I grab a mug and pour some for myself.

"Trouble sleeping?" I ask.

He nods, mashing a button on his switch.

I take a look at him and frown at his disheveled appearance. From what I know, sexual assault affects us all in different ways. Tanner's said he'll be open with me but that he wants to resolve the situation at his own pace. I'm willing to respect that, but my concern for him is only growing.

He groans and sets down the Switch as I'm pulling food out for the day. He leans his head back in the chair, and at this angle, I can see just how deep the bags under his eyes are.

"You good?" I ask, setting some chicken on the counter.

He sighs. "It happened against yesterday."

"Oh fuck," I say just as I'm about to take a sip of my coffee. "Christ, Tanner. He did it again?"

He folds his arms and looks out the back door. He just nods.

"Fuck," I say, my hands splayed out on the counter. Of course. He headed to practice right after we talked. And that's where his fucking perpetrator was.

"I wish I had fucking realized that you were going to see him later that day."

"There's nothing you could have done," he says. "Or that I could have done."

You could have said 'no', I want to say. But then there's the fucking video. Fuck. I wish I was there so I could beat the living shit out of this man. And out of all people, he chooses to do this to Tanner? No one deserves to be assaulted like this, but the sweet man who just gets excited about playing video games and playing football? Sure, he's not perfect, but he's got the genuine nature that I just adore.

"I—I know," I say with a sigh. "Fuck, Tanner."

He doesn't say a word and just keeps looking outside. I know he doesn't want me to push it, and I don't want to compromise the fragile relationship we've just been able to piece back together. But God. I want to protect this man that I love.

This man that I love.

Fuck. Well, I guess I know now that I definitely still love the man.

I sigh. "You got your game later, right?"

He nods. "This evening," he says. "But I'm benched, so it doesn't matter."

I gawk at him. "You're benched?"

He glares at me. "Yeah, because I'm a fucking loser who can't keep his weight in the ideal range."

I fold my arms. "Hey, man. I'm just trying to help."

He wipes his greasy face. "I know. I'm sorry."

We both sit in silence for a minute. If I could, I would wrap my arms around Tanner, snap my fingers, and solve this problem for him. But I can't. And I know if he could fix it, he would, too.

"But ever since I started opening up about what's happened to me," Tanner says. "It's been easier to eat, so I'll be gaining some of that weight back, which is good."

"That is good," I say.

He nods. "I've also been talking with my agent. He's going to try and convince Coach to get me off the bench for our first playoff game next week by sharing with him my progress."

"Oh, that'd be great," I say. "Finger's crossed."

"Thanks," he says.

I want to keep talking, but I also don't want to talk about Chris or him being benched since those are sore subjects. Maybe there's something else we can do instead.

"What if—" I clear my throat. "What if, while we ate breakfast, we played some games together? For old time's sake?"

He looks over at me, his face hardened.

"Just an offer," I say, my hands raised in defense.

He looks back out the window, then sighs. "I think that would be wonderful, actually." And my chest lights up at him thinking spending time with me would be wonderful.

"Great," I say, taking out a glass dish filled with eggs, sausage, bacon, potatoes, and a whole host of vegetables. "I'll plop this in the oven. Has to be in there for about an hour. I have my meditation session today, and I'll be back to take it out. And we can play then?"

"Sounds good," he says, standing up. He seems a little bit happier than before. "I'll shower while you're gone."

"Great," I say. I put the casserole in the oven, then walk around the counter and stop next to him just before walking out. I pat him on the shoulder. "You're a good man, Tanner Bash."

He lets out a small huff, as if in disbelief. "Thanks," he says.

I wish I could wrap my arms around him again and scream into his ears that he's beautiful and worthy and wonderful. But I don't even think that would fix this. I don't even think going and throwing that fucking Chris guy in jail would solve all this. So I have to focus on what I can control, which is meditating and putting my own mind at ease.

I make my way down to the beach where my meditation buddies are gathering. Yousef is talking to somebody I've never seen before.

"Oh, Jimmy," he says, greeting me. "This is my friend Derek."

"Howdy," he says, reaching out and shaking my hand. I greet him back.

"He's a friend of mine from DC," Yousef says.

"This man provided the technology that made our lives a lot easier," Derek says. "With his cyber security software I was finally able to sleep at night."

Yousef laughs. "He'll be joining us for today."

"Great," I say as I find my place in the circle.

After some small talk, Yousef pulls out her guitar and Maria her singing bowl. She starts the session by ringing the bowl, then rotating the mallet slowly around it. Once that's going, Yousef plays a riff that helps my body relax and my mind go into a meditative state.

When I close my eyes, all I can picture is Tanner. I see his sad face, his tense body. Occasionally, I get glimpses of what that man might be doing to him, and I tighten up. I try to shun the images from my mind. But they keep coming back, often times stronger than they first started.

But that's when I remember one tip Yousef gave me for meditation. You don't fight the thoughts. You acknowledge them, then recognize them for what they are. Then—this is the weird part—he says to thank my brain for giving me the thoughts, for doing its job to try and protect me by processing what bothers me. And then, finally, to let these thoughts go—to communicate to myself that stressful, dark thoughts are not necessary for my protection or anyone else's.

And, to my surprise, this works. Eventually, my mind drifts from Tanner to my mom. I hear her harsh words, but this time they feel more distant. And, by applying the same strategy as before, I can let these thoughts go, too. Until all my mind registers are the sounds of the bowl, guitar, and the ocean.

I know my friend Tanner—also the man that I love—is really going through it right now. But it won't do me any good to stress about it right now. I just have to relax and focus on myself. And once my cup is filled, I can share it with others. That, along with letting my rampant thoughts go, has been what I've learned from meditation.

Suddenly, a burst of clarity as bright as the noon summer sun hits me. I open my eyes, worried that with how strong this burst of clarity was I startled other people too. But everyone else is just meditating with their eyes closed. The only one with his eyes open is Yousef, but he's focused on his guitar. So I close my eyes again and focus on what I just realized.

Yousef's friend, Derek, used Yousef's cybersecurity resources in his own company. Which reminded me how he's rich enough to afford such a nice house on the beach in San Diego. He pioneered revolutionary software in the cybersecurity industry, changing the way that companies and individuals protect themselves from hackers and other serious threats. Now, I'm no tech guru, but if he can do what I think he can do, then he may be able to help out with this Chris situation. It's a stretch, but it may be the one thing that Tanner needs to end the molestation once and for all. If I could, I would just ask Yousef now if it's possible, but I don't want to betray Tanner's confidence. I need to present the idea to him, first.

When the meditation's over, we go around the circle and briefly share our insights as we always do. Once it's my turn, I share about how I may just have come up with a solution to a serious problem, and everyone congratulates me on the revelation. After that, I excuse myself, saying I need to take my casserole out of the oven. When, in reality, I want to race and tell Tanner my revelation as fast as possible. I'm hoping—praying—that this gives him the peace he deserves.

Chapter 32

Tanner Bash

MY BACK DOOR SLAMS open, nearly giving me a heart attack. I'm sitting on the carpet in front of my TV playing some Majora's Mask. It's perfect because Jimmy and I need to continue our save file, and I wanted something dark to play to match how I feel.

Jimmy rushes into my family room, his sandaled feet covered in sand. "Sorry," he says, looking down at them. "I needed to talk to you."

"What is it?" I ask, pausing the game and turning to him.

He opens his mouth, then pauses. "I—" he manages to get out. He sits down on the carpet next to me. "Is it okay if I talk about what's going on with you? With Chris?"

My chest tightens, and my stomach gets uneasy, but Jimmy clearly looks like he's got something to say.

I sigh. "It's alright. What is it?"

Jimmy scooches closer to me. "You say that you can't end things with Chris because then he'll post that video."

"Yeah," I say.

"Well, what if we could make sure that that video never meets the public eye?"

I squint at him. "How? Delete the video from Chris's phone? That's near impossible."

"No," Jimmy says with the shake of his head. "We get Yousef's help."

I raise an eyebrow. "Yousef?"

"You know what he does, right?"

"Yeah, I've known him for a while."

"Then you know that with the technology his company has developed, he could probably stop this video from getting leaked. Hell, he might even find a way to delete it entirely."

Blood rushes to my ears, and the Zelda music sounds like it's more distant.

"Think about it. You could tell Chris it's over. He threatens to post the video. You say whatever. Then let's say he posts it. We can get Yousef to wipe the thing from the internet. Hopefully for good. Then you're safe. You don't have to do anything he says anymore."

I stare down at the carpet, my heart racing. "You think that'll work?"

"You know, I'm not entirely sure, but I have my hopes up. I didn't mention any of this to Yousef because I didn't want to tell him your business. But I think if we want to get his help, he has to know the full picture. At the very least that you're being blackmailed. What do you think?"

My stomach curdles. The idea of telling another person about this—especially one I've known for so long—makes me dizzy. But I don't have to tell him I'm being assaulted. I just have to tell him I'm being threatened. And even though I've been shy around Yousef the entire time I've lived here, I don't see a reason why he wouldn't support me with this. Whether I tell him the truth about the assault or not. But this is a lot. I have to process it.

"I need some time to think about this," I say.

"Of course, of course," Jimmy says. "Just know that if this is what you choose, I'll help in any way I can."

"Thanks," I say with a nod. "Wanna get to playing?"

"I do," Jimmy says, laying down on his belly next to me. He grabs the controller. "Where are we at?" "I just got us to the first temple," he says. "So lots of puzzles."

"I like puzzles," he says. "Let's do it."

As he plays, I share random facts about the rooms we're in—how certain speedrunners used a strategy to get past this room in less than a couple seconds. But then other rooms had to be dealt with because they possessed keys that were necessary to reach the final boss. All the while, Jimmy's nodding and listening, asking questions when they're relevant. I don't think I've ever met as good a listener as Jimmy.

When we finally reach the boss room, the music sends me back to my childhood. But it doesn't freeze me in place like other music has. And it's not because there aren't as many bad memories tethered to it. It's because, right now, I feel comfortable and at home with myself here with Jimmy. Before, when we've played, I feel like I kept him at arm's length. I never really let him in. But now there isn't really a part of me that Jimmy doesn't know about. And he's still choosing to be right here with me as I play, listening to my every word. He's just really like that warm blanket. He helps me feel at peace.

And I can't forget the work I've been doing with Lupita in Al-Anon. As I've been attending meetings and opening up to her about my problems, the past has been less heavy and in my face. It feels a lot more distant than it used to feel. So, this growth paired with Jimmy's presence is helping me stay grounded in the present instead of jumping back to the past where my parents and brothers hurt me.

When I defeat the boss, Jimmy congratulates me, and I feel pride swelling in my chest, but it isn't just from the video game. I remember how hard this boss was as a kid. I was always so afraid as little Deku Link to jump out of the flower and fight him. But eventually I learned to defeat him, and look how easy it was to beat him today. I think the same can be said for my problems. For years, every time I was triggered by sound or something else, I was brought back to traumatic moments from my childhood. I thought this would never go away. And today is one of the first times that I haven't been completely swept up in some traumatic episode.

For months, I've thought I would never escape from Chris and his control. But maybe it's just like this boss or my traumatic episodes. Maybe he, too, is something I can overcome. And with Jimmy's little idea, it may be possible.

"I think I wanna talk to Yousef," I say as we make our way back to Clocktown in the game.

He looks up at me. "Are you sure?"

I nod. "It's time I finally end things with Chris."

Jimmy sighs through his nose, then pats me on the knee. "I'm proud of you."

My chest warms. "I'm proud of me, too."

* * *

"So, if I'm understanding you correctly, you're being blackmailed?" Yousef asks. Me, him and Jimmy sit at my kitchen table the day after I decided to go through with Jimmy's idea to get his help.

I nod rigidly. "Yep," I say. "The man's threatening to release a sex tape." For my own privacy, I left out the whole sexual assault bit. Yousef doesn't need to know, and I don't want to talk about it unless I absolutely need to.

"We were wondering if you could scrub it from the internet," Jimmy says. "With all your cybersecurity-technology knowledge."

He strokes his short salt-and-pepper beard. "Is this video online?"

"No," I say. "But it could be released any day now."

Yousef nods. "I can definitely scrub it from the internet and make sure it doesn't pop up again," he says. "But in order for that to happen, it has to be posted."

My stomach flips over itself.

"Do you know when this video could be posted?" he asks.

Jimmy looks at me, then I look down at the table.

Yousef looks between us. "Is something going on? Are you two okay?"

I look up as Jimmy opens his mouth. Then he shuts it and looks at me, so now I have the power to share what's going on. Or not.

So I decide to do it.

"Somebody is threatening they'll release the video if I don't do the sexual acts they request," I say. Luckily, Chris didn't ask for anything at the game yesterday. After almost getting caught in the showers that one time, he's careful when coach is around. But I know he'll get the gall to ask me to do something before a game again sooner or later. That's just who Chris is.

Yousef winces, and, for a brief moment, I'm afraid he'll blame me somehow. But he doesn't.

"Now that's sick," Yousef says.

"Tell me about it," Jimmy says.

And my chest warms up. It's scary to reveal what's been going on, but with each admission, I feel a little less crazy and a little more empowered.

"I really want to help," Yousef says. "Especially now that I know you're not safe."

I nod. "Thank you.""But, like I said, I can't do anything until the video's public. But once it is, you can rest assured that I'll get it taken care of."

"So we just need to get it posted," Jimmy says.

"Or do nothing," Yousef says. "He could never post it."

But I know Chris. I know that he'll keep his promise if I reject him. I just feel it.

I want this to end, and I want it to end now. There's only one way this can happen: I have to confront Chris and reject him. This will require me to be braver than ever, but I know it's something I can do now.

"I know what we can do," I say.

Both of them look at me.

"We've made it to the playoffs," I say. "And our first game is next week against the Portland Tigers."

Jimmy widens his eyes. "You're not thinking of..."

"Yes," I say with a nod.

"What are you thinking?" Yousef asks.

"Chris—the man sexually assaulting me—is going to force me to do something sexual by then," I say. "Probably at the hotel. That's when I can reject him. After that, he'll be sure to post the video. Then we can scrub it and be done with the whole thing."

"But Tanner," Jimmy says, turning to fully face me. "You don't need to see him again. You can just send him a text and reject him that way. It'll have the same effect. And that way, you won't have to be around that sleazeball again."

I pause to think about it, but then I shake my head. "I don't want to hide behind my phone. My whole life, everyone else—my parents, brothers, church leaders, and now Chris—have told me what I can and can't do. And because

I've had no self-esteem, I've let them walk all over me. But not anymore. These escapades with Chris started in person. They're going to end in person."

Jimmy opens his mouth to speak.

"This is how I'm doing it," I say. "I won't argue it."

"Will you be safe?" Jimmy asks.

"As safe as I've always been," I say. "It's not like Chris'll hurt me. I'm bigger than him, and me getting injured would surely be noticed by Seals' management."

Jimmy sucks on his lips, looking down at the floor.

"If this is what you want to do," Yousef says. "I'll support you."

"Thanks," I say. Then I look at Jimmy.

He sighs, then finally meets my eyes. "I'll support you in any way," he says. "So if this is the way, I'm behind you."

"Great," I say. "Let's fucking end this."

Chapter 33

Jimmy Dillon

ON DAYS LIKE TODAY, I wish I could just get on the apps and find some guy—or multiple guys—to fuck to keep my mind distracted. Hell, I would be lying if I didn't say that maybe trying some crystal meth could give me the preoccupation I desire.

But I don't want any of that anymore.

I lay on my couch, staring up at the ceiling, my heart pounding and stomach in knots.

Tanner's all the way up in Portland for the Seals first playoff game against the Tigers. He's planning to confront Chris and tell him that all the sexual acts are over. After that, we're anticipating that he'll post the video of Tanner and Chris on the internet. Then, Yousef will be able to work his tech magic and get the video erased.

But all this entails that Tanner talk to Chris first.

I roll over onto my stomach and turn on the TV. Of course, nothing good's on—I've never been a TV guy—so I just shut it off and turn back up to face the ceiling.

What if Chris threatens him with something else? Some other video that he took of Tanner when they were doing stuff? God, that would be awful. What if Tanner gets too scared and gives in to another one of Chris's demands? What if Tanner decides he's no longer interested in me and goes with Chris instead?

I sit up and shake my head. Okay, that last one was ridiculous. Tanner isn't going to choose Chris. Those other things, though—they are a true possibility. But it won't do me any good just to lay here and think about them. I've heard in meetings that it's not good to go down the 'what if' rabbit hole. Hell, this was why I tried to keep so preoccupied with sex. It quieted all these 'what ifs' temporarily. But that's not really an option for me anymore. I like Tanner. And besides, it's not like sex really did a great job of keeping my mind at peace anyways. It just distracted me, and the 'what ifs' always came back stronger after. Plus, I'm still taking the last couple doses of the antibiotic to heal myself of the chlamydia I could have gotten from that guy a while back. I couldn't even have sex if I wanted to.

So I gotta find something else to calm me down. Remembering what peace it brought me on my trip, I go to my travel bag and pull out the small paper bag with the metal bowl inside. I take it out then plop down on my couch. I sit upright with my legs crossed. Then, I ring the bowl and circle the mallet around the rim. As the sound fills the room, I close my eyes and lean back.

As I meditate, my thoughts calm like the snow drifting to the bottom of a snow globe. And when I'm finished, I feel significantly calmer. The 'what ifs' are less rampant in my brain, but I'm still uneasy. I just hope that Tanner's okay. And—I feel selfish to admit—I hope that after all this he chooses me.

Not wanting to sit still, I leave my bungalow and decide to go take a walk on the beach. It's a slightly warmer winter day here, and the sun is out, so a walk along the water would be perfect. That's when, over the hedges separating our yards, I spot Yousef in his kitchen. Maybe he'd like to go on a walk, too.

I make my way to his back door, and he notices me. He opens it before I get a chance to knock.

"Hey, neighbor," he says.

"Hey," I say. "You free for a walk?"

He's about to answer, but then he looks at me with a raised brow. "Today's the day, right?"

I nod.

He exhales through pursed lips. "Guys," he says, turning back into his house. "I'm going on a walk with Jimmy. I'll see you later."

"See ya!" they both say, working in the kitchen.

He steps out and closes the door behind him. "You must be stressed," he says.

"Like you wouldn't believe," I say.

"You must really love him."

I sigh. "Let's just walk," I say with a laugh. "I can deal with my feelings for Tanner after he's dealt with his shit."

But, just for good measure, I pull out my phone as me and Yousef walk down to the beach.

"You're in on my mind and in my prayers," I send. "Good luck."

And then I give it to God because that's all I can do.

Chapter 34

Tanner Bash

As I'm laying in my hotel bed early in the morning, I finally get the text that I've been waiting for.

"Come to room 4H," it says. "I wanna have some fun before the game."

My heart starts to race, but it's not completely from dread this time. It's from anticipation for what I'm about to do. I'm finally about to be fucking brave.

I get up and throw some clothes on. Last night, we arrived in Houston for the playoffs. We don't need to be at the stadium for a few hours, so Chris is using this time to get some fun in. Little does he know I'm using this time to end things between us once and for all.

I creep out of my hotel room in a shirt and some sweats and make my way to the elevator. Luckily, no one's around to see me. I take it up to the fourth floor, and it's conveniently empty, too—well, except for Chris waiting for me in his room.

When I reach his door, I take a deep breath. This is it. This is my moment. I can do this. I think about what Lupita said to me on the phone just before I got on the plane: just say what I need to say, and God will fill in the rest.

God.

I know I've had a complicated relationship with him up to this point, but after everything, I think he still loves me. After all, he's helped me see a way out of this. I just need to trust Him to get through this. But I don't believe he's punishing me anymore. He's giving me an opportunity to grow into the person I was meant to be.

Finally, I knock on the door. Chris opens it quickly and lets me inside.

"Took you long enough," he says. He's shirtless with some gym shorts on. I just stand by his dresser while he sits down on the bed.

"Was thinking we could finally have sex," he says. "Since we got interrupted last time. I'm tired of oral."

Before I can say anything, he reaches down into his suitcase and pulls out a small, leather case. From inside he pulls out a little medicine bottle with blue pills inside. He opens it up and hands me one.

"Here," he says. "Take it. Should wear off before the game."

I don't believe that, but it doesn't matter. Because I won't be taking it. And we won't be having sex.

"No," I say.

He pauses, about to put the bottles back. "What did you say?"

My heart picks up, but I stand taller and repeat myself. "No," I said. "I'm not having sex. In fact, I'm done doing anything."

He sticks his finger into his ear and rubs it. "I'm sorry," he says, taking his finger out. "I think I misheard you."

"You didn't," I say, trying to keep my voice steady. "I'm not doing anything for you anymore."

And, though my legs feel like jelly, I start walking to the door.

"Are you serious?" Chris asks so loud I'm afraid for a minute others might hear us.

"What makes you think I'm not?" I ask, my hand on the door handle.

That's when he looks at me with a glare so strong I'm afraid his eyes will pop out. "You can—you can't."

"I can," I say, my voice a little steadier.

"Why are you even doing this?" he asks. "You know how hard it is for men like us to get action. I was doing you a favor."

"A favor?" I ask, releasing my hold on the door handle. "How is sucking my dick against my will a favor?"

"How else am I supposed to get laid?" he asks.

"I don't know, Chris. Maybe find someone who actually likes you back instead of coercing them."

He clenches his fists, and he looks like he's about to cry. "But I can't just find someone," he says. "I'm a believing Christian. That's not possible for someone like me."

"Chris," I say, rubbing my forehead. Six months ago, I'd never have the courage to say this. But now with my new relationship with God, I have everything I need to speak my mind. "A good Christian doesn't sexually assault people. He stays true to himself." *And in my case, that means accepting that I'm a gay man.*

"Sexual assault?" he asks. "You think this is sexual assault?"

I take a deep breath. Lupita also said that I could be gaslit in this situation. I know I'm right at this point, but I don't think I can take this for long. This is my sign to go.

"Goodbye, Chris. After I retire when this season's over, I hope I never see you again."

I put my hand on the handle and turn it downward.

"The video," he says, his voice shaky. "I'll post that fucking video. You don't want this to happen."

My chest tightens, but I remind myself that this is all part of the plan. I trust Yousef and his abilities. I'll be okay.

"Go ahead," I say, opening the door. "Have a good life, Chris."

And then I shut it gently behind me.

I make my way back to the elevator and don't look back. Once I'm back on my floor, I greet some of the guys who are on their way to get breakfast. I think I'll freshen up and join them. After all, I worked up a true appetite talking to Chris. But in all honesty, finally ending things was like lifting up a cement block on my stomach. I could eat a fucking horse right now.

I make it to my room and shut the door behind me, unable to stop the grin forming on my face. I did it. I fucking did it.

I pull out my phone. I want to share the news with someone. Lupita, definitely. But my heart wants to talk to one man in particular first—the one who's been nothing but supportive. I dial his number, take a deep breath, and wait for him to answer.

Chapter 35

Jimmy Dillon

As Yousef and I walk on the beach behind our houses, my phone starts buzzing. Knowing who it might be, I pull it out and answer without even looking at the name.

"Hello?" I answer, stopping in place.

"I did it," he says.

My face brightens, and Yousef looks confused. 'Tanner', I mouth to him.

"Oh my God," I say, clutching the phone with both hands like a high school girl. "I'm so proud of you, man. That takes fucking guts."

"Thanks," Tanner says. "You have no idea—I just feel so fucking free right now. And so fucking hungry."

I can't help but smile at that. I know how hard it's been for him to eat. To say he's hungry means that he really feels better.

Yousef gestures me to hand the phone to him. I pull it away and put Tanner on speaker.

"Tanner, my friend," Yousef says over the phone.

"Yousef! How are you?"

"Good good," he says. "Did you talk to the asshole?"

"I did," he says.

Yousef nods. "Good for you. So we should expect the video to be posted?"

"That's what he told me," Tanner says, worry in his voice.

"Don't worry," Yousef says. "Once it is, me and my guys will be on it. The video will be down in no time. You have absolutely nothing to worry about."

Tanner sighs, and I feel just as relieved.

"Thank you, Yousef," he says. "So much."

"Anytime," Yousef says.

"I'm so happy for you, man," I say. "You ready for your game today?"

"Oh yeah," he says. "I think I may even start. My agent's confirmed that Coach Larson knows I've been eating better. So maybe he'll let me out there."

"I almost forgot about that," I say. "I really hope you get to play, man. I do."

"Same," he says with a sigh.

There's a moment of silence, and Yousef saunters away, giving Tanner and I the chance for a private conversation. I take the phone off speaker and lift it to my ear.

"Thanks for everything," Tanner says. "I don't know—I don't think I could have done this without you. Getting Yousef's help was your idea."

It feels like fireworks are going off inside my body. "Of course," I say. "But you were the one putting the plan into action. You're the brave one."

He laughs, and I can practically hear his blush through the phone. "Thanks."

"Anytime," I say. I lower my voice. "I'm excited for you to come home."

Fuck. Where did that come from? Tanner and I aren't a thing, and that's definitely a weird thing to say to friends.

"I'm excited to come home too," he says. "And see you."

Now I'm blushing.

"Alright," I say. "Well I don't want to keep you."

"Yeah," he says. "Need to go eat."

"You play like hell today, alright?"

"I will, Jimmy," he says. "You take care."

"Bye," I say. *I love you*, I wished I said. But maybe that can wait until I see him.

Chapter 36

Tanner Bash

"Bash," Coach Larson says, walking into the locker room.

"Yeah, Coach?" I ask, slipping my cleats on. Even though I'm not starting, I need to boot up in case I'm needed.

He walks and stands next to me. "I heard from your agent that you've been eating and gaining some weight."

I perk up. "Yeah, that's true."

He sighs and folds his arms. "How do you feel about starting today?"

My stomach jumps. "Starting? But what about Brian?"

"After meeting with the other coaches this morning, we want someone who has experience playing against the Tigers. I heard from your agent. Since you've been taking care of yourself, I was thinking that could be you. If that's something you can do."

I almost laugh, not believing what I'm hearing. This is too good to be true.

I nod eagerly before Coach Larson can change his mind. "I can do that."

"Alright," he says, tapping on my leg with his clipboard. And I swear I can see a small smile. "I'll see you out there." At first, it kinda felt like Coach Larson was just on my case. But now it feels like he just wants to see me at my best.

As I tie my cleats, I can't wipe the smile off my face. At one point, I thought that God was punishing me for all sorts of things: my homosexuality, my feelings for Jimmy, what I was doing with Chris. But this—it almost feels like a reward.

To start in my potential last game in the NFO? I send up a prayer of gratitude to God.

Carter sits down next to me holding out his hand. We slap our hands together, and he pats me on the back.

"I overheard," he says. "Congrats on starting again. And I'm glad. Brian's great, but we'll need you out there."

"Thanks," I say, caught up in his enthusiasm. "I'm excited."

"You're looking good too, man," he says. "You seem happier. Are you getting laid or something?"

My mind immediately goes to Jimmy, so I blush and look away. And I find it a little ironic how I very much did not get laid today. Chris can go live a life. Fuck him.

"No," I say. "Just things going well in my life."

"Clearly," he says. "Especially now that you're starting."

"Right," I say. "Thanks for being such a good friend, man. I know I haven't always been there for you. But I really appreciate what we have."

Carter extends his hand and helps me to my feet. "Anytime," he says. "Now let's go win this thing."

* * *

Our first play, I drive the Tigers linebacker so far back he falls backward into the turf. By our fourth play, he catches on to my tactics, digging his feet into the ground as I drive him, but it still isn't enough to overpower me.

I'm a fucking monster out here.

But despite my hard work, the Tigers manage to gain possession of the ball, forcing us into defense. No matter. I know I played my hardest. While I'm on the sidelines, I watch with dread as the Tigers manage to score within their first two minutes of them being on offense. This is going to be rough game.

The rest of the game goes by in a blur, but I don't let up in the slightest. Pretty soon, we're at the end of the game, and we're losing 7 – 14. We have possession of the ball. For us to win, we gotta score and then put the game into overtime. That means, even though I'm exhausted, I can't let up in the slightest.

We line up, and I put my hand around the ball to snap it. When my quarterback gives me the go ahead, I shoot the ball to him. Then I drive forward. The Tigers linebacker is pissed, and he growls as he tries to push past me.

But I'm stronger.

I dig my cleats into the turf and start driving forward, putting all my focus and strength into the movement. And then I've done my job. Because our quarterback manages to throw the ball out to our wide receiver, Chris. But the ball slips from his hand and crashes into the turf below just as he's tackled.

The crowd cheers as possession of the ball is given to the Tigers, and some of my fellow players and I lower our heads in acceptance. We'll try our hardest this last minute, but we all know the game is pretty much over.

The Tigers manage to preserve their possession of the ball, so the game ends with the score 7 – 14 in their favor. At least we prevented them from scoring any more.

So, the season is over. And so is my football career.

But as we make our way to the locker rooms, I couldn't be more proud of myself.

This last season was hell. I thought I was going to marry a woman, and then Jimmy comes along as my chef to help me eat when I was too anxious to keep anything in my stomach. He gets me feeling all sorts of ways, and then Chris comes along and blackmails me into doing sexual things with him. I get all guilty, thinking the God I grew up with abandoned me. At this point, I figured life couldn't get any worse.

But I pushed through and came out clean on the other side.

I slowly began to understand that I wasn't eating due to anxiety. Which gradually helped me eat more. Jimmy's delicious food definitely made that easier. And with his encouragement, I started attending Al-Anon, and that's where I met Lupita, the wonderful woman who helped me come to understand a God that is much more loving than the one I grew up with, one that doesn't use suffering as a punishment and loves my gay self. And then, after all this, Jimmy not only comes up with the idea for how to finally fend off Chris, but he gives me the encouragement to do so. Honestly, that's valuable more than anything else.

I sit down with my fellow players as we take off our sweaty gear and change into something more presentable. We're having a little party at the hotel tonight. Win or lose, the NFO knows how to party. But I'm just eager to get home. And I'm eager to see one familiar face in particular.

Carter rests his hand on my shoulder. "Great playing man," he says.

"You too," I say, fist bumping him. "We did our best."

"Damn right."

I glance up to see Chris changing. His head is hung low, and I swear his eyes are puffy from crying. For a minute, I feel bad for the man. Clearly, he's got a lot of shit to deal with. He still thinks that people like us can't find the love we want as football players. I used to think that too. But now I know that's a lie. Kyle Weaver coming out at the end of his career proved it false. Even if I had another year in the NFO, I would still come to the same conclusion: it's okay to be gay.

But I'll let Chris deal with his shit on his own. Now that I know Yousef can protect me from any of his blackmail, I finally feel safe.

I'm not sure if I'll ever report Chris for what he's done. I know that he could do this to someone else, but I don't think I'm ready to attract attention to this or myself in this way. Maybe someday, but not now. I'm just so happy to be out of his control. And I just need to stay that way for a while.

Coach quietly walks into the room. Before he addresses all of us, he taps me on the shoulder and gives me a thumbs up. 'Good job', he mouths. And I feel proud.

He then addresses the whole locker room and gives us some words of encouragement and how we can improve. And that's when I get a little emotional. It's like the curtains are closing on this section of my life. But it's not all sadness I feel. It's mostly excitement. Because I have a full life ahead of me, and I can approach it with a God who loves me and as a person who knows who he is. And thank God I won't be needing to find a woman to start a family.

That night, I get dinner with the team, but I don't bother partying. I'm not in the mood. I retire early and look forward to our flight back to San Diego so

I can get home and have a nice, homecooked meal—one made by the kindest
man I've ever known.

Chapter 37

Jimmy Dillon

WHEN I HEAR GIRISH'S car pull into the driveway with Tanner inside, my stomach bunches up. I frantically stir the pasta a few more times even though I know it's perfect. I've eaten more than I'd care to admit already, and I've been painstakingly thoughtful in putting it together. I want to make sure everything's right for Tanner.

The garage door closes, and he saunters into the kitchen, all his football equipment in hand.

"He's back!" I exclaim. "Sorry to hear about the loss."

He shrugs and sets his stuff down in the laundry room next to my hamper filled with dirty clothes. For a second, I think he might get a bright idea to sniff my clothes again.

Or maybe that's just wishful thinking.

"It's all good," he says, walking back into the kitchen. "I played my hardest."

"I saw," I say, leaning onto the counter. "You were a beast out there."

We both take a minute to take the other in. I swear he's at least two inches taller now—which is saying something. But it's not 'cause he's grown. It's 'cause he's more confident.

"You're looking good," he says.

I blush as I look down at the nice little polo I'm wearing with some dark jeans. "Thanks," I say. "Was gonna say you do too. Your countenance at least."

He scrunches his brow. "Countenance?"

I feel myself begin to sweat under my arms. Great. Not even home for five minutes and I'm already making things awkward between us again. God, I hope I don't scare him off.

"Countenance as in the way you're holding yourself," I say. "You seem happier. You gonna be okay retiring from the NFO?"

He lets out a heavy sigh. "I definitely do feel happier," he says. "And I think I will. It was time. And thanks for all your support with Chris. It means a lot."

"Absolutely any time," I say, stirring the pasta. "I'm so relieved that we came up with a solution that's worked."

"Has Yousef said anything about the video? I know it doesn't matter, but I'm curious if Chris has posted anything."

I prop myself up on the counter and look at him. "You really wanna know?"

He thinks for a moment, then nods.

"From what Yousef told me this morning after our meditation session, Chris did post the video just after the game," he says.

I can see Tanner tense up.

"But he took that video down the second it hit the web, and he reassured me—and told me to tell you if he asked—that no video of you will hit the internet without your permission."

He relaxes slightly, but he still looks uneasy. He even reaches up to one of his eyes.

"Hey," I say, fully turning to him. "We dealt with it. You're safe. You got nothing to worry about." I want to reach out and hug him—to bury myself in between his huge pecs, inhale his natural scent, and kiss him until he feels safe. But I know what sexual assault can do to a person. I wouldn't be surprised if he didn't want any touch for a long time. And I'm not even sure if he wants *my* touch anymore. Best not to assume so I don't get myself hurt.

"I know," he says, wiping his other eye. Christ, he's crying.

"What?" I ask, stepping closer to him. "Did Chris do something else to you? Are you okay?"

"Yeah, I'm good," Tanner says with a laugh. "I'm just so dang happy."

I lean against the counter and smile at him. "What's got you so happy? Sure, I can guess. But I wanna hear you say it."

He blushes. "My life—it's just gotten so beautiful in the last month or so. Lupita was right. God was giving me new opportunities to develop a deeper, more loving relationship with Him. And since I've seized these opportunities, my life has become so much richer."

He looks me in the eyes, fully crying now. "You and Yousef—I've never had friends, or even family, who have gone to such great lengths to help me out. And with Lupita and other Al-Anon friends, I feel like I have people who understand me. And I've even come to see some of my NFO relationships, like my buddy Carter and Coach Larson, in a better light. For so long, I've been profoundly lonely. I thought that the rest of my life would be my wife and kids and nothing else. But after seizing these growth opportunities from God, my life has blossomed into so much more. So that's why I'm happy," he says. He grabs a paper towel to wipe the tears from his face.

I stand there, my chest bursting from happiness. I'm thrilled to see Tanner so happy, and I feel now I'm able to appreciate it. Meditation has helped me slow down my racing thoughts and given me the opportunity to appreciate moments like these. Before, I woulda tried to coax a bigger confession out of Tanner about how much I've helped him so I could feel better about myself. But I'm making peace with my mom, so I no longer let her words get to me so deeply. I can provide myself with my own sense of self-worth. Which makes this confession from Tanner beautiful to hear. I can appreciate exactly where he's coming from without demanding more.

"I'm happy for you, too," I say, feeling the backs of my eyes heat up. Christ. I don't wanna cry too. But I can't stop myself seeing Tanner like this.

"I made you that pasta dish you really like," I say, turning off the burner.

"Oh, you did?" he asks, coming to the stove. "It smells great. What was it called again?"

"Marry-me pasta," I say drily, trying not to laugh.

"Hah!" Tanner says.

"It's high protein," I say with a shrug, but I'm smiling.

He walks to the cabinet and pulls out two large bowls. "Is it ready?"

I nod.

"Well, let's eat."

"Wanna play video games while we do?" I ask.

He groans. "Honestly, there couldn't be anything more perfect."

He and I serve ourselves and make our way to the family room. We get Paper Mario set up, and I eat as I watch Tanner advance through the second chapter of the game. He proceeds to tell me how this chapter is the most universally disliked amongst all players, casual and speedrunners alike.

"Why?" I ask with a laugh.

"Look at these little things," he says, pointing to the little mouse-looking creatures that are following Mario around. "They're a bitch to deal with!"

As he continues through the chapter, I ask about other opinions the community has about the game, and I'm surprised that he doesn't run out of things to say until the chapter's over. Pretty soon, he's onto chapter three. We've both finished two heaping bowls of pasta each, and I'm feeling both the warmth of a full stomach and a full heart.

"Tanner," I say involuntarily.

"Yeah?" he says, sitting down with his third bowl. The game's paused, so I have his full attention.

I sit up, suddenly regretting how much pasta I ate. Because my stomach's twisting all over itself. But as I think over what I'm about to say, I don't think it's the pasta making me nauseous.

I know I said I don't want to ask more of him. But I don't think that's exactly true. Sure, I don't want to try and get him to say things about me to make me feel better or more important. But I want more of this—more genuine connection with a man I find fascinating. And I don't want it to just stop there. I want us to be what we said we would last time we had sex.

"Earlier," I say. "You referred to me as your friend."

He squints as he eats, then he nods. "Oh, when I was talking about you and Yousef?"

I nod.

"Right," he says.

"Did you mean that?"

"Mean what? That you both really helped me? Of course I did."

I sigh. Fuck. Now it seems like he's trying to dodge the subject. Is our relationship a lost cause now?

"No," I say, playing with my fork in the empty bowl. "I meant... like friends. Like are we friends? Or are we more than friends?"

He thins his lips and sets the bowl down. He's silent for a minute, and my thoughts get so loud I have to count silently to myself to keep them at bay.

"Do you wanna be more than friends?" he asks. "Still?"

I nod, not even daring to hold back. "Of course I do, Tanner."

"Even after all this?" he asks.

"This? What do you mean?"

"After the whole sexual assault thing," he says. "With Chris and all."

I nearly scoff. "What does that have to do with it?"

"I don't know," he says with a shrug. "The whole thing turned my world upside down. At first, I was super confident and horny. Now I have to check twice if the sky's blue."

I scooch closer until I'm sitting right in front of him. "Can I hold your hands?"

He nods without pausing. I hold them between us.

"I don't think any less of you after what happened," I say. "Hell, it's made me admire you more. When I first met you, you kept running away from me. But you did one of the bravest things you could by doing what you did with Chris. You are one of the bravest people I know."

He huffs a breath out of his nose, looking down at the carpet. "You think so?"

I squeeze his hands. "I know so."

He looks up at me, and it feels so easy just to gaze into his eyes like this. He feels safe. Like he's home. I want to curl my body around his and make him cum and cum inside him and do it all over again. But most importantly, I want us both to feel safe doing this, too.

"I'd like to amend what I said earlier," he says. "About you being my friend."

I perk up.

"I'd like to level us up to boyfriends," he says. "If that's still okay with you."

It feels like there's a bonfire in my chest. "It definitely is."

He smiles. "Alright."

We both sit there, and my heart races like I'm a little school girl. I swear, no one's ever gotten me this excited before. If there's any sign that I'm with the right one—the one I want to go steady with—it's this.

"Jimmy," he says, licking his lips.

"Yeah?" I ask, my voice low. I move my hand up his arm and run my fingers over his tattoo, and I gain appreciation for it all over again. Both of us have shown that we really can heal from anything.

He swallows. "I want you fu—" he clears his throat. "I want to make love with you."

I laugh. I knew he wanted to say 'fuck', but he's trying to be all sweet about it. He's cute.

"I think 'make love' is a good word to describe what I want to do with you," I say. "I had a chlamydia scare, but I took all my antibiotics. I should be good to go if you're okay with it."

"That sounds good," he says. "So you do want to... make love?"

I scrunch my brow and nod. "That's the only thing I can think to do right now."

He nods and looks down, some new emotion appears in his eyes—a mixture of fear and worry.

I squeeze his hands. "What's wrong?"

"I don't know," he says. "Sex with you was so easy before. But now..."

"Hey," I say. "I'll be patient. Just like I was the first time."

"Right," he says with a sigh. "I'd like that."

I let go of one of his hands. "You wanna go to your bedroom?"

He waits for a second, then he nods.

So I help him to his feet and lead him there.

He stops by the bathroom. "Can I clean and get ready? I still have the bulb."

"Of course," I whisper.

"Jimmy," he says, his hand on the doorframe. "Thank you for being so tender with me."

I smile. "It's what I do."

Chapter 38

Tanner Bash

WARM CHILLS RIPPLE DOWN my spine.

'It's what I do', he said.

God, how the fuck is Jimmy Dillon so fucking attractive? He can completely unwind my body with just four words.

I douche quickly and get showered, eager to love and be loved by the man that I, even after all this time, love even more. At least I think I do. We still have to have sex, and I'm worried that after all this time I don't know what to do, or that Jimmy will see how skittish I am and decide he doesn't want to put up with broken ole me.

As I dry myself off, I try to think positive thoughts, but fear overwhelms me. God, please make me enjoyable for Jimmy. I don't want to be so bad in bed that he changes his mind. If I can just please him in the right ways, then maybe I can lock him down for good.

I exit the bathroom, and Jimmy's laying calmly on my bed with his hands over his belly and eyes closed. When I step into the room, he opens his eyes and his face lights up.

"Hey, you," he says.

"Hey," I say, smiling. I love the way he talks to me like the most special man in the world.

"Come here," he says. He takes off his shirt, and then our lips meet. He falls back onto the bed with me on top of him, and I run my fingers through his hair and beard as I kiss him, not able to get enough of him. I break hold of his lips and start kissing up his cheek to his ear. He lets out a deep moan as I stick my tongue inside.

There we go. That's it. Keep pleasing him like this and I'll have nothing worry about. He'll have no reason to leave me as long as I'm good in bed.

Feeling him harden underneath me, I quickly discard my towel and then buck my bare ass into his crotch, watching his face as I do so. At first, he looks pleased, but soon with each buck his face looks more and more pained, like I'm hurting him.

"Sorry," I say. "Let me—"

I quickly get up off of him and start unbuckling his jeans. I slide those and his underwear off, revealing his semi-hard dick. Fuck. He's not hard. I need to get on that. So I get to sucking.

"Tanner," Jimmy says, and I take that as encouragement. I take his dick deeper, relishing the taste of his manhood and scent of his crotch.

"Tanner," he says more forcefully. I stop and look up, and my chest tightens upon seeing his distress.

"What?" I ask.

He puts his hand on my cheek and strokes it tenderly. "What's going on?" he asks. "You seem... stressed."

As I take in how unhappy he looks, panic constricts my body, and it gets hard to breathe. "I—" I mutter. "I—"

"Tanner Bash," he says with open arms. "Come here."

Without thinking, I get up and rest my huge body in the crook of his arms, and he squeezes me as tight as he can. As he kisses the top of my head, I feel my heartrate begin to slow, and it becomes easier to breathe. I wrap my arms around his belly, and we hold each other like this for a while. Each time his lips press against my scalp, a rush of warmth rolls from my head to my toes, and I feel slightly more relaxed. Pretty soon, I feel mostly normal again.

"Tanner," he says. "You're doing wonderful, big guy."

Him calling me that sends a jolt of electricity throughout my body, and I'm starting to feel horny again.

"It's okay if you don't want to do this," he says. "I know you've been through a lot."

"I do want to do this," I say, playing with his chest hair. "It's just—"

"Just what?" he asks, unperturbed.

I sigh. "You don't think I'm too broken?"

He pulls away, and I look up at him. His brow is forming a deep V.

"Tanner Bash, you are not too broken. You are hurt, yeah, but so am I. As long as we're both working on ourselves, we'll be fine."

He watches me, but I stare at the ceiling, unconvinced.

"Here," he says, grabbing my arm. He lifts it in the air so we can both see my tattoo. "You said this yourself was to show how we can all heal from anything."

I nod.

"So believe it," he says. "You can heal from your past or from anything else that ails you." He pulls my hand to him and kisses it gently, his beard hairs tickling my hand and sending warm shivers up my arm and down my spine.

He looks me in the eye. "And I won't judge you for any of it. So, please, don't let your fear of your own trauma prevent you from being open with me. Okay?"

My entire body warms at his words, and I believe this truth and relish his sincerity. I don't need to worry that I won't be good enough for him because of the sexual assault. I'm good enough now.

I nestle myself back into the crook of his arm and relish the warmth of his skin. I kiss his nipple, then rest my chin on his pec. "Okay," I say. "I can do that."

He pulls my head to his and kisses me firmly on the lips. "Good," he says, pulling away. "I'll be open, too."

"Perfect," I say, kissing his hairy chest.

We lay there for a moment just looking into each other's eyes. He plays with my hair, and I run my fingers through his beard.

"So..." Jimmy says.

I laugh. I roll on top and straddle him. "Yes, to answer your question I know you'll ask. I still want to do this."

He lets out an embarrassed smile. "You read my mind."

I buck back into his dick. "You're just so predictably thoughtful."

He puts his hands on my thighs and rubs them slowly. I melt into his touch. He pushes me back onto his dick, and I moan.

"Please," I say.

He chuckles. "Please, what?"

"Please, Daddy." I lower my body and start kissing his pec. Then I slide his nipple into my mouth.

"Good boy," he says. "Show Daddy how much you want it."

"I want it," I say, my tongue lapping up his nipple.

"Good," he says, rubbing my back. Then his lips press against my ear. "Let me take control. I want you to relax. You've been through enough. Let me give you the pleasure you deserve."

I nod. "Will you please fuck me?" I ask, almost whining. "I really want you to fuck me."

In a swift movement, he gets us to switch places, and now I'm on my back with him between my legs. I'm feeling like a little princess at the feet of her handsome prince.

Jimmy's huge dick presses against my hole, and he leans over to kiss me. He reaches over to grab lube from the nightstand—the lube that I never bothered to move. As we kiss, he lubes himself and my hole up, and pretty soon, we're ready to go.

"You sure about this?" Jimmy asks, our faces inches apart. His hairy torso is pressed against mine, and his thick, hairy arms have mine pressed down, his fingers massaging my shoulders.

"I couldn't be surer about anything," I say.

He smirks. And, without a word, he sticks the head of his dick inside my hole. For a moment, my vision goes technicolor.

"That's right," he says as he pushes himself inside me, and that's when I realize I've been moaning non-stop.

"Fuck yeah, Daddy," I say.

"Ah—remember our rule."

"Sorry," I say, remembering what to call him when he's inside me. "Fuck, Jimmy."

He leans down to kiss me between my pecs. "That's good, Tanner. You feel so fucking good."

Once he's all the way in, he keeps it there and just kisses me like I'm 'marry-me pasta' and he hasn't eaten all day. And as I kiss him back, he slowly pulls out, then pushes back in. The pressure of his dick in my ass sends hot waves of pleasure all throughout my body.

From what I know, couples like to change positions a lot while they have sex—start in missionary, go to doggy, the cowgirl—well, cowboy in this case—then back to missionary. But Jimmy and I feel perfectly contented just in this one position. Having my legs spread for Jimmy just feels so hot and right, and having him hang over my body like this, rapidly and consistently thrusting into me, is a view that I could only think to be possible in heaven.

So I guess Jimmy's my heaven now.

Which makes sense with the God I've come to believe—the one who allows my idea of Him to change as I grow.

His hands cup the back of my neck, and he looks me right in the eyes. "I wanna fucking breed you, Tanner," he says.

I start stroking my own dick, wanting us to cum at the same time. "Please," I say.

He props himself up into plank position and starts thrusting harder, his huge, hairy arms and chest flexing. He pounds harder and harder, so hard that I have to let go of my dick and hold my balls to prevent them from whacking against him. But that doesn't matter. Because Jimmy's striking just the perfect zone, so perfect that just as he's moaning out his orgasm, my own cum shoots up my chest all the way to my neck—all without me touching my dick.

"Fuck," Jimmy says, his whole body twitching. Once he's gotten his bearings, he smirks down at me. "Got you to cum handsfree."

A drop of sweat falls from his face onto my cheek, and I look up at him like he's an angel. Because at this point, he really is one.

"That you did," I say.

I raise my hand to wipe his forehead, and he smiles down at me. My chest tightens, and that's when I realize what I'm feeling and that I can't keep it inside me for a second longer.

"I love you, Jimmy Dillon," I say.

He lowers himself just inches above my face and starts running his fingers through my hair, massaging my scalp as he goes. It feels so good that I close my eyes, ready for sleep to take me. But I can't yet. I'm waiting for my lingering statement to be acknowledged. Unless, of course, Jimmy doesn't feel the same about me.

Jimmy kisses just between my eyebrows, the bridge of my nose, then the tip. When he finally kisses my lips, my entire body melts into goo. I can't believe I thought this man wouldn't want me. He's treating me like I'm fucking made of gold.

He lifts up and looks me square in the eyes. "I love you, too, Tanner Bash," he says. "And I'm happy to call you mine."

I reach my arms behind him and pull him into me for a final kiss before I fall into inevitable sleep.

"Good," I say. He has his head pressed into the pillow beside me, his body resting on top of me with his dick still hard inside. It's a little difficult to breathe this way, but if I could have him any closer to me, I'd make it happen.

"And I can promise you I'll never run away from you again," I say.

Jimmy lifts his head and kisses me on the cheek. "And I," he says, his voice low and serious in my ear. "Promise to not let my own securities get in the way of our relationship."

I kiss him on his forehead. "Good," I say.

"Wonderful," he says.

And so I stroke up and down the crook of his spine until sleep overcomes me, breathing in Jimmy's scent the whole time, no longer afraid that Jimmy might not like me or that there will be some other thing to get in our way. If and when a problem arises, I have a feeling we'll be able to figure it out.

Epilogue One—Nine Months Later

Jimmy Dillon

THE OVEN TIMER DINGS, and I hurry my sweaty, apron-wearing ass over to take out the pumpkin cookies before they cook for too long. They're finicky little things, and I want to make sure they're just right for Yousef's Halloween potluck later. I set them down on an oven mitt next to the sink, and outside Tanner's kitchen window, I see a particularly big wave down on the beach, so I take a second to admire it. I'm so grateful that I got to come here and meet Tanner. I couldn't be happier with the way things have turned out.

Once I'm done musing, I return to the counter and stir the brown butter cream cheese icing I whipped up one last time, then set it to the side. I check the chicken gnocchi stew to make sure it hasn't burned, but it's perfect. After I assemble the pumpkin whoopie pies, I'll be done with nothing to do until Tanner gets home in an hour.

But stillness isn't such a scary thing anymore.

Now that I've been meditating daily for months, both by myself and with Yousef whenever I'm in San Diego, I feel a profound sense of steady peace that I've never so consistently in my life until now. And I fucking love it. I sleep easier. I no longer self-medicate with sex, and I definitely don't think about doing hard drugs anymore. My mind is calm. And, even though we're doing long-distance right now, this calmness helps me be the best partner possible for my wonderful Tanner.

Speaking of Tanner, he's been doing well, too. He's just finished Step Four in his Al-Anon recovery where he had to take a personal inventory of his actions, beliefs, and so on. So today, he's doing Step Five where he shares this personal inventory with his sponsor, Lupita. That's actually what he's doing right now. He's been real nervous about this—nervous that she would judge him. And despite my reassurances, reminding him how kind and nonjudgmental she's been with him in the past, he's still been anxious as hell.

So I've decided to do him a little favor.

We've got a while before we need to go to Yousef's Halloween party. So, I made extra whoopie pies and gnocchi stew just so we could have our own little meal, play some video games, and relax before we leave.

Oh, and fuck. Definitely fuck.

Forgot to mention that, besides the apron saying 'Kiss the Hot Chef', I'm wearing a pair of knee-high socks and nothing else.

Over the months, as Tanner has grown more and more comfortable with himself, he's been more communicative, kind, and willing to try new things. And I'd say that his libido has increased proportionally to this growth.

Scratch that. *Exponentially.*

I show up to his house fresh off the plane? Tanner wants to fuck. I get out of the shower? Tanner wants to suck me off, then fuck. We come home from a late-night walk on the beach all sandy and wet? Tanner wants to fuck. Tanner takes a red-eye to see me in Mississippi? Fuck first, nap later. He's even upped his fiber intake so he no longer has to worry about douching. Though he would explain this in more logical terms when he's not feeling frisky, he says, when he's horny, that he's my cumdumpster and should, therefore, always be ready to take my load.

And all I have to say to this is *fuck.*

Because long distance is hard, and I love how much more enthusiastic Tanner has become about our relationship, even months later, despite the fact that we live so far apart. I'm definitely still enthusiastic, but it's nice to be reminded that I'm dating somebody who's the polar opposite of Joe.

So, for the pleasure of my horny ass boyfriend who I love more than the sun loves to shine, I'm dressed like a slut for him. I didn't shower after I worked out this morning, so I'm sweaty and smelly as he likes. But I'm truly hoping that I can help him decompress from his meeting with his sponsor.

While the cookies are cooling, I clean up, then sit down at the kitchen table to play Tanner's Nintendo Switch. I'm playing the newest Zelda game—Tears of the Kingdom—and I'm still overwhelmed with all that there is to do. I could spend weeks straight playing this game and still have areas to explore.

Once I've given them enough time, I get up and grab the sheets carrying my pumpkin cookies. I take two each and place them side by side. Then, I lather one up with the brown-butter cream cheese and place the plain cookie on top, creating a sandwich or whoopie pie as I like to call them. I repeat until all cookies have been frosted and sandwiched.

Just as I'm cleaning off my spatula, I hear the garage door open, and my stomach leaps. Fuck. I still get butterflies for this beautiful man.

When he opens the door to the kitchen, I stand there and face him, leaning against the counter with my hands on my hips.

He freezes right in the kitchen doorway, and I take him in. He's kept most of his muscle but lost a good amount of fat after retiring from the NFO. Turns out he doesn't need to eat 7,000 calories a day when he's not playing a high-intensity sport. Lately, he's been letting his stubble grow out to beard-length, and he's buzzed his blonde hair off. Looks slightly different now, but he's my hot Tanner all the same.

"Christ, Jimmy," he says. "You're not wearing—and those socks."

I glance down at the long white socks that accentuate my feet and thick calves, then look back up. "You like?"

"You're gonna be the death of me," he says.

He begins to close the distance between us, but I hold my hand out to stop him. "Ah. Do you wanna talk about the meeting with your sponsor first? Or do you want me to fuck you?"

Tanner exhales through pursed lips, still checking me out. "I think I'd like to decompress now," he says. "And I'll tell you after. So, Jimmy Dillon, will you please fuck me?"

I smirk at him. "You're not getting it that easy," I say. "You gotta earn it."

He approaches, then kneels right in front of me. He his face right into the apron right where my dick is and sniffs. "Fuck," he says.

I chuckle. "I got plenty more of that."

I turn away from him and put one knee up on the counter, opening up my ass to him.

"Oh my God," he says.

"Come on," I say. "Be a good boy."

And then he shoves his face in between my cheeks.

It took Tanner a while to gather the courage to eat my ass. He always said he wanted to, but every time we got around to it, he just stuck to my armpits when he wanted to get freaky. But the day he decided to do it, he's been a changed man. Now, once he gets in there, I practically need a crowbar to pull him out.

"There we go," I say as he digs his tongue deep in my hole. "Be greedy. Fucking own it."

"Fuck," he says, rubbing his face deeper into me. His stubble tickles my hole, and paired with his big tongue lapping me up, I feel like I'm in heaven.

"You smell and taste so good, Daddy," he says.

"I know I do. Keep at it."

Tanner drinks up my hole with his tongue like I'm an oasis in the desert. I peek below me to see that he's so hard he's dripping onto his kitchen floor. He's stroking himself slowly, but we can't have that. I only want him to cum when my dick is throbbing inside him.

"That's enough," I say, standing up. I pull off my apron and toss it on the counter.

"Yes, Daddy," he says.

I turn around and find him on the floor, his jeans down to his ankles with his T-shirt thrown to the side.

I step forward and put my hand on his face. I stick my thumb in his mouth, and he starts sucking it like it's my dick.

"Look how pathetic you are," I say. "A six-foot-four man on his knees in his own kitchen eating another man's ass. Open your mouth."

I retract my hand, and he opens his mouth wide with his tongue sticking out. I spit the biggest glob of spit onto it. He immediately closes his mouth and swallows.

"Thank you, Daddy," he says.

"Fucking laundry-sniffing pervert," I say. "You like sniffing and eating my ass?"

He nods eagerly. "I do."

"Disgusting. Stand up," I say with a snap. "And bend over the counter."

"Yes, Daddy."

He obeys, leaning over the counter with his back arched and ass presented to me. I fondle his pale ass, and then I slap it hard. He whimpers but only arches his back even more, making his ass look even more plump and gorgeous.

"You wanna get pounded like the fucking faggot you are?" I ask.

"Yes, I do,"

I slap his ass, leaving a red mark. "You know what to call me."

"Yes, I do, Daddy," he says.

"Good boy," I say. I grab some lube in a drawer nearby that I left for this purpose and start lathering myself up.

As I mentioned, Tanner's been open to trying new things. One of the things we've both discovered is a degradation kink. Except, instead of him being the bully like I first imagined, I am. And it drives us both wild. Back when we were first dating, this would have never worked. We had so much shit to work through. But now? We trust each other like crazy. We know how to please the other without taking it too far or demanding too much.

After I've lubed us both up, I start to push it inside him. "Fucking pussy," I say, slapping his ass again. "Take it like the faggot you are."

To my surprise, Tanner pushes himself back on my dick all the way. "Come on, Jimmy," he says, pulling away, then pushing himself back on my dick again. "I know you can do better than that."

I dig my hands into his hips and thrust myself deep into him. He tries to hold back his yelp.

"How's that for ya?" I ask, slowly pulling out.

"That's good," he says. "Thank you, Jimmy."

I thrust in and out steadily, gradually picking up speed. Pretty soon, I'm fucking him so hard that he has to hold his dick and balls to prevent them from flopping into the counter.

"God, I love you, Jimmy," he says. "I love you so much."

"I love you, too, Tanner," I say, closer to my climax than I'd like to be right now. I want to keep fucking him.

"Get up on the counter," I say.

He looks back at me, confused, and goddamn he looks so cute from this position.

"Like on my back?"

"Yeah," I say, pulling out. "I want to look into your eyes when I cum inside you. And I wanna do it right now."

We move my cookies and stew out of the way, and Tanner hoists himself up onto the counter. He spreads his legs, and that's when I realize I woefully miscalculated. I'd have to be at least seven feet tall to fuck him like this.

"Grab chairs," he says. "I want this to work."

"Right," I say, feral from how badly I want to cum inside him.

While he's lying on the counter, I rush over to grab two chairs from the dining room table. I put them at the edge of the counter and step onto them.

"Really good call," I say, rubbing the head of my dick against his sloppy hole. "Perfect height."

"Put it in me," he says, grabbing my wrist. He takes hold of my dick and puts it inside him for me. This time, I don't go slow. I thrust it right in.

"Yes, like that," Tanner says.

So I pull out and thrust in hard again. "You are such a desperate little slut."

He grabs hold of his dick and starts stroking. "I am for you, Jimmy. I fucking am."

"I don't want you to cum until I do, you understand?"

"Yes, Jimmy."

"Good, Tanner."

My tongue sticking out of my mouth, I hold his ankles in the air as I continue to thrust inside him. And fuck. He looks like Hercules himself from this position.

"Jimmy," he moans. "I can't hold it."

"You fucking hold it," I command. "I'm getting there. I'm close."

And it feels like one of those orgasms where I'm climbing a fucking mountain. I know it's coming, but I really gotta work for it. But when I see Tanner's face contorted in exquisite pleasure, that shoots me to the top.

"Fuck," I say. "I'm cumming."

"Fuck yeah," Tanner yells.

We cum at the same time, which is wild, because I can only count on one hand the number of people where we've cum at the same time. But Tanner and I have done it multiple times at this point.

"Come here," I say, lifting Tanner up. "I want to kiss you."

He sits up quickly, then I step off the chairs and move them out of the way. I insert myself in between his legs and kiss him hungrily.

"I know I've already said it, but I love you so much, Tanner Bash," I say, taking a breath.

He kisses me back just as desperately. "I love you, too," he says in between kisses. "You are the light of my life."

We kiss until we're both tired—not of kissing, but from being in such an uncomfortable position.

"Go fire up the Switch," I tell him. "I'll get us some food ready."

"Aye aye," he says. He gives me one last kiss on the lips, then pecks me on the cheek and heads to the living room. I watch his huge ass swish as he goes, and I wonder how lucky I am to have landed this gorgeous, sweet hunk.

Epilogue Two

Tanner Bash

As I FINISH OF my second bowl of this delicious chicken gnocchi stew, watching Jimmy play Tears of the Kingdom as I lay back on the blanket we've laid out on the living room floor—my asshole wonderfully sore and full of Jimmy's cum—I can't help but think how happy I am.

Nearly two years ago, when I came out to my buddies Kyle and Michael, all I had was football, and everything else looked dark and sad. I couldn't see how I was supposed to find a woman and be happy at the same time. I just thought that I needed to do it, or else God would abandon me. But through Al-Anon and my wonderful sponsor Lupita, I've been able to develop a new, more loving relationship with God—one that helps me accept who I am as a gay man, and one that helps me continue to treat the love of my life with the respect he deserves.

"So," Jimmy says as Link ascends to the Sky Isles. "How did Step Five go with Lupita?"

"Better than I thought it would," I say without a heavy sigh or any hesitation. Because I trust Jimmy, and I trust myself to say what I feel like I need to say.

"Yeah?" Jimmy asks. "How so? If you wanna share."

"I do," I say, leaning forward. "I think the biggest thing that I discovered is that I carried so much guilt in my life: guilt for not stopping my brothers from drinking, guilt for not being the son my parents wanted me to be. Before talking to Lupita, I thought she would confirm that these things were indeed my responsibility and that I needed to apologize to these people. But that's not what happened. After sharing with her, she helped me see that that was guilt I didn't need to take on. That it was guilt for not pleasing others, and I don't need to please others to be a good person. I just need to do what's right for me."

Jimmy pauses the game and leans back to look at me. "That is a pretty good insight," he says. "Do you feel like you got it all off your chest?"

I nod. "I honestly do. And I feel so much lighter now."

Jimmy smiles, spreading the forest of his dark beard. "I remember my first Step Five. I had a similar feeling. I'm glad you feel free. You deserve it."

I wrap my arms around Jimmy and pull him close, kissing him wholly and selfishly. He lets me, leaning back and letting me take charge in that leisurely way that only makes me more hungry for him.

He pulls away and glances down at his watch. "I don't suppose we have time to fornicate before Yousef's party."

I chuckle at his use of the word. "No. It starts in ten minutes, and though I'm sure we could get a quickie in, I'd rather take my time with you."

He kisses me on the cheek, then stands up. "After, then." He extends his hand to help me up, and I take it. "Now for our costumes."

And then I can't resist putting on a giddy smile. "Oh, I can't wait."

Jimmy and I go into my bedroom and pick up the costumes we have laying on my dresser. Naked, I quickly slip on some white tights and a green tunic. He slips on a red long-sleeved shirt and some overalls. After we both don our hats, we look in the mirror, then break into laughter.

"This is perfect," Jimmy says putting his arm around me. He's dressed as Mario—specifically referencing Paper Mario—and I'm dressed as Link.

"Wait," I say. "Your mustache."

His eyes widen. "Right."

He digs into his suitcase to pull out a ridiculously large cloth mustache with some tape on it. He plasters it just below his nose.

He extends his arms. "How do I look?"

I put my arm around him and kiss him. "Like a man who can lay pipe."

He wears a cute smile and swats my stomach. "That was good."

I laugh. "I know."

"Enough dilly-dally," he says. "Let's go."

I grab our giant pot of gnocchi stew while Jimmy grabs the cookie container. We open the back door and take the five second walk to Yousef's next door, and his backyard is already filled with guests all in colorful costumes.

"My favorite couple!" Yousef yells, his arms in the air. He rugs to hug me, then Jimmy. Chewy and Xavier take our food and whisk it away to the kitchen.

"What are you?" I ask him. He's wearing a skin-tight black outfit, along with his boyfriends Chewy and Xavier.

His boyfriends come back, and he puts his arms around them. "Charlie's Angels," he says.

Jimmy laughs. "Now that's good."

"And you're... Luigi?" he asks Jimmy.

"Close enough," he says. "Mario."

Yousef nods. "And you're Link," he says to me.

"Right on the money!" I say.

As we catch up with Yousef and his boyfriends, other people come to introduce themselves, and that's when I find my arm casually drifting around Jimmy's waist. He pulls me tight, and I'm reminded of how comfortable I am with his touch. Eventually, Lupita, my sponsor, shows up with Maria, the woman who first took me to an Al-Anon meeting, and I rush to hug them. They're both dressed as witches.

After our greeting, Lupita pulls me aside. "How are you doing since our conversation?" she asks me privately.

"A little frazzled," I admit. "But okay."

She grabs my hand, her small hands dwarfed compared to mine. "You did a brave thing. Celebrate tonight. You can continue your recovery journey tomorrow. Enjoy yourself."

I nod, then reach around to hug her, and she hugs me tightly back. I kiss her on the top of her head. "Thank you for everything," I say as I pull away.

"It's my pleasure," she says. "I get as much out of this as you do."

And so the night goes. I talk, laugh, and eat more of the wonderful food that Jimmy prepared. All the while, I reflect on how, just over a year ago, I felt interminably lonely, and I never knew if that feeling was gonna go away. But, in a way that almost seems imperceptible, it has. Because, surrounded by people I love with the man of my dreams at my side, even without football, I don't feel lonely or sad about the future at all. I feel at home and full of hope.

What's Next?

Thank you for reading Tackling Tanner. If you'd like, please leave an honest review!

Still want to read about Jimmy and Tanner? Signup for my newsletter (https://dl.bookfunnel.com/44bp5x5mr7) and receive a free bonus short story! Tanner has an important question for Jimmy, and he's finally gathered the courage to ask it.

Want to read Wyatt and Silas's story? Check out Winning Wyatt!

www.ingramcontent.com/pod-product-compliance
Lightning Source LLC
Chambersburg PA
CBHW021137310726
48971CB00002B/363